"Stay with me"

He was brooding handsome, feral intensity. She understood then that here was not the man she knew—he had gone past some inner edge, past a point she could not know or even guess at.

She did not see love on him. She saw danger, and her destruction.

"No."

"Too late to deny it. You care for me too. I think it so. I saw you in the bailey. I saw your face."

"No." She shook her head again, taking another step away.

"Lily . . ." He smiled at her, that subtle grace, and the wicked curve to his lips came back, the promise of pleasure there, of heartless intent. He moved toward her, tall, stealthy, almost a threat draped across him. She glanced frantically around the room and saw no comfort—shut doors, a looming bed. A castle beyond, filled with people ready to betray her.

He caught her then, easily, almost gently, caught her up in his arms and kept her there despite her startled jerk. His head dipped down to hers.

"No!" She could not think, she could not breathe—this could *not* be happening, his words, her feelings—he was killing her, he would kill her with this, she could not feel this way for him again—

"Too late," Tristan said once more. He kissed her then, drowning her in him, tasting her, a ravishment, all gentleness gone. . . .

Also by Shana Abé

THE
SECRET
SWAN

Shana Abé

BANTAM BOOKS

New York Toronto London Sydney Auckland

THE SECRET SWAN
A Bantam Book

PUBLISHING HISTORY
Bantam mass market edition published April 2001
Bantam reissue / May 2008

Published by Bantam Dell
A Division of Random House, Inc.
New York, New York

This is a work of fiction. Names, characters, places, and incidents either are
the product of the author's imagination or are used fictitiously. Any
resemblance to actual persons, living or dead, events, or locales is
entirely coincidental.

Bantam Books and the rooster colophon are registered trademarks of
Random House, Inc.

ISBN 978-0-553-59185-9

Printed in the United States of America

www.bantamdell.com

OPM 10 9 8 7 6 5 4 3 2 1

For Darren,
who works very hard and still agrees
to take in the occasional stray bunny.

Everlasting appreciation also to
Ruth Kagle and Wendy McCurdy,
who offered splendid counsel;
and of course to Dad and Mom
and the rest of the family,
just because.

Prologue

THE LATCH TO THE GATE CAME OFF IN HIS HAND.

Tristan stared down at it in some surprise, speckles of rust dotting his skin like dried blood. The soldered seam meant to hold it in place had corroded through; he was damned lucky he hadn't cut himself on any of the flaking metal. No doubt the result of the sea air in this god-forsaken place.

He remembered now. Nothing lasted here.

Carefully Tristan dropped the ruined latch to the gravel beside him.

The gate itself did not appear much more promising. One half of the barred grille hung at a drunken tilt against the other, offering paltry defense against anyone who actually wished to enter the estate.

It made him want to laugh suddenly. Who would truly want to come here, after all? Safere was the outermost edge of the world—far, far past any prayer of civilization. Only the banished or the insane dwelled here, surely.

The thought was so particularly apt that he did laugh now, low and mirthless, but the wind merely snatched it away from him. It pushed up off the ocean nearby, a steady tearing at his hair, his skin, drying his eyes to grit. On the journey here Tristan had found himself constantly squinting against the gusts to discern the land around him, as if that might clarify matters. It had not.

He cupped a hand to his mouth and called out a greeting past the iron bars. It faded off against the bare walls of the buildings beyond. No one responded.

Perhaps there was no one here, after all. Perhaps Safere was as deserted as it appeared to be. He could not fathom why anyone would want to stay here, anyway.

If ever a land was rocky and formidable, it was this place. Whichever of his esteemed ancestors had claimed this seaside territory obviously had not been bothered by the lack of greenery. Perched on its lonely outcrop of rock overlooking the ocean, Safere seemed better suited for a prison than a stronghold: barren, remote, breathtakingly desolate. The water was a steady roar against the cliffs below. The wind never ceased.

He fancied he could hear words in it now—a thin, berating wail that wrapped around him, relentless.

She's gone . . . they're all gone . . . shame . . . shame. . . .

He gave the gate a vicious kick. The broken half shuddered in place. The other half did not move at all.

Tristan did not like Safere; he never had. Even now, in the peak of summer, vegetation was rare and trees rarer still. The farther he had ridden to it, the less and less hospitable the land became. Dirt paths, endless and winding. Pale tufts of grass struggling for life. Faraway birds, tangling into fantastic shapes amid the blue of the sky, dark against white clouds. . . .

But mostly there were rocks. White rocks, golden rocks, even ones tinted pink, which he decided were his favorite. The pink ones did something with the light, a trick of dusk and dawn, capturing the color to create a glow, suffusing the very air around them with warmth. Yes, the pink ones were—

Tristan caught himself with a mental shake, and turned back to the problem of the gate.

He might be able to squeeze through near the bottom of it. The gap from the angle of the disjointed half was just enough that he could make it, with a good bit of crawling. He would have to leave his horse behind.

Wonderful. The Earl of Haverlocke crawling back to his wife. What a pretty sight that would be. And nothing less than he deserved.

It was the reproving wind, perhaps, that made Tristan straighten, glancing around him again. Many might laugh at the sight of him on his hands and knees in the dirt, but it would not be the ghosts of this place. There had to be another way in. He thought he remembered a garden gate somewhere. . . .

He took the reins of the gelded brown rounsey and

began to walk around the walls that enclosed the estate. From here he could see the top portion of the manor house, stone and wood, bleached with sunlight. No banner flew to welcome him home. In fact, he couldn't even see the staff for it. The edges of the roof dipped and curved in places it was not supposed to; a few of those shadows might have been gaps in the beams. If the main house was as dismally neglected as the gate had been, he supposed he might be fortunate to find shelter at all tonight.

On the far side of the stronghold the salted rock wall came perilously close to the edge of the cliff, eroded away under the constant assault of the elements. He kept the reins of his horse firmly grasped in one hand, allowing the other to slide along the rough stones of the wall—a thin illusion of security. It would not help if either of them stumbled, but the feel of something solid beneath his palm gave him some comfort.

The gelding snorted and tossed his head against the wind. Tristan pulled him on.

Nothing. No garden gate—only this long, unbroken expanse of wall, stretching on and on. How ridiculous to imagine there might have been another gate. He must have been thinking of one of the other estates. Merlyff, perhaps. Or Layton. They were all mixed up in his head now, indistinguishable. Mayhap *none* of them had a garden, or a gate. Another fantasy, whirled up out of nothingness.

The wretched portal of the entrance loomed before him once again. *Full circle,* Tristan thought, and for some reason the phrase stuck in his head.

With a sigh he approached the gate, releasing the reins, grasping the rusted metal of the broken half and lifting with all his might. He was rewarded with a hideous squealing sound, the hinges protesting this rough handling. After a long while and a great deal of sweating effort, the gap was wide enough to fit through without crawling.

He dropped the gate, panting, and absently wiped his hands down the front of his tunic. Rust left smudges of darkness against the gray of it. He had no gloves.

Tristan entered his estate.

Once inside the walls, the howling of the wind was drastically reduced, a sudden respite that rang in his ears, close to pain.

No one came to greet him. There was only more dirt before him, and buildings and sky.

He took a deep breath, then called out again—and again he gained no response beyond the mournful cry of the wind.

Shame, shame . . .

An ungentle push from behind reminded him of his horse. The gelding had followed him in and now stood impatiently, tossing his head once more.

Yes. Tristan had stolen a mount—he should not have forgotten that. The horse would be hungry. He must see about feeding him. The stables must still be here somewhere.

Safere was fairly sizable, for an enclosed estate. The manor itself took up most of it, along with a modest, neat garden—*no gate*—growing along one of the walls. Here at last were living plants, herbs and vegetables, even a scattering of flowers near the back, a decent effort against the thin soil. He supposed it was some sign of hope that there might be more than just ghosts in this place.

Thankfully, he did not have to remember where the stables were. There was only one other structure of any significance on the grounds, and at first glance it appeared as abandoned as everything else. He found a reasonably clean stall and led the rounsey into it, then had to stop and think about what he must do next.

Hay. Water. Oats, if he could find them.

A rustling sound came from nearby. The delicate head of a bay topped the door of the stall opposite, eyeing him suspiciously.

When he was finished with his horse Tristan got a closer look at the other one. It was a mare, a sweetly formed thing, really, with clean lines and a shining flank. One more hopeful sign.

He left the animals examining each other with trembling hostility, walking back out into the bright sunshine of the day.

"Amiranth?"

No one answered him. There was no one here. Not a serf, not a servant. Certainly not *her*. He had come to the end of the world and found it just as he had left it so long ago—forgotten.

But the thought of seeing her again after so long apart kept him moving, listening, looking. His wife was the only reason he had managed to come so far. She was the only reason he was still alive at all. He had planned this reunion countless times in his mind. What he would say. How she would turn to him—astonished, amazed—and then laugh with pure joy, lifting her hands to him—

A small noise in the distance caught his attention. Tristan swung around, startled. It might have come from the depths of the manor. Aye. He went toward it.

The interior of this place was darker than he recalled, cool and musty. A dim hallway of stone and wood paneling stretched out before him, closed doors on both sides. He had to pause to allow his eyes to adjust, until the shadows lightened from black to soft charcoal. The scent of something that might have been beeswax lingered faintly in the air. But the only sound to be heard now was his own breathing, and the occasional creaking of the wood beams above him.

Tristan ventured deeper inside.

One by one he opened the doors, taking care to throw frequent glances over his shoulder—was he truly alone? Was there truly no one else here? No one had followed him, he had made certain of that. No one would be able to trace him here, surely, to this lonely bit of earth. . . .

There was never anyone behind him; Safere echoed with emptiness. All he found, in fact, in this soulless place were deserted chambers and scattered furniture covered in a fine layer of dust. Ashes in the fireplaces, long cold. Windows encrusted with dirt. Every single thing spoke of abandonment.

As he walked he tried to envision her living here, how her life would have been. He knew, logically, that he had hardly a chance to know her before he left. But in his mind she had blossomed over the years, all her secrets revealed; in time his unfamiliar wife had become as familiar to Tristan as he himself.

So he knew that she would have endured the wind and the heat of this place with tender patience. She might have even thrived amid it, that fair-haired girl with the shy smile. . . .

Another chamber, more dust, the creaking silence, phantom cobwebs suspended all around.

Aye, Tristan decided abruptly, closing his eyes against the sight. She had liked it here. She would have liked it. He had to believe that. And soon he would find her, and Amiranth would welcome him home, and once in her arms finally all would be right in the world. She would forgive him their past. She would accept him anew, and with her help he would become whole once more. He would never have to be apart from her again. They would have the rest of their days to truly learn each other.

In a new room he discovered his first small clue to her life, an elegant little tableau set up: a pair of chairs brought close around a low table of polished wood, the empty hearth just beyond. The edges of a wooden screen closed off a corner of it, creating intimacy. A length of embroidery lay askew across the seat of the chair closest to him, needle and thread placed neatly on top, as if the seamstress meant to return at any moment.

Tristan picked up the cloth—a dreamlike scene of the night sky and stars, a swan on a moonlit lake—then shook it. Dust erupted around him in a cloud, clogging his senses. He gave a rough cough, tossing the lot of it back to the chair.

The needle dropped from the side and swung gently back and forth, bright silver suspended by a sapphire thread.

Had his wife begun this piece? What would have caused her to discard it so nearly completed, forsaken to the mustiness of this room?

He felt a chill and shook it off, continuing his exploration.

She would be here. She would be.

There was food in the buttery. That had to be good. Not much, granted: some bread and cheese, flour, roots, dried fruits and herbs—from the garden, he guessed. Certainly not enough to feed all the people who should be dwelling here . . . but enough for a few people, for a while.

Again came that elusive noise, outside now, just past the kitchen door. Yet when he walked back into the sunshine there was nothing there—only the dirt of before, an empty sky, the mocking wind. Tristan closed his eyes once more and let out his breath, setting his teeth.

Alone, alone again. She was not here, no one was. Perhaps she never had been. Perhaps he was not even married at all—it had all been just another dream of his, a delusion conjured up by his mind, that girl, the soft touch of her hand, the sweetness of her lips—

No. It had to have happened. It *had* to have been real. He had kept her close to him every miserable day of the past eight years, had gone over and over his memories of her until each small moment was burned deep into his heart . . . even after he could no longer remember her face. Even after the pitch of her voice had faded from his mind, surrendered to the hungry silence of his cell.

Through it all, Amiranth had kept him sane. Tristan had sworn by every oath he knew that if he could just come home again, he would be worthy of her. He would change completely, he would be the best, the most devoted husband. He would make her glad every day for the rest of her life that she had wed him. By God, he would.

She was real, and somewhere, he knew, she was waiting for him. If not here, then at another estate. He would find her. It didn't have to be this place, empty Safere. . . .

But when Tristan rounded the next corner he discovered that he had been mistaken; Safere was not so empty after all. At the foot of a new garden was a statue of a marble girl seated upon a marble bench, posed to stare out thoughtfully at the few trees and bushes pressed up against the outer wall.

At first he didn't understand what he was seeing. A marble girl on a marble bench . . . but she wore a black gown that rippled in the breeze. Why had they clothed a statue? Why was her hair so golden?

The marble girl turned her face and gazed back at him, still thoughtful.

Tristan Geraint, Earl of Haverlocke, stopped in sheer surprise.

The woman—not a girl, and not marble, but flesh—quickly stood, taking a step away.

"No—wait." Tristan held out his hands, his palms streaked with rust. "I won't harm you." He scanned the area around them, seeing nothing but more of the garden, the pale stone walls beyond that. She was the only sign of life, this figure of gold and white and black.

"Amiranth?" he asked, but did not think it was she.

This woman's hair was darker than he remembered his wife's to be, more of a honeyed blonde than the silvery curls that young girl had had. She wore it loose and free—strange for a grown woman to reveal her hair so openly—but Tristan would not regret the sight of it, not when it shimmered in the sunlight as it did, shades of amber and burnished gold, richly layered.

She had not run away, but her hands had come up to shield her eyes from the bright sun; he saw only full lips stained red, like the sunset, and a sweetly curved chin. Long, elegant neck. The tail end of the wind slipped over the wall, pressing back the shadowed black of her gown, revealing a slender shape in teasing glimpses.

If God had placed a desert flower amid this vast emptiness, it could not have looked more out of place than this woman did.

He asked again anyway, "Amiranth St. Cl— Geraint?"

The woman slowly shook her head in denial, allowing the sunlight to send sparks weaving through her hair. Tristan fought a sharp disappointment. She was not Amiranth. He had battled back from hell itself only to find the wrong woman.

A new thought came to him: This could be her servant. A handmaid, perhaps.

"Where is she?" he asked, taking another step forward. The woman did not back away this time, but to reassure her he added in a calm voice, "I am her husband. You may direct me to her."

The handmaiden lowered her hands, not even blinking against the sun. She was undeniably familiar. He might have seen her at the wedding, all those years ago. . . .

"Where is she?" he asked again, motionless.

Her head bowed; a slight frown marred her forehead. He watched as one of her hands lifted, very pale against the black sleeve of her gown, her finger pointing into the garden.

Tristan turned, searching past the trees. There was no one else there. Was she jesting? Did she think to test him somehow?

When he glanced back at her she was still pointing mutely to the garden, her stare now direct to his, unflinching. With her golden hair streaming past her shoulders, she was as stern and solemn as any avenging angel.

He felt a strange sense of helplessness come over him. This was the end, then. This was what he deserved, after all.

Tristan looked again at the garden.

There it was. A simple plaque amid the plants—actually just a flat rock of that pink shade he had favored, a few words carved roughly into the stone.

Her name had been written clumsily. No doubt it had not been easy to chisel the marker.

Amiranth, Countess of Haverlocke

1326–1349

Peace, sweet friend

Chapter One

Eight years earlier: Iving Castle
1341

IT WAS GOING TO BE THE MOST GLORIOUS DAY OF
her life.

Today, Lady Amiranth St. Clare was to become a
woman. She was fifteen years old, and a bride.

His bride. Tristan Geraint, Earl of Haverlocke.

She had loved him for years already. It was deep and
heady and thrilling, and completely without reason, she
knew. Amiranth had not told anyone of it, not even her
cousin Lily, her most trusted friend. It was as if to share
this feeling with anyone else—anyone—would tarnish
it, turn it from shining silver to tin.

She did not dare risk that. It was too wonderful a suffering, too dear and delightful and agonizing to give up.

Amiranth had seen him her very first time at court, when she was just a child. Only nine years old, and the moment she picked him out from the line of squires lingering by a wall in the king's antechamber she had felt it—her breathing stopped, her heart stopped, her entire existence . . . stopped.

He was dressed as the rest of the young men around him were, in fine tunics and colorful hose, each wearing the heraldry of the lord they served. He blended in well with them. Were it not for just one stray beam of sunlight sliding along the floor, she might not have noticed him at all.

But the sunlight *was* there, slanting down from a window high above, and at just the moment when she glanced his way he took a half-step into the light, jostled by a friend, the two of them laughing softly together.

She felt as if she had stepped, unsuspecting, into a vat of honeyed nectar, thick and sweet, filling her, suspending her even as she died within it. A blissful death—or an excruciating life—to gaze upon him, to bear witness to this beauty disguised as an ordinary squire. Amiranth had never before seen such dark splendor, such grace in a boy. By heavens, she had never even noticed a boy before now.

It was in this incredible moment that she felt a recognition sound through her, resonating from the depths of her truest, truest heart: Here was the person destined to complement her soul.

She had not known his name then, of course, or anything else about him, but that he was a squire and so had to be at least four years older than she. All Amiranth had seen was a slender youth with sunlight covering his shoulders, gleaming across him. He was taller than most of the rest, with black hair that fell into dishevelment, and lips that curled up at the edges when he laughed, as if he might be holding back more than mirth.

His eyes were brown, like her own—but no—darker, closer to jet. Mysterious eyes, holding secrets and spells in their depths; intense eyes that did not laugh with him, but rather scanned the room, watchful. He was waiting for something, she could tell.

His gaze fell upon her and then skimmed past her, uncaring, and Amiranth could not even begin to summon a smile for him, so shaken was she.

She had not been allowed to stay that day to see what it was he anticipated. She had been in the company of Constanz, her sister-in-law, who kept a hard grip on her hand and smiled very tightly at the people who came near. Constanz had never been easy in crowds. When Amiranth's brother arrived, the three of them left the gathering nearly at once.

Amiranth managed to throw the sun-gilded youth one last look over her shoulder. A corner of him remained in the light, but he had turned away from it, speaking with his hands to the person next to him. She had the impression she could still see his face, tanned and alert, with his slight smile and sparkling jet eyes.

That had been the first time.

She had had to wait another year and a half for her next opportunity. She was eleven by then, and very proud that she was finally allowed to put her hair up all the time. Amiranth remembered that day with vivid clarity, because it was a very brisk October evening, and she had worn a gown just finished for her, ivory and gold, to match her hair. It had seemed almost a shame to wear a veil, but she had done it anyway, too enthralled with growing up to leave it off.

They had been on their way to London again. Her brother Augustin went to the king's court at least twice every year, and recently had allowed that Amiranth could accompany him and his wife on a regular basis. Amiranth was good with the baby, dear little Emile, and even Constanz agreed that she could be useful. Lily's parents were still alive then, so she had not yet come to live at Iving.

They put up at a rustic inn for the night. The sun was still shining rosy gold over the horizon, but they stopped anyway, because the baby was fussy. Augustin had gone to speak with the innkeeper, and Constanz had retired to the room with her son, but Amiranth was restless and soon persuaded her nursemaid to take a walk with her outside.

The air was fresh and clean. Most of the trees still held their autumn leaves, and when they caught the breeze, sunlight made them wink at her in flashes of scarlet and orange. Amiranth was lifting her skirts as she stepped carefully over a puddle of mud when the commotion began in the courtyard.

Riders, five of them, with foaming horses and thundering hooves, splashing past Amiranth and her startled nurse with nary a look.

But Amiranth had been looking. *He* was there, in the

middle of them. His hair was longer now, windblown and mussed. He was speckled with mud and laughing at something one of the others had said. His face was angled away from her. He did not see her.

Amiranth had felt time stop again, every bit of her fixed on him. The way his hands held the reins to his steed, his gloves taut over his knuckles. The ruddy flush across his cheekbones, darkening his swarthy skin. Even the faint curl to his lips, still suggesting something beyond his laughter, something bright and compelling in the black of his eyes.

No, he did not see her at all. He and his group dismounted in the courtyard and barged their way into the inn, shouting for the innkeeper, trampling mud everywhere.

The stableboys who had come out to take control of the mounts exchanged sour words, and her nurse was seizing Amiranth by the arm with scandalized exclamations, pushing her back inside to their private chamber, away from the rowdiness of his crowd.

That night, with a casually deliberate inquiry over supper, Amiranth discovered his name: Tristan Geraint. Middle son of the Earl of Haverlocke.

Wild and impetuous, Augustin had pronounced, slicing firmly into his mutton. An uncontrollable youth, the despair of his father. No good at all.

Tristan, Amiranth thought, closing her eyes, savoring the sound of it. She didn't even mind that he had splashed mud all over her new gown.

There came other times as she grew older, all of them brief, and all of them within the confines of the London court. She would sometimes see him drinking or talking, and worshiped him from a silent distance. On very good days she might pass him in a hallway with his friends, a swan amid a crowd of peacocks. If only she might reach out her hand, just a bit, she could brush against him, pretend it was an accident . . . but oh, she did not dare.

He was rarely without companions, yet it seemed to her that Tristan Geraint was always alone. It was the way he held himself, perhaps, that suggested restraint, or caution, or mayhap something darker. She could not say what. Yet even as he would smile and gesture and game with his peers, part of him looked always separate from the moment, nearly aloof. The corners of his mouth, so sensual and fine, held him back just enough.

Amiranth imagined that she alone could perceive this aspect of him, that somehow she held the magic key to knowing him, the secret to revealing his hidden heart. That only she, in fact, could banish that loneliness about him.

It was her destiny.

He never saw her. No matter how hard she prayed, Tristan never even glanced at her, save when she was in some mass of people, and even then, only in passing. And she, for all her certainty of him, never quite gathered up the courage to speak to him first.

And so Amiranth watched him from afar and dreamed and planned and practiced kissing the back of her hand, imagining how *he* might do it, were they ever introduced.

They were not. But it did not stop her from dreaming.

One year, something bad happened. No one would

speak of it openly, but she knew that his parents had died of an illness, and then, very soon after, his older brother was killed in a hunt. There were rumors about him now, unpleasant things. His younger brother was whisked away to the countryside by a distant branch of the family; some said it was to spare him the sickness . . . others muttered of more dire circumstances. She felt deeply for Tristan. Her own parents had died in an accident when she was but three. Her love was now an orphan, just as she and Lily were. Amiranth knew very well how it felt to be orphaned.

She did not see Tristan again for a very long time.

And then, by sheer luck—or as a result of all that prayer—she was in London for his knighting ceremony.

It was to be a regal, stuffy affair, the bestowing of knighthood upon a group of the most noble and worthy of young men; it happened every year, exactly the same. Heated chamber. Perfumed air. Adults in vivid colors, speaking in whispers above her head. The quiet, rumbling voice of the king, too distant to hear well.

Augustin always had seats assigned near the back of the crowded hall. Despite their exemplary bloodlines, the taxes from their estate were never enough to grant anything closer.

Amiranth sat there, bored and fitful, unable to even see beyond the massively plumed hat of the man in front of her, when the squires began their procession down the walkway.

Out of habit she searched for Tristan, and when he passed by, she almost could not believe it was true. She stood in place, prompting Constanz to press a restrain-

ing hand upon her arm, but Amiranth was staring at the
retreating back of Tristan's head, so familiar and dear
she wanted to cry out a greeting to him.

Constanz pulled her back down to her seat, scolding
softly. Amiranth only nodded as her mind whirled with
possibilities. She leaned back in her chair, fanning herself
now with one hand, murmuring an excuse. Her sister-
in-law leaned in closer, frowning; Amiranth slumped
down more, trying to look faint. Her heart was pounding with excitement, and the room was very warm. It
was not difficult to feign illness.

When Constanz dismissed her, Amiranth quickly
moved away, pretending to look for an attendant. Once
out of sight, she managed to slip into the crowd standing along the walls, using the people to hide her. She
knew that even if Augustin had seen where she went,
he could not call out for her, not during such a great
ceremony.

Amiranth ducked and weaved through the assembly
nearly unnoticed, and contented herself with a spot not
too far from the king's dais, tucked discreetly behind the
velvet robes of some royal adviser.

He was here! Her beloved, at last, approaching King
Edward. And now she was close enough to see Tristan's
profile as he bent his head before the king. Close
enough to see his hands, loose at his sides as he knelt,
tanned and elegant, and to be blinded by the quick
gleam of Edward's sword as it cut through the stained-
glass sunlight to rest upon Tristan's shoulders. Close
enough to see his glossy black hair, longer than ever, the

ends still curling past the leather strand he had used to tie it back.

Close enough to see his lowered eyes, his lashes long and dark against his skin, his expression reverent as the king spoke his name.

Her heart filled then, brimming with emotions she could not name or explain. Pride, joy, adoration, even pain. The sunlight fell across the splendid colors of the chamber and Amiranth felt it swim amid her tears, sending everything around her into a blur, only the shape of Tristan steady before her.

She had daydreamed of that moment ever since, seeing him, feeling that sharp elation suffuse her at just the memory of it.

And that had been the last time she had seen him, one year ago.

Until today—her wedding day.

"Stand up straight!" Constanz's fingers pinched Amiranth at the shoulders, forceful. "You look the very kitchen wench when you slouch so."

"Yes, Constanz."

Even her sister-in-law could not bother her. Not this morning, only hours from having her deepest, most delicious dreams manifest. He was coming for her even now. Tristan would be here at Iving Castle soon, and they would wed, and she would be the happiest woman ever to live.

So Amiranth stood patiently next to Lily in the chamber they shared, both of them listening with carefully averted eyes to this series of last-minute admonitions.

She did not dare to look over at her cousin. They would both laugh, and spoil the scold.

Constanz stood with her hands on her hips, surveying Amiranth up and down. The lines from her nose to her mouth turned deep.

"They will be here very soon. Do not disgrace us, Amiranth."

"I won't, Constanz."

"Indeed you won't! You know how much this means, child. Your brother has worked very hard to arrange this betrothal. Do nothing to jeopardize it."

"Yes, Constanz."

"And stay here in your chamber until you are summoned. I won't have you destroying your gown by tearing about the way you do. I've spent far too much time on it."

"I will, Constanz."

"Your cousin may keep you company. Be ready when you are called."

"Yes, Constanz."

Her sister-in-law waited a moment longer, scorching her with her stare, then gave a short nod and swept from the room. The door opened; for a brief moment a chorus of outside noises blared into the chamber—shouts and commands, the random furor of conversations, all frantic preparations for Tristan's entourage, the wedding feast to come.

Amiranth and Lily watched Constanz go, looking at each other only when the latch to the door clicked shut. Lily gave a slight smile.

"She is worried for you," she said, all gentle goodness.

"She is worried for her coffers," Amiranth replied, but then smiled back to take the sting out of her words. "It would not do to have the Earl of Haverlocke withdraw the sum he has promised for the distinction of my hand."

"It *is* a distinction." Lily was defensive of her, as always. "He is fortunate to have you!"

"Let us hope he thinks the same once he sees me."

"Of course he will. You look lovely," Lily said now, a most effective distraction.

"Do you think so?" Amiranth could not keep the edge of trepidation from her voice.

The betrothal had been arranged sight unseen, the result of nearly a year of offers and counteroffers, letters exchanged, the approval of the king sought and granted, the final agreement sealed. It had not hurt that Amiranth had pushed, as carefully and subtly as she could manage, for the arrangement. That when the first astonishing query came from Haverlocke, she had managed to smile and nod to her brother, and say—quite sedately—why, no, she would not reject his suit out of hand.

Augustin, who fretted constantly over his lack of funds, had pounced upon her agreement, the gleam of gold in his eyes all too visible.

Like all noble marriages, it was to be an even exchange. His wealth, her breeding. Yet, for all the Earl of Haverlocke knew, he had never before even glimpsed his future bride. They were to meet formally this afternoon—finally, at last.

Out of habit Amiranth glanced at the closed half of the glass window of her room, trying to make out her reflection against the sky. All she could see were bits of herself: the silvery sheen of her hair, swept back; large, dark eyes; a gown of blue that shone with trimming. She could not tell if she looked well in the gown. She could not tell if her cheeks were flushed or pale, or if the color of blue became her, or if the elaborate gold girdle at her waist added to her plumpness as she feared. . . .

She *wanted* to be lovely, desperately so. At least for today, she wanted to dazzle, to smile and strike envy into the hearts of all the other maidens. Today was to be her wedding day, and Amiranth fervently wanted Tristan to see her, truly *see* her, the way she had seen him all this time. She wanted so much to impress him.

What she would have given to have the looks of her older cousin—sweet Lily, without an envious thought in her, so stunning that grown men had been known to walk into walls for staring at her so hard. Even with their coloring so similar, Amiranth felt as different from her as a cod was from a mermaid.

Lily had assured her more than once how closely they resembled each other; how, when she had been Amiranth's age, her face had just the same roundness, her hair the same bright, unruly curl—even the same dimple when she smiled.

Lily was only attempting to lift her spirits, Amiranth understood that. It was typical of her generosity, to try to offer a little hope to her admiring cousin. But Amiranth had no illusions about her face or her figure.

All her life she had been plain. *Just today,* she prayed. *That's all I ask. Just today, let me shine.*

She turned away from the glass, drawing a heavy breath to test the restraint of this new gown, the ties of the girdle. She kicked up one foot, and folds of royal blue fluttered in place, falling back against her with rippling sighs.

Lily said softly, "You are as fair a bride as ever could be."

Amiranth laughed a little in spite of her nervousness. "Now I *know* you're wrong. The fairest bride ever to be will be *you.*"

"*If* I ever wed—and I certainly don't know who would want a wife with no name or fortune to speak of—I would be delighted to look half as radiant as you right now."

"You will wed, wait and see," Amiranth said. "To a prince, I am sure of it! I shall kiss you on your wedding morning and laugh and remind you of this moment."

And Lily, with her breathtaking beauty and her loving heart, only smiled again at this, modest and tender.

"Are you anxious?"

"Yes."

"I would be, as well." Lily came forward, taking her hands. "So let us not think of it. What shall we do to pass the time until he comes? Do you wish to sing? To sew?"

Amiranth gazed around the room that had always been hers, and then hers and Lily's. It was as safe and familiar to her as could be, had remained exactly the same for as far back as she could remember:

A large bed, carved wood and ornate cloth, gold and red and green. Thick rugs across the stone floors, tasseled and brightly colored. Cupboards and chests, furs and woolen blankets. A hearth of slate; the window of leaded glass, half open to show the sky. Tapestries draped against two walls, slowly swelling and falling with the breeze— scenes of castles, and deer and streams, and crowned queens out hunting on a procession of white horses.

She had lived here all her life. But soon she would reside in a new set of rooms, ones fit for a countess. Ones where *he* would come to her, and smile at her, and call her *wife*.

"I'd like to just wait for him, if you don't mind," Amiranth heard herself say. "Yes. I'll wait."

"Then I shall wait with you," replied Lily in her calm voice, and together they crossed to the window and looked out upon the unclouded day.

THEY WERE LATE. VERY LATE. THE SUN WAS WELL PAST its zenith and the riding party still had not been spotted.

As the hours passed without sign of them, Amiranth felt a slow sinking in her heart, her hopes fading.

Perhaps Tristan would not come. Perhaps he had never meant to marry her. Perhaps it was naught but a mistake, or some terrible jest, to wed the most handsome man in the kingdom to the drabbest maiden. Perhaps he had found some other noble, desperate family with an eligible young girl, one that would take a lesser settlement than the rather immense amount Augustin had demanded.

Perhaps he had decided that he did not need to wed at all, that linking one of England's oldest and most honored houses to his own—for any sum—was simply not worth the price.

A mild breeze wound around her, soft against her skin, and with it arrived the most awful thought of all, one that sent a tremor of panic through her:

Perhaps Tristan Geraint actually *had* seen her before, and noticed her. Perhaps he did not come because he knew her face, the sturdy dumpiness that had marked her all her life, common features, common wit, common, common, common—

But then the scout sounded his horn. She looked up, a hand to her throat. Lily was beaming at her, bright as a star, and Amiranth could only beam back, so happy and relieved she felt her eyes tear up.

"There," Lily was saying, patting her on the shoulder, "I told you, love, he would come . . . I told you. . . ."

At the farthest edge of the horizon came a smudge of darkness against the ample forest—a line of riders, banners flying. There were not many, Amiranth thought, squinting to make them out. Somehow she had expected more of them, though she could not say why. Perhaps it was because he had always seemed to have so many friends in London. But approaching Iving now was a mere handful of men, all in his colors, crimson and silver.

She tried to pick him out from the group and could not—again came that flutter of panic. He had not come. This was no wedding party at all, but merely a messenger and outriders sent to withdraw from the agreement. Sweet heavens. How could she bear it?

"I think I see him," said Lily now, interrupting her thoughts. She pointed, taking care not to reach past the frame of the window and be noticed. "At the lead, Amiranth. Surely that's him?"

Amiranth leaned forward, holding her breath.

The lead rider wore no helmet, no protection of any kind that she could see, not even the hauberk of the others. As they approached the outer walls of Iving, he lifted his head, surveying the castle.

"It is!" Her breath released; she leaned back against the cool stone wall, close to laughing. "He came!"

Once inside the bailey the group was no longer visible from the window. There was a rise in the noise beyond the door, from the great hall below. Amiranth closed her eyes, trying to envision what was happening. Was he inside yet? Had Augustin greeted him yet, and welcomed him in? Was he even now looking for her, perhaps?

She felt Lily place her hand on her shoulder again.

"Shall I go down and take a look?"

Amiranth opened her eyes, giving her cousin a grateful glance.

"Would you?"

"I'm so terribly thirsty, aren't you?" Lily asked, tranquil. "And we don't wish to disturb the preparations for the party. I'll just go and see if I can find something for us to drink."

And with another smile, this one just as benign as all

her rest, Lily left the room, carefully allowing the door to remain open behind her by just a sliver.

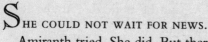

SHE COULD NOT WAIT FOR NEWS.

Amiranth tried. She did. But there was so much going on, and all of it involved her, and she could see none of it.

He was down there, somewhere! He was walking the halls—her halls!—and gazing at the rooms and talking to her brother. He was stepping where she had stepped a thousand times over. He was seeing all that she had seen, and hearing what she could hear.

She had to see him. She could not wait.

Her hallway was deserted. Even though the day outside was bright, the interior of the keep remained shrouded in cool shadows. Torches along the walls gave periodic relief from the dark, enough for Amiranth to confirm that she was alone.

Augustin's solar overlooked the great hall, where everyone would be. From there she would have an excellent view.

No one saw her; the solar was as empty as the hallway. She crept toward the balcony at the end of the room, staying in the shadows as much as she could manage. The ties of her girdle caught the faint light in golden glints, but there was nothing she could do about that. Really, she only wanted one small look. That was all. She would be done and gone before anyone noticed. . . .

The solar balcony was composed of blue stone and pillars, impressive, tall arches that ran from one end of the wall to the other. Amiranth turned sideways to fit behind one of the thick columns, then peered around the curve of it to watch the scene below.

People everywhere. Talking, laughing, shouting. She found Augustin first, because he enjoyed standing out—tall and blond, dressed elaborately today, his finest tunic and hose, a heavy chain of gold and colored gems ringing his shoulders. He stood near the dais, speaking to his steward, who kept nodding and glancing to his left.

Amiranth followed the steward's gaze.

The Earl of Haverlocke stood apart from the confusion, arms crossed over his chest, looking vaguely unhappy about something. A group of his men surrounded him in a half circle, speaking to one another, eyes fixed upon the commotion of the hall. More of them mingled about, a few already drinking. But Amiranth was focused on the man she would soon join in marriage.

He wore no beard, and she could not help but be glad about that—to see the clean slant of his jaw, the true shape of his lips. It made him look younger than he was, perhaps, but she liked that about him. What good fortune that she was not to wed a man twice her age, as had happened to so many girls she knew. What wonderful, wonderful fortune instead to wed the one she adored.

He was so handsome. Even now, standing relaxed with his weight on one foot, with his distant gaze and reserved manner, he was clearly superior to every other man in the hall. He remained rare and fine to her, exquisitely male in his crimson tunic with silver, the slight curl to his lips subdued.

Without warning he looked up, straight at her. Amiranth froze.

He can't see me. He can't.

But it seemed that he could. Tristan's face remained very serious, his dark eyes shuttered. He showed no surprise at what he saw, nor did he look away. Instead he gave a very small frown, still staring. Amiranth felt completely exposed, even pressed back into the shadows.

She was safe. There was no way he could pick her out from the row of pillars; the solar was very high, and darkness curved and arched around her. But she felt a flush begin crawling up her neck anyway, caught in her childish game of spying on him.

She stayed where she was a moment longer, partly to test her bravery, partly because she feared to stir, and allow the movement to reveal her. He really did seem to be staring right into her eyes, even from this distance. It was a strange moment, growing stranger as Tristan maintained his stare, penetrating.

Amiranth felt her flush turn warmer, dizzying, and even the stone against her body was not enough to cool her. Tristan's gaze was keen and knowing, relentless. She felt connected to him, their eyes locked together, and in this long, tense interlude Amiranth felt a new emotion growing in her, something beyond her wild anticipation of their marriage. For some reason, what she felt right now was . . . apprehension.

He was so serious. Formidable. She was completely

vulnerable to him, held in place in her brother's solar, fixed by the severity of this man she was to wed.

Someone walked up to speak with him and he turned away, releasing her without another look.

Amiranth scrambled back, heart racing, a metallic taste in her mouth. When she was safe in the hallway again she raised a hand to her lips, trembling.

Her fingertips came away dabbed red with blood. She had bitten her lip that hard to fight his spell.

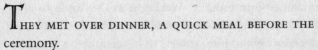

THEY MET OVER DINNER, A QUICK MEAL BEFORE THE ceremony.

Augustin drew her close, his arm heavy around her shoulders, and introduced her in hearty tones.

Tristan Geraint, love of her life, took her hand and bowed over it. His lips came nowhere near enough for a kiss.

"I am honored," he said in a bored voice. He dropped her hand, and looked away from her again.

IN THE FINAL HOUR BEFORE THE WEDDING, AMIRANTH sat alone in her chamber, staring at the mantle of cloth she held to her lap, worrying at the cut on her lip with her tongue.

Should she do it? Would he like it?

She had labored many an hour upon the design, meticulously stitching it together: Tristan's family colors and hers, chevron patterns of crimson and indigo blue in alternating folds, velvets and satins, white ermine lining the hood. It had taken many months to complete. In fact, she had finished it only a few days ago. She had begun it on the very day Augustin had told her of Tristan's missive of proposal, her dreams at last coming true.

When it was done, she had thought the mantle truly worthy of royalty. How pleased Tristan would be to see her thoughtful efforts for him, to note how gracefully she had combined their two houses in this design. She imagined him proudly wearing it as they rode back to his castle, how the wind would catch it and let the colors flare behind him, tribute to his elegance.

But now, gazing at the bunched material on her lap, Amiranth was filled with doubts. Perhaps her work was too clumsy. Or she would look too eager, to present it to him now, like a pet begging for approval. She had meant to give it to him later tonight, or tomorrow. After they were wed.

But something in her urged her to reach him before the wedding. It felt like a peace offering, although she certainly could not say why she needed to broker peace with him.

Yet he had been so quiet at the dinner. He had not even met her eyes.

Yes, Amiranth decided, standing. She would give it to him now, in this fragment of time before their union, and tell him how pleased—how *very* happy—she was to be marrying him. She would let him know, in no uncertain terms, that she did not begrudge this arrangement.

That it did not matter to her in the slightest that he was paying for her good name, to blunt the rumors that surrounded him. That he did not love her . . . yet.

Indeed, given the chance, she would tell him she had never believed any of the rumors anyway.

He could not be a murderer. Not her love.

Lily was downstairs, consulting with Constanz about the final details in the chapel. At any second Amiranth would be surrounded by women come to attend her. If she did not leave now, it would not happen.

Carefully she draped the mantle over her arm and left her chamber.

The Earl of Haverlocke would be housed in the finest of the guest quarters of Iving; Augustin would not put him anywhere else. It was a series of chambers not so very far from her own, ones that opened out into the larger of Iving's two enclosed gardens. At this time of year the garden was at its prime, with masses of blooming flowers that perfumed the air. Today it would be colorful and impressively lush, and Augustin knew it.

Tristan was not in his room. The squire there scowled at her, startled to see her as he answered the door, and took a good long moment before bowing to her. At her inquiry he claimed not to know where the earl might have gone.

Amiranth clenched her teeth and gave a strained smile, asking again if he was *quite* certain he did not know, did not have *any* idea where the earl might be, because her *brother*, the *Earl of Iving*, desired to see him. . . .

The squire scowled again and rubbed his forehead,

looking uneasy. At last he conceded that he thought the Earl of Haverlocke might have gone to the garden, and offered to look for her.

"No, thank you," Amiranth replied, and turned smartly away. She did not quite dare to sweep past him into Tristan's room. Besides, there was another access to this garden, through one of the main hallways.

The sun was lowering now, not quite dusk but nearly. As she stepped outside the light grew soft all around her, throwing purpled shadows across the grass and trees. She listened but at first heard nothing beyond the gentle splashing of the fountain Constanz had installed a few years ago. Birds sang, low and sweet; leaves rustled. There was peace in every corner.

". . . nervous?"

A man's voice, not Tristan. Amiranth hesitated, looking around her, still seeing no one.

"Hardly." This was Tristan. She recognized his honeyed tone instantly. "I merely want it to be done with."

There was a pause, more leaves rustling nearby. Something moved behind a mass of tamed shrubbery directly ahead of her, great bushes cut into fanciful shapes. The men were in the heart of the garden there, Amiranth realized, hidden behind the thick brambles. They could not know she was near. She stared down at her feet, feeling awkward. Perhaps she should go.

"Mayhap it won't be as bad as you fear," said the unknown man.

Tristan laughed, sardonic. "Mayhap."

The other man lowered his voice. "You know what the king said, Tristan."

"I'm not likely to forget. 'Marry well, Haverlocke, and marry soon.' "

"Edward has strong ideas about the redeeming value of marriage."

"Aye. He was even so kind as to give me a list of acceptable families. This was the first one"—another laugh, bitter—"the *only* one to respond. And there you have it."

"It is a wise course, to wed."

"Indeed. I'm neatly trussed and dressed, ready to be served unto that blessed state."

"You make it sound like prison."

"Isn't it?" Tristan's voice came suddenly closer to her, behind a bush shaped as a fat rabbit. Amiranth looked up, but she was unable to move otherwise. She could nearly make out his figure behind the leaves, the shape of a man against the green. "The king handed me an ultimatum. If I wish to remain in his circle, I must obey. So, I obey."

Leave, Amiranth thought. *Leave. Don't hear this.*

"Everyone marries, Tristan."

She heard him sigh. "Aye. I suppose."

"Well, what did you expect?"

"I don't know. Something . . . different."

The other man chuckled. "Different? How?"

"Better."

"Love?" suggested the other, now sounding perfectly serious.

Amiranth bit her sore lip, waiting for Tristan's answer, her fingers tightening over the mantle.

"No," he finally said. "Of course not. How could

there be love? We've never even met before. But at
least—familiarity. Companionship."

"Those things will come."

"Listen to you," Tristan grumbled. "As if *you* know
aught of it."

His friend laughed. "I've stolen love's fair favor more
than once, I'd say!"

"Aye, but I wasn't thinking of *your* sort of love. I
meant—"

"Oh ho! So you *do* want love!"

Tristan's reply was exasperated. "Not at all. I'm not
an idiot. All I wanted was—a choice, at least!"

Silence followed this. The two figures stood motionless behind the bushes, each apparently lost in thought.
Amiranth remained focused on Tristan, her thoughts
racing.

He wanted love—he had nearly said it, he wanted
love, *her* love! It was perfect—she *did* love him, she had
always loved him, and now all she had to do was tell
him so—

"All I mean," said Tristan suddenly, "is that I'm marrying her because I must. She is marrying *me* because
she must. I assure you, she's not becoming the Countess
of Haverlocke because she loves me. This is business,
that's all."

"How very cold of you."

"I'm certain she's a pragmatic girl. *She* won't have
any illusions about it."

"Do *you*?"

He sighed again. "Not any longer."

Another silence, unbearable. She had to do something,

say something. Amiranth lifted her chin and took a deep breath, ready to pretend she had just arrived, when the other man moved, tossing up his hands.

"Oh, cheer up, my lord. She looked presentable to me."

"She's a plain little damsel," responded Tristan, in his gorgeous voice. "She'll lead a plain little life somewhere away from me, I'm certain. That's the way of things."

Amiranth grew cold—instantly, horribly, like ice in her veins.

"Cynical," noted the other man.

"Honest. Did you really think I could bring her with us to France? She's like these pampered English blossoms, my friend, coddled and spoiled. She'd wilt in a sennight. I'm off to war. She's got no place with me."

Amusement threaded the other voice. "Your wife has no place with you?"

She could almost make out Tristan's shrug. "I'll be back. Someday."

Go, Amiranth thought. *One foot at a time. Start with the left. Go.*

"What if she wishes to accompany you? She seemed quite smitten."

"I'll take her as far as Safere. It's on the way." Tristan sighed once more, the sound of it frustrated. "We'll call it a wedding trip."

She heard the *pop* of a cork coming free from a bottle, the shallow clinking of rings against glass. The friend spoke again.

"Too bad it's not her cousin. Did you gain a look at her?"

"Cousin?"

"The attractive one. Iris or Lily, something like that. Fair hair, hazel eyes. Slightly older. Poor relation, I heard. Some distant kin."

"Aye, I saw her." Another pause. "Pity. I suppose we know where the beauty of the family resides."

Amiranth moved her left foot, and then her right. She turned and retreated from the garden as silently as she had entered it.

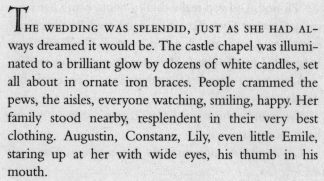

THE WEDDING WAS SPLENDID, JUST AS SHE HAD AL-ways dreamed it would be. The castle chapel was illuminated to a brilliant glow by dozens of white candles, set all about in ornate iron braces. People crammed the pews, the aisles, everyone watching, smiling, happy. Her family stood nearby, resplendent in their very best clothing. Augustin, Constanz, Lily, even little Emile, staring up at her with wide eyes, his thumb in his mouth.

It was a most exceptional gathering. Sumptuous—because the Earl of Haverlocke was one of the wealthiest men in the kingdom—and impeccably royal—because her own family had ties of blood to the king himself.

It was a wedding worthy of a princess. Even Amiranth's gown incited awe, pearls and gold and rich blue velvet, a precious circlet of garnets and sapphires across her forehead.

And when her groom repeated his vows, just slightly unsteady on his feet, he was near enough that only

Amiranth could smell the wine on his breath. Only Amiranth could see the redness in his eyes as he blinked and swayed, and held the look of a man who was not fully certain of what was taking place around him.

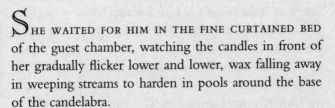

SHE WAITED FOR HIM IN THE FINE CURTAINED BED of the guest chamber, watching the candles in front of her gradually flicker lower and lower, wax falling away in weeping streams to harden in pools around the base of the candelabra.

A shiver took her; Amiranth was cold, completely undressed in a bed for the first time in her life. It felt odd and painfully defenseless, her bare skin against the sheets. She really didn't like it at all. But she knew that soon Tristan would come, and it was expected that she would greet him in this state—Constanz had told her so. She had gone on to mention other things, strange and disturbingly vague, telling Amiranth that she must submit to her husband, and allow him to do things to her no matter how much it hurt. The look on her face alone had set a seed of terror deep in Amiranth's stomach.

She kept the covers up to her shoulders now, but they did little to ward away the chill that permeated the room.

The sounds of the feast in the great hall remained undimmed, hours after her discreet departure. From her position in the bed—half hidden behind the curtains—she could not actually see the door to the chamber, but she could hear very well the noises beyond it. The festivities appeared nowhere near ending.

At the wedding feast they had eaten beside each other, she and her new husband. They had shared food, and a goblet of wine—though Tristan had drunk most of that. His fingers had brushed hers only once, very lightly, as if he could not bear her touch.

Amiranth had smiled and replied to all the good wishes in the happiest tone she could manage. Tristan had merely nodded occasionally, looking around for more wine.

With the quiet urging of Constanz she had retired here to his chamber, fussed over by a series of women who undressed her, and perfumed her, and combed out her hair. Lily had held her hand, very tightly, and then kissed her on the cheek before leaving with everyone else.

That had been four candles ago. There were still three left burning on the candelabra, but their flames were turning a dull yellow. They would die out very soon.

Amiranth watched them, concentrating on them and nothing else—certainly not the sound of masculine laughter that still rang from the great hall—until her eyes burned so much she had to close them, slipping lower and lower into the bed. . . .

The sharp *crack* of the door slamming open startled her awake. She sat up abruptly, gasping. The room was nearly dark—one lone candle remained lit, the flame of it swaying with the draft.

Voices at the doorway; Amiranth shrank back into

the depths of the pillows, clutching coverings around her, panicked that he had brought others with him. What should she do? She was undressed, alone—if he brought them in farther they would all see her, and they would laugh at her, looking so silly here waiting for him in bed, the plain little bride—

But she heard Tristan telling them to leave now, and—thank the Lord!—they did, shouting out things that made no sense to her, their words choked with laughter. The door closed again.

She heard him move around the room, stumble into something and mutter a curse, then move on. He seemed to be taking an amazingly long time to come to her.

Amiranth gave a small cough, in case he did not realize where she was. Then he was there, a dip in the mattress, sitting on the edge of the bed, his back to her. He dropped his head down into his hands. She heard a low moan.

She waited for him to turn, to say something to her, or at least to look upon her, but he did not.

He was drunk. He found their marriage so unbearable that he had abandoned any notion of public dignity and immersed himself in wine. And now his head hurt.

Good, she thought, sitting up straighter. *He deserves it.*

Another moan came from him, deep and miserable.

The single flame beyond them wavered and dipped. It created shadows in his hair, faint glossiness across the ebony of it. His fingers, threaded through the mess of his locks, were long and refined, the tan of his skin looking now close to golden brown.

In spite of herself Amiranth felt a curl of sympathy for him. This was still her Tristan here before her, weary and unwell. It was not his fault that she did not appeal to him; he was merely a man. Naturally he would be disappointed in her appearance. Naturally he would compare her to other women—to Lily—and find her lacking.

He could not know her secret heart, or her thoughts. He could not know how she had hoped for him, had cherished his face each night in her dreams. He was the man she had loved for ages, though he could not know that, either. Tonight really changed none of that, no matter if she wished it to or not.

Amiranth reached out a hand to him, placing it on his arm.

"Would you like some water?"

"No. Thank you."

She took her hand away. Tristan didn't move. He didn't do anything else, in fact, for a very long while— long enough for the last remaining candle finally to extinguish, the flame sputtering out in a twist of smoke.

Thin moonlight was all that lit the room now, spilling in from the open windows that faced the garden. It hid his face as he turned toward her, shifting suddenly, much swifter than she had thought he could be, silent now, a dark shape against the dark.

She felt him loom up close to her, his hands at her shoulders, pressing her back into the bed, and then he was over her, still fully clothed, pushing aside the coverings between them, his breath a rush against her neck, his form covering hers.

Amiranth let out some small noise of protest, but he seemed not to hear. She felt his hair against her cheek, silken. His tunic, the material of it warm against her, solid heat from his body. His hands, sliding from her shoulders down the curves of her, his palms against her bare skin— and it was happening so fast, all of it so fast, she did not have time to understand it, what he meant to do to her.

The seed of fear from before grew suddenly stronger in her, shortening her breath, and when Tristan bit her earlobe she jerked against him, stiff. But then he paused, perhaps taking in her faint trembling. When he nuzzled her there again she felt him kiss her: a light kiss, his lips barely there, like a whisper but better, more thrilling. It stilled her as he did it over, his tongue against her skin, amazing. He tasted her while his hands still moved, feeling her, touching her in places that sent very singular sensations rippling through her.

What was happening? He seemed to know her body better than she did, caressing her in a way that should have sent her scrambling for modesty . . . but instead Amiranth found herself arching into him, closing her eyes. He moved again, was now kissing her throat, her face, her mouth—harder, more intense. When he spoke against her lips it was dreamy, the opposite of his touch.

"Soft, soft . . . you're so soft . . ."

Her hands were sliding up around the width of his shoulders, tracing his form beneath the tunic. Past the weight of him she was beginning to feel something new, something almost fine—the way he was moving against her, between her legs, a budding warmth. Even the pressure of his kiss became nicer, heat and urgency, the way he teased the shape of her lips with his tongue.

It was startling and strange. It was so—agreeable.

Hesitant, she framed his face with her hands, kissing him back, and he grew still over her, allowing her careful inquiry of him. She knew his lips, the contours of his cheekbones, every aspect of his features. How delightful, to brush her mouth across him, to feel so intimately what she had only seen all these years. How exciting, to note the faint roughness of his cheek, his new beard already growing in—to inhale the scent of him beneath the wine, to stroke his hair as he stroked hers. How incredible, that she could do these things to Tristan Geraint, her *husband*—

He moved swiftly again, rising between them, and Amiranth let her hands fall away, puzzled. He was fumbling now, adjusting his tunic, his hose. When he lay atop her once more there was something new between them, something hot and rigid . . . and then it was no longer between them but against her, pressing slowly and astonishingly inside of her, unyielding.

Her pleasure of before instantly vanished. What he was doing now hurt—so much that she gasped aloud, unable to stifle it. But instead of stopping, Tristan took a deep breath and then pushed against her, quick and hard.

The pain exploded within her. Amiranth barely managed to cover her mouth with her hand to stop the cry—what was happening, oh God, was he killing her?

He kept moving in that sharply painful place, stretched over her, their bodies connected in a way she never could have imagined. The hurt of it slowly began to lessen, but the shock still numbed her; tears streamed down her face, hot against the cold night.

Tristan's breathing was ragged, rough. He kissed away the tears, still moving, his face lost and dim to her.

His rhythm changed, slowed . . . he tensed above her—pausing at last—and with one final, long groan collapsed across her, limp.

Amiranth lay very still now, weeping silently even though the pain was mostly gone, her hand tight over her mouth. Tristan's breathing began to lengthen, become more regular. It sounded almost as if he might be . . . falling asleep.

Please, yes! Let it be over!

He stirred finally, lifting his head. She felt his lips against her cheek, another kiss, warm.

"Don't cry, sweetheart. I'm sorry. Don't cry."

She took her hand away, fighting for control as he kissed her once more and then pulled away from her, leaving behind a stinging ache in the part of her he had invaded. The night air seemed clammy now, dismal. Her body throbbed with grief.

Tristan rolled away, taking the covers with him. He muttered something unintelligible, nestling deeper into the mattress. Then he said it again.

"Love you."

Her breath caught in her chest, mid-sob. Amiranth sniffed, looking over at him, flat on his back now across the bed, covers tangled across him. His eyes were closed. He looked very peaceful.

She wiped away the wetness on her cheeks, then leaned up on one elbow to see him better.

"What did you say?" she asked, hushed.

Tristan yawned, rolling over once more, giving her his back.

"Love you," he mumbled again, his words slurred with sleep. "I love you, sweet Bess."

And then he began to snore.

Chapter Two

Safere Manor
1349

THEY ATE IN STIFLED SILENCE IN A DARKENED, EMPTY room, seated at an immensely ugly table Tristan hazily recalled from his youth here.

The golden-haired maiden kept her eyes downcast, serving him and then herself from the meager dishes before them, all vegetables—spiced, broiled, boiled or stewed.

She had prepared them herself, apparently. He had seen no one else around to do it for her.

After their meeting in the garden she had led him back inside the manor, watching him warily, still silent. Tristan had followed her because he could not think of what else to do.

Amiranth was dead. He had come all this way for naught.

The handmaiden had turned to him once in the great room and bidden him to sit, in an attractive, husky voice. Some old habit had him choose the chair at the head of the table; he saw her notice it.

"Who are you?" he asked of her at last, when all she did was stand in front of him, pinning him in place with that somber stare of hers.

Now that they were inside the manor he could see that his initial estimate of her beauty had been quite accurate. She was lovely in a way that teased the back of his mind for some reason, younger than he, but not too much so. An exquisite face, nearly too perfect to be true. But for the colors of her she really could have been a marble statue, an ode to some artist's worship of Venus, mayhap.

Her hair remained that wonderful hue even in this light, like gold darkly polished, very long, curling at the ends. Her eyes were not blue, as he had expected, but a rich brown, a startling contrast to her blondness. The depths of them glowed with some emotion Tristan could not name as she gazed upon him now.

"You don't remember me," she said, not a question at all; there was no expectation in her voice to imply that he should. Nevertheless, Tristan felt himself flush.

"I'm sorry," he said. "I'm sorry."

Her head tilted very slightly, her eyes judging him. Her expression remained impassive.

"I am Lady Lily Granger. Amiranth was my cousin."

Tristan felt a burst of embarrassment come over him

again, stronger now. "Of course," replied, trying to conceal it from her. "I beg your pardon."

"It is not *my* pardon you must beg," she replied.

He could not think of what to say to this. Her gentle, direct accusation was devastating enough to slice through to his bones. She was correct. The fact that he was too late ever to apologize to his wife was a sin of unforgivable proportion.

She let him languish there for a while longer in his remorse, apparently waiting for him to say something new. Nothing came to him beyond further apologies, however, and she had already spurned his feeble attempts at that.

So Tristan only stared up at her from his chair, knowing it was rude, unable to stop. She was a tie to Amiranth. She was the first person he had met in years who had not openly scorned him.

Her gaze shifted from his face to his clothing, bringing a bare frown to her forehead. He knew how he looked: his tunic was shabby at best, filthy and torn, years old. His hose were ripped. Only the boots he wore were fit—he had stolen those from some unsuspecting Frenchman who had left them out to dry behind his cottage after a rainstorm. More apologies owed, Tristan knew. His whole damned life seemed to necessitate them.

The woman before him arched a regal brow. "You certainly look . . . different."

He felt a smile take him, dark and pained. "People do change, don't they?"

She did not smile back. Tristan had the sense that she

was judging him still, that her mind was not quite made up to accept this ragged, bearded man claiming to be an earl. Her voice echoed softly around them, so refined.

"We thought you dead."

"So did I," he replied, and laughed a little.

"Is this a matter of jest, my lord?" she asked, very grave. He sobered, shifting in the chair, avoiding her look.

"No."

"Not dead," she said, unmoving before him. "Merely truant, is that it?"

Tristan examined his hands. "I was—occupied."

"For eight years." A faint hint of incredulity crept into her tone.

"For eight years," he concurred softly, "as you say."

She fell silent once more, arms crossed over her chest, hair still flowing past her shoulders. When he looked up at her again he noted the light surrounding her from behind; she seemed more than ever like one of those righteous angels brought to illuminated life in texts, or chapel windows. Tristan half expected her to smite him with a burning sword at any moment.

"You've come a long way, no doubt," she said.

"Yes," he agreed again, unable to say anything further.

"All the way from France, I suppose."

"Yes."

Once more her gaze traveled up and down him, then back to his face, a gathering assessment. He could not say why it should be, but Tristan almost felt some of his agony diminish, looking into the profound depths of her eyes, such a warm brown. . . .

"When did you last eat?" she demanded abruptly.

He shook his head. "I don't know."

Her stare turned hard again.

"Yesterday," Tristan tried, fumbling for the memory. "Or the day before."

The arch to her brow was back. "Remain here."

She left the room.

He followed her anyway, drawn to her, the sight of her black skirts brushing the floor, her hair swinging at her waist. Once in the kitchen she threw him a pointed look, clear disapproval, but he had waited a bit longer, lingering awkwardly at the doorway.

He did not want to be alone. He had spent too much time alone already.

But she obviously did not want him there, so he retreated, finding his way back to the main room of his manor, slouched down into his chair, counting the seconds until she reappeared.

She brought him those dishes of vegetables, the delicious, steaming scent of them making him slightly dizzy. He watched her serve him, practiced and smooth. When he inquired about meat—he had dreamt of eating meat again, years and years now—she replied in a dispassionate voice:

"There are two chickens left. You may try to catch them and kill them if you like. I will not."

Tristan ate the vegetables.

There was wine as well, liquid ruby contained in cut-glass goblets, very fine. He was vaguely surprised by that, to see such delicate glasswork here in this place of stone and dust. The shining, elegant goblets seemed so misplaced, another segment of his past that had slipped away from him, unnoticed. He scowled down at the one in his hand, swirling the wine, trying to remember.

She noticed his scrutiny. "They were a wedding gift." She paused, then added bluntly, "For *your* wedding."

"Yes," Tristan replied, as if it were the most obvious fact in the world.

Her gaze returned to her food, cool as an autumn lake.

It occurred to him, over the course of the meal, that the entire situation was probably very peculiar. He could not say for certain—he did not seem to recall much of the intricacies of genteel manners—but surely there should be some other people here—serfs, at least.

Of course there should be serfs, came a sudden thought, one of those unexpected moments of clarity that still fell over him. *This is Safere. It has a staff of twenty-three.*

He glanced at the woman sitting to his left, two places away down the table.

"What happened to the serfs?"

She did not look up from her soup.

"Is that truly what you wish to ask me first, my lord?" Her voice was very composed.

He glared at her, abruptly infuriated. How dare she defy him? Who was this bold servant, with her comely face and strange lack of deference?

She did look up now, meeting his eyes.

"Do you care to know nothing of what befell your wife?"

Tristan blinked, the rage gone in an instant. Amiranth.

That's right—he had come for Amiranth and found Lily instead. Cousin. Not a servant.

He was too hot. Why was the room so hot? There was not even a fire lit in the hearth.

"Yes," he rasped. "Tell me."

She rested her hands beside her bowl. "As it happens, there is one answer for both questions. The plague came. Everyone died—or fled."

"Plague . . ." He rubbed his temple, so tired now, trying to make sense of the word.

"Yes, the plague," she snapped, her composure at last appearing to fracture. "The Black Death. Mayhap you've heard of it? It's killed half the kingdom, from what I understand. Safere was no exception. It arrived here seven months ago. My cousin was one of the last sickened. She was naught but a pampered English blossom, after all—she died two months past."

Her words were biting, strangely familiar, yet he could not bring his thoughts together clearly enough to imagine why that should be. He felt quite removed from himself, from even the heat of the room.

Tristan heard his own reply as if from a distance, saying the right things, trying to placate her.

"Sorry. I didn't know. How awful."

"How awful," she repeated, in a carefully empty way. "Indeed."

He was at a loss, trying to make sense of what was happening, all the things that had already happened without him. Plague. Death. Amiranth.

The dish of sauced peas before him, so enticing moments ago, became repulsive suddenly, completely inedible. Even the smell of it, garlic and spice, was turning his stomach. He was starving, he was dying for food—and he could not take a single bite.

The irony of this seemed blackly humorous; he could not stop that dark smile from returning. His voice spoke again, still coming from some place beyond him . . . close to the ceiling, perhaps.

"Well, this is a dilemma. I have come to find me a wife, and now I have none."

"Restrain your grief, my lord," she said sharply, "lest you harm yourself."

"Certainly," he murmured.

Tristan was remotely aware that he was behaving badly. He couldn't think of why he was doing it, or even how to halt it. He sent the golden-haired cousin an entreating look, wishing she might understand—how hot it was in here, how her words were becoming like silk to him, sliding along him, slippery and thin. She had turned her face away, no doubt quite angry.

Another instant of cold clarity shone at him: Here was someone who had actually known his unknown wife—her habits, her likes, her foibles. Here was one who had loved her. She truly was *gone,* that girl he had met so briefly.

He recalled the inscription on Amiranth's gravestone. Lady Lily obviously had been more than just a cousin to his wife, she was also a devoted friend.

Not like you, said a cruel little voice inside him.

"In France, you see," he was saying to her, speaking quickly over that other voice, to drown it out, "they did not allow me out. I stayed alone until the end, and the door opened. They took me and I ran—it was night-time, and I ran, and they did not catch me. . . ."

He was babbling, making no sense. He could see it in her face, her newly focused attention on him, the widening of her eyes.

He was frightening her. He had not meant to, but he was.

"Well," Tristan said ponderously, still from that great distance. He felt his head fall back against his chair, and curiously enough he did not care to raise it up again at all.

Without warning her face was above his, alarmed. Her golden hair fell down around him like beautiful rainfall, framing her, touching him, cool and bright. He tried to reach up a hand to feel it better; she knocked his fingers away. Her breath became a hiss against his cheek.

"You are ill!"

"Perhaps," Tristan agreed, dazzled by the colors of her. "Perhaps."

"The plague," he heard her say, her words echoing in his ears, and, oddly enough, he sincerely hoped so. The plague would do to him what no one else could have, or would have. The plague would be an end with no uncertainty at all. Aye, let it be the plague.

But for her—

"Go away," Tristan said.

"Don't be a fool." She was already pulling him from the chair. "Do you see anyone else around here to aid you? You may have me or no one, my lord."

"Oh," he replied, very rational as he staggered against her. "Then you, of course."

I T WAS NOT THE PLAGUE. AMIRANTH HAD SEEN ENOUGH of that to know that the signs were all wrong; he was feverish and flushed, and thinner than she remembered. But there was none of the dreaded swelling at his throat or under his arms. No boils. It could not be the plague.

Her diagnosis was not merely the result of her yearning for it to be true—far better if it *were* the Black Death, at least for her. For some reason, the plague did not touch Amiranth. As the people all around her at Safere had begun to drop and die, only she remained healthy, appalled, watching the bare control she had maintained all these years on the estate crumble away to nothing, until all was naught but dust around her.

And now from that dust had risen a phoenix of sorts—her missing husband, returned at last to Safere.

It had taken her eight years to believe she had finally banished him from her, that she had cleansed the ache of him, the longing for him, from her soul. And with the skip of just one heartbeat he had shattered that belief.

One moment she been seated in the garden before Lily's grave, secure in her outcast world; in the next she had looked up and seen him before her, watching her.

At first she had thought him a dream, an illusion. How could he be real?

He was bearded and frayed, filthy as a beggar. He might have been some madman, wandered past the gate.

But she had known him in that very instant as he stood alone in the sunlight—his eyes, his voice. Even his hands, bloodied and torn. It *was* Tristan Geraint, the lost and late Earl of Haverlocke.

Eight years she had spent living in his manor, branded with his name, her very existence shaped by his thoughtless decision to take her to Safere. Eight years, and he had shaded her life in one way or another every single day, even after they had all thought he was dead.

How God must be laughing at her now, finally answering her prayers from years past: her husband had come back for her, and he had not even recognized her. Not at all.

He thought—he truly thought—she was Lily.

Amiranth realized that the passing of time had whittled her looks. Lily had been the first to remark upon it, just a few years into their exile, how Amiranth's hair was turning darker, becoming more like her own. Her face, her smile . . . even her hands, all of her slowly evolving to become Lily's shadow. That girlish plumpness that had cursed her for so long ended up melting away amid the steady heat of Safere. She even grew another three inches, until she and her cousin stood eye to eye, perfectly matched in height.

They were not exactly alike, of course . . . but close, so close. Lily's hair was more a pale golden brown to Amiranth's deep gold. Lily's eyes were a shade lighter; Amiranth's lashes a shade darker. Little things, larger differences slowly changing to become more subtle ones, and Amiranth could only wonder at her strange fortune.

It was a cosmic joke, perhaps—now that it no longer mattered, she was finally gaining a portion of her cousin's beauty.

Near the end they had been almost like reflections of each other. Lily had made that comparison once, laughing, and Amiranth could not help but agree—mirror images. But she knew that mirrors could only reflect the truth, a dusky suggestion of the real person in front of it. Lily would always be that bright reality, kind and good. Amiranth could only ever hope to echo her, and fight the shadows that dwelled within her.

In dim rooms even the servants had confused them for each other. It was the only reason she had thought to do it, such a mad idea: become Lily. Take hold of her destiny, and leave behind this life Amiranth hated.

She took Tristan to the room that would have been his—that *was* his, she reminded herself—the master chamber, and let him fall into the bed there, a dark shade of the man she once knew. Then she stood back and just watched him, studying his face, both angered and awed by the fact of him before her: a hard-vanquished ghost somehow returned to astonishing life.

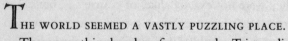

THE WORLD SEEMED A VASTLY PUZZLING PLACE.

There was this chamber, for example. Tristan did not know it at all, but at the same time he knew it so well that even the corners of it he could not see were familiar to him.

And there was the woman. She was no one he had ever been introduced to, he was very certain of that. He would remember such wicked beauty, a face of pure innocence, and eyes that shone with worry even as her hands did those terrible things to him. She was torturing him, this evil spirit disguised as a saint. She was nearly killing him—taking him to the edge of death and leaving him there, because it would not do for him to die. If he died, the pain would stop, and none of them wanted that.

He tried to fight her off and that only got him tied to the bed when he was not looking, sly maneuvers that had him screaming at her, that he would kill her himself once free from here, that she would suffer as he did, by God!

But she ignored his threats, carrying on with her diabolic acts, pretending at times to care for him, wiping his face, whispering soft words—then later on hurting him again, sending fire through his blood, agony, broken glass behind his eyes, knives in his skull.

She was a witch, a harpy. He would kill her for this, he would.

But those times when she touched him tenderly, and blew her sweet breath across his forehead, it made him want to weep, his love for her was so great. How could she do this to him? What had he done to deserve such torment?

Tristan did not know, and grew too tired to try to reason it out. The best solution, the only real escape he had, was to sleep, and leave her behind. In sleep she could not touch him, for better or worse. In sleep, that darkest place of quiet, there was no pain at all.

———————— ⟁ ————————

H E HAD A DREAM OF HER COMING INTO THE ROOM, pale and stricken against the gloom.

"Your horse!" she exclaimed, in a voice that trembled. He could make no sense of that. He had no horse. Did he? Only that little gray pony as a boy, the one on which his father had taught him to ride, and then his destrier, killed in that very first battle in France—a dirty deed by some damned French knight, to slay his steed beneath him, until they both fell to the mud, bleeding—

"You did not latch the stall!" the woman cried to him, anguished. She came closer to the bed, flow and movement, gold and black, her face tight with emotion. "You did not latch it!"

She seemed utterly dismayed, even distraught. Tristan felt a happy malice bubble through him, triumphant. He didn't know what she meant, but the witch was hurting—finally, after hurting him so badly. *Yes,* he wanted to sneer at her, *the stall, damn you!* But his mouth was not yet working, and so he could only stare at her, hoping that his victory over her showed in his eyes.

She appeared not to notice, sinking to her knees before him, her hands over her face. Her shoulders were shaking.

"The garden," she was saying, over and over, incredulous. "Oh, my garden, gone, gone . . ." Her hands fell away; her face was shining with tears. "All the food is gone."

A WOMAN OF EXCEPTIONAL BEAUTY WAS SEATED beside him on a stool. Her head was bowed over a needle and a fold of cloth in her hands. She was sewing by candlelight. She did not appear to notice he was awake.

Tristan studied her, recognizing her features from a place lost within himself long ago. It seemed so odd: He could not say where he was now, or why he was here, or why he felt so hellish. He lay upon a bed that had a particularly hard lump right at the base of his spine. There were blankets over him, up to his shoulders, soft against his bare skin. It must be night out—the window beyond his silent companion was utterly black. The air was very cool.

He should certainly have been alarmed, at least, to awaken to find himself alone with this woman in this place, so exhausted he was unable even to lift a hand to rub his eyes. But he was not.

Instead, Tristan was remembering her.

It had been at a castle, not his own. A crowded hall, people talking, dressed well, speaking in jovial tones. The smell of food in the air, and of rushes beneath his feet. People kept trying to speak with him, fawning, pretentious. He had hated that. He recalled wishing he might be somewhere else, somewhere calmer, where he might relax, no one to stare at him. And that was when he had caught sight of her.

Now he remembered. She had been above him, somehow . . . up some stairs . . . or a balcony. Aye, that was it—a balcony, the edge of a solar. She had been standing alone amid the shadows and he had noticed the gleam of her hair, this particular shade of darkened gold, distinctive even in the half-light.

At first his eyes had tricked him; he had thought it was just a girl up there, peering down at him owlishly, hardly more than a child. But then the shadows had seemed to change before him, shifting, and when he blinked and looked closer the girl had transformed into a vision of a young woman—*this* woman—remote and lovely, set high above the confusion.

Iving Castle. Betrothal. Wedding. And her . . . something to do with a flower . . .

Tristan found his voice, broken and hoarse.

"Lily."

The woman started, dropping the needle and thread to her lap. He heard her let out her breath, a rushed sigh, and then she leaned over to place a hand on his forehead.

"Are you in pain?" she asked, in that husky voice that sounded so dulcet to him. When he tried to answer her it came out as a cough instead, a sharp twisting that lanced across his entire body. She was there, close to him, supporting his head and pressing a mug of cool water to his lips, telling him to drink.

He accepted the water, bliss on his tongue, humiliated that she would see him in this weakness. What had happened to him?

Lily laid his head gently back on the pillows, the

thick braid of her hair falling over one shoulder to graze his chest.

"You've been very ill," she said, answering his unspoken question. "Do not attempt to talk yet."

But he had to know if his vision had been real. He had spent so many days and nights imagining things—the course of his life, how it was, how it might have been with only a few wiser choices, wishing he could have it back to do over again. . . . Years of dreaming, because there had been nothing else left to him. Let this dream, at least, have been truth.

"I saw you in the solar, didn't I?" he asked her, his voice very rough. "Before the wedding. That was you, wasn't it?"

"Rest," she replied, picking up her sewing, rising from the stool.

She was leaving! She would leave him here like this, not knowing what was real, unsatisfied! Desperation gave him strength—Tristan lifted a hand to stop her, a tug at her skirts. When she looked back at him, impatient, he spoke again urgently.

"It *was* you! You were at the castle, for the wedding. I saw you from the great hall. You were watching me."

Lily paused, studying him, candlelight lending warmth to her cheeks. She said slowly, "Yes. That was I."

He smiled, releasing her gown. He remembered her. She had not been a dream.

"What were you doing up there?" he asked, hoping she might sit again, talk to him, or just stay quietly with her sewing, so that he might admire her, this fair maiden who gave him water. . . .

She gazed down at her hands, the embroidery she held, not replying. The light flickered; he saw something new in her now, a glimpse of some other person, a girl with paler hair, a similar nose, small and straight.

"My wife," Tristan said, a revelation. "You're her cousin."

Lily's gaze returned to his. "Your fever has broken."

"I had a fever?"

A very slight smile curved her lips, delicate irony. "Yes."

He managed to bring up one hand to his face, testing for heat. Instead he felt only the smoothness of his skin, cool as the night.

"You shaved off my beard," he said, bemused.

Her brows raised. "To fight the illness. You are fortunate that was *all* I shaved."

Tristan stared up at her, uncomprehending, but as soon as she said the words she had looked away again, as if suddenly shy.

He turned his head to see the room—he knew it now, looking upon it with fresh eyes, the furniture, the shape of the window, even the stool she had drawn close to the bed. It used to be over there, by the armoire. This was his father's room. This was the master chamber of Safere. . . .

He was at Safere! *England!*

His attention went back to Lily, still paused before him. More pieces of memory fell into place—a hot sky, the empty manor, the marble girl in the garden . . . the chiseled marker bearing the name of his wife.

His elation dimmed, then drained away to nothing.

Amiranth was dead. Aye. After all those years of dreaming of her, she was gone. There was only her cousin left in this deserted place.

"What are you doing here?" he demanded abruptly.

Her gaze met his, a spark of indignation in her eyes. "Tending to *you,* my lord."

"No, no." He struggled to sit up. "I meant, what are you doing *here,* at Safere?"

"I . . . came to be with my cousin, not very long after you left. I was Amiranth's companion."

"Amiranth needed a companion?"

"She was lonely," Lily said, exquisitely neutral.

She did not have to add what they both knew: *And it was your fault.*

Just the thought of it brought back the fatigue. Tristan was too late to reach his lonely young wife. She had died forsaken here, just as he almost had, and there was no one to blame but him. He recalled now Lily's coolness to him, her careful reservation. He was fortunate that she had bothered to save him at all. Why had she? He was too tired to ask.

Lady Lily walked to the flickering candle on the table nearby. She brought her face close, her hand cupping the flame. He saw her lips purse, golden light flaring across her profile, and then the flame vanished. Blackness took the room, true night. The ebbing scent of smoke drifted across his face.

"Rest," came her voice, close to the door. He could not see her, only hear the soft rustle of her skirts as she left him, her light footsteps fading away down the hall.

Chapter Three

Eight years earlier:
en route to Safere Manor
1341

A CHALLENGE, MY LORD!" THE YOUNG KNIGHT named Gilbert cried. "To the edge of yon field and back!"

Amiranth watched as her husband grinned and spurred his horse on, matching the pace of his friend as the two of them raced ahead of the caravan, a rising line of dust on the road marking their passage.

"Splendid," she muttered, and dropped the curtain beside her, ending her view with a swish of scarlet and purple cloth.

She sat alone in the small carriage, occasionally shifting from side to side to prevent her legs from growing completely numb. With the curtains loose the sun turned her world a muted violet, filtered through the heavy material and wood surrounding her.

The roll and sway of the carriage left a constant queasiness in her stomach, but when she had asked to ride horseback, as Tristan and his guard did, all she received were incredulous stares. Clearly a countess would not do such a thing, and the fact that she had been a countess for only just over a week appeared to make no difference in the matter.

So all of her husband's men rode beside her, green knights as young as he was—surely none of them older than twenty—and their squires, exchanging jokes and comments, free to set their own pace, while Amiranth was left to swelter in this torturous enclosure, hidden from such rash and dangerous things as sunshine and clean air.

She swiped an angry hand at the curtains, sending the fringed tassels along the edges dancing. She hated it here. She hated traveling like this, she hated the cramped carriage, and the guards outside, and most *especially* she hated Tristan Geraint.

And for all she could tell of it, he felt the same way about her.

Amiranth had awakened alone in her bridal bed the morning after the wedding, blankets messed and rumpled, Tristan nowhere to be seen. She had risen from the covers, wincing at the ache in unexpected places, hiding it from the maids who had come to her, and helped her bathe, and exchanged smiles over her head.

She had spent the day almost in hiding, alone, too

shamed to face Lily, or even Constanz, with her brisk questions. What could she say to them?

She had given her heart to a man wholly unworthy of it. Her marriage was a mistake. A dreadful, dreadful mistake. Most dreadful of all, there was nothing she could do about it. Amiranth had pleaded a headache until dusk, when she finally grew too miserable to remain alone any longer.

Tristan did not reappear until supper that evening, when he had blown in from a hunt with the August wind, surrounded by his men, offering her only a quick bow of acknowledgment.

To her very great relief, he had not come to her bed later that night—or any night since. She had no idea where he had stayed, or with whom. She didn't care. It didn't matter. As long as it was not with her.

They had left Iving and her family a mere day later. Apparently her fine husband was in such a rush to get to France that he had no time to spare for her sensibilities, the long farewells Amiranth suddenly had wished to make.

She had stood there in the bailey of the castle, watching Tristan's men mount up, tremendous steeds, quick movements, barked orders. It was all so foreign to her, these men and their ways, their leader, that young man she once thought she knew so intimately.

She had stood there and felt herself begin to quake, sick with fear of what was about to happen, all her days and nights to be spent in such a way, with strangers, in a strange world—a world where she seemed not to merit an ounce of true attention, much less affection. Lily stayed close to her, reassuring, holding her hand, even helping to shield her face as Amiranth wiped away one desperate tear. Lily had told her she loved her and embraced her tightly as they said their goodbyes.

Amiranth had to bite the inside of her cheek, very hard, to hold back the whimper that wanted to come. She did not *want* to leave Iving! She did not *want* to be wed! Not to *him,* not any longer! Sweet Mary, she did not want any of it, and could not imagine how she ever had.

But Tristan had come for her then, his stride brisk and impatient, and Amiranth had gathered her courage and walked away with him, toward his entourage and the carriage that awaited her.

Her husband handed her in, saying nothing, touching her fingers gingerly, as if she were fragile enough to shatter. Feeling a flash of defiance, she met his gaze openly, daring him to note her reddened eyes, but all he did was nod to her, sober. He stepped back and released the sash that had restrained the curtains, ending her final view of her home. And that had been the end of it.

She had been trapped in this carriage for nearly a week, enduring the heat and her woe. She had only a vague idea of where they were going—to one of his estates, she knew. The one closest to France.

Once, it would have filled her with despair, the idea of being torn away from him. Now she could only count the days.

Outside the carriage the echo of hooves pounded closer now, the race returning. Amiranth lifted the edge of the curtain to watch the two riders gallop toward her, crouched low in their saddles, wild exhilaration on each face.

Sir Gilbert had turned out to be that other voice in the garden at Iving, the one who had mentioned Lily. Amiranth hated him, as well.

Tristan held the lead but his friend was a close second, both of them flying along the road, horses foaming, coming so close so fast that even a few of the guardsmen were exclaiming, pushing off the path. A rough rocking took the carriage; Amiranth heard the horses cry out nervously, the call of her driver, trying to restrain them. Men were beginning to shout outside. Without warning the carriage gave a hard jolt to the left. Amiranth slammed against the side there, winded, and then everything seemed to jump and she found herself on the floor, twisted sideways, her arm crushed against the edge of the seat.

The curtains were now dangling loose above her head. She blinked up at them, dazed, not understanding how she had come to be beneath the window.

The outcry beyond the carriage had not abated, louder now, peppered with oaths. A face appeared in the rectangle of the sky that was the window, darkened against the light.

"My lady! Are you hurt?" A man's voice, worried. It was not Tristan.

"No," she replied. "I don't think so."

The face was gone, and then the window, too. The door above her opened. Hands reached down, lifted her free from the wreck of the carriage and into a cloud of dust on an uneven road. The knight who had helped her quickly withdrew, disappearing among the men milling about.

Amiranth raised one hand to her head, looking around her, seeing the wreck of the carriage, flipped neatly onto its side in a large ditch by the side of the road, the free wheels still spinning in slow circles. The back left wheel, crushed against the ditch bottom, had split several spokes. A number of men were attempting to unfetter the panicked horses from the twisted harness that held them, having no easy job of it.

"That was a near thing!" someone said cheerfully.

Sir Gilbert, still mounted, drew his sweating destrier close to the carriage, surveying the mess of it. He turned to the figure who had just ridden up beside him and grinned. "Nearly made yourself a widower, my lord, while as yet barely a groom!"

The dust began to settle, and the other figure took on the shape of Tristan, twisting around in his saddle until he finally found her. For once he did not turn away from her, but met her gaze steadily. He was not smiling.

Amiranth rubbed her sore arm, glaring back at him.

"You might have killed me," she blurted.

He looked down, actually appearing chagrinned. His hair was now streaked in light brown waves, dust and dirt mingling with the perspiration she could see running down his temples. When he looked up at her again she was struck anew by his beauty, dark and stunning, the features of a man with rogue perfection, that curl to his lips unrepentant.

"Sorry," Tristan said. It was the first word he had spoken to her all day.

Perhaps it was the heat, or the shock, or just her sour spirits—Amiranth felt her temper snap.

"Sorry? Sorry? Why, my lord, whatever for? Surely *I* am the one who must apologize to *you*! How terrible of me, to interrupt your silly games! How inconsiderate, that I might have my carriage here in the path of your race! I am the worst kind of wife that might be, to deny her husband the pleasure of his reckless behavior! I do most humbly beg your pardon, dear lord—"

Tristan had dismounted smoothly, coming very near to her, unexpected. He took hold of the hand she had been using to gesture wildly at the broken carriage.

It emptied her of words. She was left dangling there, midsentence, as he leaned in even closer and spoke again softly.

"Amiranth. I said I was sorry."

She felt her anger scatter, her thoughts as splintered as the sad carriage wheel. She could only stare up at him, the endless black of his eyes finally fixed on her, finally seeing her, here in this dust and ruin, her hair falling down around her.

He looked very serious. Almost leisurely his free hand reached up, his palm pressing lightly against her cheek—not quite a caress, but a sensation of gentle interest. She froze, entranced.

It was a dream come real before her, at last, at last. He saw her now, right enough—all of her, mussed and flushed, mute with wonder. She was held fast in time, lost to him, dazzled by even this simple touch. She could not have moved to save her life.

The slightest frown came to him as they stood there, his gaze searching hers. Gleaming strands of her hair floated up between them, rising with the sultry breeze as if they were not even part of her, ivory pale.

With his hand still against her cheek, Tristan closed his eyes and lowered his head. His lips covered hers, firm and warm, sweeter than heaven itself.

So then Amiranth closed her eyes as well, afraid to think, to breathe, lest she dash this splendid dream.

When he ended the kiss his expression had not changed; the slight frown was still there, as if he were not quite certain of what he had done. He looked dazed, almost perplexed. He blinked at her, pulling back, glancing around at the green countryside, the carriage, the road. The men surrounding them, gone still and silent.

Tristan looked back at her and smiled. Her heart melted into a puddle of liquid heat.

"I'm glad you weren't hurt." He gave her hand a squeeze and then was gone, moving away from her with the same speed and grace he had used to come close, as if the kiss had never happened. As if nothing at all had happened.

She watched him retreat to his companions, all the men talking now, somber and low. Only Tristan kept his smile, saying something to Sir Gilbert, who laughed suddenly, throwing back his head.

Amiranth stood alone in the middle of them all, still

feeling the warmth of his lips against hers, sparkling magic amid this rough day.

THEY CAMPED BY THE DITCH THAT NIGHT, CLOSE to the useless carriage, beneath a vast sky of indigo and silver. Amiranth ate alone, as she had every evening— although tonight, at least, it was Tristan who brought her her meal, roasted pheasant and hard cheese.

He had lingered beside her after handing her her portion, and she had waited, looking up at him from her seat on a mossy log, trying not to expect anything at all. Starlight brushed him from above, hiding his features. Even the campfire kept throwing shadows across them both, so that she could not truly see his face. Amiranth knew it so well she did not need the light. But it would have been nice to perceive his eyes.

"Are you well, my lady?" he asked, almost hesitant.

"Aye." *No. I miss you. I love you. I still do.*

"I—I am sorry about this afternoon. I want you to know that."

She couldn't tell if he meant the accident or the kiss, and tried to smile over the pained confusion within her. "It's forgotten."

"Safere Manor is but a few days' away," he said, as if to reassure her.

"Oh."

"I'm sure you'll enjoy it there. It has gardens, like your brother's castle."

She nodded, still smiling.

"And—the ocean. Do you like the sea?"

"Yes," she said, although she had never set foot on a beach in her life.

"And . . ." He rubbed his cheek with one lean finger, apparently searching for something else to interest her, but after a long pause added only, "The kitchens are excellent."

"How wonderful," she replied, trying to sound sincere.

"Yes," Tristan agreed, and fell silent once more.

They remained like that a bit longer, he standing, she sitting, letting the night stay between them. For one endless moment she thought—she *hoped*—that he might kiss her again. But finally all he did was bow, supple and low, and back away.

Amiranth pretended not to watch him rejoin his men near the fire, settling down with them, becoming one of them so easily. She was the lone outsider here; never was it more evident than at night, when she slept in the middle of their circle, surrounded and solitary.

Amiranth decided, upon reflection, that she hated the night as well.

As she began to pick at her meal she heard them talking, exchanging stories of war, and of France, and the king's will. Their voices rose and fell against the constant song of the crickets in the woods.

". . . invincible, I say!" This was Sir Gilbert, speaking ardently to the group. "We cannot lose!"

"The problem with the Scots has taken a toll," said one of the knights, a note of caution. "We should not go marching blindly into France, no matter what the king says."

"King Edward has the right of it," insisted Gilbert. "The French crown should be his—"

"And so it will be," said another man. "And we'll be the ones to hand it to him, won't we, lads?"

Approval met this, the passing of wine flasks. A plume of sparks spiraled up into the sky, gold against velvet blue. Amiranth turned her gaze down to the charred pheasant, chewing resolutely. She tried, without much success, to block out the rest of the conversation, focusing instead on the crickets.

"English forces waiting . . . reinforcements . . ."

". . . eight hundred men . . ."

". . . as little as five months for the siege, to take all of Calais . . ."

". . . to ransom . . . I'll take some of that French gold—"

"—jewels!"

"—women!"

Laughter took them all, drowning even the forest sounds. Then Tristan's voice came clear, cutting through the others.

"We've bested them at sea, and now we shall best them by land. In a fortnight we'll be there, in battle. Winning."

"The French have seen none such as us, I wager, by land *or* sea!" declared Sir Gilbert.

"I wager not," agreed Tristan, and they all laughed again.

"To honorable war!" proclaimed one of the knights,

and the others stood to salute this, a tight circle of men in mail, lit with yellow fire.

"To war!"

"To war!"

"To glory," Amiranth heard her husband add, and everyone cheered.

———— ◦〜〜◦ ————

NEVER BEFORE HAD SHE SEEN SUCH A DESOLATE place.

Safere Manor seemed formed of naught but hard stone and burnt colors, singed by the sun above, crouched defensively against the sea below.

They approached it slowly, in great procession. From her vantage atop one of the carriage horses Amiranth had a perfect view of her new home, pushing up against the flat of the land. Only the air seemed lively here, smelling of sea and salt. She could hear the ocean Tristan promised writhing against the cliffs below, crashing against the rocks. Even it seemed intent on assaulting this walled estate.

She tried not to show her dismay at it, her sense of loss—no lush greenery, no gentle hills or winding creeks. No family awaiting her. She would not have even the comfort of her own clothing—her trunks had been left behind with the broken carriage, to be sent on in a few days after the repairs were made. So all that Safere seemed to offer her was the heat, and the dirt, and the vast, strange boulders that littered this land.

Amiranth made certain her face was as neutral as she

could manage before she looked over at Tristan. She did not wish to reveal her true thoughts to him: that she dreaded this place already, that she could not imagine living here at all—how could anyone? She knew he meant to rest here a night and then move on, off to his glorious war in the name of the king.

She would not be the one to break down. She would not beg him not to leave her here, no matter how awful it seemed.

But her efforts at cool indifference were wasted upon Tristan; he was not looking at her. Hardly unusual. Instead, he held a hand to his eyes to block out the sun, examining the place much as she had. His mouth lifted to a handsome smile.

"There!" he said, as if none of the rest of them could see it. "By God, look at that! I have not been here in years—it is just the same!"

"Last outpost to France, eh, my lord?" said one of the knights, and Tristan nodded, pushing his steed to a trot down the road.

Amiranth thought resentfully about keeping her horse to its plodding walk, but they would most likely only leave her behind. She touched her heels to her mount. The carriage horse gave a tired sigh, moving to catch up.

The gate was scrolled iron, ornate and thick, patches of rust dotting it along the curves. Two boys, no older than pages, were struggling to open it as they approached; the gates swung wide with a groaning sound. The boys bowed as all the group filed past, Amiranth near the end.

The interior of the estate seemed hardly more promising than what she had glimpsed from the outside. She knew the Earl of Haverlocke had properties ranging across half the kingdom. Surely this had to be the most bleak of them all.

Someone helped her down, one of the servants of Safere, a man with a weathered face and curious eyes, openly staring from her to the carriage horse she rode, to Tristan, who was already walking away. A short line of bowing serfs stayed silent as he passed.

In spite of his impudence she thanked the man in a murmur, hurrying to follow her husband and the rest of his knights, trying very hard to appear that she belonged with them. They all headed for what had to be the manor house, long and winding, a sprawl of stone and wood and shuttered windows. Just outside of it spread a dusty garden, wind-battered trees and gaunt shrubs, green plants laid out in careful rows. Tristan looked behind him then, finding her, nodding to the plants, and she could only nod back, still trying to catch up past the other men. He kept moving, disappearing into the manor house.

It was a relief to be inside a real building again, away from wind and heat. The manor was very dim; Amiranth found herself in an extended, narrow hallway, walking with everyone else toward the room at the other end. She could hear Tristan talking ahead, others responding, although she was far enough behind that she could not make out what was said. She thought she heard a woman's tone, and walked a little faster.

The room at the end of the hall was quite large, like

a great hall, but with fewer tables. In fact, there was
only one table in here, long and heavy, benches along
both sides, a chair at either end. Tapestries drifted above
them, draped from the tall beams that crossed the ceiling. A lone window in the far wall allowed in the only
light, nearly blinding against the shadows.

Amiranth paused, taking in the space of it, gloom
and coolness, another line of servants pressed back
along one of the walls. These did not bow—or perhaps
she had arrived too late to see it. They remained as they
were, staring at the floor, hands clenched into skirts or
tunics.

The knights were already seating themselves at the
table, looking about them, talking loudly. Only Tristan
remained where he was, speaking with the woman
Amiranth thought she had heard earlier, an older lady in
a simple gown of gray, a veil of cream. She was nodding
her head, curtsying over and over as Tristan kept talking. He appeared not to see Amiranth enter the room.

She squared her shoulders and approached the two of
them, standing patiently near her husband as the
woman—the chatelaine, Amiranth assumed—began to
speak.

"Of course it is a great honor to greet you, my lord! If
only we had but known of your arrival— I pray you will
find all to your liking! I will see to your rooms myself, my
lord! If only I had had time—"

"We have not yet eaten today, mistress," said Tristan,
flashing his devastating smile at the woman. Amiranth
watched with interest as the chatelaine grew flustered,
her eyes lowering.

"My lord! We have a fine meal already in the making! Potage and shallot tarts—I only wish I had *known* you would come, my lord! I might have had a banquet for you—"

"No need for that," said Tristan graciously. "Whatever is ready will do. We may banquet tonight."

The chatelaine curtsied yet again, beginning to back away. Tristan turned, then caught sight of Amiranth, close behind him.

"Oh," he said, his face lighting up. "There you are."

She began to smile at him, almost ready to forgive his negligence for just the glad look in his eyes now. Tristan touched the back of her hand, calling out to the chatelaine.

"Mistress!"

"Yea, my lord?"

He gave Amiranth a little push forward. "Here is my wife. She may aid you in the kitchens."

------- ◦〜〜〜◦ -------

H E WOULD BE GONE IN THE MORNING.

Amiranth held on to that thought tonight, a sliver of comfort here in this strange darkened chamber, a narrow bed, a lack of stars outside the closed window.

She sighed and tossed the blankets off her, too warm despite the cool night. The chatelaine—her name was Agnes—had led her here to this room for the night—for *every* night, Amiranth supposed—saying that this was the chamber the previous Countess of Haverlocke had used. It was small and filled with pretty things, painted screens and bright rugs, the bed a jumble of jewellike colors, and furs that smelled musty with age.

Agnes had declined her help in the kitchens. It had become very clear, as Amiranth stood awkwardly next to the hearth, that she had no idea what to do, despite her husband's casual offering of her services. She could plan a menu with ease; enacting one was another thing entirely. The chatelaine appeared to take pity upon her, bidding her to sit, bringing her food, wine, as the grand new Countess of Haverlocke sat alone at the servants' table, hunched over her meal.

The noises of Tristan and his men in the other room had remained quite merry, even as they finished their dinner and wandered back out into the sunshine, practicing their warrior arts in the courtyard. Clearly spirits were high as they anticipated their quest to France.

"Go, then," Amiranth muttered now, to the canopy of the narrow bed. "Go and be gone with you. I'd sooner miss a blister on my heel than you, Tristan Geraint."

Gone in the morning. Fine. Let it be. She had no cause for sorrow, especially right now, as her husband ate yet again in his hall, a finer feast for supper, the banquet Agnes promised fulfilled. Out of spite Amiranth had withdrawn to her room, refusing to endure another long meal of being ignored. Better she remain here, alone in spirit and company, and rest after the tedious journey. Better to sleep early and wake late, and perhaps even miss his leave-taking.

He would not even notice. She knew he wouldn't.

She had married a boy. A mere boy, not a man, despite

his comely grown looks. A man would not disregard his wife so. Surely a man would not.

Gone in the morning. And she would be stuck here until he made up his mind to return.

Amiranth rolled over and clutched at a feather pillow, hugging it to her.

I am not *sad,* she thought, setting her teeth. *I am* not. *Let him go.*

He would whether she willed it or no. Better at least to be at peace about it.

———————— ⟨⟨⟨⟩⟩⟩ ————————

S HE AWOKE AMID THE GRAY OF THE DAWN WITH A start, wondering what it was that had brought her out of her dreams. Nothing stirred; no noises about, no movement that she could see. The room lay traced in the pallid light creeping past the sill of the window.

For a long second Amiranth could not recall where she was. She remained motionless, afraid of this unfamiliarity—what was this place? But then she remembered all that had happened, and what this morning meant.

She was tired. She wished to go back to sleep. She did not wish to face this day. Her eyes closed.

A sudden, rolling sickness overcame her, rising past her stomach, tightening in her throat. Her eyes snapped open again, her hand pressed over her mouth. She stumbled out of bed and found a basin barely in time.

When it was over Amiranth lay back on the hard floor of the room, panting, wretched. She had already lost her home, and soon her husband. And now, on top of all that, something in the meal last night had spoiled—she had thought the jellied fish tasted off—and this terrible day was to be made worse with malady.

A sly thought took her, sneaking past her misery: perhaps Tristan was ill as well. Perhaps all of them were. There had been plenty of fish. Perhaps they would not leave today after all.

But by the time the sun had slipped over Safere in full force, golden bright, Amiranth saw that she was the only one afflicted. Tristan and all the others were cheerful and hale. Their very excitement seemed to hum and swim about them.

She stood off to the side in the courtyard, leaning against the manor wall with her arms hugged over her stomach, watching as they packed up their steeds. They remained as boisterous as always, these bold young knights with their brave futures. It seemed to take them no time at all to finish the preparations. Half the men were already mounted, banners waving, shields lined up along the destriers in polished fields of color.

Tristan was standing in heavy counsel with Sir Gilbert and a few of the others. She saw their discussion end, all of them bowing to him, then scattering to their horses. Her husband walked over to his stallion, and now she moved, pushing off the wall, crossing to him as he mounted.

She stopped before him, quiet, gazing up at him. He gave her a friendly look.

"Come to see me off, my lady?"

Yes, she meant to reply.

"Don't go," was what she said, a pathetic plea.

Tristan leaned down from his saddle, placing a hand on the top of her head, as he might a favorite hound.

"I must go, Amiranth. It's war. You understand."

"No."

His look turned restless. "I'm sorry. Try not to worry about me. I will return for you soon enough."

"When?" she asked, holding her arms tight to herself, so that she would not grab his foot.

"Soon," he repeated, and drew up straight again, so high above her on his destrier that her neck ached as she watched him. Warm sunlight gentled his face, lit his eyes to deep brown as he gazed down at her. He offered her that handsome smile she so adored.

"Farewell, my lady. God keep you."

"And you," she managed to reply, but he did not hear her, because he was already riding away.

———— ◦❦◦ ————

THE GLORIOUS BATTLE HAD TURNED MADLY WRONG.
They had killed his destrier first thing—his destrier!—and that had left Tristan stumbling about in the fog and the mud, swinging at men who remained high above him on their war horses, out of his reach but for flashes of them as they rode by, maces and lances and swords of their own, dripping with blood.

He fought as well as he could beside his downed steed, searching past the chaos for any friendly shield, any crest of England that might aid him. But there were only the French, so many of them, riding up out of the mist with guttural cries, appearing from nowhere, vanishing again as he did his best to fend them off. Tristan was half blinded by the fog; sweat and water mingled to sting his eyes, running down his face. He had lost the protection of his helmet in the fall—the nasal bar had bent so far it cut into his cheek. His shield remained trapped beneath the bulk of his horse.

God's blood, where were his knights, his squire? How could they have been so outnumbered so quickly?

"Gilbert!" he bellowed, fending off another blow. "Cyril! Morley!"

Only the indistinct screams of men and horses answered him past the wet vapors, sounds of battle and death.

The French meadow was a muck of filth. Three days of rain had turned it to a swamp, sucking mud and putrid grass, bodies scattered throughout. King Edward's commander had seemed so certain of this battle—a first, important step toward gaining control of Calais. They had planned this so carefully, gone in with such vigor. Yet the French had seemed to expect them, expect every damned move they made, and within hours they were surrounded on all sides, fighting an army as fierce as their own, and twice as large. Losing.

"*En avant!*" came a shout through the fog, very close. Tristan managed to turn just in time, ducking the lance that would have speared him, falling to the wet ground, too heavy with his hauberk and plates to roll. He struggled back to his knees as the knight turned his horse, circling around to try again. The pennon of yellow and green attached to the lance fluttered with bright menace.

"Have at you!" Tristan cried, enraged, finding his feet again. The French knight lowered his shield and held the lance ready once more, galloping toward Tristan at a truly astonishing pace. He deflected the lance this time, had the satisfaction of feeling the jolt of connection, his sword splintering the wood of it. The force nearly threw him to his knees again but he managed to stay upright, staggering.

"My lord!" A voice close-by, muffled by the fog. Tristan jerked around, seeing only blank mist, the ominous form of the knight returning.

"My lord! God's mercy!"

It was Gilbert, an anguished cry. Tristan barely noticed the Frenchman bearing down upon him. He raised his sword, still searching.

"Gilbert!"

The staccato thud of hooves drew him back to his foe—too late. Just as the mounted knight reached Tristan the lance twisted in his grip; a rapid, wobbling move Tristan had never before seen.

Tristan swung at him—and missed. The blunted lance struck him hard on his left side, tossing him backward as easily as a straw dummy on a quintain, emptying the world of all its air.

He lay stunned, sinking into the oozing mud, strangely feeling it seep into his ears, although he could feel nothing else. A blur of movement passed by his head, hooves splashing more mud over him, but he could not even wipe his eyes clean. Tristan took a terrible, gasping breath and then released it.

The whole of the battlefield turned dark around him.

———⟨ೲ⟩———

He AWOKE IN A CRAMPED SPACE, CHILLED AND MUD-died, sprawled across a floor scattered with what smelled like rotting hay. Manacles, cold as ice, bit into his wrists.

The first dazed thought that came to him was that it was an unusually black night. However, as his eyes adjusted, Tristan noted a narrow, crooked line of light falling close to the floor: torchlight, thin and wavering, sliding past the uneven planking of a closed door.

He was in a room. A tower room, from the rounded looks of it, rough stone, no windows, not even an archer's slit. It might truly be night—or day. He had no way of knowing such a thing, not without a window, and it was this realization that made him attempt to stand, to see the chamber better.

A devastating pain sliced through him, from his chest to his knees. He could not catch his breath from it. He heard himself gasping, still crouched against the wall, when a faint voice sounded against the stones.

"My lord?"

It was a ghastly tone, nearly unrecognizable. But Tristan had spent so many years with this friend, in good company and poor, that he recognized the speaker within a heartbeat.

"Gilbert!" His own voice was hardly better, a low hiss. "What has happened?"

"Defeat," replied Gilbert, still faint and lost to the darkness. "Prison."

"Calais?"

"No—I don't think so. Someplace south. It took us days to get here. I heard them say it—Mirgaux, I think it was."

The name meant nothing to him. Tristan attempted to rise again, much more cautious now. He used the wall against his back to support him, to take his weight when he felt the agony creep back, clenching around his chest. When he could he pulled at the manacles around his wrists—locked tight. The clinking rustle of chains came from near his feet. He noticed, with a sense of resignation, that his ankles were secured as well.

"What of our soldiers?" he asked, searching the shadows. Gilbert made some small movement; Tristan caught it, a faint blur against the stone. He was chained to the curve of the wall exactly across from him—not far in this small space. With effort Tristan thought he might be able to reach him—

"Dead," whispered Gilbert. "I saw it. They surrounded us. They slew Morley right away, and then Lewis, and Harold—we fought, my lord . . . but there were too many."

"Aye." Tristan turned, following the thick chain from one wrist up the wall. It was embedded into the stone high above him. He yanked at it as hard as he could. The chain rattled and bounced around him, bruising, holding fast.

"I'm fair relieved you're alive," said Gilbert, a trifle

stronger now. "For a long while I thought you dead as well."

"Not yet," Tristan replied grimly, still pulling.

"They did not take many of us, that I saw. No more than thirty."

"Where are the rest of the prisoners?"

"I know not." Gilbert stirred, sending his own chains into a metallic clatter. "I heard them speak of ransom. If they know your name, that may be why they keep us here."

"Perhaps."

Tristan released the chain with an angry sigh. His boots were missing, along with his armor and sword and even his gambeson, all of them obviously pilfered by the damned French. The floor was almost bitter cold against his unprotected feet. He tried to bring them closer to his body but the cramping around his chest would not allow it. Instead he sat hunched, awkward, trying to breathe through his mouth to lessen the ache.

"Tristan," whispered Gilbert, in his softest voice yet. "Think you we will survive this?"

"Aye," Tristan lied. He exhaled around his teeth, and tried not to consider what would happen next.

<hr />

THEY CAME WITH TORCHES, AND DAGGERS, AND IRON tools. They spoke with accents so thick he could not make sense of their words. All had the same face, long and thin and lined with black shadows, the smoking light of the fire reflected in their eyes.

When he did not respond to their questions, he discovered that their fists were effectively ruthless. He could not recall much of it; only the taste of blood in his mouth, and the pain in his chest became a crunching sound with each breath.

He tried not to listen as they turned to his vassal, noble Sir Gilbert, a steadfast friend. He tried not to watch but they held his face and forced him to, Gilbert stretched tall on the wall across him, his mouth an open gape, his eyes rolled up to whiteness.

He tried to forget it, hours later, days and years later—and could not: the sound of Gilbert's screams, devouring his very soul.

Chapter Four

Safere
1349

TRISTAN'S HORSE WAS DEAD.

Amiranth stared down at it in dismay, a hand over her mouth.

It was only two days ago that she had discovered the gelding in the middle of the travesty of her garden, busily finishing off the last of the sweet pea vines. After her initial shock she had managed to capture him and lead him back to the stables. He had followed her docilely for the most part, growing restless only when they passed Jorah's stall.

Jorah lifted her fine head over the door and bared her teeth at the other horse, letting out a squeal of anger. The gelding had responded in turn, and it had taken all of Amiranth's strength to get him into a stall. At last it was done; she had made certain there was water for him—no food, certainly not any longer—and then left the stables, dazed, intent on returning to Tristan, still in the grip of his strange fever.

The garden had been her only hope for survival in this place. As the servants had started to disappear, one by one, she had begun to concentrate on maintaining it: watering every day, weeding, even praying over it. She was not familiar with plants—Constanz had been the one in the family who gardened—but now she was the only one left to nourish the tender spring shoots.

The fleeing servants had taken most of the stores of food with them. They left by night, and there was nothing she or her cousin could do to stop them. Only a few of the faithful remained—a handmaid and two kitchen boys, who were brothers. They had all banded together in those last few weeks, every one of them working until they could not work any longer.

In the end, when the shadow of the plague had draped across Safere once more, Amiranth had let them go with her blessing, retreating to their villages, trying to reach home before the end came.

It became just she and Lily at the estate, and then she alone.

And the garden. It kept her fed; if she concentrated on it well enough, it kept her safe from insanity.

She had known from almost the first signs of the dreaded scourge that she would be forced to leave Safere. Were the circumstances less miserable it might have been cause for celebration—she had never loved this place or even liked it. Events beyond her control had forced her to live here, and now events beyond her control were forcing her to flee.

But she did not want to go alone.

Bandits roamed the land, everyone knew that. A woman traversing the countryside by herself would be an easy target for thieves, or worse. Though a good distance from any sort of village, Safere could hardly be termed safe, with its empty rooms and broken gates. But it was most assuredly safer than no haven at all.

She had been waiting for the traveling priest who served the estate to return. He was due in two months. He could consecrate the grave of her poor beloved Lily; he could absolve Amiranth of her sins—*resentment, anger, fear, trickery*—and then they could leave here together. If she could wait until then . . . if she could manage to stay alive until then, she would have a chance.

Tristan's horse had removed that chance. And now it lay dead in its stall, bloated with the last of her food, and she could only stare down at it, her entire being gone curiously numb.

Abandonment and plague and ruin, and now this.

It was not enough that it had eaten everything in sight. Now it was useless as well, and there would be only one horse for the two of them. They had too far to go to ride double on Jorah the entire way, even if she wished to do so, which she did not. She would have to walk while Tristan rode; he was too ill to do anything else. And dear Lord, she was so tired already. . . .

All at once the emotions flooded back to her, bright

and strong, piercing. She wanted to fall to her knees again, as she first had in her ruined garden, and weep. She wanted to scream and tear at her hair and shake her fist at God, who kept sending death back to her, taunting, leaving her to suffer life alone.

Jorah clenched her teeth around the edge of her stall door and shook it fiercely. The stench was truly awful; even the mare could not abide it.

Amiranth composed herself. She threw an old blanket over the gelding, then led Jorah to the stall farthest away, saying words in a soothing voice, telling the mare that everything was fine. Everything was absolutely fine, and all would be well again. She could not speak the truth aloud, even to a horse.

It was over now. Her last hope was gone.

TRISTAN SAT UP IN HIS BED, SAVORING THE LAST OF his broth. When he finished, Lily took the bowl from him, brisk and impersonal, as she tended to be.

"It was excellent," he announced, hoping to elicit one of her scarce smiles, but all she did was nod and place the bowl on the tray she had brought for him, turning to hand him a slice of heavy brown bread.

"I couldn't," Tristan said. "I'm quite full."

"Eat," Lily said flatly, still offering the bread.

"My lady, you will make me fat." He smiled now, enticing, still looking for her to favor him with her own. But his playful words had no effect upon her; or rather, not the effect he had hoped. Her lips grew thin as she met his look, her brows lowering. She tossed the bread back upon the tray.

"Fine," she said, in a voice that did not quite mask her anger. She turned her back to him, gazing out the window. He listened to her breathing, only slightly too fast, her arms clasped tight around herself.

"I'm sorry," Tristan said, puzzled. "Lily. I'll eat the bread."

"Why bother?" she asked coolly. "Waste it if you wish. It doesn't matter any longer."

And with that, she left the room.

Tristan stared at the doorway, empty and open behind her.

Without question, Lady Lily Granger was a riddle to him, deep and complex. He had known her only five days—only five days that he could remember—and with each new minute of being with her he discovered some new facet of her: a flash in her eyes, quick humor there and gone; a tilt to her head, sign that she was thinking hard about something; her hands, usually calm and relaxed, so delicate yet capable. Even the way she wore her hair—bound or free, offering clues to her mood; the beginnings of her day, when he was not there to see her rise, and dress, and seize the morning.

And her smile, that thing of rarity and pure loveliness, bestowed upon him only three times—he had counted each—the slight curving of her lips, a sweet happiness that found a chord within him, echoing it.

She even had a dimple, a fleeting mark of mischief that filled him with surprised pleasure.

Perhaps it was not right. Certainly it was not appropriate, to notice such things about his late wife's cousin. He hardly knew her at all. Was she wed? Betrothed? In love or out? She would not appreciate the direction of his thoughts, Tristan knew that well enough.

Yet she disarmed him. She fascinated him, for so many reasons he could not straighten them out in the muddle of his head. It was something about her, a sense of who she was, this woman named Lily, with her voice and her face and her hands, astonishing strength beneath astonishing beauty.

She had not even asked him about his past—not yet. Instead she had merely accepted his presence with a kind of patient grace. It left him even more indebted to her than he was before.

But he had displeased her, and he did not know why. Fair Lily, who had done nothing less than save his sorry life.

Remorse took him, holding tight to his tongue, to any smooth words he might command to charm her with. The old Tristan would have known exactly what to say to soothe her temper, no doubt. But that young knight had died years past.

The man he was now could only stare, silent, at the space where she had been moments ago.

What to do about her? He had no idea.

Tristan closed his eyes, frustrated, and then opened them again, looking restlessly around his father's room. He had already memorized every possible way out—*escape*, his mind whispered, *be ready, know the way*—although logically he knew that there would be no need for such a precaution. But he could not overcome that push within him, the fearful urgency that had to know, that *needed* to judge the doorway, how wide, how far it opened. The window; glass, breakable if need be, large enough to fit through. The garden outside, corners to hide around, places to run . . .

Ridiculous. He was in England now. There was no need to worry about escape.

The door, the window, the glass, the garden . . .

He shook his head, fighting that voice, glancing away again. For the first time he took note of the smaller things around him that had eluded him before, all signs of Lily's presence:

The basin of clean water, close to the bed, an ewer and mug next to it. Spare blankets, neatly folded across the top of a chest, a pile of men's clothing beside them. The stool she used, hard polished wood, her resting place while she had nursed him. Even, astonishingly enough, a small, framed portrait of himself on the wall next to the door. Tristan squinted at it, trying to make out the dusky colors that composed it.

He pushed back his covers and carefully stood. The room did not swim as it had the last time he attempted this, two nights ago. His body ached, his muscles were as sore as if he had just taken a fall from a horse, but he was standing. He took the plain tunic Lily had found for him and shrugged it on, enjoying the cool feel of it against his skin. A peasant's outfit, it seemed, thick cloth, sturdy hose. They were such a glad change from the rags he had worn these past years he felt like nothing less than a prince.

Tristan gave a small, ironic smile. If only those exquisite courtiers he used to run with could see him like this.

More memories—unpleasant to him now, to contemplate who he used to be, the frivolity of his life then. To distract himself he walked closer to the portrait, examining it curiously.

It had been done when he was just a boy, seven or eight, he thought, some indulgence by his mother at the time. He could not help but marvel at the child staring back at him, so stiff and formal. What a smooth face that boy had. What solemn eyes. What a dignified masquerade it all was, with a dog seated obediently at his feet, a bird in its mouth. He remembered posing for it, how the dog would not sit still, and the bird had been stuffed, empty holes for eyes. The missing eyes had made him cry, as he recalled.

He rubbed at the slight ache to his forehead, turning away, and his gaze finally fell upon the discarded slice of brown bread Lily had left upon the tray. He picked it up and went to find her.

It was eerie, walking along the empty halls once again. His arrival here days ago seemed strange and distant to him now; the fever had distorted what he did remember. He supposed he had caught it in one of the numerous French villages he had encountered—probably from one of the taverns he had slept in. He had lodged for weeks with the poorest of the poor, all of them stacked like kindling on the floors at night, huddled for warmth. There was anonymity in poverty, Tristan had learned that very quickly. But he had stolen enough money by then to afford the luxury of the floor, filthy as it was. He knew, from experience, that it was far safer than sleeping outdoors.

He had to stop for a moment, leaning hard against a doorway, and push away the dredges of that time. No matter that it had been just weeks ago. It was done now. He would not think of it any longer.

The pain in his head expanded, became more intense. He rubbed at it again, finding his way out into the sunshine.

The air outside Safere was exactly as he had hoped, warm and tinged with brine, surprisingly pleasant. He inhaled deeply, feeling better already, appreciating for perhaps the first time the uniqueness of this place, heat and salt and the pulse of the ocean, how just the breeze could make him feel glad to be alive. Why had he ever thought it inhospitable? Right now Tristan felt as if he could stay forever.

If only . . . if only . . .

If he had only one dream, one wish left from the storm of his life, this would be it: to remain here, enclosed behind these walls, safe from the whole of the world, from war and France and dank prisons. Just he and Lily, dwelling amid this rugged serenity, far from the eyes of anyone who might condemn them.

Tristan shook his head. What fantasy. Of course they would leave here—eventually. As much as he wished to deny it, he had a life beyond Safere, an earldom calling out to him, demanding him. He would see to it.

Eventually.

Until then, though . . . he had this secret dream.

When he found Lily the feeling redoubled in him, a hidden pleasure. She was seated on the marble bench in her garden, exactly where she had been when he had first discovered her—and aye, that was what it felt like, that he had *discovered* her. That in some mystic way she had not existed before he had stumbled to Safere. That as he entered the gates she had been swirled together from the sun and the sea and the cooling breeze, a woman of perfection formed in this very garden to greet him, and care for him—

He came out of his reverie, appalled. This was his wife's cousin. He owed both her and Amiranth far more than these unsettling, selfish thoughts.

Her head turned to him, just as before, and in spite of himself Tristan felt that dangerous whimsy slip over him again, that she was there just for him. That she had been waiting for him.

But just then something new about her arrested him: the angle of her head, the darkness of her eyes. He had a flash of memory of another woman—his wife, a girl who by all rights should still be alive here now. Shame took him; it should be Amiranth on that bench awaiting him. It should be Amiranth who sent this feeling of strange longing through him.

"You should not be out," said Lady Lily, not rising. Sunlight fell past the leaves of the tree above her, dappling her hair, casting her with a glow of molten gold.

Tristan felt, alarmingly, an urge to go to her, to touch her, to feel the softness of that gold. He stared down at the bread he held instead, fighting this yearning inside him.

Wrong, wrong, this is wrong. . . .

"I would prefer company to eat," he said at last, not quite an invitation, but close.

When he looked at her again, she was regarding him steadily, hands on her lap. He found it almost painful to meet her eyes, and so Tristan was the one who glanced away, finding the telling pink of the marker near her feet. He walked closer, concentrating on this.

Someone had done a passable job of carving the stone. The words were clear, if rough. The earth around it had become a mass of vines, ivy and something else, a flower he could not name, petals of deep lavender that reminded him of dusk.

He moved even closer now to see better, forgetting all else but the marker, Amiranth's name and title before him, nearly lost to the green. The wind took the branches of the tree above, sending patches of sunlight swaying across it all.

In his daydreams he and Lily might stay here. But there would always be a ghost to haunt them. . . .

"Did she suffer?" he asked, hating the question, that he had to know.

"Yes," Lily replied, almost careless.

Tristan rounded on her, guilt spurring him. "Why was she buried out here?" he asked fiercely. "She was a countess! She should be in the chapel, at least!"

He thought her face turned a little paler, but that might have been an illusion of the light. "The dirt here is soft, my lord. And I could not move the chapel stones by myself."

Replies froze in his mouth. He stared down at her,

realizing what it was he had said, and she. The guilt began to twine around him, sharp as steel, ruthless as those
ivy vines. He heard the *plop* of the bread he had held,
fallen to the dirt from his numbed fingers.

Tristan turned back to the stone, going to his knees
before it, close to Lily's feet. He traced the grooves with
his fingers, feeling the shape of them, trying to gain
some deeper meaning through this touch. Such simple
words, for a girl who had seemed simple to him, straight-
forward and kind.

He could not recall her face, her voice. What he
remembered more was the way of her, how she had
walked, the glow of her skin, the pink softness of her
lips. That time he had kissed her in the middle of the
road . . . how strange it had felt to him then, like a slow,
gentle awakening.

He thought that her hair had fallen free during that
kiss; he wasn't certain about that now, but he seemed to
remember it drifting between them, long, bright strands
that defied the dust and heat. What he *did* remember
was Amiranth's response: still and hesitant at first, but
when she had moved . . . when she kissed him back,
something inside him seemed to shift, almost to thaw.
He had become aware, for perhaps the first time, that
the girl before him was truly his wife, and that she
tasted only of trust, and utter faith.

Aye, that was the memory he had kept deepest
in his heart. That was the memory he had savored more
than any other over the years. That kiss, and how good
she had made him feel—like someone he did not know
at all.

Tristan noticed, with wonderment, that his hand was shaking.

"Amiranth," he whispered. He could not find words beyond her name, nothing adequate to express his sorrow to her, the apologies he wished he could make, all nothing but useless noises. There were so many things he would never be able to tell her.

In time, he heard Lily stir.

"Did you care for her so much?" she asked, light again.

He shook his head, hopeless. "I wanted to. I didn't know her . . . I could not *know*. . . ."

"No. There was no time for that, was there? You were so eager for your war."

Now he laughed, a low, bitter sound. "It was not mine, my lady."

"Oh? I thought it so—you seemed so impatient to leave this place." He glanced up at her, and she added, "Or so I heard."

"I wish," he said quietly, "that I had never left Safere. That I had stayed here with her until we were both gray and gone, and buried here together."

A frown came to her, dubious, barely there at all before it vanished. He looked away once more, going back to the fact of the marker before him, the pink of the stone, the green of the ivy, the little flowers.

"This was Amiranth's favorite place," Lily finally said, milder than before. "I chose it mostly for that reason, my lord. We would spend hours here, together or apart. She said she always found it . . . quite peaceful."

"I understand," he said, and turned away from his wife's grave, wearied.

A bird began to sing above them, delicate against the wind and sea beyond.

"You are still recovering from the fever," Lily said at last, beneath the notes of the song. "You must rebuild your strength. We don't have much time."

Tristan found the bread he had dropped and reached for it, brushing off the dirt. He began to break it apart in his hands, watching it crumble into his palms.

"Time for what?"

"We have to leave soon. You must be well enough for it."

"Leave?" His hands lowered, caution shading his tone. "Why?"

"Because," she said, enunciating each word carefully, "your horse—your *dead* horse—has eaten all the spare food. I told you this before, but I suppose you were still too ill to understand."

The caution turned to something more severe within him. "The food is gone?" he asked, incredulous. And then, "My horse is *dead*?"

"Yes, to both."

"How?"

"I *believe* it consumed too much of my garden."

He looked around them, at the vines and drooping flowers.

"Not this one," Lily said, with a graceful flick of her wrist. "The vegetable garden, my lord."

"My God." Tristan glanced down at the bread again, suddenly precious, every single crumb of it, dry and falling to pieces around him, against the ground, the simple tunic.

He had an image of her suddenly, crying before him, her hands over her face, an outline of golden Lily surrounded by darkness. At the time he had felt a strange satisfaction at it—he had no idea why that should be, what had been running through his mind. But she had cried before him. Lily had cried.

"So you understand now why you must eat," she said, perfectly composed. "Do not waste what we have left."

"How much longer?" Tristan asked.

She looked away, her lips drawing thin once more.

"How much longer, my lady?" he demanded again, standing.

"I don't know," she confessed, for once sounding uncertain. "Mayhap a week, or a little longer."

He began to laugh, prompting her to quickly rise. Tristan caught her hand before she could touch his face.

"No. I am well enough. Merely . . ." He couldn't find the words to explain it, his black amusement at their situation, his tenuous fantasy already shattered. So much for remaining at Safere. They would have to leave here together, and brave the very world he wished to hide from. Somehow he would have to find the courage to do that.

He was still holding her hand, his thumb now absently skimming her skin, close to a caress. They glanced down at this transgression together, both of them apparently realizing at the same time what he was doing.

Tristan released her as if she had scorched him. Lily

swiftly tucked both hands behind her, her face down-turned.

"Very well." He took a step back to put some distance between them, pretending to concentrate on breaking the bread into smaller pieces. "We'll go to my castle. We'll go to Glynwallen. It's the closest to us. It shouldn't take us much longer than a fortnight."

"Your castle," she repeated, in a voice so bland that he knew something was wrong. His gaze to her was sharp.

"Aye, Glynwallen. We'll be safe there."

Lily looked back at him, her face as calm as stone, increasing his alarm. Tristan actually scowled at her.

"Why, lady, what's amiss?"

"My good lord," she responded, very formal, "I had not thought—that is . . ." She sighed and moved away from him, toward the trunk of the leafy tree. "I have told you we thought you dead."

He answered her slowly. "Aye. Yet here I am."

"Yes. But the Earl of Haverlocke resides even now at Glynwallen."

"What?"

"Your brother," she said. "Your younger brother, Liam."

He let the words sink into him, taken aback. Liam—Earl of Haverlocke? Of course. If he were dead, Liam would inherit the title.

He had not seen his brother since he was a child. He could barely remember him—only a little boy, skittish and shy, the opposite of how Tristan had been at that age. After the deaths of their father and eldest brother,

Liam had been taken away by distant family—cousins—to the countryside. . . . Tristan had been so overwhelmed with his new duties and prestige—*so pleased,* his mind whispered—that he had barely even noticed the boy's absence.

But now Liam was earl. Tristan had not considered it before—all that time locked up in France, he had not allowed himself to think too much about why he remained a prisoner, even after the damned French had discovered his name and title. He had not allowed himself to question why he was never released, why what he had assumed was a demand for ransom had never been paid.

Liam had thought him dead. A miscommunication, a body from the battle claimed to be his own; some poor butchered knight resembling him, perhaps even fallen next to his horse, his shield. . . .

Great God, it made perfect sense. No one had thought to rescue him because no one had known he was alive.

It should have gladdened him. Why did it not? He could only stare into the hidden depths of Lily's eyes, collecting his thoughts.

"No matter," Tristan said at last. "We shall go to Glynwallen, and greet my brother, and clear up this business. Certainly he will welcome us."

"Oh, certainly," she said, very dry. "Nevertheless, I cannot accompany you there."

"Why not?"

"It would not be appropriate. You and I are unrelated. We should not travel alone together, although it seems there is no choice. In truth, we should not even be at Safere together. And we absolutely cannot arrive at your castle together, without proper accompaniment—"

"We are related by marriage," Tristan said firmly. "No one may fault us for—"

"In any case," she continued without pause, "I have an endowment with the sisters of Our Lady of the Blessed Faith. I shall be going to their convent."

"Convent?" He couldn't believe it. "You're going to join a convent?"

"It's been arranged for years."

There was almost a dare to her stance, defying him to contest her. Tristan felt betrayed, although there was certainly no cause for it. He had no right to feel the sense of loss that now overtook him. No right at all to say the things that came to him at once: *No, no, of course you can't. You will stay with me. I command it.*

"A convent," he managed to say again, past all the unseemly protests within him. He gave her a stately nod of his head, a token of false acceptance. "Then pray allow me, my lady, the honor of escorting you there. I am sure the nuns will not fault such a precaution, not with the plague ravaging the land."

Lily only nodded in reply, then turned her eyes away from him, staring out gravely into the garden once more.

———— ✺ ————

THE DAYS MELTED TOGETHER FOR HIM, ONLY THE shifting of the light telling Tristan another hour had passed, another minute, another dawn or sunset with Lily beside him, or away.

He knew there was something wrong with him. He knew that the feelings he was experiencing were beyond reason, beyond what anyone might think fitting. How to explain it, the way he felt around her? He could not fathom it himself. All he knew was that being with her was like being in the room with a spray of stars, tame and glowing, soft illumination.

Perhaps it was that she was as close as he would ever find to Amiranth, that girl he had not had the chance to know or love. Perhaps it was just guilt creating these feelings in him, a need for his late wife misguided, distracted to the living woman with him now.

Tristan found himself inventing pretexts to bend close to her, to lean in near where she sat or stood, and adore her scent. His hand might touch her braid when she could not see or feel it. Even the whisper of her skirts did something to him, sounding like poetry in a language he could not speak.

And her eyes . . . he was finding it more and more difficult to stare into them directly. Such great, glorious brown eyes, knowing and wise, fringed with dark lashes. He loved it best when she had been working at some task, and her hair would come loose from its knots. Strands of burnished gold would fall across her face and brows, a lovely complement of colors.

Besides the fact that her words to him became sparser

and sparser, she treated him exactly as she had since he had first arrived. She appeared to notice nothing of his infatuation with her, but instead went about Safere with her usual efficiency, preparing for their departure. He spent his days trailing her, helping as he could, even though she scolded him for not resting.

"If you fall ill as we travel it will be a great misfortune," she said, fretful as she watched him haul water from the well to the kitchen.

"You will only have to nurse me again," he replied, spilling water from the bucket around them both.

"I am aware of that," said Lily tartly. "And it is something I would prefer to avoid if possible."

"I will do my best not to disappoint you, my lady."

And he would. The last thing he wanted was to spend his final days with her in a stupor, unaware of what was about to leave him, the loss that would soon come. No, he wanted to live each moment with her, truly *feel* it, in pain or pleasure or both. Only then might he be ready to go back to his own world.

The food dwindled. Lily had let the vegetable garden begin to die, no longer bothering to water it. The stubs of the plants the gelding had left turned a shriveled gray.

They agreed to leave within two days. There was slightly more food than that, but they would need it for the journey. She directed him and they worked together in the kitchen, making rows and rows of sweetened cakes of oats and dried fruits, until their hands were sticky with honey. Baked pies, loaves of bread, the last of their reserves spent.

On their final night at Safere they had a feast of sorts,

the end of the fresh food. They ate it in grand silence together, alone with full plate and ceremony in the great hall, wine and gleaming glass around them.

Tristan had come to cherish the silence between them; there was no strain attached to it, no reserved emotions—except his own—no secret messages in the quiet. Indeed, he had never before known such a tranquility as he had found with this lady. She dined and drank and even smiled at him once as he took a bite, brightening the herbed tart to something beyond splendid in his mouth.

They said their good-nights with equal formality, each withdrawing to retire to their own chambers.

He had noticed days ago that she was staying in Amiranth's old room, the quarters of the countess, connected to his own. When she saw him pondering her going to the door, she had explained, with a bare hint of a blush, that she had used this chamber since he had arrived, the better to hear him in the night, when he had been ill.

"I shall move back to my old quarters, if you like," she added calmly.

"No," he had answered, only a trifle too fast. "Please don't. Stay where you are. It's better this way."

"Better?"

"You're already there," he said easily. "It makes no sense to move now."

And she had agreed, and left, and every night since then he had listened to her move beyond their connecting door, imagining what she might be doing . . . wearing . . .

what her dreams would be about, surely something far, far more innocent than his own.

Tonight was no different. He lay in his father's bed—when would he be able to think of it as his?—and strained to hear the slight rustling that betrayed her movements, staring up at the ceiling. Very soon the noises faded until there was only the night around him, the insects outside, the distant moan of the wind.

He slept.

When Tristan opened his eyes again the room had changed, orange and pink across it all, highlighting the paneled walls. He sat up quickly, listening, as he always did, for any sign of Lily's awakening. Because he had asked, he knew that she tended to rise just after the dawn. Every day he had meant to do the same, but the remnants of the fever made him sleep late, rousing him long after she had left.

Not today. A short glance out the window showed him that the sun had not yet cleared the horizon, only those vivid colors heralding its arrival. There were no sounds coming from Lily's room—perhaps she still slept. Surely there could be no harm in checking on her. It had nothing to do with the fact that he had been envisioning her in her bed all these endless nights. He was merely ensuring that all was well with her. If he happened to see her in slumber, her hair loose and free, her face unguarded, well, it would certainly not be his fault. . . .

Her bed was empty. The entire room was empty. He took a few short steps into it anyway.

"My lady?"

There was no response.

Tristan felt a strange warning sound within him, unwarranted. There was nothing alarming about this. He had simply missed her again, that was all. She would be in the kitchen, probably, preparing their breakfast. Or the stables, seeing to the mare.

He dressed quickly, still feeling that sense of unease, an unpleasant chill crawling down his back.

She was not in the kitchen. Nor was she in the stables—the mare stood fitfully alone—nor the garden. Tristan was searching more hurriedly now, calling her name. As the rising sun began to warm the morning he made himself pause, trying to think clearly.

She had to be inside the manor. There weren't that many places she could go, and the easiest place to lose herself would be the manor, with its labyrinth of rooms and darkened windows.

Unless . . . she had left him.

No! Tristan slammed his palm against the wall outside the main doors, hard enough to hurt. She would *not* be gone. She would not have deserted him, after all they had done together, all they had planned. If nothing else, she would not have left the horse. But she might be ill somewhere, in a faint—or trapped somehow, needing him. He had to find her.

But Lady Lily truly was not in Safere. He searched every room, every corner, behind every screen and chair. Finally Tristan sat, exhausted, at the table in the great hall, cradling his head in his hands, staring down at the wood before him, feeling nothing but despair.

He was alone again. He had never deserved her—he

had known that all along. Lily had only done to him what he had done to Amiranth. He could not even fault her for it. She might have been planning this from the beginning, but that seemed so cruel, so unlike the woman he thought she was. . . .

"Ah, God," he said, and laid his head upon the table.

He could not count the times in his life he thought he was about to die; there had been too many of them. Times of danger and desperation, his capture winding out to long years of imprisonment, a painful and barren eternity before him at Mirgaux. Even during his escape, when he had managed to wrest free of his guards and leap—from a third-story battlement—into the liquid sludge of the river running past the prison, Tristan had honestly thought it would be his last act on this earth.

He had survived that leap. Shock and the current had dragged him to the bottom of the black water; he had crawled, choking, to a hidden shore hours later. He had lain upon the stinking mud of that bank and stared up at the night clouds above him, and truly contemplated the pleasure of his death then.

And none of that hopelessness, none of that despair and rage and sorrow that had swept him that night, compared with what he felt now, with Lily's abandonment of him.

His head was throbbing with pain, a familiar torment. Tristan pressed the heel of his hand against his forehead, squeezing his eyes shut.

He would have to chase after her. She would not thank him for it, but he could do no less. She was unprotected now, traveling on foot, vulnerable to all kinds of harm. Despite what she thought of him, and what she had done, she did not deserve that.

He pushed back his chair, wandering down the main hallway again, toward the entrance of the manor. He stepped outside and raised his face to the sun, trying to gain strength from it, and when he looked down again a flash of light over glass blinded him for a moment. Tristan frowned and walked to it—a window of long panes, set back into an arch.

What room was this? It had its own outer door, small, unnoticeable, the same color as the stone.

It was the chapel, dim and narrow, a single row of pews running up to the altar in front.

And Lily was there, in the first of the seats, a figure garbed in solemn black, her head bowed in prayer.

Tristan stood motionless for a moment, overcome with emotions he could not name. The chapel! Of course! He had not been here since his boyhood— sweet heavens, he could not even recall the last time he had attended Mass, or even thought to.

She was *here*, his Lily, silent and unhurried. She had not left him!

"I wanted to ask you something, my lord." Her words resounded against the close stone walls, hollow. She showed no astonishment at his sudden appearance, did not even look back at him.

"Ask," he replied, striving to sound normal, to keep the wild relief from his voice. He began to walk toward her, admiring the nape of her neck, long and lovely, her hair loosely pinned up, little strands of amber curling close to her skin.

"Why did you come to Safere?"

Tristan took a seat in the pew just behind her, moving slightly to the left, so that he could see the curve of her cheek. "It is my home."

"You have many homes, I believe. Why this one?"

He drew a long breath, not answering.

"Was it that it was closest to France? The most convenient for you, on your journey back to England from your great war?"

"No." He looked up at the fresco beyond her, the painted figure of the Lord on a cross, red blood and thorns. "I remembered my wife. I was thinking of her."

"Were you?" She sounded almost cynical. The portion of her face that he could see showed him nothing of her expression, only the smooth whiteness of her skin. He must have imagined her jab.

"I was. I could not help but remember . . ."

"What?"

"Nothing." He shifted, uncomfortable. "Nothing. Just . . . her touch. That was all."

"Her touch?"

"Like—innocence. That was what I remembered."

She made a small, scoffing noise.

"I know how it sounds," Tristan said. "But it is the truth, my lady."

"Truth," she echoed, low. "Shall I tell you what is true? How about this: death. Desertion. That innocence in your young wife you recall slowly turned to rancor over the years, as month after month you did not return for her. She watched for you every day, my lord—I'm sure you do not care about such a trivial fact, yet she did. But of course you never came, and eventually she was declared a widow, and told to remain here forever. Safere became her dower house. And her doom."

Tristan stared down at his hands, clenched tight around each other, scarred and rough.

"I don't suppose I deserve any better than that," he said into the hush.

"No," Lily agreed, more composed. "I don't suppose you do."

He stood, unable to remain in place a moment longer, her words still circling his heart, harsh justice. He moved to stand in front of her and held out his open palm.

"We should leave now, my lady."

She did not accept his hand. Nor did she rise from the pew; only her gaze shifted, going to the floor between them. He followed her look and noticed that he stood over a small, engraved stone, a marker for a crypt. Tristan moved his feet and read the whole of it: R.G., 1342.

There was a single stem of flowers across the stone, tiny bluebells. He had nearly stepped upon it.

He looked back up at her and noted for the first time the unusual pallor of her face, the contrast of two spots of color high upon her cheekbones.

"Who was this?" he asked, very gently.

She was silent for so long that he thought she meant simply to disregard him, but then she said quietly, "My daughter."

Tristan concealed his shock. "I did not realize you were wed."

Her look was almost wrathful. "I am not."

She stood and pushed past him, her steps sharp against the floor as she walked outside, her back straight and stiff.

He could not help slanting a look back at the little stone, the scripted initials somehow both lavish and sad. He bent down, adjusting the stem of bluebells to a more careful angle. Then he followed Lily.

A child out of wedlock—it would better explain why she was here, a far more likely reason to be sent to Safere than merely to companion Amiranth. If what he remembered about her was true, she had been living off the generosity of Amiranth's brother, a cousin several times removed. Her affair would have caused quite a scandal, he knew that. And the results of that affair must have been hidden with all due haste. Impoverished or not, an unwed noblewoman with child could not quite be tossed away—so she had been banished instead, and left to languish here, forgotten by the mannered world.

Tristan had grown up in that dangerous, rarefied society, where words and actions often contradicted each other, and complicated lies abounded, waiting to trap the unwary. It was a gilded snare of rogues and princes and courtly debauchery—he remembered it clearly . . .

. . . and she was so beautiful, fairer than any woman he could recall. How simple it might have been to take advantage of her faith in some suitor. How cleverly it might have happened, the seduction of Lady Lily.

He wondered, with a rising sense of outrage, who the father was and why he had not been forced to take responsibility for his dishonor.

He found her now in the stables. It was no mystery

where she had gone; the sound of her voice led him straight to her, crooning words to the bay mare, both of them ignoring him as he walked closer.

"Lily," he said, uncomfortable. "I did not mean to—"

"It was a long time ago." She spoke over him, still looking at the mare. "And I will thank you not to mention it again, my lord."

"Of course."

He bowed to her, a half-forgotten convention, and at last she glanced at him. Her eyes were very bright. The circles of feverish color on her cheeks stood out all the more in the daylight.

Tristan came closer to her, concerned. "Are you well?"

"Perfectly," she replied, freezing cold. "Shall we be off, my lord?"

She was lying. He recognized this flush only all too well. But there was nothing he could do to persuade her to stay, Tristan knew that right enough. There was no food at Safere anyway, and no future.

He argued with her when she insisted that he ride the mare. She would not listen to his protests, grew more than unreasonable: her voice rose, her eyes filled with tears, and the alarming spots of color began to spread across her entire face. He only calmed her by agreeing to ride part of the way, allowing that she could walk, at least the first few miles.

But he was watching her closely, and waiting.

They were two days out when it happened. She had steadfastly refused to change places with him, muttering something about how they had to move on as quickly as they could, to reach the convent. The one time he had attempted to force her onto the mare she had ended up screaming and striking at him, and the damned horse had nearly bolted.

She was right about one thing—they had to keep going. If they hurried they might reach an inn soon, and that could be invaluable for what was to come. So he placated her and rode while she walked, all the while expecting the inevitable.

Tristan was thinking quite seriously about tying her up and gagging her to keep her on the horse, when his fears became reality.

It was midday, and they had just crossed a sullen creek, a few lone trees at last appearing again at its banks. Lily stepped off the bridge and suddenly released the reins of the mare, her hand falling limply to her skirts. His attention to her was so acute that he was already leaping down from the horse as she began to crumple in slow, graceful folds to the ground. Tristan caught her in his arms before she fell completely, and gathered her close to his racing heart.

Chapter Five

———————⟨∿∿∿⟩———————

IT HAD COME TO HER IN THE DARKEST MOMENT OF them all, in the deep of that last dreadful night of the sickness, as her cousin lay gasping for air on her bed at Safere.

What if . . .

Amiranth had clutched Lily's frail hand and stared, dry eyed, at the ravaged figure before her, distorted shadows dancing across them both with the torchlight.

Even death could not take away Lily's beauty. Even this monstrous disease could not rob her of her fairness. The gold in her hair was undimmed. The light in her eyes had been just as loving past the pain. Those eyes were closed now—probably forever.

Poor Lily, to die so young and kindhearted, abandoned to this place.

Poor Amiranth, to be left here without her.

What if . . .

It was such a wicked idea. It was unforgivable, what she was thinking. Selfish. Shocking.

But who would ever know?

A spasm of pain took her cousin; for a moment Lily's fingers tightened hard over her own, squeezing. A wet cough followed, convulsing her body. When it was over Amiranth helped her back down to the covers, both of them breathing too quickly.

Amiranth ran her fingers over the heated brow, clearing back a tangle of hair. She could no longer tell if Lily was awake or asleep in her torment. She had not been able to speak, or eat, for days. It had to end soon. Please.

If . . .

God curse the thought! She was a wretched, horrible beast to be thinking of herself in this moment. She should be doing nothing but attending to Lily—praying for her, helping her. Wishing for the end to this agonizing madness.

But the wicked idea did not go away. Born of this darkness, saturated in desperation, it gained strength from it. Too late to avoid it now, or wish it unthought. It had taken hold of her, crafty and creeping, hiding amid the shadows of her soul.

And now, even as death lurked closer—*yes, come! hurry!*—in this forlorn little room, Amiranth knew she would succumb to the shadows in her, after all.

She gazed down at her dying cousin, the only friend she had ever known.

What if it were I?

Lily took one final, thin gasp, exhaling so slowly that

Amiranth could feel the very last warmth in the world departing the room with her. Her fingers went lax in Amiranth's hand.

She truly was alone now. God help her.

───────── ⟨⟩ ─────────

AMIRANTH SIGHED AND TURNED IN HER SLEEP, TIRED of remembering, tired of the heat that drenched her, and the sorrow, and the fear. When she tried to push it all away from her she found her arms constricted, bound tightly to her sides, and this sent her to weeping, because she could not even do what she had always done, and force away the pain.

Someone was speaking to her, a man, his voice soothing and low. She could not hear him well enough to make out his words; he was all but drowned beneath the rushing in her head, a steady, rapid cadence that sent ripples of pain through her body.

She was cold, and then she was hot. There were only extremes around her, nothing sweet or mild, nothing to rely upon, save the steadiness of that man's voice, familiar yet so obscure. Who could be speaking to her in such a tone? Who could be touching her in such a way, soft whispers across her face? Who would stroke her so gently?

She opened her eyes and saw him, disheveled black hair that fell to his shoulders, sparkling eyes that smiled at her. Those lips, with their enticing curl at the corners, a secret mirth . . .

Tristan was dead. So now Amiranth supposed she

was as well, for never had he looked at her so kindly in life. She grew still, staring up at him, blue sky beyond his face—that made sense, for heaven would be blue, wouldn't it? And there was sunlight on him too, falling across his shoulders . . . she had seen him like this before. . . .

Amiranth saw her hand reach up and touch his cheek, a test; his own hand caught hers there, pressing her closer. He turned his head and kissed her fingers, his eyes closing.

She said, marveling, "Why, death is surely a wondrous thing."

His eyes opened again. He leaned down closer to her, dark and handsome as the blessed night.

"Sleep now, Lily. You'll feel better soon."

"No," she said, struggling to make him understand. "I . . . I'm not . . ."

But the rest of her sentence faded away, and she felt the dusk of heaven come up around her, as safe as his arms, enfolding her with velvet and satin, utter stillness.

───────── ∘୨ৎ∘ ─────────

TRISTAN WRAPPED HER MORE SECURELY IN THE ELEgant mantle he had found in one of the bags, tucking the corners in around her so that she could not easily shiver it off.

It was a rather amazing piece of work, velvet and ermine, crimson and blue chevrons forming bright lines. It had been a lifetime since he had seen such finery, felt such luxury between his fingers. The colors of it seemed almost too rich to him, too deep, too sumptuous. They spoke to him of things he had not dared to consider except in his dreams: wealth, power, privilege . . . gifts from a stolen life, one he thought he had lost forever.

He could not imagine why Lily had wanted to bring this cloak with them—it was meant for winter, without doubt—but could only be glad now that she had. It was imperative that she stay warm, despite her fever. And the summer nights could cool considerably.

Tristan sat back and watched her, her breathing more even than it had been yesterday. That was good. She would recover. He was determined that she would.

He thought they were not too far from a village. He seemed to recall, from the depths of his memory, that the first signs of life beyond Safere were about three days away from the estate; that would mean only a day's travel from here to find it. If only he knew for certain, he might dare to leave her, ride out and summon help. . . .

But he couldn't do that. He would not risk leaving her while she was still lost in her fever; without him she would be defenseless. Yet he had to do something soon, or she might fall so far into the illness that there would be no return, no matter where she rested. It was a damnable mess however he considered it.

Tristan glanced around at their crude campsite. It was the best he had been able to do with it—they were cradled beneath the shelter of two twisted trees next to the creek, on a sandbar that was dry and soft. It had been adequate until now. There was water, and there was shade from the relentless sun. He actually felt somewhat relieved to be out here in the open, nothing but warm air around him.

Escape would be easy from a place such as this. It would not be difficult to flee with Lily on the mare, emptiness stretching in every direction. No harm could come to them here, no enemy could approach without warning.

Yet he found himself constantly checking the area, rechecking it, confirming what he already knew: open air, empty sky, flat horizon. No one coming for him, for either of them.

And every time he verified their security he felt a jagged pain in his chest begin to ease, loosen its hold on him—but it always came back, building slowly through him until it felt as if his ribs had splintered again, until he had to raise his head and scan it all once more. . . .

Safe here, his mind would chant. *Safety here.*

Yes. It was good. But they would have to leave soon. There simply wasn't enough food.

For the past four days he had fed her watered bread until it was gone, and then boiled the oatcakes they had made to mush. With a great deal of cajoling and no little threatening, he had gotten her to eat from his hand in the midst of her fever, the softened oats and fruits keeping her alive. It was not going to be enough, however, and he knew it.

She needed proper shelter. She needed a bed—a pallet at least. Broth. A warm room. A physician, if he could find one. If only they were at Glynwallen, he would know precisely what to do. At Glynwallen he could offer her the care due a queen . . . and he knew all the rooms there by heart, all the hallways, every path to safety. . . .

Tristan snapped his head back up, rubbing his face, fighting to stay awake. He was not yet completely well himself. He spent more time than he should napping, no doubt. He should remain wary and alert. He should be on constant guard for danger. But the slow music of the creek beyond him was a constant lull to his thoughts, sending a sleepy haze over him. Better, surely, to mend as he could, to regain his strength that much more quickly. And they were still far enough from civilization, no one would come. . . .

He lay down on the ground beside Lily, keeping his eyes fixed upon her face, relaxed now, serene. He had shielded her from the sun as best he could under the trees, but the world around them still flared with brilliance. Shimmers of silver danced across her form, reflections of sunlight from the nearby stream.

His gaze shifted from her face to her chest, noting the rise and fall that marked her breathing, still constant, still calm.

She was better. It would be up to him to ensure she remained that way.

———— ᨆᨆᨆᨆ ————

AMIRANTH AWOKE WITH A FIERCE HEADACHE, AWASH amid bright light that seemed to burn behind her eyes. She tried to lift a hand to block it and felt the constriction of something wrapped tightly around her; with a bit of a struggle she had her hand free. She covered her eyes with relief, sighing heavily.

Gradually the noises of her surroundings crept past the pain. Wind whistling, as it might through the branches of a tree. A murmuring, liquid sound, like water passing over rocks. Frogs. An occasional rustle from above, the movement of some small creature amid leaves—a bird, or a squirrel.

A man's voice, hushed. Horse's steps against dirt, restless.

Amiranth moved her hand, turning her head to take in the sight of the man and the horse not too far away, face to face, his hands on the bridle.

She knew him. Didn't she? He was very familiar. How strange to find herself here, lying as openly as could be beneath the sky and the trees. How immodest of her, to have fallen asleep in such a place, in front of this stranger. . . .

But he wasn't a stranger.

No. It was Tristan. Yes, *Tristan* over there, her husband standing with her horse, looking for all the world like he might be arguing with the mare.

Amiranth squinted, propping herself up on her elbows, studying the scene.

It was he. It certainly was. He looked almost exactly as she remembered, tall and leanly muscled, tousled black hair that curled and lifted in the wind, a princely profile, masculine grace in his very posture, the air about him.

He had come back. After all this time, he had

returned from the dead, and thrown her world upside down once again.

She felt a curious amusement come to her, caustic. How very like Tristan, to reappear when she had least wanted him to, still so ruthlessly handsome that it sent a painful stab of recognition straight through her.

And how ironic that his recognition of her was not nearly so keen. It was coming clearer now, her memory returning despite her headache. To save herself, she had enacted a desperate lie: Amiranth was dead, and Lily lived. . . .

Lady Lily Granger was nearly no one to refined society. She had no fortune, no significant family name, and thus no future to speak of.

Lady Lily Granger was not tied to Safere, as her unfortunate cousin had been. In fact, through her very lack of distinction, Lily could do nearly what she pleased with her life. She would never have to wait for a lost husband to reclaim her. She would never have to choose between spending the rest of her days at Safere or remarrying some old man of the king's choosing.

Lady Lily could simply slip away, off to a convent, unmolested, forgotten—free. It was everything Amiranth desired.

A desperate lie, indeed. How could *she* be Lily, who had walked in beauty, who had never raised her voice or said or thought an unkind thing about anyone? No one would believe it! Yet Lily had died . . . and Amiranth had done it anyway.

And it had worked. Her wild plan, her one grasp at salvation from her life, had worked! Thank God she had

had wits enough to maintain the charade in front of her newfound husband.

Now, watching Tristan in the bright sunlight, Amiranth wondered for the first time what Lily would say of her deception. She pushed away the twinge of guilt that spread through her. Beloved Lily was dead, and all her gentle beauty and grace—and the need for truth—had died with her.

Amiranth had only done what she had to. She would not regret it now.

Jorah tossed her head, and Tristan lost the reins. The mare pranced out of his reach, her steps quick and irritated. Even her horse, it seemed, had sense enough to dislike the earl.

She watched as he chased after the mare, his voice coming to her with the breeze, commanding. Jorah only snorted and skittered sideways, stirring up little plumes of dust.

It might have been amusing, but for the fact that Amiranth was beginning to recall the rest of the past few weeks: Illness. Starvation. Sanctuary awaiting her at the convent.

They needed the mare. If she didn't stop him, Tristan would end up chasing her away until she was truly gone. Jorah was faithful to her, she always had been. But she didn't like men, and Amiranth didn't want to risk her panicking and running off into the vast countryside. She would make a excellent prize for any thief.

"Stop," she called out—or meant to. Her voice was scratchy and breathless, impossible to hear.

Jorah stood deliberately just beyond Tristan, the

black of her tail swishing high across her flanks. She curled her lip at the man edging slowly toward her, then snapped at his outstretched hand. Tristan pulled back hastily; Amiranth heard him curse.

She sat up, moistening her lips, and gave a low whistle. Jorah's ears pricked toward her. With another toss of her head, she trotted daintily over to Amiranth, blowing warm breath against her hair.

Amiranth reached up and touched the nose lowered to her, stroking it, watching as Tristan approached, his eyes dark and concerned.

"Lily."

She heard many emotions in that single name, a velvet tumble of inflections that never would have been there eight years ago. In spite of herself she felt a response building in her—how nice it would be to warrant such favor. But he was speaking to another woman, not to her.

Amiranth looked down so that she would not have to see him, sun-splashed and charming, and feel the need for him again.

She heard him come nearer, his steps across the earth and stone, and then he was there in front of her, kneeling, taking her hand in both of his.

"My lady." His fingers tightened. "Do you know me?"

She almost laughed, but stifled it in time. Amiranth nodded instead, not trusting her voice. He released her hand; she felt his fingers touch her chin now, lifting, so that she had to look into his eyes.

"Are you certain?" he asked, searching her face. "I am Tristan."

She pulled away from his touch. "I remember you."

Her voice came out broken still, but her words were clear enough. Something in his face eased.

"Thank God," he said, sounding very sincere. "Last night I feared—" He stopped, not finishing the sentence. Their eyes locked. The tension returned to his features, a subtle tightening that almost as swiftly relaxed into a faint smile.

"You're better." He shifted, moving to sit before her. "I'm glad."

Amiranth looked around, noting the stream, the gnarled trees, a sky the color of lapis. Something flickered in the corner of her vision; when she turned her head too quickly to see, her balance was gone. The world dipped and swayed, streaks of color. She found herself caught in Tristan's arms as it all began to settle again, sky above, ground below. He eased her back to the sand.

"Relax. You're not yet hale, my lady. Do not attempt to exert yourself."

The movement came again—Jorah, wading off into the stream, slurping at the water.

"We must keep traveling," Amiranth said.

Tristan regarded her from above, intent. His hands were firm on her shoulders.

"Not yet."

"How long have we been here?"

"Five days."

"Five days!" She pushed at his hands. "We have to leave immediately! We haven't enough food for—"

"I know." He had not released her, overcoming her

weakened struggles with ease. "Lily, listen to me. There is food enough for two more days."

She lay there panting, trying to understand.

"I think we're close to a village. If we can get there, we'll be fine, I'm certain of it."

"Village." She frowned, remembering. "Yes. Haverton. It's closest to Safere."

"That's right."

"But—it's still three days hence. We need to leave to-day if we're going to manage the food."

"I estimate we're only a day away now, more or less."

Amiranth had forgotten they had already gone some distance from the estate. Her memory of their travels was patchy at best—she recalled walking, but not where she had gone. Glimpses of Tristan now and again, watching her, silent, withdrawn. Feeling the endless heat, eating her whole, still walking, always walking. . . .

They must have covered quite a bit of ground, to be only a day out of Haverton. How odd that all she could really remember was the heat, and him.

"Very well. I can be ready to leave in a moment."

Tristan leaned back. "Don't be absurd. I'm going alone."

"Certainly you're not!"

"Certainly I am." She saw that hint of a smile again, against her will felt the appeal of it travel through her. "You're in no condition to ride. I'm going to get help for you."

A tingle of dread began in her fingertips, spreading up her arms, to her chest. If he left—if anything hap-pened to him—a fall, a thief, an accident—who would ever know? They would both die out here after all, death would come just as she had always feared it would. She would never escape this place, not even with the man who had first delivered her here.

Amiranth sat up again, and this time Tristan did not attempt to stop her. Her words came firmly now. "You cannot leave me here."

"I won't be long. If I can keep that beast up to a good trot, I'll be back for you in no time at all."

"We must go together. It's the only way."

"Lily." He shook his head, then touched her hand again, gentle. Sunlight and shade mingled across him, playing off the clean lines of his face. "I would not abandon you, my lady. I *will* be back."

I will return for you. . . .

She had believed him once, all those years ago. Back then he had owned both her heart and her faith. She would not make the same mistake again.

Amiranth drew herself straighter, pointing to her mare.

"Jorah won't allow you to ride her without me."

"We shall see."

"No—I'm quite serious. She responds only to me. You won't be able to manage her."

He glanced back at the mare standing in the mud of the stream, deceptively placid as she watched them.

"It's why the serfs did not attempt to take her as they fled," Amiranth explained. "She was too faithful for them to overcome, and they knew it."

"Too malevolent, you mean," Tristan grumbled. He sighed and bowed his head, running both hands through his hair. She granted herself the luxury of admiring him then, when he could not see her do it; how his hands were still so elegant and strong, his hair such shining ebony. Amiranth recognized this pose from years past—their wedding night, when his distaste for her had not allowed him even to look at her face.

Tristan raised his head again, and she returned her gaze to the horse.

"We will go together," she said softly, adamant.

"Aye," he agreed reluctantly. "I suppose we will."

⁂

HAVERTON. WHAT A KINDLY NAME FOR SUCH A squalid set of huts, thatch and whitewashed mud baked by the sun, inhabited by fleeting ghosts of people wrapped in cloaks or blankets, staring at them as they passed.

Tristan led the mare down lanes that sent heat rising to the sky in waves, carrying the stench of garbage and human filth with it. Occasionally he would glance back at Lily, hunched in the saddle, her hair tangled down her arms in golden streamers. She had not fallen. Not yet. Where the hell was the local inn?

When he tried to stop one of the villagers to ask, the man jerked away from him, his reply garbled, almost a shout. Tristan watched him retreat into an alley, close to a run.

They waited but nothing else happened, and so they walked on.

What an odd place. There were other people here,

he knew it, but he saw almost none of them. He might have heard whispers as they passed doorways. He could see the gleam of eyes amid some of the shadows. But as they drew closer to the village center the lanes were empty. Even the marketplace was deserted, vacant stalls, tattered awnings swaying with the wind.

He paused there to examine it, bits of rotted vegetables rolling around with the dust, closed doors, shuttered windows.

A faint sound behind him made him turn. Lily was slumped even lower over the mare now, a hand up to her face. What he could see of her skin was flushed to a deep rose.

"We are looking for the inn!" he called out into the empty courtyard before him.

No one answered him, although he heard a scraping sound nearby, perhaps a door opening. When he faced it he saw nothing new, only the shadows and blank walls of before.

"The inn!" he called again, as loudly as he could. "We seek shelter there!"

Another noise from Lily; her head had lifted, her hand lowered. She was breathing shallowly through her mouth.

"My lord. We need . . . to leave."

"Try not to move too much," he cautioned her, and then faced the buildings again. "Come out, you people, and guide us to the inn!"

"My lord—" Lily's voice was a faint gasp.

He turned to her just as the first rock struck his shoulder blade, a sharp stinging. Tristan whirled and the second rock hit him in the forehead, hard enough to send sparkling stars into the center of his vision.

"What the—"

"Leave!" Lily wheezed, tugging at the reins of the mare.

"Leave!" came an echo to her, a man's voice close-by, and then several more, a menacing chorus, hidden behind walls.

"Leave!"

"Leave us!"

"Go!"

Another rock flew by his head, clattering off the wall behind him, spooking the mare. Lily swayed alarmingly in the saddle as the horse twisted and whinnied, her hooves ringing across the cobblestones.

"Leave off, you fools!" Tristan shouted, fighting the mare. "Are you all mad?"

Another rock, and another. He felt one hit his leg, and then his lower back. Something warm and wet was sliding down his face; he wiped it away, and saw blood on his palm.

"Get out! Plague! The plague!"

"Carriers!"

More stones, a hail of them. The mare let out a pan-icked squeal, beginning to spin in circles around his grip on the reins. Tristan pulled the horse down with brute force, snarling with the effort.

"Plague carriers!" was the new chant, and the rocks came more quickly, striking him, the horse—Lily. She gave a muffled cry and hid her head in her hands.

"God curse it!" He pulled the mare out of the courtyard, as fast as he could manage it, praying that Lily had the strength to keep her seat. The rocks followed him, striking walls, flying past him down the narrow lane. The mare was kicking and screaming and still the stones did not stop, the chanting growing stronger behind them.

"Plague carriers!"

"Plague!"

"Begone, plague!"

Tristan was running, and either the horse was pulling him or he was pulling her, both of them skidding over the ground. Lily's form was a blur of black skirts and golden hair, clinging to the mare.

They left the last of the huts behind them and kept on, bolting out into the open day, the shrieks of the villagers finally fading behind them.

Chapter Six

———— ❧ ————

THEY CAME TO REST BENEATH A CLUTCH OF PINES, sparse shelter against any who might wish to find them, but the only shelter of any kind to be seen.

At some point during their flight Tristan had leapt up onto the horse behind her. Amiranth had felt his arms come hard around her waist, probably the only thing keeping her seated as Jorah streaked across the earth.

And then they were slowing, halting, ducking the limbs of sticky sap and sharp needles. Both of them slid from the saddle at nearly the same time. Tristan caught her again, and together they sank to the ground.

"Lily!"

She opened her eyes and saw him, too close. He brought her even closer then, holding her to his chest as they sat together. His heartbeat became a rapid drumming against her cheek. She was breathing too hard to protest this, feeling strangely limp and muddled. Her hair had tumbled across her face, strands of dark gold in her lashes, almost hiding her—from him, from the world. How odd it was, to have him hold her.

Amiranth closed her eyes again, and the beating of his heart grew gradually slower against her, somehow reassuring. She felt his hand begin to smooth her hair, long, gliding strokes from her crown to her shoulders.

She did not feel well. It was the only reason she allowed such an intimacy, his touch upon her. She was ill. That explained what was happening to her now, this very unwelcome sense of pleasure in being so close to him.

She lifted her head to clear the hair from her eyes. But she made the mistake of looking up at him then, his face just above hers, his eyes endless black. The curl to his lips was gone now, and in its place was a hint of something new and enticing, an expression she had never before seen on him.

The change in him transfixed her. All this time she thought she had known Tristan so well, almost better than her own self. She had spent her girlhood studying him, learning him and observing him, casting out the net of her dreams for him. How astonishing to realize she had overlooked any part of Tristan Geraint.

Yet she had. She did not know this man before her. What was this slow, darkening look about him now?

His hand came up, sliding across her cheek just as his head lowered and his lips touched hers, a tentative warmth. Amiranth exhaled the last of her sanity, so faint she barely noted it.

She was a young girl again, and here at last was her
hero, the man she loved. Here was Tristan truly kissing
her, his touch sweet and soft and yet hard as well. It was
nothing rushed, nothing urgent, more of a slow, languorous fascination, the unique feel of him, his scent.
His mouth opened a little over hers; he tasted her with
his tongue, wicked delight.

Amiranth felt a distant amazement at it, that he could
be doing this to her, that she might feel his arms pressing her tight against him, that she clutched at him and
returned his kiss and reveled in it.

They were breathing heavily in tandem now, quick
gasps of air around the kisses, cool against hot. Her fingers curled into the cloth of his tunic, bunching it
across his arm. She felt the heat of his skin beneath the
material, the strength of him, his muscles flexed and
taut with holding her, a very slight trembling encom-
passing them both.

She knew this feeling. She remembered this, the sensation of magic and stillness, of slow suspension in a
dream. She had felt this way with him untold nights before, but he hadn't really been there with her—he was
gone by then, far from her in France, and she had been
left alone in her bed with nothing but her twilight fan-
tasies, aching and inconsolable. She had passed through
this illusion more times than she could count: the hope
of him come back to her, her husband returned from
his war, returned to love her.

Her husband.

Amiranth slipped out of this dream . . . out of his

arms, away from him, and felt his touch leave her as easily as rain flowing over glass. His arms fell to his sides.

They faced each other in mutual consternation, the magnitude of their embrace expanding between them.

His gaze shifted; a hand reached up to her cheek. Amiranth turned her head away, allowing her hair to sweep across her face. Tristan paused, not touching.

"You're bleeding," he murmured.

She felt her skin, the moisture there. "It's not I," she said, still hiding behind the fall of her hair. "It's your blood. It must be. I'm not hurt."

When she glanced up at him he had not changed, intense as he met her eyes, troubled. She noticed now the cut on his forehead, how it left a trickle of deep red across his face. It looked painful. Why did it hurt her to see him wounded?

His lashes lowered—long and very black, as lustrous as the rest of him.

"Lily," he began, and faltered. His mouth tightened; he stared down at open space between them, taking a heavy breath. "Please accept my apologies. I had no right to do that."

"Yes," she said, feeling the strangest urge to cry.

She heard him sigh a little, and waited for him to say something more. But without another word Tristan rose and walked away from her, going to the other side of the trees, until his form was nearly lost to her amid the trunks and boughs.

Amiranth looked back at the smear of his blood on her hand. In that moment the crimson of it seemed to take on a heavy new meaning to her, becoming both dangerous and splendidly beautiful.

———— ⟨⟩ ————

THERE WAS NO STREAM IN THIS LITTLE COVE OF TREES. Tristan regretted it very much, that they had no water save what was left in the skins. No soothing liquid lullaby to counter his thoughts, or drown them, whatever might distract him from the disaster to come.

How sweet Lily had tasted. How fine it was, to kiss her. How wrong, how corrupt, how he wanted to do it again.

She had accepted his apology for it. Would she be so kind a second time—a third, a fourth? The hundredth time, when he would capture her and contain her solemn passion and keep it fast for himself? She would not stay solemn long if he did, he could guarantee that. She would blossom and enfold him, he could teach her about these feelings . . . he could show her how to wield them, and bring them to shining brilliance for them both.

Selfish, arrogant thoughts.

He was doomed, and he knew it.

His apology was already vanquished in his mind, thin as beaten gold, dissolved to fragments in the searing heat of his desire for her.

What was an apology to this: the eager, dark edge within him that clamored for her, that howled for her and scrambled his thoughts, turning his body to hunger and fierce wanting? The need to touch her again ate away at him, an almost physical craving that *hurt,* hurt so brightly that he had to grit his teeth against it.

But no, he had apologized and she had bowed her head and accepted it—yet he was *not* sorry. He would do it again if he could. He would drag her along with him even farther down this forbidden path. He would lie with her and celebrate her—lovely, radiant Lily— until she cried out his name with her own passion, and understood the terrible depths of his heart.

Tristan looked at her in the wan light of the moon, seated what she must surely think was a safe distance from him in the little nook of the trees. She should be sleeping now. It had been a strange, arduous day: a stoning, a chase, a near seduction. And she was still battling the fever. She should at least be trying to sleep—and perhaps she would have been, were he not here. Had he not kissed her.

He could not see her well in this light. He could not tell if she was looking at him, as he was at her. Her hair glinted milky pale beneath the moon and stars. The silvered light on her lashes sent curling shadows down her cheeks, masking her eyes. She was wrapped in her velvet mantle; the ermine around her shoulders seemed almost to glow, a celestial collar.

She had eaten only half an oatcake. She would not eat any more of it, not even when he raised his voice and called her a fool. There were just four of the cakes left, she had pointed out in her carefully calm way. And they did not know how much longer they must go before finding more food. When he had taken one threatening step toward her she had called his bluff, staying firm and resolute, her eyes shining with fever—or something else. Tristan had backed away, unable yet to come too close to her.

Half an oatcake. At this rate, even if he ate nothing at all for the next few days, she would be dead within the week. And he did not need another death to drag upon his soul.

He stood too abruptly; he saw her start back.

"Get some rest," he said, and walked to the hulk of the mare, drowsing nearby.

"What are you doing?"

They had left the horse saddled for the night, agreeing that it would be better to be prepared to flee immediately if they had to. Tristan now loosened the reins from their knots around a tree branch, working quickly. The mare took a cautious sideways step but otherwise remained calm. He climbed into the saddle.

Lily had stood, clutching the mantle around her.

"What are you doing?" she asked again, alarmed. "Where are you going?"

"I'll be back."

"What? No! You can't—"

He was already wheeling the horse around, clearing the trees.

"Rest!" he called behind him, and urged the mare into a gallop.

⟨✦⟩

SHE LAY BACK ON THE GROUND AND WATCHED THE midnight heavens while he was gone, cursing him, cursing herself, and even Jorah for refusing to throw him.

The night sky was swept with stars, an endless glitter of silver hanging above her, looking near enough to touch. The moon had set and still he had not returned.

What sort of lunatic had the Earl of Haverlocke turned out to be? What could he being doing now, out in this cold and silent night, with no supplies or friends, and certainly no welcome from any village?

If he harmed her horse she would kill him. She would. Despite Jorah's startled acceptance of Tristan tonight, the mare had been her loyal companion. She did not deserve to be ridden to her death by a madman.

He might be hurt out there. He might be stoned again, beaten.

Amiranth felt a bitter tremble take her lips and fought it. She did not need to feel these things for him now. She did not need to indulge in worry for him. She was not worried. He had survived years of war. Clearly he did not require or even merit her concern.

But what could he be doing?

It didn't matter. She would not care. The stars of the sky were so close . . . they promised secrets to her . . . peaceful slumber. . . .

The world was a rumbling storm beneath her ear, a muffled, distant thumping that was rhythmic and familiar . . . like thunder, but deeper, denser.

Amiranth sat up, awake again, glancing around wildly until she spotted him, riding low and fast on Jorah.

Starlight threw sloping shadows across them both, high-lighting Tristan's face, sending Jorah's legs to a blur. For one disconcerting instant they seemed fused as one: horse and rider, pagan and feral, a mythic creature risen from the enchanted night.

She blinked and it was only Tristan and her mare again, fleet over the dust and stones. Amiranth rose as he came nearer, waiting with an outward composure she did not feel as he brought her horse to her.

Jorah came to a gradual halt in the high, dancing steps she favored, blowing air through her nose, shaking her head, pressing close. Amiranth reached up to rub her cheek and the mare nudged her back, breathing heavily.

Tristan's cut was bleeding again. It had sent threads of black down his temple with the wind, across his cheek, thin as cobweb strands. He was smiling at her, almost jubilant.

"My lady fair," he greeted her, and leapt from the horse, landing before her with effortless grace.

"What have you done?" she asked, dreading the answer.

In response he went to the burlap sack hanging from the saddle, untying it with a flourish. When he turned back to her, that handsome curve to his lips was still in place. Tristan reached into the bag and pulled out—a loaf of bread.

Amiranth stared at it, taking it wordlessly as he handed it to her. Next came something about the size of her fist, wrapped in thin white cloth. He unfolded it for her, revealing a coarse-hewn block of cheese. He gave her that, as well.

"And now, my Lady Lily . . ." Tristan lifted the bag higher. His hand dipped in again, all the way to the bottom. She watched, amazed, as he lifted out a whole covered pie, the crust of it only a little crushed along the edges.

Tristan held it up to his nose, inhaling deeply.

"I think it's meat," he said, the yearning in his voice clear. He brought it close to her face.

"Pigeon," she said faintly.

He nodded, handing her the pie, going back to Jorah, walking her, leading her to the trees. "I've got water, too. There was a well."

"What have you done?" Amiranth asked again, stronger than before.

"Saved us." He tied the mare to a branch, patted her on the neck.

"Sweet Lord." She stood there, burdened with the food in her arms, staring from it to him, the scent of the pigeon pie sending a sharp pinching to her stomach.

Tristan watched her, his smile fading. Cast in starlight and shade, his eyes remained hidden, the line of his jaw shown lean and strong. With his wind-tangled hair and elegant darkness, he looked once again like some pagan creature—a brooding god now, regarding her silently.

"Did you steal it?" she asked.

"They weren't likely to just give it to me, were they?" He took the pie from her, seating himself beneath one of the pines. "Come eat, my lady."

"You should not have stolen." She looked at him in agitation. "I have coin. We might have paid for it."

"Oh yes," he said, sardonic. "I can imagine how delighted they would have been to take my coin. Never mind that they tried to kill us this afternoon merely for breathing their air."

"But—"

"Come, Lily. Do not waste what we have. Look here, I'll give you half." He held up the pie to her, inviting. Her stomach gave a sharper pinch. She saw him smile again, very slight, a roguish temptation.

"I only did what I had to. It was for you, my lady. Don't make my work for naught."

Amiranth shook her head, tired again, wavering.

"When we're at Glynwallen," he said softly, "and things have settled down, I'll send a man to pay the baker for his inconvenience."

"When *you're* at Glynwallen, you mean," she said quickly.

"Of course." His expression was perfect innocence. "When *I'm* there."

They exchanged a long look, her heart beating in odd thumps, recognition of a sense of peril from him, nearly undefinable. But then Tristan released her gaze, turned to the pie again. He produced a dagger from his waist and began to slice through the crumbling crust.

The scent of the food overcame her doubts. She sat beside him, still clutching the cheese and bread, her skirts puddling around her in a circle. Tristan handed her half the pie, still in the pan.

"Pigeon," he said blissfully, and took the first bite.

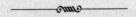

THEY LEFT AT THE PEARLY RISE OF DAWN. HE WOKE her with a heavy touch to her shoulder, and Amiranth moaned and tried to turn away from him.

"Sorry, Lily." His voice was hushed and sweet, close to her. "We must be off."

She felt so wretched. It seemed this illness would not be shaken from her. She wanted nothing more than to sleep for the rest of her life. But he was pulling at her arm; Amiranth stumbled to her feet, bleary.

"Awake yet?"

She rubbed her eyes, sighing, looking past him to see Jorah, already packed and saddled, her ears twitching with the breeze. Tristan unfastened the mantle from her shoulders, folding it rapidly into layers of velvet and fur.

"I apologize for the haste, but I rather think we should be away from here by the time the villagers wake."

She muttered something that came out as consent, then blinked and took a closer look at him. "What's amiss with you? You look terrible."

He was red-eyed and scruffy, almost pale beneath his tan. "Nothing."

"Oh, God—are you ill again?" Her heart sank. "Do you feel feverish?"

He pulled sharply away when she went to touch his forehead. "I'm well enough, my lady. It's nothing more than the baker's evil work."

"Baker?"

"The pie." He was lifting her into the saddle, straining with the effort, even though she tried to help.
When she was in place he stepped back, wiping a hand
across his brow. "At least it didn't sicken you as it did
me."

"No," she said, and then, after only a small hesita-
tion, offered him her hand.

He looked at her palm, unmoving.

"If you're ill," Amiranth said, "you must ride with
me."

His eyes returned to her face. He might have turned
slightly paler.

"If you're ill and they are coming," she said patiently,
"we must ride together." She waited, then added, "At
least for now."

He glanced around them, at the spindly trees, the
path to the plague village a straight line to the east, clear
in the dirt.

"Come," she said, trying to sound firm.

Tristan climbed into the saddle behind her.

They left the grove at a brisk trot, jarring the ache in
Amiranth's head to a thumping pain. Tristan was a supple support behind her, his arms at her waist, lightly
now—not like yesterday, when he had seized her to him
as they fled for their lives. She closed her eyes, remembering the fear of those terrible minutes, how it felt to
have him keep her clenched to him, his chest to her
back, his chin above her shoulder.

Eventually Jorah slowed from her trot to a walk, slow
and not as painful. Amiranth straightened a little, and
Tristan's grip grew even lighter, barely there at all.

The sun was rising at an angle across the sky, thin clouds drifting near the edges of the horizon. The heat had already begun; she felt slightly dizzy with it. There were no sounds beyond the *clip-clop* of Jorah's hooves, the creaking of the leather saddle. Even Tristan's breathing seemed muted behind her, faint.

She felt herself grow gradually detached from the moment, considering their options with the part of her mind that was still capable of such a thing as rational thought. The rest of her was floating somewhere, almost outside of her skin, painless.

If he was ill again—if he had the fever as she did now—they were surely going to die.

"I have heard that when one consumes meat after a long time without it, it sickens the stomach," Amiranth said.

Tristan seemed to grunt but otherwise did not reply.

She continued. "You said at Safere you had had no meat. Perhaps that is what happened to you."

"Perhaps."

His voice was strong enough, though his tone was curt.

"How long had it been, my lord?"

"What? With no meat?"

"Yes."

He said nothing. She waited, then turned in his arms. He was too near to see clearly; she had a glimpse of his jaw, the slope of his cheekbone, curling black hair. Then he moved, shifting her firmly forward again, so that she could not see him at all.

"I don't know," he said.

"Well, I would think it must be some time. Months? Half a year, even?"

He was breathing more rapidly. His arms tightened slightly against her, then loosened again.

"I don't know," he repeated.

Amiranth sharpened her tone. "If you have the fever again, my lord, we must take steps now to prepare for it. The two of us sickened at once——"

"Years," he interrupted, his voice low, almost harsh.

"Oh. I see."

Silence again. She found herself examining Jorah's mane in front of her, the way it parted neatly down the horse's neck, to the left on top, to the right along the bottom, long and black, bouncing with each step.

"How many years?" she wondered aloud.

Tristan did not answer.

"I find it very strange," she said, "that a king's knight would have no meat at all. It seems a very poor situation, my lord."

He laughed, mirthless.

"Indeed it was, my lady."

Something told her to stop—his words, the suppressed tone that sent a prickle of warning across her skin.

He had said nothing of France, save that odd, rambling speech the first night in the great hall at Safere. She had dismissed it at the time; it was nonsense, only the fever speaking. Yet she had seen for herself that whatever had happened to him had hardly gone well—he had arrived alone, bedraggled, ill—a far cry from the manner in which he had left years before.

Amiranth had allowed him his silence because as much as he seemed not to want to speak of it, she did not want to hear of it. He had chosen his glorious war over her, and damn the consequences. She did not need to know the details of it—the insult had been clear enough. And it was easier not to know, certainly. Easier to not care.

But the Amiranth floating above her, pale and sheer as the wind, wondered at this, his reticence of his past . . . her acceptance of it. Surely there was something wrong with that. Surely she had the right to know more. . . .

She asked again, "How many years?"

Clip-clop, clip-clop. Jorah's steps filled the silence, rhythmic and plain.

"Eight," Tristan answered at last.

The warning expanded within her, filling her, battling even the floating sensation. "Eight? But—how could that be?"

"I will not discuss it."

"But—"

"Enough!"

Clip-clop, clip-clop . . .

"Did you forsake the king's men?" she asked quietly. "Is that why?"

No response. Only that slight tightening of his arms at her waist again, his breath a little more ragged than it should have been.

A fugitive from battle. Of course.

It explained much—why he would have been without meat; why he had returned alone to Safere, and in such pitiable condition. Above all, it explained why they had had no word of him over the years, how he had been assumed dead all this time, but he had only been running, hiding, leaving her to lament his death alone—

He interrupted her thoughts, his words slow, labored. "Eight years gone. I would say that the king's men forsook *me*."

"What does that mean?"

Tristan sighed. "Nothing. It is unimportant now."

"I only wish to understand—"

"Lady Lily." His voice turned tense, close to savage behind her. "If you value yourself or me, you will honor me in this. Leave it be."

She bit back her protest, hearing for the first time proof of the steely element in him, a glimpse of the hard will she had always suspected about him made real. It gave her pause, even in the midst of her own strange delirium.

He was hiding his past, not trusting her enough to reveal the intimacies of his war—or the lack of it— dismissing her now as easily as he had always done.

Yet it seemed so unlikely, that the Earl of Haverlocke would desert his king, his own vassals in battle. It seemed so incredible, that the man she thought she had once loved would so completely abandon the ideals of his knighthood. It could not be true. It couldn't. But why didn't he deny it?

Her head ached fiercely; she could not reason this out. Amiranth felt a grieving sorrow begin to filter through her—for him, for herself, for this unwanted moment between them—and told herself it was the illness rising in her again.

To hell with him. Let him keep his secrets. She had her own, as well.

Behind her Tristan held his silence, his hands firm around her now, steadfast.

And so slowly the silence unfolded to become long minutes, and then hours, and then she didn't know how long, because the floating part of her had become all of her, and Amiranth could not figure time any longer.

They rode on beneath the shining sun, staying in the shade of the trees when they could, otherwise enduring the open road. It seemed to her she slept some, but it was not a true sleep; it could not be, sitting up in a saddle, sore and hot and uncomfortable.

She was thirsty. Tristan gave her the waterskin and she drank heavily from it, the liquid heated and fetid. It did not satisfy her. It did not help.

When they rested he gave her bread, a little of the cheese. She ate what she could. He did not allow them to linger long in any one place. They kept riding.

Eventually Amiranth became aware of leaning against him fully, uncaring, her head beneath his chin. Tristan braced her easily, holding the reins now, and Jorah *clip-clopped* on and on and on. . . .

Twilight. The sky had turned brilliant scarlet and violet-pink, the most beautiful colors she had ever seen. They were stopped again in some woods—real woods, she noted with sudden amazement—hidden amid green trees, and ferns, and grass.

He was helping her from the saddle, easing her to sit

against an oak, and Amiranth began to cry, because she was so happy to see grass again, after all this time.

"There," he was saying, drying her eyes, crouched in front of her. "My love, my heart, no tears . . ."

This startled her into stillness. She gazed up at him, and Tristan gave her his slight smile, his fingers cool on her face.

"Take a nap," he said. "Right here, Lily. Lie here, and sleep."

And he helped her to the sweet-scented grass, so welcome against her heated skin. Her eyelids felt heavy, gritty.

"Sleep," she heard him say, such a soothing temptation. "Sleep now, and I'll be here when you awaken."

So she let go of her worries and fell into the soft grass, sinking swiftly and certainly into its green, green depths.

⌘

IT WAS A TOWN, NOT A VILLAGE. A VERY SMALL TOWN, Tristan conceded, even a rather shabby one. But a town nonetheless.

A town might be more open to strangers than a village. A town might not even take note of two newcomers in its streets.

He watched it for a while, staying back in the trees on top of the hill nearby. The town had been built in the lush valley below, two streams bordering it, then disappearing into the maze of streets and alleys. People walked about—that was good, he thought. Everyday business was still taking place. There was no air of desperate solitude that he could see.

He racked his memory for the name of this place, without success. He must have been here before. As a child, at least—aye, surely then. But it seemed the same as the countless other towns exactly like it that dotted the kingdom.

A smithy. A slaughterhouse. A bakery, a mill. A tavern.

Tristan concentrated on the area around the tavern, watching the flow of people going in and out of it, straining to hear the rumble of noises that sometimes wafted up the little hill. Night was nearly upon them; lamps and torches lit the entrances of the buildings now, cheerful welcome.

Where there was a tavern there would be an inn. There must be. He was counting on it.

He made his way back to Lily, still sleeping embraced by the tall grass. She looked so lovely in her tumbled gown and her hair falling free, dusky gold over green, gentle shadows about her. A nymph, caught in her slumber. Only the tint of rose across her face betrayed the mortal weakness that beset her now.

Tristan knelt before her and woke her as gently as he could.

"Time to go again. How are you? Can you sit up? Excellent. That's wonderful, Lily. Here's the horse. Let me help you."

He mounted behind her, keeping her near. She was warm in his arms, soft curves and sleepy befuddlement. Tristan steered the mare out of the woods, down the hill toward that tavern.

At the edge of town he tried to get her to sit up straight, and she did, pushing her hair out of her eyes, gazing around them.

"Let me speak for us," he whispered. "Do you understand? I'm going to get us a proper room tonight, my lady. You'll be better there."

So help me, he thought, determined.

No one stopped them. He had covered Lily with the mantle before they entered, drawing the hood close around her face, a show of modesty that would serve to hide her telltale flush. They gathered curious stares down the streets but no one disturbed them.

Now that they were actually amid the people, he recognized the lean, hungry look to most of them; he had lived with such a hunger for years now. But the majority of the gazes seemed to be aimed at the mare, in fact. Tristan had to admit she was a fine piece of flesh, and despite their hardships of the past few days, she was obviously no common rounsey. He had not considered it until just now, how much the steed stood out in this ordinary place.

They did not need to stand out.

At the corner of some busy street Tristan dismounted, leaving Lily alone in the saddle so he could walk the mare himself, keeping his hands tight on the reins. He met the gawking of the people with a warning look of his own. Most turned swiftly away.

When he glanced back at Lily, she was watching him with her great brown eyes, very wide now, the curve to her lips turned down at the edges. He tried to smile at her, to reassure her without words. The worry on her face did not ease.

He found the tavern without having to ask directions. From the distance of the woods it had held a kind of comforting familiarity: noise and bustle, the hanging sign out front depicting a fat pig and a mug of brew. He had seen a dozen taverns just like it in his youth—a hundred, more like. There would be plenty of plain food and sour ale, or watered wine. There would be rooms above the bar for rent, hard pallets—a fireplace, if they were lucky.

And he could see now that all of these things were still likely to be true. But as he turned to check on Lily again he had his first, belated notion of just how out of place she was here, a noblewoman on a noble horse, both as rare as diamonds in these parts, no doubt.

Still he drew them forward into the courtyard fronting the building, concentrating on the thought of shelter ahead.

As a boy came to take the horse, a man stepped out of the tavern door, a swell of smoke curling after him. He walked to Tristan, eyeing him, then Lily.

"Help you?"

"My lady requires repast. Give us your best room, and send up a meal at once."

"Lady, is it?" sneered the man, coming closer, staring.

Tristan blocked his path. He was larger and over a head taller than the other man, and knew how to make good use of both.

"Your best room," he repeated, with soft menace. "And a meal. At once."

The innkeeper took a step back, his look surly.

"Need payment for that. In advance."

"Show us the room and we'll discuss your price."

"Payment first," insisted the man, taking another step away, edging toward the door.

"Do you know who I am, sir?" Tristan began, incredulous. "I am—"

"John," interrupted Lily, her voice slightly hoarse. "Pay the man."

"What?"

As one he and the innkeeper turned to her, still mounted. Lily leaned down from the saddle, holding out her hand to Tristan, a pile of coins in her palm. The hood remained around her face, but the faint light from the tavern was already revealing her flush. She met his eyes steadily, spoke again in a firmer voice.

"I say to you, good servant, pay this man his price and let us enter. I am fair weary, and in no mood for your haggling."

Tristan had never heard her speak in such a tone, complete command, crisp aristocracy. When he continued to stare at her, she arched a brow at him, lofty.

"Pray do not tarry. I am in need of my meal."

He reached for the coins, an outrageous sum—far, far too much for such a simple place.

The innkeeper knew it, too.

"At once, my lady," he said, smirking up at her.

Without comment Tristan dropped the coins in the

other man's palm, ignoring the smirk. He turned to help Lily from the horse.

She slipped from the saddle too quickly, nearly fell against him but recovered, her hands tight on his forearms, her steps shaky.

"This way, my lady," said the innkeeper, and they followed him into the haze of the smoky tavern.

Chapter Seven

———— ⚬⚭⚬ ————

Amiranth maintained the charade as long as she could, leaning heavily against Tristan as they climbed the stairs to the inn's only room with a private parlor.

"The best in town," the innkeeper boasted, throwing her frequent, assessing looks over his shoulder. "My lady won't be disappointed."

"I should hope not," she replied coolly.

Beside her, Tristan walked with steady steps, his eyes cold, unreadable. The strength of his arm beneath her hand was the only thing that kept her from sinking to the floor.

He took her immediately to the chair by the fireplace, helping her to sit, urging her loudly to keep warm and rest after their very long journey. She heard him move away, confer with the innkeeper, but their voices were strange to her now, seemed to reach her through a heavy buzzing sound that filled her head, mingling with the sounds of the tavern beneath them. She thought once that Tristan might have asked her something, and could only lift one hand lazily in response, a dismissal, hoping he would understand what was happening to her.

The fire burned and burned, so bright . . . she had to close her eyes, just for a moment. . . .

A touch on her shoulder. Tristan was there in front of her, blocking out the flames.

"Supper for my lady," he said, and helped her to rise. The world was not quite as unsteady as before. The buzzing sound had sunk away to a low hum.

With her hand on his arm she crossed to the small table nearby, meat and condiments already laid out upon it. A serving woman was directing the meal, a jug of something in her hands. The woman spoke briskly to the other servants, pouring ale into Amiranth's cup. Her eyes were sharp green, inquisitive as she glanced from Tristan to Amiranth.

"Leave us," Amiranth said to her. "My man will serve me."

The woman curtsied, mumbling a response. Only when all the servants had left the room did Amiranth dare to give in to the weakness trembling through her. She sighed a little, leaning back, closing her eyes again. The smell of roasted lamb drifted over her, making her queasy.

"Drink," said a voice close to her ear.

She opened her eyes to Tristan, holding a cup to her

lips. She accepted the ale, tasting the bitter sting of it, allowing it to soothe her thirst, settle her stomach. When she finished he took it from her, then returned to hold out a morsel of bread, dripping sauce. She pushed away his hand.

"I can feed myself."

"I think not," he replied, in a voice as low as hers. "You have claimed me your man, my lady. I would not be much of a servant if I allowed you to handle your own food."

A touch of sarcasm, so slight she almost missed it. Amiranth bristled. "You could not very well tell them you are the Earl of Haverlocke, my lord."

"Why not?" He abandoned his pretext of feeding her, sitting back on his heels. "It would gain us a better measure of respect from that thief of an innkeeper, I can tell you that much. Now we are merely a spinster and a servant."

She felt a measure of her energy return. "A spinster and a servant with a *room,* and a *meal. You* would have gotten us tossed out at once."

"Clearly you have no real understanding of the power of a title."

"I have understanding enough to realize when a title would do more harm than good!"

"The Earl of Haverlocke is an old and valued—"

"The *Earl of Haverlocke* is not here. Although most certainly he has been here before, so his face would be known. But your brother Liam is most likely now at his castle, enjoying his life, surrounded by many who will vouch for his identity. *You,* my lord, are naught but a stranger in poor man's clothing."

She saw him consider her words, once more discerning in him that trace of the cold arrogance of his youth—affronted now, as if she had committed some mortal offense merely by pointing him to the truth. His elegant brows were lowered in a scowl, his eyes narrowed. Aye, she remembered this look about him.

Strangely, it did not impress her as much now as it had years past. Perhaps it was merely that she had grown, and saw him now without stardust in her eyes— but there might have been uncertainty behind his pride, a narrow fissure in his vanity. Or perhaps it was merely the light.

Amiranth said nothing further, pursing her lips together. Let him stew. She was correct, and she knew it.

With a sound of disgust he abruptly stood, crossing back to the hearth. One hand reached out to touch the stone, his palm gradually flattening against it, as if to test the strength of it. Against the fire his form turned dark, muscle and man, supple lines.

"All these years away," he said slowly, to the flames. "And when I return, nothing is as it should be. My wife, my title, my home—all taken from me." He shook his head. "I cannot comprehend it."

"It is a simple situation," she offered, still watching him, the light around him. "Tristan Geraint is dead, and has been for many years. It is going to take a miracle to bring him back."

He gave a short laugh. "I fear I've already used up my share of miracles, my lady."

"Have you? I'm sure I would not know about that."

He hunched his shoulders just slightly, and stared down at the wooden planking of the floor. His hand looked shadowed against the stone, his fingers tan and lean. He pushed harder at the rock, until the skin around his nails turned pale.

What struck her then was that he seemed so vulnerable, a man pitted against a world he did not know. Something in her softened, close to empathy.

"You should think of your future. You must plan now," she said, trying to combat this feeling.

"I have, Lily. God's truth, I have." His voice had become gravelly, rough. He dropped his arm and turned to look at her at last, gold and orange around him, a halo of fire against a tall knight. "I think of it all the time."

She felt that odd skip in her heartbeat, meeting his gaze, so severe, almost . . . imploring.

Amiranth had to glance away, down to her lap. In time she heard him stir.

"And your future, Lady Lily. Have you truly considered it?"

"Of course."

"A convent," he said, smoother than before. "Such a sheltered life, secluded away, prayers every day, nuns all around you . . ."

"It will be pleasant," she said firmly.

"Indeed."

Now he had that bored tone, the one that used to wound her so. She kept her gaze lowered, studying her hands, her fingers locked together. Her nails were very short, suited for work. For survival.

"I saw it once," Amiranth said suddenly, defiant. "On a visit. It is a lovely place. Green. Wooded. There are gardens and trees and birds, and a stream that winds around the chapel. There is a little bridge to cross."

"How nice," he said, in the same voice.

"Yes," she agreed, and then said it again, resolute. "Yes. I'm sure it will be."

He had turned his back to her, as if the conversation were no longer of even the mildest interest. His next words were spoken down to the fire.

"Shall I serve you now, my lady?"

"No. I will serve myself."

Tristan approached the table, then moved to her, ignoring her gesture of protest, kneeling at her side. There was a bite of lamb in his hand.

"They'll be in and out, you know." His face had slipped to a mask again, expressionless. "Bringing the courses."

Her gaze went from the door—unlatched, slightly open—to his hand, waiting with the food. The noise from the tavern below was a steady din.

"Beware the meat," Amiranth said.

"I know."

HE HAD STAYED BESIDE HER, FEEDING HER AS CAREfully as he might a child, and she had allowed it, despite the strong objection that lingered within her. She accepted his offerings in small bites, hungry, not hungry, contemplating his profile as he deliberated over the platters.

The fever seemed to have its own life within her, surging at times, receding, a slow, steady cycle that gave her long moments of lucidity before losing her again, letting her thoughts drift free.

What a silly lie, to call him her servant. It had done its purpose, it had gained them entrance to the inn, but she still couldn't quite believe that it had worked.

After the meal was done she examined him anew, garbed in the peasant clothing of Safere, tall and beautiful, golden with firelight. How had the innkeeper ever believed such a thing, when everything about him spoke of nobility? His face, his posture, even his voice proclaimed his ancestry as clearly as a banner flag. He was an earl, lost and now found again, moving around this little room tonight, preparing the pallet for her as she lounged by the fire, idle as a queen.

The serving woman of before reappeared, two others with her. They cleared the table with much clacking and thumping of dishes, little comment between them. The green-eyed woman kept throwing Tristan sidelong looks.

For a moment Amiranth feared the woman had grasped what the innkeeper had not—but no. She leaned back in her chair, resting her cheek on the back of her hand, watching the woman watch him.

Had she ever had such a look on her own face for her husband? Amiranth wondered. Had she ever studied him so carefully, so hopefully, even as a girl?

He *was* too fine for a servant. He was too fine for this room, for the lie she had set up for him. Yet he worked so easily at his tasks, pouring water in a basin for her, ordering more towels brought up, more blankets for my lady, more wood for the fire.

No doubt he had been waited upon countless times before in such a way. That was why he knew what do, what to say.

She tried to imagine him in battle, and could not. She tried to imagine him fighting, turning, running away—and still could not. What was true and what was false? She couldn't say. She was so tired.

She let him undress her to her undergown, peeling away the heavy layers of her bliaut, his fingers light and brisk against her. He led her to the pallet, moving with her slowly across the chamber, her spine very straight against the curious stares of the women. She lay upon the furs and he covered her with blankets, impersonal. As he turned to dismiss the others from the room, Amiranth closed her eyes, letting the sweetness of his voice carry her, all at once, to sleep.

———⟨⟩———

THE DAMNED FLOOR WAS TOO HARD.

Tristan couldn't sleep upon it, even with three blankets piled under him and a cushion beneath his head.

There was a strong draft coming from the doorway, the door ill-fitted against the jamb—

—would it stick in a hurry? were the stairs wide enough to run down? how high was the window? how far the ground?—

—and the draft chilled the left side of his body, no matter how he arranged the covers over him.

Lily slept so peacefully just a few feet away, surrounded with softness. He should be happy for her now. He should be relieved that she had the succor he had so desperately wanted for her. That, for now at least, she would gain a full night's rest.

He had stretched out on the floor at the foot of her pallet as any true villein might, part guardian, part servant. He knew the role; he had lived the guise of earl for years before it was taken from him. He remembered what to do, how to act, what to say to remain convincing, to follow Lily's lie and hide his true self from the people here. . . .

But he could not sleep. Not like this.

Tristan sat up, rubbing his eyes, smiling grimly. He had slept in a cell with no heat or decent covering for years. This room was an extravagance of solace compared to that. Yet he had been alone then, always alone. Tonight *she* drowsed nearby, wrapped in the comforts of civilization.

Beneath warm blankets.

In a gown very loose.

In a pallet clearly large enough for two.

The fire had all but gone out; the room now was dusky with night, only a faint, reddish glow coming from the hearth. Hours had passed since she had first lain down. The tavern below was largely silent now, only an occasional snore from the men sleeping there creeping up through the floorboards.

He looked at Lily, fair in the night, her hair loose and

free, long curls arranged around her like a pillow of spun gold. His eyes were still used to years of darkness—he thought he could see her better now than even in daylight, with her brilliance dimmed, slumber and dreams taking away the caution that always seemed to shade her.

Shining Lily, locked away for the rest of her life in a convent. Inconceivable. How could she choose such a life for herself? How could she hide her spirit that way?

He found himself kneeling beside the pallet, examining her face, her hands against the blankets, the way her wrists seemed so slender, such fine bones, soft skin. Her closed eyes, her lashes long and winsome, as if they belonged to a little girl and not the grown woman who had saved him. The delicate slash of her brows, strong yet feminine, relaxed now. Her lips, sweet and pretty and full. He remembered how they tasted, how they felt. . . .

All other thoughts seemed to melt away from him, fading into the dusk. As Tristan stared down at her a new word came to him, just one, repeating itself—a dangerous word, encircling him, and her, until it was all he could consider:

Mine, mine . . .

He leaned down closer to her, slowly, slowly, never taking his eyes from her face. Lily slept on, unaware of his thoughts, his very presence, the peril near her now.

He let his face linger over hers, their lips close to touching, but not quite. The scent of her came to him, subdued and infinitely pleasing, filling him. He felt almost dizzy with it, heady now, lost.

Tristan lowered his lips to hers.

She was warm and luscious, for all her sleeping

peace. He kept the kiss soft, so nearly not there, teasing himself with the contact between them, allowing his lips to glide across hers, feather light.

His eyes closed. It was heaven.

He felt her take in her breath in a sigh and paused, hovering, but she did not awaken. So he continued the kiss, still gentle, fighting the craving within him for more of her, for what was *not* his, despite the throbbing ache of his body. And because that thought made the craving turn unbearable, Tristan allowed his tongue to savor her lips, to slide along the smoothness there, a deliberate torture.

She sighed again but this time he didn't stop. Greedy now, he curled close over her in a tight arch, his hands clenched against her pillows, tasting, tasting, and oh, she was so good, so sharply beautiful to him, and he was so hungry for her—

Tristan pulled back, breathing too hard, raising his face to the ceiling, to the wall—looking anywhere but at her.

Lily lifted a hand to her mouth, still sleeping, brushing her lips with her fingertips, turning her head. She let out her breath in a long, languorous murmur.

"Tristan . . ."

What an appalling mistake. This was not heaven—this was absolute hell. He stood, pacing away from her, turning to the door. He was afraid that if he looked at her now he would give in to the craving and go back to her . . . and awaken her in a way that would turn his name from a sigh to a plea.

He heard the rustle of her blankets. When he could

finally face her again he saw that she had rolled away, her back to him, her hair still gleaming gold, falling down her back to whisper across the covers.

How would it feel, to touch her hair. . . .

Tristan took the few short steps he needed to leave the room and closed the door quietly behind him.

He had been too long without a woman. That was all this was, he told himself. Eight years—and the last time he had enjoyed the pleasures of the flesh he could only barely recall: his wedding night, a blur of memories, too shadowy to recover.

His wife. Amiranth.

Shame came back to him, cooling the lust, clearing his head enough that he could lower it against the wall of the hallway, grimacing.

Amiranth, he thought bleakly, trying to summon her face, her eyes, anything to clear the spell of Lily from his body. *Amiranth, Amiranth.*

She was the innocence lost to him. She was the reason he was here now, fighting his basest self. She was the only reason, in fact, that he knew her cousin at all, that he traveled with her, and longed for her.

What would she say about this? he wondered. What could she say? It was too late to reach her—despite his noble intentions, he had failed all those fine oaths he pledged to her in France. She had died too soon. He would never have the chance to make her happy.

But would she offer her blessing now? She had loved her cousin, he was certain of that. If he could make *Lily* happy, if he could wed her, and win her, and spend his life trying to please her—would Amiranth still haunt them?

Tristan let out a laugh, curt and hushed. Wed Lily. Not bloody likely. Not without a miracle, a papal dispensation at the very least, to marry the cousin of his deceased wife. Not without a long and arduous journey through the courts of Rome, payments addressed, official petitions made to deflect the laws of consanguinity. . . .

If he could convince the world that he was who he said he was.

And *if* she would have him.

Tristan thought, glumly, that most likely she would not.

Even if he managed to push away the ghost of his wife, it was perfectly clear that Lily never would. She wanted her convent, nothing else. He was dreaming, to think he might have her. He was crazed, indeed. Perhaps this was all just an intricate new nightmare of his, and he was still locked in his cell in France, waiting for death, hoping for it.

He opened the door to the room again, finding the shape of her against the night. *Real, this is real,* he thought, and let the spiral of relief unwind through him. No matter what the sins of his life, Lady Lily Granger was real before him.

He shut the door, beginning a slow walk down the hallway.

Ale, that's what he needed. A good mug of ale, perhaps some of that lamb to go with it, aye. Rebuild his appetite, prepare for the journey ahead—

He descended the stairs too quickly, almost blundering into the conversation of lowered, sly voices coming from the tavern room.

". . . her clothes are fine enough, I can tell you that much. And that mare! Did you see her?"

A man's voice—the innkeeper, Tristan was quite certain, coming from near the bar, where he could not see. He slowed on the stairs, then stopped just outside the room, out of sight. From here he had a view of a good slice of the tavern, the tables, the hearth. Men lay strewn across the floor, fast asleep—weary travelers and the servants of this place, clustered next to the fire.

A loud snore from one of the sleeping men drowned out a woman's reply. The innkeeper spoke again, furtive.

"No trouble at all, I tell you. Think on it, Moira. It's just a woman and a serf. No doubt she's been whoring her way to the city. They'll have plenty of coin to go around. Who are they to complain? Who'd believe them, anyways?"

"Sheriff might, that's who."

The serving woman, the one with the unpleasant eyes. Tristan remembered her, the veiled looks of speculation she had thrown at him.

"What? The sheriff? Doubt *me*? Believe them over *me*, what's been his good friend all these years?"

"Friend," the woman snorted. "Aye, you're a real friend, you are. You took with his wife like the dog you are first time he blinked. And keep your voice down, fool."

"Now, Moira, pet, you know you're the one in my heart. . . ."

The innkeeper's tone deepened, turning intimate, prompting an appreciative murmur from the woman. Tristan stared at the wall before him, thinking quickly.

He had no real weapon—no sword, merely his dagger, good enough only at close range—and there were many of them, all those men asleep just beyond him, no doubt as greedy as the couple speaking now, as eager for bounty—

"We'll do it, then," said the man, still low. "I'll take the mare to the old shepherd's hut in the woods. You take care of the coins in the room."

"*Me?* Why should *I* risk goin' up there? *You* take the coins, and I'll take the mare."

"Moira, my sweet, you're the one they won't suspect. . . ."

Tristan didn't wait to hear more. He was already racing up the stairs, fleet as a cat. He found the room and closed the door again quietly, inspecting it. A flimsy lock, easy to pick. Easier still just to break.

He dragged a chair over to the door, token defense, better than nothing.

The woman would not dare break in to the room so openly. But the mare—it would not take the innkeeper long to remove her. Once taken, Jorah would not be easily located again.

And then the man would return, and perhaps he had been right, perhaps the sheriff of this shabby little town truly would believe an innkeeper over a serf and a whore—there had never been a horse, or coins. Perhaps the innkeeper was adept enough to convince his friend that *they* were the thieves. He had heard such tales before.

Tristan would not suffer another night imprisoned—not another minute, in fact. Death was a happier fate than that.

"Lily! Wake up!"

He had her by the shoulders, hauling her upright, ignoring her moan of protest.

"Wake up," he whispered again, urgent. "Stand! We must leave."

"What? Why?"

He left her sitting on the edge of the pallet, rubbing her eyes, bewildered. He found her bliaut, tossed it at her, then her shoes, moving rapidly through the room, throwing together the rest of their meager belongings.

"The window," he commanded. "Open it. Quietly."

"Tristan?" She sounded more alert. "What's happened?"

"We're leaving this place. Now."

"We are not," she countered, finally standing. She clutched the bliaut to her chest.

"Look out the window to the stables," he invited her, dragging her along by the elbow. "There, to the far right—do you see? Recognize that horse?"

She gasped at the scene below, a man in a cloak tugging at a reluctant steed near the stable door, his stifled oaths floating up to them. "Jorah!" Lily turned to him, her eyes a soft gleam in the night. "What is he doing?"

Tristan thrust her cloak into her arms on top of the

gown. "Not taking her for a pleasant walk, I assure you."

He opened the window, letting in the cool air. I brushed against him, stirred the curls around Lily' shoulders. The innkeeper wasn't making much progress the mare began to fight him, angry squeals the mar tried to hush.

"Out," Tristan whispered, and began to push her to the ledge.

She resisted. "Stop! Stop it! We must go downstairs raise the alarm—"

He clapped a hand over her mouth. "Downstairs is woman preparing to rob us, surrounded by her fellows She won't take much longer coming up, either."

She pushed his hand away, but dropped her voice to match his pitch. "We'll summon the innkeeper—"

He pressed her down to the ledge, lowering his face to hers. "That *is* the innkeeper, my lady. He thinks u naught but a whore and her serf, ripe for plucking Hurry."

To her credit, she did not argue with him again. He saw the change come over her, indignation turning to ire, and then determination. Lily dropped the cloak and pulled the bliaut over her head; he had to pause to help her, tugging the material down over her body, tightening the laces as quickly as he could while she struggled with her shoes. She was still a confusion of loose ties and ribbons when she stooped to sweep up the cloak, flinging it over her shoulders. He helped her swing her legs out over the edge of the sill, easing out to the short,

slippery thatch of the roof. She faced him, holding tight
to his forearms.

"Careful," he urged, supporting her. "It's a steep
drop, but to the left is a bed of turned dirt. Do you see
it?"

"Yes." Her voice was faint, thin.

"Can you make it?"

"Yes." A tiny quaver in the word, less certain now.

The mare screamed again, her hooves clattering
against stone. Tristan could no longer see the man or
the horse. They would not be far, not yet—but how
close was the sheriff, how soon could he be here, bribed
to injustice, a waiting cell—

He leaned out more, lowering Lily carefully, slowly,
his grip sliding from her arms to her hands, until he
could go no farther with her. She dangled in the air
now, nothing below her but the ground.

"Don't worry." His words were clipped with strain.
"It's not far."

She looked up at him suddenly, her eyes very dark
and wide, golden hair drifting around her.

"Don't let go—" A whisper, choked.

"I'm sorry," Tristan said, and released her hands.

———⟲∿∿⟳———

SHE FELL WITH A RUSH OF COLD AIR PUSHING UP
her skirts, a short howl of wind in her ears, followed by
a crushing impact to the ground.

Dirt puffed up gently all around her, settling over her

in speckles of bark and peat. She lay there, stunned, until she realized there were stars above her, and the awning of a thatched roof.

From near that roof a man's voice called out quietly, her cousin's name.

Amiranth rose to her elbows, inhaling the earth, staggering to her feet. She could not reply to Tristan. She could not breathe yet—

A flash of something before her, a man falling, Tristan, landing with a grunt and a clever roll, coming to his feet again almost before she could take it in.

He clutched a pair of bags in his arms, unkempt, as winded as she was. They stared at each other for a moment, the dirt rising between them.

Jorah called out again, distant.

Tristan took her hand. "Come with me."

She ran with him, trying to manage her loosened gown with her free hand, to keep from tripping over the layers of material that bunched between her legs. He moved quickly, half pulling her along the uneven stones.

Jorah was at the end of the courtyard before it led out to the open road, panting and snorting, dancing on the cobblestones. She reared, and the innkeeper dragged hard at the reins, his oaths much louder now. When she landed again, the man struck her across the nose.

Amiranth had no sense of breaking free of Tristan, or even of time or distance—only an instant, frenzied rage, to see the abuse of her horse, the rolling whites of Jorah's eyes, the bit tearing at her mouth. She came upon the innkeeper so suddenly that she had only the impression of his startled face as she flung herself at him with all her weight, assailing him with both fists, a howl in her throat.

The man lost the reins and stepped back, yelling as she hit at him, and they tangled together for a moment before he shoved her off with a vicious blow, sending her falling to the stones.

"Bitch!" he cried, taking a step toward her.

The form of Tristan blocked her view, deft violence unloosed. The two men became movement and harsh, ruthless sounds, fists striking flesh. Amiranth scrambled up and ducked around them, searching for her mare.

There were new sounds now, light coming from the tavern, people spilling out. Jorah had bounded across the enclosed courtyard, still panicked, the reins slapping at the ground around her forelegs.

The new people moved between her and her horse. Amiranth limped to a halt, watching with dismay as they approached—large men, burly.

"Here now," called out one. "What's the trouble, Nigel?"

The innkeeper and Tristan stood clutched together, frozen in a moment of brutality. Tristan had his fists clenched in the man's tunic; the innkeeper had braced one hand against his shoulder, holding him off, and the other cupped his nose, blood dripping around his fingers.

"The sheriff," he called back, eyeing Tristan. "Get the sheriff! Got a couple of thieves here!"

"The hell you do," Tristan snarled.

Amiranth looked quickly back to Jorah, backed near

the wall of the tavern, quivering with fear. One of the men had taken up her reins. There were at least half a dozen of the newcomers, with more beginning to fill the doorway. Someone held up a lantern; it cast mad shadows across them all, swaying in his grip.

"Tell them to release the horse," Tristan said now to the innkeeper, fierce. "Release her, and we'll be gone."

"Aye, no doubt you will!" The man tried unsuccessfully to shake Tristan off, then turned his face to the men again. "Caught them myself, lads, stealing my new mare! Bring the sheriff, I say, and we'll deal with these two properly!"

"*Your* mare, Nigel?" asked one of the men, cynical.

"A beauty, she is," said the innkeeper quickly. "Fetch a fine price on the market, and you know it, Will Stone. More than enough for a few good men like us."

The others exchanged looks, slowly nodding. A few of the stableboys had crept to the edges of the yard, watching with open-mouthed fascination. The serving woman of before had slipped outside as well, standing next to Jorah.

"Right, then," said the man with the lantern, and began to approach Amiranth. "What's a charmer like you doing thievin', love? Too bad for you, I reckon. Mayhap we can work something out . . ."

She shifted but then Tristan was beside her, in front of her, swift and dark, like one of the shadows streaking across the yard.

"Touch her," he warned, "and I'll kill you."

"Bold fellow," taunted the lanterned man. "You against me? And my brothers here?"

"I'll take all of you," Tristan vowed, in a voice Amiranth wholeheartedly believed, wilder than before, utterly fearless.

The other man very deliberately put the lantern on the ground, cracking his knuckles.

"Oh!" Amiranth cried out, clutching at the clasp of her cloak. "Oh, my head—the pain!"

No one paid any attention to her; Tristan and the man were beginning to circle each other around the flickering light, crouched low.

"The plague," Amiranth moaned, louder than before, and approached them both, shrugging back the cloak to reveal the slack folds of her gown, laces fluttering around her. "That last village—two days ago, John . . . we lingered too long—"

She had their attention now, right enough. Tristan's adversary paused, flicked his eyes to her, wary.

"The blacksmith," she said, stopping, holding out one trembling hand to Tristan. "Remember the smith—how he sickened afore he left me—"

"What's that?" Now the other man straightened completely, staring at her. Amiranth kept her gaze on Tristan, her hand still outstretched.

"God's blood, look at her," someone said, and she made certain to step closer to the lantern, pushing back her hair from her face with splayed fingers, hoping the flush of before had stayed with her.

"John," she cried again, in a voice that cracked with real fright. "Take me from this place! The pestilence—it comes here too, I know it, I *see* it on their *faces*—"

The other men had begun to edge out of the circle of

light, plainly unnerved. Only Tristan remained where he was, gazing back at her, his eyes still too wild.

"Away," she moaned, and swayed to him.

He had sense enough to catch her, hugging her to him, hard and fast.

"My lady," he murmured, close to her ear.

"Plague," she heard the others repeat. "The plague, by all that's holy, look at her—"

She pulled away from Tristan, swinging around to the man who restrained her horse. "My mare!" she cried. "The smith touched my mare, he shod her, remember, John!"

"Aye," replied Tristan, just behind her.

The man released Jorah's reins as if they had turned white hot, jerking out of Amiranth's path. Of all the people around them now, only the serving woman seemed unconvinced, her face pinched with emotion—anger or greed, Amiranth couldn't tell.

No matter. She caught the reins again; Jorah moved toward her, ears pinned. Tristan flung the bags of their belongings across her withers, then quickly lifted Amiranth onto the mare's back—no saddle, she supposed the innkeeper meant to sell it apart, or keep it—following her with rapid grace, a solid warmth behind her.

"Nigel," snapped the woman, near their feet. "What's all this? She's a cunning whore, that's all it is!"

"Pity's sake, Moira, get back—"

"It's not the plague," the woman insisted, shriller than before. "I watched her all night! I would know!"

Amiranth looked at her, imploring. "I pray you,

mistress, protect yourself from this death! Burn your clothes, the bedding—oh, that it's not too late—"

"Cunning slut!" The woman came closer, her eyes turned flat gray in the light. "It's *not* the plague! It's *not!*"

Without warning she reached for the bridle, startling Jorah into a sideways leap, whinnying. Amiranth fought to regain control as the woman persisted, still reaching. Out of desperation Amiranth bent down and spat at her.

The men cried out together; the woman stumbled backward, shrieking.

Tristan made some urgent sound, leaning in to her, and the mare responded. Jorah lunged for the road so suddenly that Amiranth toppled back, nearly falling, caught only by the crush of Tristan's arm across her ribs.

They raced off across the black countryside, soon lost to the night and the fell world around them.

———— ⚬⟊⟊⟊⟆ ————

BY DAWN THEY HAD FOUND A NEW SHELTER, WOODS again, thick and dark. They stayed there, watching, waiting to see if they were followed. No one came after them.

As daylight crept across the sky they moved through the pines and elms, silent, weary and awake, no words between them.

They lunched on a portion of the cheese and bread he had stolen before, still mounted, still moving. At a stream flickering with light they paused to map out the rest of the journey to the convent. It could well be their only hope for respite, both understood this. Tristan thought he knew the way to it; Amiranth nodded and said it sounded right. They would make it there soon. They would be safe there. The church would protect them, she was certain of it. There would be time to heal, to rest.

They did not speak of what would happen after that.

———————— ❧ ————————

TWO DAYS LATER THEY ARRIVED AT OUR LADY OF the Blessed Faith. The outer wall was crumbling, neglected, the scent of smoke ghostly in the air. The gate was ajar. They dismounted together and entered the grounds.

All around them were only the blackened shells of buildings, ash and soot smudging the stones in fantastic, whirling patterns.

The convent was deserted. It had been scorched to the ground.

Chapter Eight

⟨∞∞⟩

HE WALKED ALONG THE PAVING STONES CHOKED with weeds, stepping carefully over the rubble of a broken sanctuary, Aves and benedictions forever gone.

The sweetness of the day seemed almost a mockery of the convent ruins around him, a soft blue sky, a clement breeze stirring the branches of the old trees that still lined many of the paths here. But for the charred vestiges of the chapel before him, Tristan might have convinced himself he was in some idyllic country estate, enjoying a sleepy summer day.

He crossed the wooden bridge Lily had described to him that night at the inn. It was a charming thing still, spared the flames that had consumed all the other structures. It arched over a winding creek that fed patches of milkwort and vetch, bright flowers against green moss and stones.

He found Lily in the courtyard past the chapel, seated on a bench that had tendrils of ivy winding around its base. She was staring down at the ground, her empty palms turned up in her lap. All around her spread clusters of rosebushes in full bloom, a rainbow of hues to frame her, brilliant colors against the dark of her gown.

Tristan sat beside her, not close, and watched a pair of blackbirds exchange nods atop a shattered beam.

"Glynwallen is three days' away."

"I cannot . . ." Her voice faded off, shaken.

"Be sensible, Lily," he said, in his hardest tone yet to her. "What else is there to do? You might go to Iving to stay again with Augustin—"

She looked up now, close to stricken.

"But Glynwallen is closer," he finished. "We need shelter, and food and rest. We'll go there. You may consider what to do next after that."

She shook her head slowly, almost stunned. He had the sense that she was not actually refusing him, but rather this place, what had happened here—her careful and cloistered future turned quite literally to ash.

He felt a curl of satisfaction at it, of wicked hope, and crushed it before it anchored too strongly within him.

"The sisters," she said, in her lost voice. "They must have gone somewhere. I can find them . . ."

He sighed and spoke again, kinder now. "Have you seen the field behind this wall here?" He knew she had not. "It's a graveyard. All of it. I fear your sisters are there."

A wordless sound escaped her, thin and cut short, her hand pressed over her mouth. She would not look at him, instead blinking rapidly at the ground.

"It was not vandals who did this, my lady. Not pagans or mercenaries. I think it was the church itself. I think the plague ravaged this place, and they burned what they could, to contain it."

It made sense. He knew it did, but that did not gentle the stark truth of it.

He stood. "I've found a cellar, I think. There might be food there. Come with me to see."

She rose slowly, almost languidly, and followed him to the battered wooden doors he had discovered, set at an angle against the ground. Tristan had glanced only briefly at the darkness of the cellar from above; down the stairs it was dim and damp, surprisingly chilly. He didn't actually think there could be food stored there, not any longer, but there could be no harm in looking.

He watched her covertly as he opened the second of the heavy doors, letting out a sweep of musty air from below. Her lassitude disturbed him deeply. She seemed dazed, remote, nearly unaware of her surroundings. If danger came . . .

The need to keep her near him was strong and binding, even though it was plain no one had been to the convent in quite some time. There could be no danger in this sad and desecrated place. But before they descended the cut stone steps, he paused, glancing around them again.

Sooty walls, empty fields. The bridge, the water. The

mare standing docile nearby, feasting on the long grass
and clover beneath the shade of a walnut tree.

Lily, pale and flushed together, her lashes moist, her
hair catching the sun and turning it to sweet amber. She
was staring at the darkened space before them, not
meeting his gaze.

She seemed suddenly very frail to him, a lone woman
in a haunted garden, relics of a vanished world all about
her.

He took her hand, and led her down the stairs.

Such a familiar setting, close walls, a finite space;
such familiar shadows and coolness, though he had not
been here before. Familiar smells, of dirt and dust, a
lack of living things, combined with that ever-present
tinge of smoke. The doors above them let in a square of
sunlight that slipped down the slick stones, revealing pits
of moss and orange lichen. He stepped carefully, mind-
ing the shadows beneath his feet, his hand firm on hers.

At the bottom of the stairs the light ended. Beyond
him stretched the unknown confines of this cold place,
black shapes amid blackness. He wished devoutly for a
lamp.

"Why are we stopping?" Lily's voice was hesitant, as
if the darkness had touched her, as well.

Tristan took a deep breath, then walked forward.

A ground of hard earth, a low ceiling. Soft, whispering tendrils of something sliding along his hair, brushing his cheek . . . dangling roots from above, or
cobwebs . . . the smell of winter down here, of cold
death, in fact, lurking in the corners, wherever the corners were in this black and hollow place. He could hear

the rats now as well, sly skittering sounds, hungry, crawling toward him—

He stopped again, closing his eyes, fighting this.

Not real, not real—

"Tristan?"

Lily was close behind him. She was the only heat to this place, the only true thing at all around him. He tightened his hand over hers.

"Do you see something?" she asked, hushed.

He opened his eyes. The darkness began to break apart, to dissolve into a dusky new shape, something close and dreaded.

There was a stone wall in front of him, aye, he could see it now. And were those . . . *chains* hanging from it? Chains, long and heavy, thick with rust, blood on the manacles, blood on the floor—pooling, spreading oily and viscous, right to his feet, the rats running to it, squeaking, greedy for it—

Tristan turned and walked swiftly back to the square of light, pulling Lily with him. He took the stairs two at a time, ignoring her gasps, yanking her up without pause when she stumbled.

"Slow down! What—"

They emerged into the brightness of the open sky and only then did he release her hand, his fingers stiff and clumsy, as if it were some other person who had dragged her out here to the sanity of the day.

Lily faced him, rubbing her hand, glaring.

"What were you doing?" she demanded. "Have you lost your wits? We might have fallen down those steps—

broken our bones!—and then what would become of us?"

He had no response for her; he only kept his teeth clenched together, concentrating on her face, the color in her cheeks, the heat in her eyes.

Not real. Not real! Breathe slowly . . .

He saw a change come to her, a gradual thing, uncertainty taking the place of her anger, her frown fading. She took a step back from him, holding her hand to her chest, assessing him with a long look. Her gaze drifted over him, across his face, lower, to his throat. When she spoke again her voice was calmer.

"Did you see aught amiss, my lord?"

Tristan felt his mouth shape into something like a grin. He gave one short, awkward jerk of his head, no.

"It was fair cold down there," she said, still mild. "I believe I need to warm up again over there, on that bench in the sun. Will you accompany me?"

He took her hand as she offered it, careful with her now, pretending to lead her to the damned bench, splashed with light, although in reality it was she who led.

They sat together in the yellow sunshine, the rustling of her skirts very loud to him. Birds celebrated in the trees; the soothing trickle of the creek nearby was a constant ballad over the stones. The scent of roses came to him with a whisper of wind, warm and heady.

Lily, beside him, stayed quietly tranquil, a seamless part of the light and the vibrant day.

Tristan felt the tightness in his chest begin to unclench. Slowly the feeling returned to his feet and hands, a prickling heat. He became aware, eventually, that the sun was quite hot on his head; that a tense, pulsating ache was pounding near his temple. He raised a hand to his face and wiped at his brow with his sleeve.

A bee, fat with pollen, hummed by them in a lazy, spiraling flight.

"What did you see, my lord?" Lily did not look at him.

"Nothing. Darkness. That was all."

"Oh."

He couldn't tell if she believed him or not. It didn't matter. He would not speak of it. He would not *think* of it any longer—

—*rats, blood, death*—

Lily said, "You do not look well."

"I have—a pain in my head."

"Oh," she said again, less cautious now. "Merely that?"

"Aye. Merely that."

He rubbed at his temple, at the ache that did not diminish, like a demon come to life inside him.

She stirred, a sideways look he did not return. "Perhaps I might go see if there was food, after all. I thought I might have seen a storage bin."

She moved swiftly, gracefully, and was already a full five steps away before he realized she meant to go back down there by herself.

"Lily! Wait!"

He caught up with her next to a battered gray pillar, part of a covered path. She turned, placing her fingers over his, where he had grabbed her wrist.

"I won't be long. I remember where it was, I think."

He felt the coldness of before begin to slither over him again, up his feet, up his spine.

"You can't go down there," Tristan said, trying hard to sound rational.

"Why not?"

"It's unsafe."

She tilted her head, studying him. "It was safe enough a few minutes ago."

"I was mistaken. There's nothing there. There's no reason for us to go down."

"*We* are not going down." She removed his hand from her. "*I* am."

"No," he said past his clenched jaw, and the cold burrowed deeper into him. "I forbid it."

"You are not my master, my lord," she replied, a hint of temper. "I will do as I please." She walked away again.

"Dammit, Lily!" He caught up with her once more, blocked her path. "We should leave this place. There is nothing for us here. We need to make haste to Glynwallen, to the shelter there."

"With no food? I'd rather not. This won't take long. If you are right, then I'll be back very soon. And if I'm right, then at least we won't starve."

"Starve?" He bit back a harsh laugh, reaction to this winter-cold thing in him. "We have—oatcakes, and bread—"

"A very few oatcakes, and even less bread," she said firmly. "We need food. You know we do." And she lifted her chin and met his gaze, a challenge, so beautiful with her tattered gown and uncombed hair, so remarkably foolhardy.

She would do it. He knew she would—easily, thoughtlessly, with no idea of what dwelled in the shadows. He felt the winter pierce his heart, the image of her alone in that death trap, the rats, the blood.

Tristan swallowed the mindless dread in him. The pain in his temple turned ferocious and bright.

"Very well, my lady. We'll go together."

"You don't need to come—"

"I said we'll *go,*" he growled, and began a blind walk back to the gaping cellar doors.

———————⌒⟳⌒———————

THAT NIGHT THEY ATE WALNUTS FALLEN FROM THE trees, and blackberries found growing in hedges around the convent walls, hidden behind green leaves and thorns. There were also pears and apples from the ragged orchard beyond the chapel. The grapes were not yet ripe enough, and the birds had gotten to nearly all the plums.

But Amiranth had discovered treasure in the cellar, after all: wine, jugs of it, and half a wheel of moldy cheese, the edges of it gnawed away, most probably by rats.

She carefully sliced away the mold and those edges, and tried not to think of what else had tasted this cheese.

They had decided to camp in what was left of the chapel, since it had sustained the least amount of damage from the fire. The nuns' cells had collapsed into mountains of stone—but the chapel still had four walls, and the beams of its roof. They built a fire near the altar from the green wood scattered on the grounds; the smoke whorled around them in billows of white, vanishing up to the stars. Amiranth sent a quick prayer for forgiveness up with it, hoping God might understand why they slept in His home on this night.

Tristan ate silently, almost sullenly, ignoring her for the most part, which suited her well. His hands were scratched from the blackberry thorns, his fingertips stained dark with their juice. He had finished eating before her—largely because she was the one who had prepared the food, she thought, vexed—and now slouched against a wall opposite, methodically tearing off the petals of a yellow rose he had stolen from the garden.

Amiranth watched him from beneath her lashes, discerning what she could of his humor through the smoke. The curl to his lips was still there, still comely, but there was something else to it now: a suggestion of the moody displeasure she knew so well of old.

She granted him his mood. She sensed that in some way he deserved it. Clearly he had not wished to return to the cellar. He had acted so strangely about it, had seemed almost panicked. She could not fathom what he was thinking; it was only a cellar, nothing very unusual at all, certainly the same as most others. Yet he had gone so cold in there. Cold and still, as if the life had drained straight from him, and left behind a man deathly pale, every aspect of him turned brittle and sharp.

Aboveground again he had only stared at her when she

demanded an explanation, and she had seen it then, the savagery in him, a wild creature cornered and desperate.

How curious it had made her feel. She had not welcomed the sensation of tenderness in her at this; she did not want to care any longer about the enigma of Tristan Geraint. Perhaps he did not like the dark. Perhaps he was averse to the cold, or to the specters of this place. . . . Yet, no matter what the cause, she had to think that accompanying her back to the cellar had been naught but an act of bravery.

He had not wanted to go. But he had gone.

She had found the cheese and they carried it up the stairs together, back into the light, and he had taken it and nearly thrown it down to the ground. Then he walked away from her, pushing his hands through his hair, moving briskly to the rose garden.

She had slipped back down to the cellar by herself for the wine.

So tonight they ate their unlikely meal, and Amiranth, at least, thought it fine enough. They had food, drink. The cheese was excellent, the berries plump and ripe. There were apples and pears and walnuts enough to carry them on a few more days.

They drank wine from two large scallop shells she had found lining one of the paths. There were no remnants of plates or mugs left in this place. The shells were a pleasant discovery, washed clean in the creek, inverted to cup the wine. Amiranth had thought it rather clever of her to suggest using them. It made her feel exotic, almost daring.

But Tristan had only shrugged and turned away, shunning her again.

The petals of his ravaged rose swirled past her feet now with the night breeze, pale yellow mingled with the pink and coral of the ones he had already destroyed. Smoke followed the breeze, drifting over her, making her close her eyes against it. She turned her head away and took another blackberry from the pile nearby. As the smoke cleared she brought it to her lips, tasting the juice of it first with her tongue, pleasing and pungent. She closed her lips around it, looking up to find Tristan watching her past the haze, his eyes dark and intent, his whole being arrested, the tattered rose dangling from his fingertips.

She bit down too quickly; the blackberry exploded into sweetness, a rush of flavor that flooded her mouth. She brought a hand up to her lips, feeling the liquid there, swallowing, embarrassed.

"A *nun,*" Tristan said, almost in disgust, and tossed the rose into the fire.

She kept her eyes averted, watching the stem of the flower singe brown, the leaves begin to curl with the heat.

"Tell me this, Lady Lily." He stretched out his legs, crossing them before her, the light glowing along the curves of his muscles past the hose. "Why did you wait so long to come to your convent?"

"I . . ." She shook her head, trying to think past the wine and the potency of the look he had given her. "I did not wish to leave my cousin."

"Yet you would have left her."

"Eventually, yes."

"Rather heartless of you, don't you think?"

"What?" She stared at him, indignant.

He regarded her with a faint smile, derisive, arms crossed over his chest. "Well, after all, you did come to companion her. Yet you were so ready to leave."

"The arrangement with this convent was established long past, my lord. She—I would have waited for Amiranth's permission to leave."

"And left her alone."

"She would not have been alone very long," Amiranth retorted. "The king had an eye for her next husband, I assure you."

His arms uncrossed. "Really?"

"Aye." She looked down, toyed with the scallop shell near her, red wine pooled in the bottom of it.

"Who?"

She shrugged. "I know not. Some old man, I'm certain. She had already paid a forfeit to the royal treasury to remain unwed for five years. That time was about to expire when . . . when the plague came."

"He never came to Safere to see her, this prospective husband?"

Amiranth lifted her head, spoke with deliberate meaning. "No one ever came to Safere."

"Except you," Tristan finished slowly.

"Aye. Except me."

She let her gaze fall again, unwillingly troubled by his expression, feeling a guilty pang at the remorse that might have flashed behind his eyes. She resisted this odd feeling within her, reaching for another blackberry, putting it back.

Tristan spoke quietly, musing. "So, Amiranth had no wish to remarry."

"Why should she? Her first experience was hardly encouraging."

He said nothing to this, leaving her to study him once more from beneath her lashes. He seemed so distant, almost a ghost to her in truth, as handsome and solitary as he had ever been, whether in her dreams or in true life.

She asked, "Would you have minded, if she had wed again?"

The faint smile returned. "I should say so. Two husbands are one too many."

"I meant, *if* you had not come back—rather, if you *had* died . . ." She trailed off, then tried again. "If you could not return, and she were alone, would you mind if she wed another man?"

He stared at her from the shadows, glimmers of firelight still caressing the edges of him. "Aye," he said at last. "I mind."

"But what if she met a kindly man, one who would take gentle care of her?"

"She was my wife," Tristan said shortly. "The fifth Countess of Haverlocke. And although you may not believe it, my lady, that matters to me."

Another look sustained between them, thick with smoke.

"What would you do," Amiranth heard herself ask, "if she were still alive?"

"Do you mean—here, now?"

She shrugged again. "What would you do if, say, Amiranth lived—but wanted to be apart from you?"

He looked away. "A foolish question, my lady."

"What would you do?"

He scowled, tapping his fingers against one knee. "Why should a wife live apart from her husband?"

"If she did not love you, and you did not love her," Amiranth said softly.

"Love," he echoed, surprised. "Love? Why should that matter?"

"If it did," she insisted.

"I would . . . speak with her about it. I would ask her why she wanted to leave, where she thought to go."

"And would you let her go, my lord?"

"No," he said, decisive. "Of course not. A wife belongs with her husband, all else aside."

There was an ache in her chest; she let out her breath, only now realizing that she had held it. "A most curious response, considering your past," she murmured to the floor.

"Then let us merely say I have learned a lesson from that past," Tristan replied, curt.

She felt his gaze and finally found the nerve to study him again. His hair fell in waves about his face, the black of his eyes remained shuttered. Firelight and smoke combined to make him seem unearthly, remote.

Without warning he rose. "It's late. You should be asleep."

And he turned and left her alone with the flames and swirling smoke, rose petals drifting softly around her.

————— ◦⁓⊙⁓◦ —————

He tried to ignore her the rest of the journey to his castle.

Her hair, her mouth, her eyes. The way she had
looked at the meal in the ruined chapel, with blackberry juice staining her lips a darker crimson, beckoning him, glossy with light.

Her body, pressed against his on the bare back of the
mare whether he willed it or no, until at last he could
suffer it no longer and got down to walk, insisting it
would be better for the horse this way.

Her voice, low and dulcet, a tantalizing lure to him,
the heated reaction of his fervent imagination.

It was driving him mad, if he wasn't already. It was
making him crazed—more crazed—being near her,
touching her, talking with her, learning her.

She was beauty and thought perfectly joined; she was
passion and logic melded together, put on this earth
solely to torment him for the rest of his days.

He admired her intelligence, her courage, her inge-
nuity. He imagined growing old with her, playing chess
with her by firelight, ruminating over their lives, eating
together, sleeping together, sipping wine from *scallop*
shells, for God's sake. . . .

Tristan held on to his reason one breath at a time,
each step, each moment taking him closer to his home,
and the finish to this misery. He needed patience for the
conclusion of this, that was all. He needed merely to

bide his time, and then she would be gone from him, and he could reclaim the life that used to be his.

He would not think irrational thoughts. He would not wish for something that could never be. He would not dwell on the loss of her, on how soon she would be gone, and that he would be facing the uncertain world alone.

He tried to remember who he was, and what he was meant to do. He had a castle, manors, tenants. He had a title and a surfeit of duties that he would soon attend to. He had a brother, and explanations to demand.

But for now there was only Lily, perched astride her mare, her skirts rising up past her ankles, her feet small and dangling, as careless as a milkmaid, as lovely as a dove.

Patience, patience . . .

By mutual agreement they avoided villages completely. It wasn't difficult; this part of the kingdom was heavy with woods, and the population was sparse. He knew it better and better each hour, coming closer to his childhood home. It gladdened him in spite of all his other troubles, and when the first bright turrets of Glynwallen came into view over the treetops, Tristan had to stop completely and take it in.

Glynwallen. A tremendous castle—some of the more cutting wits at court termed it monstrous—formed of buff-colored stone and heavy buttresses, thick and imposing, nothing so much of elegance about it as absolute strength. There was no moat; it wasn't needed. A high wall ringed the whole of it, seemed to stretch on forever, guarding the buildings inside, the bailey, the keep itself. It had circular towers and rectangular ones, stones upon stones, from cream to dun, reaching up to heaven itself.

It was not attractive. It was home, imposing and real.

Lily leaned forward, her hands woven into the mane of the mare.

"Is that it?"

"Aye." He began to move them on.

"Wait." She slipped from the horse, sliding down to the ground. He watched as she pulled off the bags holding their belongings, setting them before her. She looked quickly around, then back at him.

"We need to change."

"What?"

"Clothing."

She indicated her dusty gown—torn in places now, the hem of it tattered along one side—then knelt, rummaging through the bag. "It won't take long."

Tristan turned away when she told him to, keeping his focus on the turrets of his castle, trying not to listen to the telltale movements behind him. Trying not to picture in his mind what she might be doing . . . shedding her gown, the undertunic, fine linen and long ties, fanciful, feminine things.

When she said his name he looked back at her, and saw before him a lady he did not know.

Gone was the old gown of black. On her now was a garment of shining brilliance, the palest green, like summer leaves under ice. Embroidery of silver and gold gleamed along the sides of it, enclosing countless tiny pink flowers, rimming the bodice and hem. A gown of darker green peeked from beneath the slit sleeves and the split in her skirts. The colors perfectly suited the gold of her hair, the warm brown of her eyes.

She looked like a princess. An exquisite faerie, drawn from the ether. He stared at her, unable to say a single word.

Lily pulled back her hair, twisting it over her shoulders. "Now you," she said.

He kept staring. She bent down, oblivious, to the bags.

"We haven't any clothing fit for an earl," she said, "but there *is* this."

She pulled out the winter cloak, shaking out the folds of it, letting the light illuminate the scarlet and indigo velvet, jewel tones, bright against the forest.

He cleared his throat. "I—I couldn't wear that. It's yours."

She threw him an impatient look. "Actually, it's yours. It was made for you." She flung it over his shoulders before he could protest, the weight of it coming down against him in satin smoothness, heavy and cool. Lily adjusted the clasp at his throat, concentrating, and he was so close he could make out the very tips of her eyelashes, honey dark in the light.

Her fingers paused; her eyes met his. He felt the heat go through him, smothering, the way her focus grew soft and gentle, the way her lips parted, and he could breathe her now, he could nearly taste her—

She stepped back, her hands falling to her sides.

"Good enough, I think." Her words were slightly

breathless. She hesitated, then added, "Shall we go, my lord?"

Tristan glared down at the ground. "Aye."

He found the side road that branched off from the main one, leading straight to the castle gate. He walked Jorah slowly, taking in his surroundings, examining this place he had left so carelessly eight years ago.

He knew it all, the fields and the huts of the peasants who dwelled here. He remembered this, the color of the earth, the wheat and barley, the hedges and trees—even the homes they walked past, unchanged for generations.

Yet he led the mare on without pause, even when a few of the people stepped out of their homes to stare at them. He saw no one he recognized—not that he would know these folk, in any case. He had not bothered with them back in his thoughtless youth. They had been merely his workers, his serfs and villeins. They did their part in the intricate workings of the estate—toil, labor—and he did his. Or so he had thought at the time.

It pained him today, seeing their faces, worn and curious, their simple clothing and tools. Tristan thought he understood them a little better now. He understood it all a little better.

He took care to meet their eyes, nodding, but none nodded back. He saw only surprise on them, speculation and interest.

The last of the woods grew thin, less and less of the forest between him and his castle. They traveled through it slowly, a man on foot and woman on a horse, no accompaniment—no banners, no squires or knights, no fanfare of any sort. Only a ragged tail of peasants behind them, following at an almost fearful distance.

Right before they cleared the trees he turned to give Lily a final look. Lady Lily, a princess fair, was seated like a gentlewoman on the mare now, both feet to one side. Her hair stirred slowly with the breeze; feathered clouds floated by above her head in shades of luminous pearl. She did not return his gaze. Her face was lifted to the castle ahead, her expression unreadable.

Tristan surveyed her one last time, trying to memorize this moment, the sight of her against the radiant sky and the woods of his home, the colors of her gown and her hair glowing with the sunlight. Soon she would be gone, but at least he would have this—this, and Glynwallen.

He drew the mare forward, and approached the gate.

Chapter Nine

⚬⚬⚬⚬

THE GATEHOUSE WAS MASSIVE, TRULY THE LARGEST Amiranth had ever seen, nearly as big as all of the manor house of Safere. It was the only part of the castle she could see that had any sort of decoration on it: the stones around the portal had been arranged according to color, from dark to light to dark again. At the top of the tall archway a carved stone tablet revealed a chained unicorn standing with its head high, the spiraled horn pointing straight to heaven. One hoof was raised, as if in warning, or in flight.

The gate was raised, inviting entry, but the portcullis was firmly lowered. She glimpsed the buildings now past the grid of it—a chapel, a granary, stables, gardens. Over there, in the corner, a gentle motte that led up to the keep—

"Halt!" A guard, posted high at the top of the gate-house.

Tristan stopped, turning to hand her the reins. Amiranth took them, searching his face, finding naught of his emotions there. She hoped he was not as nervous as she.

"Who comes?" called out the guard.

"The master of this place," called back Tristan, his voice deep and ringing. "I am Tristan, Earl of Haverlocke. Raise the portcullis!"

From behind them came a hushed fury of sound, as if all the peasants had gasped at once, followed by excited whispers. Tristan did not turn, so neither did Amiranth.

"Your name again, sir?" questioned the guard, incredulous.

"Tristan! *Earl—of—Haverlocke!* Now open this portcullis!"

The guard disappeared from view. The voices behind them rose again, a babble of sound, disbelief, thrill, agitation. Amiranth focused on the man before her, standing relaxed by the mare, looking around, perfectly composed. She dug her nails into the center of her palms, trying to appear serene.

Half a dozen men came back into view at the top of the gatehouse. One leaned down from the battlement, peering at them.

"My man tells me a brash story," he said in a loud drawl. "He tells me a stranger has come calling with the name of a dead man. Since I know this cannot be true, tell me your true name and purpose here."

"Who are you?" Tristan demanded. "I do not know your face!"

"Nor I yours! Get you gone from here, villain, and do not waste my time."

The man began to withdraw.

"By all that's holy," Tristan began, a rumbling shout, "I will not stand for such insolence in my own demesne! You are not Charles Bingham, my castellan! Send forth that man, *and* my brother Liam, at once!"

All the men paused, then turned to one another. Amiranth heard them begin to confer in quick, worried tones, too low to make out. The lead man broke apart from the group and spoke again.

"Charles Bingham, you say? That is the name of another dead man. And I would like to know how you know of it."

"I *am* the master of this place. I do not know you, but there are a good many men I *do* know, and who will know me! Send forth my brother, and let us settle this."

"The Earl of Haverlocke is away," said the soldier briskly.

"Then send out the steward of my estates! Send Silas James to me!"

"Silas James no longer resides here. You still waste my time, knave. Get you gone!"

"Alain Grayson!" Tristan roared. "William Fremont! Gaylord Roswald! Jacob Wentford! Dylan of Trent! Show me these men, and I will prove you my true name, soldier!"

More conversation among the guards, a few nodding

their heads, appearing to argue with the leader. As a group they disappeared, hidden behind the stone.

Behind Amiranth came a new current of sounds, the peasants speaking louder, their excitement rising. She turned her head and glanced back at them. They had given her a wide berth, not coming too close to the gate, staying in a distant half-circle. A few were returning her look, but more were facing away, toward the end of their gathering, focused on something she could not see.

"Those names are well known to us," said a voice just ahead of her, no longer shouting. She found the entire guard had reassembled behind the portcullis, staring at them past the bars of it. The castellan spoke again. "Yet any man might have learned of them. This is no proof you are Tristan Geraint."

"Where are they?" Tristan took a step forward. "Ask them themselves!"

"Alas," said the castellan, with a malevolent grin. "All those soldiers are gone, I fear. They left this estate with the demise of their lord."

"Convenient," Amiranth muttered.

The castellan's eyes flicked to her, dismissive, then back to Tristan. "Indeed. And so—for the final time—I ask you to leave this place, sir. You are not welcome—"

"Is it true?" A new voice, a new man, behind them, pushing through the crowd. Amiranth and Tristan both turned to see an older man coming toward them, a peasant with long white hair and eyes of brilliant blue. "Is it so?" he continued, walking straight to Tristan. "My Mother Mary, I never thought it could be. . . ."

"Silas!" Tristan went to the peasant, plainly shocked, taking him by the arms. "Silas James, by my soul!"

"My lord!" The man began to tremble, staring up at him. "My good, good lord!" He dropped to his knees suddenly, picked up the hem of the colorful mantle, and buried his face in it. Tristan attempted to lift him up again.

"What has happened to you?" he asked, scowling.

"It *is* he!" The man named Silas broke away from Tristan, rising to face the guards. "It *is* the right and true lord of Haverlocke! By my life, I swear it!"

"The word of an old peasant man—" began the castellan, uncertain.

"The word of an honorable man!" Tristan interrupted, furious. "An honest and faithful man, who by all rights should be behind that gate now himself! Who has done this to him? Tell me!"

Now the castellan looked uneasy, his gaze going from his men to Tristan, shifting. "He withdrew himself from his position. He left the castle so that another might serve. He is old. 'Twas all it was."

"Open the portcullis," Tristan ordered coldly. "And I will set to right what has so clearly gone wrong in my absence."

The castellan hesitated, backing up a step. "I—I cannot. One man's word is nothing. You have no proof. . . ."

"Proof!" Tristan thundered. "Proof, is it? Here is proof, soldier!"

And to Amiranth's horror, he pointed straight to her, still seated atop the mare.

"Here is my lady wife to confirm me—Amiranth, Countess of Haverlocke!"

She felt the blood drain from her face, her body turned to ice, her stomach dropping to her feet. She blinked down at him, speechless, and tried not to faint.

He knew! He knew, he knew, oh God, he knew all along!

Tristan left the portcullis and walked to her now, giving her a formidable look, his mouth turned grim and flat. He reached for her and she felt herself slipping from Jorah's back, lighter than ash, everything in her turned hollow except for a quick beating panic in her chest—

He caught her to him and bent his head to her ear, a soft rushed whisper, as if an endearment.

"Please, Lily. I'll give you whatever you want. Just do this—whatever you want . . ."

He leaned back to see her. His eyes captured hers, fierce and dangerous, wild once again.

The panic slowed, fading. She gazed up at him, bewildered, as he took up her hand and pressed his lips to the back of it, then leaned in again, still speaking swiftly under his breath.

"I'll give you your own manor—Merlyff, the fairest estate of them all. I'll leave you be for the rest of your life, if you wish it. Just—*please.*"

He *didn't* know. It was a trick—a cunning and desperate one. She understood him suddenly, what he risked, what he wanted from her, what it would mean. She knew well of tricks and the unkind ways of fortune. The advantage was entirely hers. Unfair, perhaps, to take it . . . but too few advantages had come to her so readily before.

She spoke around a clenched smile, just as hushed as he had been.

"Promise me."

"I promise."

Amiranth took back her hand. She ran her palms down the fine silk of her skirts, leisurely, sending them straight again, then lifted her voice to everyone around them.

"Here is my husband, the Earl of Haverlocke, home from long battle with the French, bringing back the glory of England! Who in this place would not receive us?"

"This woman—" sputtered the castellan.

"Is the *beloved* sister of the Earl of Iving," she interrupted, speaking coolly, smoothly, the way she knew to do. "The strong and *vengeful* Earl of Iving, whose holding is but days from here, I believe."

"But you are—"

"Also the dear *cousin* of his majesty the *king*," she continued, imperious. "Our sovereign lord, who would be fair grieved to hear that I had been mistreated in any manner." She paused, and gave the castellan a withering look. "Any manner *whatsoever*."

The man said nothing, his expression darkening. Amiranth strolled up to the portcullis, resting her fingers lightly against a slat of wood. All around them the silence rang, every eye fixed on her, every ear turned to her.

"My good man," she said indifferently, "would *you*

be the one to begin a war between the rightful Earl of Haverlocke and his brother? Would *you* be the one to explain to King Edward the *very* grave error of your thoughts on this day?"

The man's face grew ruddy, sweat beading across his brow.

"Open the portcullis and let in your true master," she said mildly, "and mayhap we might forgo the telling of this tale to my cousin the king."

"I—"

"Or, begin the war that will provoke King Edward himself," she finished, and then smiled, steel and ice. "You decide."

———— ⚭ ————

GLYNWALLEN WAS A CAVERNOUS PLACE. TRISTAN loved that about it, he had missed it so dearly—God, he was so happy now, to be back here, to walk these halls again, and see these chambers!

He escorted Lily through the keep, and she walked beside him, so sweet, so temperate that he nearly could not believe the threat she had enacted outside the gatehouse.

She was wondrous. Magnificent!

He felt as if nothing could stop him, as if the power of the sun had come to him and suffused his limbs, his mind. He remembered every path as if he had left here but yesterday. He was truly *home*! At last, at last . . .

He took Lily to the great hall, both of them trailed by his brother's chastened men, completely silent now but for the metallic *chink* of their hauberks sliding against their scabbards.

The great hall. It was not quite as he remembered it, but close enough for the bright feeling in him to expand again. A huge and imposing space, with the cream stone and heavy wood that suited this castle. Four enormous hearths, two of them with fires blazing, tapestries and benches and the stately steps of the dais of the main table, where the carved chair of the Earl of Haverlocke still awaited him.

Tristan crossed to it, Lily at his arm. He seated her and then himself—forgotten luxury, cushions and colors and gilt—looking down at the people gathered below him, staring eyes, whispering mouths.

"Food," he ordered. "Ale. Now."

A few bowed to him, slowly, and backed away. Tristan picked out the castellan of before, a short man with wispy red hair. "You, sir. Where is Silas James?"

"I am uncertain," the man replied, frowning.

"Find him and bring him to me. Immediately," he added, when the man remained motionless.

Lily leaned forward and brushed her fingers across the wood in front of her, as if to test the polish. Tristan watched the man's eyes go to her; he gave a terse bow, and left.

More people were crowding into the great hall, men and women, serfs and nobles. He wanted to examine them. He wanted to search for a friendly face, anyone who might spark his memory. But the joy in him was too great in this moment. It was beyond joy, a strong, barbarous thing—like pain, in fact.

Mine, he thought, and felt that flood through him, clear and powerful, a reawakening that spread through his soul. *Yes, mine, all of this.*

This time it was right, this time it was *real:* the ferocious longing for it all—every stone of it, every bit of wood, every pebble, every chair and table and cup. It sang through his beating blood, the pounding of his heart, a call to him, ancient and true and deep.

He glanced up to the arched ceiling, dim and distant with tapestries, a hollow heaven above his head. He knew each beam. He could place each strut, each archer's slit in the walls, memorized without his knowing in the wilderness of his youth.

Mine! Finally. Forever.

He would never give this up again.

Serfs began to place trenchers on the table, goblets brimming with ale. Someone put a platter of fish before him, grilled steaks of pink salmon, so hot that wisps of steam twirled up into the coolness of the chamber.

Tristan smiled.

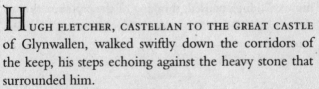

HUGH FLETCHER, CASTELLAN TO THE GREAT CASTLE of Glynwallen, walked swiftly down the corridors of the keep, his steps echoing against the heavy stone that surrounded him.

He had known Liam, Earl of Haverlocke, a good five years, had held his current position for three. He was the son of freemen, a mercenary at the age of twelve, living a life of hard gains and taking the rewards due him as he could. Liam Geraint had found him in London one night at a tavern that made even the gutter whores look fine. Hugh had accidentally stepped into a brawl involving the earl, and finished it for him. He had been the earl's man ever since.

He did not know this stranger claiming to be Tristan Geraint. He did not care to know him, or to let him stay. It seemed impossible that the earl's older brother might yet live, but if it were so . . . he was clearly alone, no knights beside him any longer, not even the retainers who would have served him years before. A man who stood alone, Hugh thought, would not remain standing long.

The woman was a problem, but the one thing he had learned over his years was that all problems had solutions, even if they were ugly ones.

The bailey was filled with people gathered in groups of gossip, everyone talking, everyone staring up to the keep. He motioned for a circle of his soldiers to join him near the doors.

"Send the swiftest man for the earl. He should be at Staffordshire now—tell him what has occurred. Tell him . . ." Hugh paused, thinking of the earl's reaction to this news. "Tell him we await his command," he finished grimly.

THE CHAMBER THEY WERE SHOWN TO CLEARLY WAS not the quarters of the Earl and Countess of Haverlocke. Amiranth entered first, examining the furnishings: a pallet, a chair, one simple cupboard. A single window of leaded glass let in the light in watery waves across the floor. At least the rushes were fresh, she noted. The floor was well swept, the walls barren.

The girl who had escorted them here stooped to a low curtsy, her face downturned. Tristan entered the room behind them, an imposing shape against the frame of the door, the colors of the mantle muted against the cool shadows.

"What mischief is this?" he inquired, dark and silky to the poor maidservant. "Is this where you would place your lord, girl?"

"Please, my lord," she whispered. "This is where I was told . . ."

Her words ended with an audible tremble. Amiranth took pity on her.

"No doubt you will need time to prepare the proper chambers of the earl," she said, with a stern glance at Tristan. "No doubt the earl's younger brother has personal goods in place that require much tender care for moving."

The girl said nothing, staring miserably at the rushes on the floor.

"Be certain to tell the castellan we expect Lord Liam's belongings to be handled well in the move," Amiranth continued, regal. "Naught will be broken, or lost. Tell him we shall expect to be in the appropriate quarters of the earl and countess within a day."

The girl curtsied again, beginning to inch away.

Tristan threw Amiranth a dry look, shrugging out of the mantle. She crossed to him and quickly took hold of the edges of it, keeping it wrapped around him, then called out again to the maid.

"Another thing, child. My lord requires fresh garments, fitting to his station. See to it."

The girl curtsied once more, very deep, then almost fled the room.

Amiranth released the mantle after the door shut. "Best not to give them further reason to doubt you. These clothes were well enough for travel, but they won't do any longer."

Another look from him, even drier now, as he pushed back the folds of the cloak and worked free the clasp.

"A man would do well to keep such sharp wits as yours around him," he commented, pleasant.

"Your wits will be sharp enough." She went to the door, opened it a crack, and peered through. Nothing; only an empty hall, faint echoes from distant chambers. She closed it again and leaned back against the wood.

"Tell me of this estate you have promised me, my lord."

He turned away from her, taking care with the mantle now, folding it up slowly, precisely, his head slightly bowed. "Are you so eager to leave?"

Amiranth felt a warning within her, reaction to the silkiness that had returned to his voice. He looked up at her now, still holding the cloak.

"First my wife, and now myself. Tell me, Lily, what is it about us that makes you want to flee?"

"I am not fleeing," she replied, striving for calm. "You made me a promise, my lord."

"So I did." But he did not move, and he said nothing further, only gazed at her with a flat, measuring look.

"Merlyff," she tried, combating that look. "I believe that was the name of it. Where does it lie?"

"North," he said shortly. "Distant north."

"How long will it take me to travel there?"

"Weeks, I fear."

A surge of dismay took her. Weeks of travel—and she was so weary of travel. He knew she was; he knew that much about her, at least. His expression grew veiled.

"A rough journey, as well," he added. "Through moors and marsh and bog. It is no trip for the light at heart."

"You said it was fair!"

"Passing fair," he granted, with a shrug. "Once there. But getting there . . ." Another shrug, careless.

"You have tricked me!"

He faced her fully, sobering. "No trick, my lady. I meant what I said, by my honor. You saved me. I owe you everything."

Her protests died away within her. He stood quietly, waves of light rippling over him like sunshine under the sea, turning shining blue in his hair, radiant against the lines and sinewy curves of his body. He was so handsome, her lost husband. He was still so comely to her, dark and tall, elegant enticement.

"Don't go," he said. "Don't leave me yet."

She opened her mouth to refuse him, but the air was suddenly too thin in her lungs, and all that came was a sort of sigh. A strange weakness befell her: She could not look away from him, from the heat in his eyes, the unspoken question on his face.

Tristan moved toward her in the light, his shadow thrown long across the floor until it overlapped hers, and the shape of them together grew blurred and indistinct. He reached for her hand and she allowed it, slipping deeper into this fleeting folly. His grip was loose, no pressure, just his fingers warm against her skin.

"The danger has not passed," he said, gazing down at their hands, then up to her eyes. "I still need you."

She frowned, fighting the pleasure she took from this, trying to hold on to the warning within her from before. But it was so hard to think of it now—with Tristan before her, focused on her, asking her to stay . . . *wanting* her to stay. . . .

"Lily. Please."

He had a gentle smile now; his look was sweet honey. His voice was so tender, soft as a lover's, intimate and rich. With a sense of familiar dismay, Amiranth awoke out of this treachery.

He was talking to Lily. Everything about him now—his smile, his touch, the light to his eyes—was for the illusion of her cousin, not for Amiranth. Not his plain, forgotten wife.

She pulled her hand free from his. "In truth, you don't need me any longer, my lord. You served at Edward's court. The king can vouch for you, can he not?"

"He might. If he remembers. I cannot know that he would. But either way he will not come here, Lily. I would have to go to him in London." He met her gaze, still so enticing. "If I leave Glynwallen now, chances are very good I won't be able to get back in. Not without storming the gate."

She sighed, frustrated, realizing the truth to his words. "Very well. I'll stay a while longer, to be certain of your place here again. Then I must go."

"I'll escort you there myself."

"I'm sure that will hardly be necessary."

"It would be my honor."

"Your honor would be better spent in this castle, my lord, than with me."

The light to his eyes dimmed; the gentle smile vanished. He gave a slow nod.

"As you say, my lady."

She drew back, stepping out of the watered sunshine, feeling a sharp regret zing through her even though she knew she had done what she should.

A knock sounded on the door.

"Come," Tristan called, tossing the mantle onto the pallet.

Amiranth rolled her eyes at his recklessness. The door eased open, a weathered hand wrapped around the edge of it.

"My lord?"

It was the man named Silas James, the old peasant from the gate. Behind him was the maidservant of before, and two other men. Guards, she could see, dressed in the colors of the castle, caution and distrust all about them.

"Enter," said Tristan, waiting near the pallet. He did not look at her again.

Silas James did so. On his heels were the guards and then the maid, who darted forward, setting a heavy jumble of material at the very edge of the chair.

"Garments, my lord," she mumbled, and fled again.

The guards did not follow her. They lingered near the entrance, shifting on their feet.

Amiranth turned to them. "That will be all." The soldiers only exchanged looks; she placed her hands on her hips, eyes narrowing. "What, do they not understand me? I did not realize, my lord, that the vassals of your demesne would be so ill trained."

"Nor did I," said Tristan, and there could be no mistaking the danger that had come to him, swift and certain, shading his tone, his posture. "My brother appears to rule with a softer hand than I. I beg your forgiveness, my love. It is a fault I will soon remedy. Glynwallen still has a dungeon, I presume."

The guards looked to each other again, clearly uneasy.

"Your pardon, my lord," said one, and together they bowed, backing out of the room.

She returned to the door, listening closely for the sounds of their steps to fade away.

"Silas James," greeted Tristan, same as before, but now with soft regret.

"My lord."

The man was on his knees again before Tristan, his hands over his heart.

"Rise," Tristan urged, helping him. He pushed impatiently at the garments on the chair, sending them spilling to the floor, then led Silas to sit. He gestured to Amiranth, still lingering by the door.

"My lady wife."

Silas began to stand.

"Stay," she ordered, using her regal tone again, because she was uncertain whether this man would need to see her fine authority.

"Most gracious lady." His voice was muffled; he kept his head low, his hands over his heart again. "I greet you, and welcome you." Silas glanced up, his gaze going from her to Tristan again, and the raw hope on his face made her look away from him.

Amiranth went to the careless heap of fine clothing, whisking up the garments, busying herself with straightening them, spreading them flat on the pallet as Tristan and the man conversed.

"How can it be?" Silas was saying. "How can you be, my lord? We were told you had died—the war—"

"Aye. I know it, friend. Yet you see me here. At times I do not know it myself how, but I do live."

"Praise God!"

"Aye," Tristan said again, a touch of irony darkening his tone. "But explain to me what has happened here. You were steward to all my estates! You served my father and me with the same devotion. What has my brother done?"

A pause, followed by a short cough. "Naught. Only what was wise, my lord. I have grown older—"

"We are all older," interrupted Tristan. "What else?"

"Well . . ." Another pause. "Your brother is . . . a younger man, my lord. At his ascension to the title he brought with him a steward from his home in the country. I chose myself to leave. It is true."

"And you chose yourself to live outside the castle, as well?"

No answer.

"Where are my men?" Tristan asked quietly. "Where are the faithful who served me? Has *everyone* gone?"

"After your death, my lord—the new earl came, and with him his own men . . . many left Glynwallen. They found lives elsewhere. A few remained you would remember—Appleby, Sherman, Dorset, and Manning— but they succumbed to the pestilence, my lord, not a year past. Many did."

The tunic in Amiranth's hands was fine wool, thin and lightly woven, like the down of a thistle. She pretended to study it, listening for Tristan's response to this ill news. From the corner of her eye she saw him standing steadily, rock calm in the light.

"Where is this new steward?" he asked abruptly. "Why has he not come to greet me?"

"He travels with your brother. They have gone to direct the other estates for this half year. Layton, Ergonbury, Staffordshire, Merlyff—"

Amiranth turned, dropping the tunic, watching them openly now.

"—and Yaverling. They are due back this Michaelmas, my lord."

"Michaelmas," Tristan mused. "A distant time, indeed."

"Aye," agreed the old man, nodding.

Tristan straightened, going to the window, staring

out at the view. Amiranth and Silas both watched him, a
shadow against the sky.

"You are steward now," said Tristan, not turning.

"My lord?"

"And find me a competent castellan. I do not like the
eyes of the man my brother has employed."

"But, my lord . . ."

"Yes? Is there aught amiss with my orders, steward?
Do you not know of a trustworthy man for the position
I named?"

She had seen a grizzled man seated before her, the
wear of his years evident from his face to his feet. She
had listened to her husband's orders and felt a mild
alarm thrill through her at this, the beginning of his
command in this place. Silas James seemed an unlikely
choice for steward—whatever his experience, he *was*
old now, bowed and thin with time. It seemed a gamble
at best, to throw their lot in with this fellow.

Then, before her very eyes, Amiranth saw a small
miracle take place. The man in the chair transformed,
his back growing straighter, his head held more high.
She looked into the blue of his eyes and was struck
again with their brilliance, a keen and lucid light shining through. He seemed years younger to her now, in
just the space of a single breath.

"My son," said the man. "My son Evan works in the
stables, my lord. Yet I swear to you he has served honor-
ably in the king's own army. He knows well the ways of
war, and would be a worthy castellan."

"Done," announced Tristan, and when he turned he
had a smile that matched the sharpness in the other

man's eyes. "Has he friends? Men to trust, to serve with him?"

"Good men," affirmed Silas, a new strength to his voice. "Friends and sons of friends, I promise you."

The sharpness about Tristan grew finer, hardening to calm assurance. "I like it well, this new beginning for my castle. We'll go find your son and then the man who used to be castellan. I will inform him of what fresh order has come in his stead."

Silas said, "Methinks Lord Liam will make haste home now."

"Yes," replied Tristan, very composed. "I think it, too."

Chapter Ten

———⟨◦⟩———

THE MAN IN THE EARL'S CHAIR AT SUPPER THAT
night was a stranger with Tristan's face.

Amiranth entered the great hall slowly, mindful of
her position now, of the stares that would be pinned to
her, and the words flung fast behind her back.

She had spent the early evening alone, without the
company of Tristan or servants, using the time to bathe,
to unpack what few belongings she had brought with
her on this wild and unexpected journey.

Three more gowns, shaken out. Undertunics, combs,
belts, garters, a precious few baubles from her life that
she had not the heart to leave behind her at Safere.

Her jewelry, resplendent and heavy, flashing colors in
the sea light of the room, tinted with the faint blue of
the window.

To bathe again felt like the most sinful extravagance

she had ever dreamed; the water was warm and soapy, fragrant with primrose and honeysuckle. She had washed her body and her hair and felt, for the first time in months, a sense of pure relaxation. She felt almost happy again, healthy. A screen of painted birds and trees hid her from the rest of the world, from even the rest of this simple room. She had not wanted it to end.

But women came to attend her. Amiranth tried to recall the lessons of her youth, how to act, what would be expected of her. She chose the most sumptuous of her four clean gowns for her first supper as the Countess of Haverlocke. It had a bliaut the color of autumn, impressive shades of scarlet and flame and gold, a refined yet bold pattern over a long tunic of bright white. She knew it suited her well; she knew it moved with her in a way that spoke of subtle delight, flowing and opulent.

She wore her mother's pearls with it, twined in loops about her neck, and had the satisfaction of noting the handmaidens' awe when they were finished with her.

Amiranth declined a veil, allowing instead that her hair be arranged in soft braids and curls. She wanted to hear everything said tonight without the distraction of covering over her ears.

The handmaidens had stared at her with wide eyes and she had gazed back at them, wondering at what they saw, if she truly looked the part of a countess. She hoped so.

They offered to brush and press her gowns for her; Amiranth consented to this, knowing full well she would need new clothing soon if she was to stay here in this place. Four gowns would not be enough to last her charade. Perhaps she might borrow some. Perhaps she might even have some made, to take with her to Merlyff. She had not had a new gown in a very long time. . . .

As they were leaving, one of the women had discovered the mantle, crumpled across a corner of the pallet.

"Shall I clean it for you, my lady?"

Amiranth examined it, thoughtful. It had worn well throughout their adventures, only a few stains marring the colors of it. The white ermine remained as fine as the day she had sewn it to the hood, all those years ago.

"Can you?" she asked.

"Aye, my lady. Surely."

"Do so."

The women had curtsied, and swept it up with the rest of her clothing, all of it gone to somewhere she could not know, down to the inner workings of the castle.

Amiranth waited and waited, and still Tristan did not return for her. So eventually she had left the room and began to roam the halls of the castle by herself, taking in her new surroundings.

She had gotten lost almost immediately. Glynwallen, it seemed, was as vast as a city. She encountered few people, only long corridors, and voices that seemed to disappear when she rounded a turn. She became acutely aware that she was treading the territory of the enemy, that her position here was anything but secure, no matter who she claimed to be.

That this place was actually to have been her home almost made her laugh out loud. She could not imagine living here. She could not imagine attempting to rule, to command the serfs and freemen and all others except Tristan. How incredible, that she had nearly stepped up to this station. How astonishing, that plain little Amiranth St. Clare had nearly, nearly become the empress of this castle-city.

She finally rounded a corner where the voices did not dim, and found herself in the great hall, facing a chamber filled with people, and that stranger with her husband's face seated in the earl's chair.

Everyone quieted, staring at her as she stood alone at the entrance.

The man at the earl's table remained distant, as fine and forbidding as the king himself. She hid her fears and began to walk toward him, the autumn gown trailing the floor behind her.

The stranger—Tristan—stood, watching her approach.

All at once she knew him. Of course. Of course she did.

Here he was, the Earl of Haverlocke she used to behold. Yes, here, in the silver and ruby robe she herself had laid out for him, a heavy belt of midnight stones gleaming near his waist. Here was the boy she had given her heart to, dark splendor full grown into a man, still aloof, still cool and reserved, every inch a noble knight.

His eyes locked on hers, his face half masked with shadows. Was that a glimpse of misgiving behind his gaze? Surely not—not when he approached her with such a firm, confident step. Not when he greeted her in his calm, pure voice, an earl indeed, and took her hand, and bowed over it.

She was transported back in time, to their first intro-duction. Only this time, she felt his lips against her skin. This time, he truly kissed her hand, warm and linger-ing, his fingers tight on hers.

Amiranth felt a flush begin.

When he looked up at her she could see directly into his eyes. There was nothing at all of misgivings there. There was pride. Possession. A knowing, subtle heat.

"My countess," he said, in a voice that carried.

"My lord," she murmured back to him, sinking to a curtsy.

The hush over the hall had not broken. She was cer-tain that she could hear the rapt breathing of them all, scores of people absorbed in the drama of the scene.

Tristan helped her to rise, led her to her seat. "We have awaited you."

They had indeed. There was no food set out, only wine and mead, plenty of it, in flasks and cups of pewter and gold.

The goblet in front of her seat was of gold. She ig-nored the page who had pulled back her chair for her, instead taking up the goblet, lifting it high so that the flames of the torches lining the hall glowed along its golden curves.

"A salute, good people," she said, not even trying to raise her voice.

The hush extended, avid attention from every cor-ner, every single face.

"To our right and merciful lord, our most beloved liege, Tristan, Earl of Haverlocke. Good welcome to him back home from his long journey away. May God grant him peace for the rest of his days."

She—she alone—took a sip of the wine, her gaze a dare to the rest of the hall over the rim of her drink. She set the goblet on the table, then curtsied again to Tristan.

"A fair salute," he said, once more helping her to rise. She could not tell if there was amusement in his voice or not. "From a fair lady. I thank you."

They sat together, Amiranth moving carefully, very aware of the set of her shoulders, the straight line of her back. Tristan remained cool and quiet to her left; to her right was a nobleman she did not know, and beyond him a woman she did not, and then another man, and so on, a row of new faces feigning consummate interest in their drinks, their laps, or the table. The only sound to be heard in the room was the subdued bustle of the serfs beginning to bring out the meal.

She accepted the bread a boy handed her, nodding thanks. The child ducked and dashed away.

Tristan took his first bite; everyone began to eat in strained silence. Amiranth could feel the stares aimed at her, but when she looked up all she discovered were averted faces, passing glimpses of judging looks. Only one man met her gaze straight on.

Silas James stood apart from the crowd of the room, against a wall not too far from the table, watching her, Tristan, the chamber. Now that she noted him she saw others stationed like him—not soldiers, but men who held a common look of ungarnished strength and restraint. The son Evan and his friends, no doubt.

She wondered how Tristan had handled the surly castellan of before. Although she searched the chamber, he did not appear to be in the assembly. That worried her; an absent enemy was not to their advantage, not now, so new in this game they played. He might be off with his fellows, stirring a rebellion. He might be anywhere, saying anything—

"A celebration," Tristan announced suddenly, startling her. Amiranth turned to him, forcing an inquiring smile.

"Aye," he continued calmly, as if she had responded, "that's what is due, my lady. We'll give thanks to be home. A feast for our people. For our neighboring lords."

"A feast," she repeated, cautious. "Indeed, my lord? Do you think it wise, so early into your return?"

"All the more reason to celebrate. As soon as may be, in fact." He had been speaking straight ahead of him, to the chilled air and unnatural silence of the hall, but now he looked back at her. "We'll invite your brother."

She could not summon a response for this, for the warring emotions that took hold of her: *discovery, disaster, ruin—*

Tristan leaned in closer, dropping his voice. "You said yourself he never came to Safere, my lady. He has not seen you since our marriage—no doubt he will be eager to greet you again, and witness how you have changed."

She understood immediately what he was about. Tristan apparently remembered his bride enough to know at least that Lily had similar coloring. If Augustin had not seen her for years—and he had not—then he could not know how she looked now. If she claimed to be Amiranth . . . of course he would believe it. It was naught but the truth, after all.

But since Augustin would know her for her true self, he could easily betray her with just a simple word. It was a grave risk . . . yet he knew Tristan Geraint, as well. He would not forget his wealthy brother-in-law, even if he *had* let his sister languish in seclusion at the far end of England for years.

To have Augustin acknowledge Tristan as her husband would be tantamount to ensuring his place here. Amiranth had not lied to the castellan when she claimed the king as her cousin. Distant, yes, but her family was still blood. If the Earl of Iving accepted Tristan as the true Earl of Haverlocke, only a fool would step in to refute it.

Indeed, the deepest danger would be to herself. Augustin was not a man given to subterfuge and sly reason. He would see and believe Amiranth for who she was and confirm it to all who asked—even Tristan, if circumstances turned dire enough.

How could she escape this tangle?

She saw the resolution on Tristan's face, how the secrets in his eyes grew brighter, the handsome lift to his mouth determined. He touched her hand atop the table, a slip of a caress, his fingers there and gone.

"A fine feast," he said, deliberate and composed. "And your brother will be well met, I'm certain."

Amiranth bowed her head in assent, closing her eyes, praying.

Let it work. Let it all work.

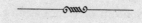

HUGH FLETCHER WATCHED THE PROGRESSION OF THE meal from the small vestibule overlooking the great hall, the man claiming to be Tristan Geraint sitting boldly at the lord's table, in the lord's seat high upon the dais. The woman next to him held her haughty air even from this distance. If she was not actually nobility, she was actress enough to fool the common eye.

Hugh did not consider his eye common.

The interview with the usurper had been no more than what he had expected. This man would want anyone faithful to Liam to fall quickly out of power—Hugh understood that. Yet he had been dismissed as easily as any simple serf, a clear humiliation in front of all who heard. The usurper had taken care to arm himself with a group of peasant men—had *elevated* them to the status of personal guard—even as he had calmly informed Hugh he would no longer serve as castellan.

It was an outrage. Who was this pretender to dismiss *him,* Hugh Fletcher, loyal man of the true earl?

But Hugh had no choice. To protest publicly would be a mistake at this point. When Liam returned, all would be set right again, he knew; and besides, there were other ways to humble a man without open warfare. So he had choked on his anger, holding on with bare restraint to the sudden hatred that had flared through him.

The woman below turned her head and addressed

her husband. Hugh had a glimpse of the pearls around her throat, heavy drops of cream against her skin. Half the men in the hall were gaping at her, clearly besotted.

Without looking away from the scene, Hugh addressed the man at his side, another of Liam's deposed guard.

"Tell me. The wife of Tristan Geraint—she stayed at Safere, did she not?"

"Aye. So I heard."

"A young widow in mourning, it was said," Hugh continued, thoughtful. "Resisting the will of the king to rewed. My lord Liam never visited her?"

"Nay, I think not."

Hugh rubbed his chin, still examining her, the golden crown of her hair, the graceful movement of her hands.

"And we've had no word from Safere in months, I know that much," he murmured. "Strange. One would think that *if* an earl returned from the dead—especially an earl so desperately mourned—that word would spread rather quickly. Servants love to gossip, and this certainly would be worthy news. Yet we heard nothing at all."

The other man glanced at him, and Hugh looked back, considering.

"A most intriguing mystery, don't you think, soldier?"

"Sir?"

"I believe a visit to the country is in order. My lord's estate of Safere has been neglected far too long."

————————⟆∞⟆————————

It wasn't until the supper was done, and the food was reduced to scraps of greasy bread and empty bowls, and the people grew restless on their benches, that Tristan at last deigned to rise and end the night.

The conversation in the chamber had gradually grown looser over the courses, as wine flowed and cups were refilled. Amiranth had not been able to make out precise words, but she took it as a good sign, that at least some were beginning to relax enough to converse.

Yet as they left she finally managed to understand flashes of what was being said. It was the name of her husband, and that of his father, his older brother—and another word, one she had not considered for many, many a year:

Murderer.

————————⟆∞⟆————————

She slept in a gown so voluminous that the folds seemed to follow their own will around her, twisting and turning against her body as she tossed on the pallet. It had been brought to her by one of the maids, a makeshift gift from the chatelaine of the castle, Amiranth assumed—a lady who had tried unsuccessfully to hide the scandal on her face when she learned that Amiranth had not brought a sleeping gown of her own to Glynwallen.

Amiranth had been too tired to attempt to erase that

look. She wanted only to fall into her sleep, and bid this long and onerous day farewell. She was grateful for the gown, as simple as it was, for the length of pale blue linen that rucked up in pleats by her feet, and the drawstring at her neck that pulled it modestly tight.

Tristan managed to be elsewhere while she changed, entering the room just as she was slipping into the pallet. He dismissed the maid with a short nod, then closed the door and stopped, staring at her. From beneath the covers Amiranth had stared back at him, still splendid in his tunic and robe, feeling the blood come rushing to her cheeks.

"There is but one pallet," she blurted—such an obvious fact that she was shamed as soon as the words left her.

But he only nodded, still fixed on her face, his own carefully blank, unsmiling.

"I'll sleep on the floor," he said.

She broke away from his look, pinching a wrinkle in the blanket beneath her hands. "Are you certain?"

"It's better than the chair." He moved forward, already beginning to free one arm from the robe.

She had taken the lamp quickly and blew out the flame, sending blackness across the little room. He was no longer visible to her, but the thought of him so near—undressing—kept the blush warm across her body. She peeled away the top two blankets on the pallet, and one of the furs, and placed them on the floor beside her.

"For your warmth," she whispered, and had gotten

no response, only the shadow of him close by, the stir of air from his movements gliding over her.

She heard him bed down, the sound of the blankets being rearranged. Amiranth settled back into the pallet and tried not to think of him, waiting for sleep to come.

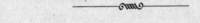

Dreams. dreams upon dreams, both vivid and dark, memorable and not. Amiranth had the odd sense of knowing of her state, that none of it was real, but it seemed not to matter. She dreamt of waterfalls, and of flying as a bird, and of swimming deep into the ocean. She dreamt of light and stones, of colors and sunsets over rich fields of wheat.

She dreamt she was gliding through that wheat, at peace, admiring the shades of nature around her, so many golds, such a beautiful sky, such warmth.

Aye, she was warm, happily so. She felt safe and serene—she could not recall such a feeling of satisfaction that filled her, here in this field with delicate stems that danced and swayed as far as she could see.

She sighed with contentment, turning, and felt the warmth shift around her, tighter and then looser, still there, still close, a breath at her shoulder, a stroke across the delicate skin of her wrist.

Amiranth opened her eyes and found Tristan beside her in the pallet, covers tossed over them both, masculine heat against her. Beyond him a pair of maids moved about the gray of the room, dim to her, nearly noiseless.

She blinked and it all stayed just the same: Tristan pressed close; two women lighting lamps, setting out trays of food.

She gazed at him for a long moment, uncomprehending, then opened her mouth to speak.

With fluid ease he leaned over her, placing his fingers lightly over her lips as his own grazed her cheek, a brush of a kiss.

"Good morn to you, love." His voice rumbled through her, intimate, playful even with the note of caution beneath. "You slept late. I fear we've missed Mass already."

The maids did not pause in their work, but Amiranth knew they listened anyway, that every bit of this moment would be remembered and retold. She sat up, keeping the blankets high over her, noting that the floor appeared undisturbed, all coverings back upon the pallet.

Tristan sat up with her. He was tousled and impossibly handsome, his ebony hair even more disheveled than usual, his smile beckoning, his eyes sleepy—though *that* was merely an act. He knew full well what he did. So did she.

One hand reached up; he brushed her cheek again, this time with the backs of his knuckles.

"Dream well, my wife?"

She pushed his hand away, wary of the easy appeal of him, the feel of his body too familiar against hers, sculpted muscles, a pleasing warmth.

"Until this moment, my lord."

"Such a sour mood!" The look in his eyes did not

abate. "You never did like waking. Mayhap I can change that for you."

When he leaned in again she pulled back, but he caught her at the nape of her neck and she had nowhere to go, with the wall flush behind her. His lips came down over hers, soft while his grip stayed hard, almost a tenderness to it, close and far too potent for her comfort.

His hand changed, his fingers sliding up through her hair, massaging. Amiranth squeezed her eyes shut and tried not to succumb to this, his mockery of a kiss, her emotions reeling out of control, elation and fear and hope and misery swimming through her.

Oh, it was a dread thing, an arrow to her heart. Oh, it was so sweet.

She stayed that way, hunched and frozen against him, as he moved his lips to her cheek, a path of little kisses, soft as whispers, over to her ear.

"Merlyff," was the word she heard him breathe. "Think on that, my lady. . . ."

She heard her own reply, far too faint: "It had better be more than passing fair."

Tristan found a place beneath her ear, the pulse of her throat; she felt his mouth open over it, as if he could taste even that. His voice was muffled by the fall of her hair. "Fair enough to make a king weep . . . fairest of the fair. . . ."

He came back to her face, trailing golden strands that tickled between them, and somehow they were both slowly easing down in the pallet. A new kiss, lingering, feeling like satin against her skin, a lazy burn that found some response deep, deep within her; a song she had forgotten once again beating through her blood.

A distant part of her heard the door softly closing, the maidservants leaving. But Tristan's hands were at her shoulders, sliding down her arms to bring her closer, and Amiranth found that her own were encircling him—someone else's arms, surely, that pulled him to her. Someone else's lips that returned his kiss, that tasted him and found him like nectar, unfairly forbidden—as if she had been told she could no longer breathe the air again, or drink clear water, or see the bright sun.

Someone else's body, welcoming his, the weight of him, all supple tension and comely lines. Someone else who felt the most intimate shape of him, lithe and fine, skimming against her, accenting the desire between them.

Someone else who closed her eyes and shut out the world, allowing him the curve of her shoulder, where the drawstring had come loose, and lower, to the rise of her breast, where he made a harsh sound in his throat and tugged the gown even lower still.

Someone else who shivered and gave a soft cry as he savored her skin, drawing her nipple into his mouth with tongue and teeth, a hard, ferocious ache that turned the song within her to a darker pitch.

Someone else who bent her knees and kept him with her, feeling the rhythm of them together, a new thing, as urgent as all the other newness he gave her.

She would not think beyond this moment. She would not think beyond his touch, the press of him against her, his hair soft against her face, his eyes as he raised his head and kissed her lips again, quick and fervent, as if he could not decide which part of her he liked best.

Amiranth broke away and made her own study of him, the column of his throat, the hard slope where his neck met his shoulder, the flex of his arm. He wore no heavy garments, only the thin, thin tunic of thistledown, nearly translucent. She could feel him through it; she could almost taste him as he had her, and rubbed her face against the pale cloth, pushing it up and away from her with her palms.

Tristan grew still, tense, the force of his breathing rocking them both as she repeated what she had done before, and rubbed her cheek against his now-bare chest, turning to kiss him there, finding salt on his skin, delicious.

His hands came firm around her head, urging her upward, to a kiss that hurt from the power of it, bruising, wonderful. He clutched her close to him—all of her, to all of him—and pushed against her hips in a way that made her score her teeth against his neck. He did it again, straining, his entire form ardent against hers.

"Lily," Tristan muttered, thick and dazed. He felt as if his life would end if he could not complete this act. "My God, Lily . . ."

He moved to the neck of her gown, ready to pull it all the way off her, ready to find the beautiful, bare flesh of her and bury himself in her. The simple kiss he had begun whirled out of control, so fast, so severe that he could not even recall how it had happened—how they both had come to be entwined in this pallet, skin to skin, cumbersome gown and tunic all that was left between them.

He said her name again, and something else—her breasts, so perfect, her legs around him, yes, yes—but then she changed.

Utterly. Completely. Changed, stopped, that lissome sensuality that had welcomed him so well, and so sweetly, turned to rigid resistance.

His body did not believe what his mind understood: She was rejecting him. That quickly, that ruthlessly. She pulled away from his hands and sat up amid the blankets, her hair clinging to them both, then scrambled to the edge of the pallet, her feet on the floor. The blue gown drew tight over her shoulders again.

He did not try to stay her. Tristan lay back and stared at the ceiling instead, enraged, impassioned, hating himself and her in this moment. Hating the world.

Christ, what a mistake. What a stupid, *stupid* mistake. What the hell had happened to him?

She would leave him now, he knew she would. She would go—she had every right to go. He had used her—*attacked* her—his sanity turned as dark and murky as his soul. He had felt only Lily before him, an erotic dream turned real, holding him, responding to him. He had gone mad with it. He had lost all reason.

A bewildered panic seized him: She could not leave. She would. What would he do to stop her? He could not even move yet, for fear that he would lose his control again.

But she did not rise from the pallet, only sat there,

bowed and small as a child might sit, her hair falling down to conceal her face. Finally, she spoke.

"Who is Bess?"

He exhaled around the clench of his teeth. "Who?"

"Bess. Sweet Bess." A lone lock of gold curled down the center of her back, all he could really see of her, a glossy temptation. "My cousin mentioned her to me once. She thought—you loved this Bess."

Now he did sit up, staring, astounded. Bess? He had a vague flash of a face, a dark-haired girl, laughing. A tavern wench? A servant?

"I have no idea where she got such a notion," he said honestly. "I can't think of anyone by that name."

Lily kept her head lowered. "She did not say how."

"Why does it matter?"

"It doesn't."

She stood, walking away from him, from the mess of the pallet, finding a robe, holding it to her.

He spoke to her back. "Lily, I apologize. I—"

"It doesn't matter," she repeated, thin and distant. She hesitated, then wrapped the robe around her, hugging her arms across her chest. "I'm going to sleep in the ladies' quarters until we finish this."

"No—"

She turned. "I am!"

"No, listen." He did not attempt to stand, to reason with her up close. She had a brittle look about her now, tight and fragile. He did not want to be the one who shattered it. "You won't need to. Today we'll move to the master chambers of the castle. You'll have rooms of your own. You won't have to—" Tristan choked on the words, then said them anyway. "You won't have to see me at all, if you wish, except in public places."

She made no assent to this. If anything the tension about her increased. Her eyes were stormy and dark, reproaches shining through.

"There is a lock on the door," he offered, desperate. "You may hold all the keys."

Finally she gave a short nod of her head. But the storms in her eyes did not diminish.

———————— ⟲⟳ ————————

SHE AVOIDED HIM FOR FOUR ENTIRE DAYS, AND IT was no easy feat.

Moving into the quarters of the countess was a tricky thing. The old castellan, the surly man with red hair, had done nothing to prepare the rooms, no doubt planning to rid himself of them instead of making them more at home. It had fallen to Tristan's new man, Silas, to set the chatelaine upon it, and she had done so with clear reluctance.

Lord Liam had not yet wed, Amiranth knew. When she inspected her rooms that afternoon she found dust so thick she could draw pictures in it, covers over the furniture, a bare stone floor, and an iron grate empty of wood or even coal to burn. A glance into Tristan's quarters showed little better: Someone had started the transfer of Liam's belongings—they were piled in a heap in the center of the chamber, clothing and bottles and jewelry treated with the same careless disregard.

She sent the women to clean her rooms and went to work on Tristan's herself. She would not want his younger brother to have more cause for complaint than he would already.

Tristan traveled in and out. She did not meet his eyes at all; he had a distracted look to him anyway. Well enough. Let him deal with the suspicions and questions of his vassals. She would do her part, and hope that soon all would settle here so she could leave without a backward look.

She obtained the keys to her quarters from the chatelaine. She tested the lock herself, made certain it was well oiled and solid. The click of the bolt sounded very cold to her ears.

So then Amiranth slept apart from him, from all the population of this place, in a real bed with diaphanous curtains drifting around the frame of it, an embroidered canopy that shimmered with the summertime breeze.

It was her bed. She tried not to consider that, but the thought continued to creep back to her, persistent. It was her bed in fact. It was her room. This was her proper wedded home, even if no one but she knew the secret truth of it.

By day she did what she could to aid Tristan in his precarious claim. She supported his decisions, she greeted him with the utmost courtesy whenever they met, granting him all sorts of favors with her words, implying that his blessing was as vital as any overlord could hope. She could not tell if any of it was working. She could not tell if what she glimpsed on the faces of the scattered nobles of this place was fear, or respect, or just a dreaded patience, everyone waiting for the day that Liam Geraint should arrive again.

She dreaded it herself. But the sooner he came, the sooner she could leave. And then the problem of Tristan Geraint would fade from her life, and she would never have to fear love destroying her again.

On the afternoon of the fifth day a riding party was spotted. When the horn sounded everyone gathered in the bailey, amassing near the gate. Amiranth had left the keep with a great crowd and jostled her way through them, less careful than she should have been, but they were woven so tightly against her, not letting her through—

Tristan was suddenly beside her, taking her arm, and magically a path cleared before them, people bowing and bending out of their way like flowers in a windstorm.

It was a pleasing day; a morning rain had come and gone, so everything still smelled dewy fresh, and the stones of the outer wall were darkened to taupe and brown, the earth damp before them.

"Who comes?" called Tristan to the man at the top of the gatehouse.

"A great party, my lord! Two score men, at least!"

"Their colors?" demanded Tristan.

"Too far yet to tell, my lord! A dark and light, that's all I can say!"

Crimson and silver, Amiranth thought, the colors of Haverlocke, and felt the excitement of the crowd around her.

Tristan's face remained cool, determined. He waited s they all did, for the party to break past the forest and pproach the gate.

"Blue and snow, my lord," cried the watch suddenly. 'Blue and snow!"

Not Liam—Augustin. Amiranth felt her stomach ighten; her fingers momentarily clenched over Tristan's rm. He covered her hand with his own, looking down t her now, eyes of jet black, a sorcerer's sparkling mystery. His words to her were barely audible.

"Courage, my lady. Can you remember enough of our life at Iving to convince him you are his sister?"

She bit back the urge to laugh. "It's rather late for hat worry." When he did not release her from his stare, he added, "Yes," on a sigh.

"He may test you," Tristan murmured, watching the woods now, the first of the riders coming clear of the rees—outriders in her family colors, banners and horns and shining weapons. "Question you with anecdotes, or people. Try to remember—"

"Do not fear on this account," she whispered, impatient. "I am full at ease with Amiranth's memory."

He gave her his faint smile, approving. "Excellent. Then we have nothing more to fear."

She wanted to laugh again, and still managed to control it.

At Tristan's command the portcullis was raised, and here came the group from Iving, crossing the threshold. Amiranth searched the riders until she discovered Constanz and a few of her women, looking uneasily at the gathered people before them.

Beside Constanz was Augustin, plumper than she re
membered, his beard cut shorter, dressed in the full her
aldry of his station, glorious beneath the sun. It almos
made her smile.

She knew him well, her brother. He would display
the best of his finery in this moment. He would ride
here with the most noted of his knights, as a show—not
of force but of status, lest anyone think he could not af
ford their loyalty. He would smile much and say more
but beneath that outward humor would be a man full
aware of himself, the situation he entered, and his rank
within it.

She even knew the horse he rode, a gift from King
Edward, a mighty bay stallion—Jorah's sire, in fact.

Augustin had not changed much over the years, after
all. She could only hope he would find the same of her.

Together she and Tristan approached. Before she
could even rise from her curtsy Augustin had bounded
from his saddle—mail and all—and nearly leapt upon
Tristan.

"By my word!" he exclaimed, grinning. "By my word,
here is my brother, back from the depths of hell!" He
pulled Tristan into a hug, laughing, and Tristan laughed as
well, his face transforming from its usual intensity to
something that made Amiranth's breath catch: a look of
joy, of boyish delight.

"Augustin! It is good to see you again."

"And you, I daresay! I could not credit it—your mes
sage seemed a jape, my lord, but I could not imagine
why anyone would jape on such matter! Tristan Geraint

alive! And with my sister! It was such news to take years off my life, I swear to you!"

"And mine, I promise!"

They laughed together again, two men matched in height, one fair, one dark, the sunlight slanting across them both. Augustin drew back slightly, glancing around.

"Where is she, by the by? Where is Amiranth?"

Amiranth took a deep breath and cleared her throat. Augustin turned to her; surprise scrolled across his face, then happiness again. "Why, and here is my fair cousin! I had not thought you here, as well. Good day to you, Lily!"

She heard the complete silence of the crowd, a drop in all noise that gave even her brother pause. Amiranth offered a silvered laugh, holding out her hand to him. "Has it been so long, Augustin? I cannot conceive that you do not recognize me! I am your sister."

His grin faded, replaced by a watchful expression. Oh heavens—it was worse than she had feared, he was as simple to read as a child! The doubt on his face echoed clearly in his voice. "Amiranth?"

She kept her smile firmly in place, hand still outstretched. "Aye."

Everyone gawked. Everyone waited, from the steward to the serfs, focused on the two of them, her proffered hand, the motionless man before her. The sound of her heartbeat was thunder in her ears.

"Come," she said, her voice so normal. "Will you not greet me properly, brother? I would like to say my welcome to Constanz as well. It's been a very long while."

Augustin changed again, his expression going from astonishment to pleasure. He took the final steps between them, enveloping her in a hug.

"By heavens, how can this be you?" He leaned back, examining her. "You have the face of our cousin, I vow!"

She set herself gently away from him. "A strange world, is it not?"

"Indeed it is! Indeed it is!"

He embraced her again, and she gave in and held him as well, thinking how peculiar it was to have her head reach his shoulder, his beard pricking her skin. The last time she had seen him she had been hardly more than a girl.

Constanz dismounted, and there were more greetings, these with a great deal more restraint to them. Beneath her tempered demeanor Constanz threw Amiranth long, dubious looks, and Amiranth could only meet her eyes, willing her to stay quiet out here, at least.

The rest of her brother's knights had begun to dismount, men talking, consulting, a mass of them surrounding them. Augustin and Tristan began to move toward the keep, Amiranth and Constanz on either side of them. Augustin was speaking again.

"Where *is* Lady Lily? Did she not accompany you?"

Tristan looked at her, alert. Amiranth moved close to her brother. "The plague, my lord," she said, as quietly as she could.

He stopped abruptly. "The plague, you say?"

"Hush!" Amiranth looked around them. "It was

months ago! You are safe. We would not have had you come were it otherwise."

Constanz made some shocked murmur, edging close to her husband. Amiranth glanced at her, frowning. To her surprise, Constanz was the one who lowered her eyes.

"A perplexing state," Augustin said slowly, his gaze going from Tristan to her. "A *most* perplexing state—the earl alive, Amiranth looking as Lily—and Lady Lily herself dead."

"I cannot explain it," she said helplessly. And then, in a rush: "Are they not glad tidings anyway, brother? Vast fortunes have turned. Much had been lost, but now all will be well again. Think on it, Augustin."

She *did* know her brother. He was kind at heart; if money was his weakness, well, he would not be the first man to succumb to such a vice. He had loved her enough to care for her when their parents died, and not enough to visit her in all the eight years of her exile. He had sent Lily to her when she wrote letters pleading for company. He had always ensured her health, if not her happiness. She knew where his thoughts would now lie.

Augustin looked about at the city-keep, the massive bailey, the fine stables and granary and all the good things here before them that bespoke the uncommon wealth of this demesne.

The advantages of having the Earl of Haverlocke in the family were as plain today as they were eight years ago. Augustin had to realize this; despite his vanity, he was no fool.

His gaze came back down to hers, considering.

Just then the scout sounded his horn again. As one, everyone turned to the sight of the lowered gate.

"New riders, my lord! Crimson and silver! Lord Liam returns!"

Chapter Eleven

———— ⚬₥₥⌒⊘ ————

AUGUSTIN WAS THE KEY. TRISTAN HAD REALIZED it long ago.

He had been anticipating this moment. He had been keen for it, in fact, the confrontation with his brother that had been bound to come. For days it had been eating at him. He had envisioned it a hundred different ways: Liam angered, Liam delighted, Liam riding for war. He did not know his younger brother. He had not seen him in centuries, a thousand years. He remembered the boy his brother had been, but could not even imagine a face on the man he would grow into.

But here was the man, and here was his face—not so dissimilar from his own, as it happened, lean and wakeful, his hair as black as Tristan's, his seat on his horse as certain.

Different eyes. Different mouth. No sign of welcome

or delight on his features as he found Tristan before him in the great stretch of the bailey, flanked by the Earl of Iving's knights and his own newly sworn men.

If it was to be war, Tristan was ready for it.

Liam picked him out easily from the crowd, his eyes going straight to Tristan. "You, sir!" he called out, still mounted. "You are the man I was told of—the man claiming to be my brother!"

"Liam." Tristan nodded once, folding his arms over his chest.

"By what right do you make such an outrageous claim? By what right do you come here, to my demesne, and grasp at my title?"

"By the right of God and law," Tristan responded. "I am your older brother. Haverlocke is my demesne, not your own."

Liam's face grew grim. He kept a hand on the hilt of his sword as his steed turned a nervous loop in prancing steps.

"My brother is dead! He died a hero, in the battles of France!"

"A fetching lie," said Tristan, with a cynical smile. "How unfortunate for you it is not true. I lived in France all this while."

"We would have word of such a thing!"

"Indeed, I should think you would. So I must wonder, brother, why my ransom went unpaid."

He heard Lily's sharp intake of breath; he did not spare her a look.

"Ransom!" Liam scowled. "There were no demands for a ransom!"

"God's wounds—" Augustin swore, but Tristan cut him off.

"No demands? How astonishing. It seemed to be all the French spoke of to *me*."

Liam seemed flustered, his scowl fading to uncertainty. "If there were demands to ransom my brother, I would know of it. I would have paid it!"

"So I had hoped," replied Tristan, with a deliberate darkness. "And yet it went, alas, unpaid."

"There was no ransom," Liam insisted, adamant. "They told us what happened—Tristan was dead! He was slain in the first wave of the battle for Calais. That's what we were told!"

"Felled in the first wave of battle," Tristan corrected him, "but not slain, Liam. Not slain."

Lily had taken his arm. He didn't know why, if she meant to hold him back or needed his support, but still he did not look at her. He kept his eyes fixed on his brother, looking much younger on his destrier than he had a minute ago.

"There was no ransom," Liam said a third time, quieter, discomfited.

Tristan studied him anew, the green youth of his features, unlined, unscarred, the flesh of his jaw already growing loose from an excess of riches. His brother was almost still a boy in truth, even with his bluster.

He thought of the life Liam would have led back here in England—security, entitlement, abundance—all the things Tristan had so readily abandoned on his quest for glory. It was not difficult to see traces of himself in this young man before him. How he might have been, had he not taken such a wild and disastrous turn with fate.

Had the French truly failed to deliver their demand? It might be so. Anything could be true of that black time, he thought; they had bungled it, or never actually understood whom they had held.

Tristan decided, abruptly, to throw the child a bone. "Will you come down, Liam Geraint, and greet me as your lord? I swear to you my word is true. I am your brother."

Liam stared at him, and then at all the men surrounding him, knights fully armed, his guard, all the people of Glynwallen, it seemed, clustered in this bailey. Liam's men were not inconsiderable. Tristan knew they might do some harm if they wished it, at the very serious risk of treason. Even so, they would not win. Not against Augustin's forces, combined with his own. He hoped they were not all so hot-tempered as his brother.

"I fail to see," Liam said at last, "why I should take faith in either your name or your word. You speak of things that did not happen. I know nothing of you or your tale."

"Then you will listen to mine, pup!" barked Augustin, a growling baritone. "You know *my* name, I trust, sir? Then hear me well! Here indeed is Tristan, Earl of Haverlocke! He has more patience with you than I would, young cur! Get you down from your horse and bow to your lord—or get you gone from here, at peril to your life!"

"My lord." Liam glanced at Augustin, his expression wary. "I do know you, of course. Yet this man could be anyone! He has the aspect of my family, I admit, but even you could not have seen him in years. This talk of ransom—it might be a trick, a confusion, sent to deceive us."

"I know the man's face," pronounced Augustin, calmer. "And I know my sister." He indicated Lily, standing stonily between them, white as alabaster, her fingers still clenched around Tristan's arm. "To the great joy of the land, Tristan Geraint has returned, along with his lady wife. Greet him as you should, as any man of honor would do."

Tristan watched his brother grapple with his choice, the flush of his cheeks marking anger, or frustration, or embarrassment. He rather thought all three.

A new voice sounded across the bailey, clear and high, only slightly too thin. It was Lily.

"In three days Glynwallen will host a feast, Lord Liam. Our guests are old friends from far and near. It would look ill upon you not to recognize the Earl of Haverlocke as they will surely do. If you wish to stay, we welcome you. If you will not, then go now, and spare yourself this dishonor upon your name."

Liam narrowed his eyes, considering. His horse took another agitated sideways step. Instead of calming him, Liam vaulted from the saddle, passing off the reins, approaching Tristan.

They stared at each other a long moment, toe to toe. Then Liam went to one knee, head bowed, and spoke to the ground.

"I am grateful to be able to greet you again. Welcome home . . . my lord."

Tristan touched him on the shoulder. Liam stood, young and flushed with emotion—a lifetime younger than Tristan had ever felt.

"I am well pleased to be home, my brother."

———————— ❦ ————————

S HE FELT ILL. SHE FELT BETRAYED, UNDONE.

A *ransom*! He had been held for *ransom*—then in a *prison,* all this time—and he had not *told* her, said not one word to her about it, not even when she had asked.

It was a struggle to keep walking beside him, not to shriek at him and push at him and demand explanations. Damn him! He had not told her, had let her think the most awful of things. . . .

Somehow Amiranth got through the moment. Somehow she spoke, and smiled, and directed all the people to where they were supposed to be. She sent the chatelaine scurrying, to prepare chambers and food. She moved as if through drifts of snow, jagged ice cutting her with every step, her face frozen, her words ringing in her ears.

Then she was alone, in her rooms. Benumbed. She stood there, staring at nothing, reliving the scene in the bailey over and over, Tristan's words sliding back to her, almost indifferent—a ransom, unpaid!

A noise behind her. Tristan appeared in the doorway, closing the door to solid wood against his back. She felt clumsy with her movements, turning to see him. The curl to his lips was gone; he looked at her moodily, dark as night.

"Prison," she hissed, in a rage, in a fury.

He did nothing.

"You never said! You let me believe—"

"What?" he asked, mild.

She stopped, almost panting, trying to find her control again. "You did not tell me," she finally managed. "You should have told me."

"Why?"

"Why! Because I had the right to know! Because I thought—all this time—"

He waited, but she could not finish the sentence. She could not tell him what she had actually thought. Amiranth raised a hand to her eyes, hiding them, feeling the anguish splinter through her. Her entire body was shaking. "I cannot fathom that you did not tell me."

"It would have served little purpose."

She released her breath, a scoffing sound. He came closer in slow, measured steps.

"You had no need to know my past, Lily. It would have meant nothing to you."

"How could you say such a thing to me?"

"I would have told my wife," he said, deep and hushed. "Amiranth would have had that right. But you are not . . . my wife."

She bit her lip, fighting back more words, a babble of accusations. She could not believe the turn her life had just taken. It was inconceivable.

"You did well, Lily," Tristan said, another step closer to her. "Very well. You fooled everyone."

"Prison." Amiranth shook her head, seeing the dark

beauty of him, despairing. She felt wretched and sick, everything spinning by too fast for her—he had been imprisoned—forsaken, as he had told her once, gone from the world as surely as if he *had* died, or run away. Imprisoned! Her Tristan—

"Stay with me," he said, his voice turned to velvet.

It took time for his words to come clear to her, as if she had to translate them in her head from some arcane language, strange and cumbersome.

"What?" she whispered.

"Stay with me. Become my wife in my home, in my life. Live with me. I love you, Lily."

Her hands came up to cover her heart, to shield her from the grief of his words. She took a step back and he equaled it with a forward one, pinning her with his look. He was brooding handsome, feral intensity. She understood then that here was not the man she knew— he had gone past some inner edge, past a point she could not know or even guess at.

She did not see love on him. She saw danger, and her destruction.

"No."

"Too late to deny it. You care for me, too. I think it so. I saw you in the bailey. I saw your face."

"No." She shook her head again, taking another step away.

"Lily . . ." He smiled at her, that subtle grace, and the wicked curve to his lips came back, the promise of pleasure there, of heartless intent. He moved toward her, tall, stealthy, almost a threat draped across him. She glanced frantically around the room and saw no comfort—shut doors, a looming bed. A castle beyond, filled with people ready to betray her.

He caught her then, easily, almost gently, caught her up in his arms and kept her there despite her startled jerk. His head dipped down to hers.

"No!" She could not think, she could not breathe—this could *not* be happening, his words, her feelings—he was killing her, he would kill her with this, she could not feel this way for him again—

"Too late," Tristan said once more. He kissed her then, drowning her in him, tasting her, a ravishment, all gentleness gone. He held her and engulfed her, and Amiranth fell into it, helpless, suffocating, letting him win, carrying her back to her own abandoned dreams.

"I love you." He spoke against her cheek, his lips tracing the words over her skin. "Beautiful Lily, I love you."

"Stop!" She tore out of his embrace, her vision blurred with tears. "You can't do this to me! I will not allow it!"

"Too late," he murmured, his eyes bright upon her.

"It is not too late! I won't—" She lost her breath, a sob in her throat. "I *won't* let this happen again!"

"I love you."

"Get out!"

He did not move.

Fear made her wild; she ran to the door. "Get out! Or I promise you I will tell them all the truth! I will!"

He turned his head away, only that, so that she could

not see the shine to his eyes, the terrible dark look he
had for her.

Amiranth lost her nerve, and fled the room herself.

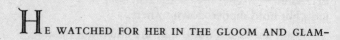

HE WATCHED FOR HER IN THE GLOOM AND GLAM-
our of his castle.

Tristan tested his senses, seeking clues of her in the
everyday, a hint of her perfume, the flutter of her skirts,
a long golden hair coiled across a pillow in her room.
And she hid from him, swift as a rabbit in the hunt, as if
she eluded him for her very life.

Perhaps she thought she did. Perhaps she did in truth.
Tristan almost did not know himself, this passion that
had come over him. He felt light and heavy at once
with the thought of her. He felt the depths of his love,
untested, and let it wrap itself around him, a lure to call
her, to bring her back to him.

He discovered layers of emotion within him, a burning for her, a desire above all costs. He was almost at a
loss with these raging feelings, still trying to consider
coolly how best to keep her, and capture her faith in
him.

Sometimes it chilled him, when he might come
across her, enough so that he could think of no words
to speak. He became as gauche as a country squire, staring at her, watching the blush come to her cheeks,
thinking only of how she would look after he had loved
her, mussed and sated in his bed.

Each occasion was most public—at meals, in hallways,

and once in the inner garden of the keep, when he had found her in quiet discussion with the chatelaine, the two of them going over menus.

Both women curtsied; Lily said hushed things, words that sounded right, in a voice that told him clearly of her fears.

Tristan had granted her mercy, knowing the leverage was all his, and none of hers. Despite her threat she would not betray him. She could not. He knew her better than she thought. So he would let her fly again, and could only linger in the space she had left, finding the imprint of her in the dark of his imagination.

They spent two nights far apart, each ensconced in the elaborate quarters of the earl and countess. Tristan had not bothered to test the lock on the door between their chambers. He knew it would be secured against him.

She did not know he had another key, purloined from the master chain. He would not use it. Not until he had to.

He wanted her. He needed her. He would make her forget the past, her cousin, his wife . . . he would make her think only of the two of them, and what could be between them.

She loved him too. He was certain of it. Tristan had seen it in that moment in the bailey before his brother, with her fingers pressed hard into his arm and her face turned stark. It was like a rainbow flashing clear of a prism, a burst of revelation, there and gone.

She loved him, she did, and that made all their other problems thin as paper. He was going to vanquish mountains of memories to win her. All he needed was time to gain her confidence, to let her realize the truth.

These were the things that mattered to him: his name; his home; and her, Lady Lily, circling ever closer to the careful trap he had laid for her heart.

THE NOBLES ARRIVED IN MAGNIFICENT STYLE FOR THE feast, carriages and steeds draped with pageantry, the greetings of horns, curious strangers Tristan barely recalled from his days at court. A few old friends—very old—men grown fat with life, or thin with avarice, talking to him, picking apart his words and actions, ready to devour all that he did and spread the stories back across the kingdom.

Where had they been, these joking fellows, while he had rotted in a French dungeon in defense of their king?

Tristan played their game with deft assurance. This much, at least, had stayed with him: how to laugh with them and jest about their ignoble pasts, say the things it would be expected he would say, act as the Earl of Haverlocke would act in his keep. He traded quips and sporting insults with the lords, threw false compliments to their ladies. He cared for none of them beyond what they could do for him—secure his rule here. Rout out the last of doubt around him.

When they questioned him about France he always managed some light response, as if that time had been nothing to him, a minor inconvenience in the splendor of his life. No one pressed him; it was just as well. He had nothing for them beyond this facade.

Liam walked heavily around the keep, quiet, reserved. Tristan kept a man on him at all times, held to a discreet distance. He was not careless enough to fully trust his brother yet. Liam had lost much. Tristan knew how that hurt.

And as the new people arrived, Lily managed to stay away more and more, until it seemed she was no longer with him even at the meals, only a shell of her, her eyes empty, her words too dry for meaning. At times her hands would tremble as she ate; he contemplated that, wondering what it was, in fact, that she feared so greatly.

Let the celebration finish. Let these japing crowds depart, and he would conclude his hunt for Lily. He would set her right, and convince her he was naught to fear. That she needed him. That she would stay, and they would find their delight in each other forevermore.

The feast day arrived, great bustle and cheer among the guests. Minstrels wearing his colors played and sang, performing along the length of the great hall.

The sight of the tables laden with food sent a great cacophony echoing around them. Tristan escorted Lily through it all, past the musicians and frankly staring nobles to their places at the main table, her touch on his forearm cool, her fingers pale against his tunic. She wore a gown of violet gray—*storm clouds,* he thought— rich with trim, a necklace of lilac stones clasped high around her throat.

She stood with him silently as the noise began to die, a sea of expectant faces turned to them.

This was his time. This was his moment: home again, his title regained, his life held once more in his own hands. This was the place, the chamber, the castle he had never relinquished, not even in the deepest moments of misery. Through all the madness of the past, this was his again. He saw no skepticism on the people before him now. He saw interest, greed, curiosity, engrossment—but they all acknowledged his name.

"My friends," Tristan said, hard victory singing through him, "I thank you all for joining us here. May God save you and keep you. My lady and I greet you, and pray the Lord's blessing upon each of you and your houses. Noble sirs, gentle ladies, enjoy our great bounty."

Augustin, two places away, stood, seconding him, and so Liam could do no less. He raised his goblet and commanded a toast to Tristan, to his wife, and Tristan turned his head just enough to see Lily beside him, her eyes almost feverish with emotion.

She glanced at him once, then swiftly away again.

They ate.

It was a lavish meal, all the foods Tristan had savored in years past and had tried not to consider in the years since. He knew it was Lily who had planned it all; he was not astonished to find that she had read his dreams in this, that she had plucked from his thoughts the very dishes he craved. She had not asked him anything. She had known.

It gratified him. It kept him laughing in his seat, anticipating the end of the meal, the finish of this long test—when he could find her alone again, and taste her, and let her feel the true beating of his heart.

Conversations were loud and hearty among his guests. He kept a choice few acquaintances of old at his own table, men and women with quick mouths and an ear for gossip. Soon the story of his successful return would be circulated all over the royal court, from the king down. Tristan had fortified the arrangement well; in addition to the gossips he had placed both his strongest ally and his potential enemy near—Augustin and Liam, seated across from each other, where Tristan could observe their faces.

Waves of laughter would take the room, as if some joke was passed from table to table. Tristan paid it almost no mind, his thoughts distracted by the soft glow of violet beside him, the vision of a single, perfect curl falling over Lily's shoulder, ending at just the tip of her breast. He was following the rise and fall of it from the corner of his eye, imagining the lock freed from the glittering pins that held it in place, all of her hair falling loose over her shoulders, amber and darkened gold against her skin, against his. . . .

Augustin was speaking over the gentle strumming of a lute. A maiden was tucked away in a corner by their table, playing a quiet ballad. In the depths of his fantasy Tristan was kissing Lily to the notes of it, a bit of her at a time.

". . . amazing, I must say. I never conceived you might grow so close to your cousin Lily's looks. None of us did, did we, wife?"

Tristan looked up quickly, his attention honing back to the moment.

The Countess of Iving shook her head. "No, I daresay not."

Lily spoke, the first time Tristan had heard her all day. "Well, we are all family, are we not? Such things happen."

"Aye, true enough," Augustin conceded. "Why, you should see Emile, Amiranth! He has the face of our father already, if you can believe it."

"I can," said Lily, in a steady voice.

Augustin turned to Tristan. "I tell you, my lord, there is nothing like a child to remind a man of his mortal fate! I see my father in my son—my cousin in my sister! All the family repeated, from old to new again." He laughed. "You'll find that out soon enough, I warrant."

A high, delicate blush was overtaking Lily's cheeks. She lowered her lashes, modest, but Tristan had caught the flash of her eyes. It had not looked like modesty to him but something rather more vibrant.

She ignored them all, very deliberately reaching for her goblet, taking a small sip.

Augustin continued, picking over his food. "Of course, you had a child already, didn't you? A little girl. You named her after our mother, as I recall."

Conversation at the main table dropped, eyes widening, faces turning toward them. The Countess of Iving murmured something in a reproving tone.

"What, my dear?" Augustin looked at her, frowning, then slowly began to redden. He darted a glance back to Lily, and then Tristan. "Oh. My apologies, my lord."

Tristan began an instinctive denial, brushing aside this uncouth comment, imperiously, the way a lord should do.

But something stopped him. Something in him quickened to frost, the pit of his stomach, his mind seizing upon Augustin's red face, the line of consternation across his wife's forehead.

With a sense of slow wonderment Tristan felt himself split apart—quietly, even invisibly, a total wrenching of his soul. He watched the hall turn flat before him, become like a painting, a portrait of some elegant, unknown place: the men and women in their finery, feathers and velvet and luminous colors. Bloodred wine shining in goblets. Everyone motionless at the table, each person staring in a different direction, refined and still against the rich backdrop.

Augustin, bearded and florid.

The wife Constanz, veiled and bejeweled, pearls and gilt all about her.

Lily beside him, her hair up, her face averted, pale, expressionless . . .

. . . her fingers clenched so tightly around her goblet they had turned pure white.

Oh God. Oh God.

From that split in the chasm of his soul Tristan felt a glimmer of his old self reemerge—the boy he used to be, so many lifetimes ago, a sharper wit, arrogant and filled with contempt for this softer version of himself.

Of course, the younger Tristan said, mocking him. *Of course it's her. You knew it all along, didn't you?*

No. No! How could he have known?

Of course it was your child. Your daughter.

A little stone in the chapel floor, scripted initials, a single date. Bluebells. *Her* daughter—*his*—

He was standing. He did not remember doing it but he was, his chair pushed back from the table, and they were all staring at him now, all but *her*. An awful smile stretched across his face; he could not seem to erase it.

"Pray forgive us," he said, barely an excuse at all, and calmly took her arm and left the great hall with her.

They were walking. They walked and walked until Tristan realized the surroundings again. They were alone in the inner keep garden, and she was staring up at him, white-faced. Everything about her was empty and smooth, still as a painting, so perfect. Her hair shone with golden fire in the sunlight. He had both hands at her shoulders, as if to push her away yet keep her close at once.

"You," was all he could think to say.

"You," he said again, not even managing her name.

He was sinking to his knees before her. His arms wrapped around her, holding her so hard he was almost trembling, but she wasn't trying to push him off. She had turned to marble before him, just as she had been the first moment he saw her at Safere. The accidental brush of her hand was icy cold, even in this heat.

Her skirts whispered beneath his cheek, soft violet. He placed a hand over her stomach and she didn't protest even this, the pressure of him against her, drawing his palm downward over the folds of her gown, following the bare curve of her there.

His mind chanted, *A little stone, a little date, a little girl. . . .*

His wife. His daughter.

"What was her name?" Tristan asked, closing his eyes.

She took a ragged breath, the only sign of life to her.

"Rose," she said at last, her voice fragile. "I called her Rose."

Bluebells, his mind responded, irrelevant, befuddled. Not roses; slender bluebells across her stone, tiny flowers for his daughter.

The woman before him took another breath, speaking up to the sky, away from him, the words soft and hurried, floating off into the blue.

"She opened her eyes just once—they were dark like yours, so beautiful. And then she fell asleep in my arms. And that was all. She came too early, you see . . . far too early."

A strangled sound came from his throat, bitten short. His clenched fists made a mess of her skirts.

"I want to go now," she said. "I want to leave."

"No."

"You promised me! You said I could!"

Tristan stood, releasing the gown, staring down at her, the familiar features that had haunted him, lovely and cold right now, the sunlight brilliant upon her. "I promised Lily Granger she could leave. I did not promise you—*Amiranth.*"

Her lips began to tremble, true tragedy on her face. He looked into her eyes and couldn't believe all that he had not seen. How stupid he had been. How blind.

"You let me be sorry for your death," Tristan heard

himself say, incredulous. "You let me *apologize* for kissing you."

"You *should* be sorry," she snapped back. "You *should* apologize!"

"For kissing my *wife*!" His emotions spun and turned, vast beyond his control. "For what is mine, by all rights!"

"I am not yours!"

He proved her wrong because he had to, because the contempt and frenzy in her voice goaded him to. He pulled her to him and kissed her, hard and ruthless, painful. They broke apart, gasping.

"I am well enough sorry for that," he said, low, almost vicious. "But no more, my lady. We have played enough games between us, you and I. It is finished."

"What do you mean?"

"I am delighted to find you alive, Amiranth, and that is a fact. We are wed. We will begin living together as true husband and wife."

He had thought her face pale before; now it blanched even whiter. Only her hair remained bright, framing her with color.

Her voice was stricken. "You promised . . ."

"Not to you."

"I don't want to stay with you! You must let me go!"

"No. Absolutely not."

She began to back away from him into the garden, into the trailing wisps of a verdant willow, long leaves gliding over her shoulders. "I will tell everyone I am Lily! That you are a fraud!"

"I will do," Tristan came close, menacing, "whatever it takes to stop you. Whatever it takes, Amiranth."

"Why?" she cried. "What difference does it make to you? You were willing to let me go before, even as everyone believed I was your wife!"

"That was before I knew who you truly are." He found her in the willows, stalked her until they were both beneath the canopy of green, isolated. "We were joined before God. We will remain together."

"I don't love you!"

He smiled over the pain of that, keen and sharp. "Do you truly think that signifies? It doesn't. You will stay with me."

He came closer still, taking up her hand—limp now, as if the life had fled her. She stared at him with luminous eyes, her lips turned down, tears falling like stars down her cheeks. She seemed transfixed on him, appalled, terrified and fascinated, his prey finally cornered.

Tristan leaned in to her, another kiss, softer than before, more persuasive.

"This doesn't have to be love, Amiranth. We have this." He touched his tongue to her, tasting the tears, feeling the warmth of her through her gown, the hitch in her breathing. "This will do."

For now, he added silently.

"God help me," she whispered to his chest.

"Too late," Tristan told her, and felt a wild and dark anticipation spread through him.

Chapter Twelve

——————⟁——————

MIRANTH HID IN THE CHAPEL, THE ONE PLACE she knew he would not go. She sat and then knelt, kneading her hands against her stomach to fight the queasiness there, her loss of balance that set the world on its head.

The great party carried on without her. She could not hear it, but knew it continued, because the nobles had not yet poured out of the great hall.

Tristan had gone back alone. He had not pressured her to return with him—had not even asked, in fact— so he must have sensed the panic that lived within her. It was a savage, raw fear, and she could not say what would come of it.

Now he knew about her. Now he did.

The castle priest had approached her twice so far, asking questions, was she ill, did she need help? Amiranth had refused him—she wanted only to pray, please, let her be. Since she could not seem to stop her tears she knew he would come again soon, and this time perhaps with her husband, or one of his men, or her brother—she would be paraded before the entire assembly of shrill and dazzling people Tristan had invited here, and she would not be able to hold her composure at all.

The man four rows behind her knelt as she did, but Amiranth was not fooled. He was one of Tristan's guard, sent to watch her, to contain her if need.

What should she do? What was she going to do?

She remembered being with Tristan in the chapel at Safere. She remembered fragments of that day, that morning, rising before dawn, finding the last perfect stem of flowers left in her garden. Placing it on her daughter's grave and then remaining there, adrift in her thoughts, dwelling on the brief spark of life that had been her child.

No one ever spoke of it at Safere, the tiny, precious secret entombed behind stone, missed by none but she, it seemed. Her baby, blonde and fair and so very, very small. Rosine had not been meant for this world. That's what they told her. And Amiranth could only weep and agree as she lay in her bloody sheets, clutching her daughter. She had let them take her from her. She had held Rose for her first and final breath, and then let them take her away, wrap her in shrouds and give her over to the darkness. Forever. There was only the crypt to remember her by, a flat stone, not even her full name.

For a long time afterward Amiranth had considered joining her daughter there. Only Lily saved her. Only

Lily had been too stubborn to let her go, and nursed her back to health.

And now Lily was gone, just as Rosine was. There was only Amiranth left, and the man she used to love.

She had truly thought no one would remember, after all those empty years. She had thought that all had forgotten. Then Tristan had come to the chapel and stood right above his daughter, asking about her as casually as could be.

In that one strange moment Amiranth had not lied to him. It had been the fever making her speak, or she knew not what. Perhaps she should have lied, but she had not. Now he knew all.

Her love for him had led her to disaster, over and over. She could not risk such a thing again. She would not.

"God keep you, my lady."

The quiet voice echoed through the chapel. Amiranth started, looking around to find Liam sitting behind her on the bench. He stayed awkwardly near the edge, as if he meant to spring up at any second. His glance to her was short and uncomfortable.

"I beg your pardon, my lady, if I disturb you."

She swiftly faced forward again, wiping at her face.

"I did not come to disturb you," Liam continued, after a pause. "I merely noted . . . that you were so quiet at the feast. You left so quickly. My brother told us you felt unwell. And now I find you here. . . . I cannot help but notice that you do not seem at ease."

"I am well at ease," she said to her clasped hands, an obvious lie.

"Your pardon," said Liam once more, and fell silent.

They stayed like that, she kneeling, he sitting. She wondered if Tristan's man was still behind them, but did not turn around to see.

The priest walked before them, preparing for the Mass to come. She caught the scent of incense as he passed. It mingled with the beeswax that saturated this place, a smell that always reminded her of death and heaven together.

Liam did not stir. Finally she spoke without looking at him, keeping her words faint.

"Why did you come here?"

"To pray," he responded gravely.

She almost sighed. "A worthy endeavor."

"Aye. So I hope."

There was something strange in his voice, but when she dared to glance at him his face held only gentle inquiry.

His eyes were brown, lighter than her own, flecks of hazel in them. He was much younger than Tristan, she thought, but right now she clearly saw his brother in him, the raven hair, the set of his mouth.

"Has the meal done?" she asked.

"Nearly so." He glanced downward, and she saw now that they had the same lashes as well, sable thick. "Or so I think. All were steeped in wine and ale as I left. The food was finished."

"Do you not drink?"

A wry smile took him. "Not that much."

A part of her wanted to return his smile; she turned forward again to disguise it.

"I must leave," Amiranth said. But she did not. She did not want to walk out into the day and see all those people again. She did not want to see Tristan.

"I know it is not my place," Liam said, interrupting her thoughts. "But—I wondered if there is aught I might do to help my lady."

She lifted her head. "Help me how?"

He stood, rocking on his feet. "Ah—forgive me. I misspoke." He offered her a short bow, then walked away. She followed his form until she met the eyes of Tristan's guard, watching her, and turned around again.

She could not hide here forever. Even if she could, her knees were aching, her eyes itched, and a chill had crept through her from the stone of the floor.

Amiranth rose and left the chapel, pretending not to see the bowing guard she passed, walking as quickly as she dared into the courtyard, the bailey, and then the welcome shadows of the keep.

She managed to avoid the great hall—where the sounds were indeed quite merrily drunken—and finally found the solace of her chambers, empty of people and words and prying looks.

Tristan was not there. When she peered past the door into his rooms, he was not there, either.

She was left alone, undisturbed, until a knock on her door revealed a maid, holding a damp cloth wrapped around loose stems of lavender.

"From Lord Liam," the maid said. "A soothing balm, for the relief of my lady's eyes."

The maid curtsied and was gone. Amiranth was left

to stare down at the fragrant cloth in her hands, pondering what it meant.

THEY WOULD NOT DISPERSE, THESE REVELERS HE HAD invited into his home.

Tristan had stopped drinking hours ago, and now only watched the wine flow into cups, spill on the tables, as the laughter and conversations reached astonishing heights.

The empty chair beside him was a silent reproach. He did his best to act as if nothing were amiss, and all else did the same.

His wife was indisposed, he had told them, and silently let them draw the obvious conclusion from that. It sent knowing looks around the tables, a few covert smiles. He had his own smile, he knew, a slick disguise over the true emotions roiling through him.

Rose, Rose— But he would not think on that here. To think on that was to invite disaster, to allow those emotions free reign. He could not afford such a thing now.

Later. When he had privacy, and the sanity of mind to absorb the truth.

So he had made her excuses and to his hidden amazement the words did not stick in his throat—*my wife,* he had said, smooth as honey. He had called her that before, when he thought it naught but a clever lie, or a senseless hope. But it was truth.

Amiranth lived. By God, she lived!

All this time—through all the past days when he had been drawn to her, had condemned himself for wanting her, thinking she was forbidden—all this time, she had been his all along.

Perhaps in some deep, dark corner of himself, he had known it. Perhaps that secret part of his heart—the part that had kept her close throughout the ordeal of France—had recognized her pure spirit, unchanged over the years. How else to explain his feelings for her, this sense of overwhelming relief mixed with pain?

Amiranth alive, not Lily at all. He bit back the laugh that wanted to come, the crazed joy of it, the bitter ache.

He could not trust himself to be close to her yet. There was much at risk today: there were questions to appease, and quick lies to conjure to dismiss any lingering suspicion over his strange actions before. In any case, he could not merely abandon the grand celebration he had created, even if he wished to do so.

He needed time to think, to sort through what had happened to him . . . his wife restored to him. The woman he loved turned out to be the only woman he *should* love.

It was too sweet. It was too much a miracle to believe—but he did.

He sent a guard after her and let her alone; the sight of her weeping did disturbing things to his heart, a pinching hurt. He would rather she recover before he went to her again. He would rather she calm, and think of what he had said to her, and begin to accept their union once more.

Finally the people began to tire. It was his signal to rise and end the feast, allowing them all to stagger off to the places assigned to them.

Augustin was beside him, still laughing and hale, his wife a colorful shadow at his side.

It was only when Tristan looked both ways down the main table that he noticed that Liam had stolen away.

No matter. There wasn't much his brother could do to him now. Tristan smiled at the cheerful mob before him, wishing them well, accepting their wishes, confident at least in this place, in his home.

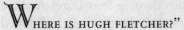

"WHERE IS HUGH FLETCHER?"

Liam Geraint leaned back in his chair, thumping his fingers against the plain wood of the arms. It was a simple chair in a simple chamber, the furnishings austere, the hearth too small, the window too narrow—nothing like what he was used to.

"At your estate of Safere, my lord." The soldier before him kept his head lowered. "He left just before you arrived."

"Safere? What the devil is he doing there?"

"He did not say precisely, my lord." The man looked up. "Yet I believe it has aught to do with the reappearance of your brother."

Liam frowned, staring at the space beyond the man's shoulder, his eyes distant.

"Safere," he muttered. "Gone all the way out to that miserable place. He must have had an excellent reason."

"Aye, my lord."

Liam sank back into silence, contemplating the unadorned wall before him.

———⟨∞⟩———

Silas James walked the hallways of the castle he loved, listening with trained perception to the words that came to him past walls and doors, from knots of people that scattered as he approached.

These were not the nobles his lord had brought to Glynwallen. These were the remnants of Lord Liam's rule, sharp faces, caustic glances he met evenly.

He had never liked this fawning crowd, and they had never liked him. That the balance of power had shifted back in his favor was a boon that no one—least of all he himself—had anticipated.

Silas knew the man standing idle next to the storeroom; that man had mocked him once, when Silas had tried to persuade him not to take a wounded hawk on a hunt. When the hawk had sickened and died, Silas was blamed.

He knew the two men speaking next to the fire in a sitting chamber; for a lark they had chased his granddaughter one fine day, and only relented when half the men of the village stepped in to shield her.

He knew the three women speaking behind the door of the ladies' quarters; one had slapped his wife when some trifling need had not been met, and the others had threatened her with more if she complained.

Ill people, ill content. They looked to Lord Liam for

relief, and that they were finding none troubled them mightily, Silas knew.

It troubled him, too. He knew Liam well enough. That he had not acted beyond the most obvious means to discredit his brother was a worrisome thing. Silas had Evan to warn him of crisis. He had his own senses to guard the castle. But it was a vast place, with corners and crevices that were always just beyond him, and whispering words that faded before he found their source.

He heard the rumors resurfacing—stories of the deaths of the old earl, the eldest son—fleeter than he could crush them, and could only stay ever more vigilant, fighting to ensure the rightful rule of his lord.

———⌇———

THE NIGHT WAS VELVET BLACK. TRISTAN HAD EX-tinguished all the lamps in his chambers, so that only the fitful glow of the dying fire illuminated the space. The air was cool all about; he hardly felt that against the heated tumult that had taken him. He himself would warm the room. He himself would warm her bed.

He held the key to Amiranth's chamber in the cup of his palm, feeling the long weight of it, brass forged to a simple pattern, tarnished with age. It gleamed mysteriously in the light, promising a world beyond his dreams, just past the door that separated him from her.

Still, he waited. He waited until he could hear nothing from the hallways, nothing beyond the occasional poem of the nightingale roosting in the eaves above his window.

He did not know the time. All he knew was his body, his heart . . . and Amiranth, in her bed beyond the wood of this door.

He slid the key into the lock, and turned it.

The door opened without a squeak, only the dull click of the bolt announcing him.

Her room was nearly as dark as his own, but she had left a lamp burning on a table, its flame a meager slip of gold against the blackness. She had drawn the curtains around her bed; they were translucent to him, folds of phantom paleness surrounding her in eerie elegance.

He walked to her on soundless feet, crossing rushes and rugs with equal care, intent on her, the shape of her behind the sheer material—smudged colors, amber hair and the soft blue of her gown, the covers hugging her figure.

Tristan paused just before her, allowing the thin fabric of the curtain to drift against his face, cool on his skin. He closed his eyes and then opened them, finding the split in the cloth, pushing it back with one hand.

She watched him from her pillows, calmly, as if she had expected him. Her eyes glowed dark; her skin seemed touched with a trace of the fever she had had before, pinkness high on her cheeks. Golden hair waved all about her to form a halo, richer than any he had seen in paintings or stained windows.

"You said I could have all the keys." Even her voice stayed flat calm, unsurprised.

He sat at the edge of the bed, finding his balance on the downy mattress. "The rules have changed."

"Your rules. Not mine."

He smiled at her, faint. "Same rules, my love."

She stared at him, very serious, the slightest trace of unhappiness to her lips. "I did not invite you here. I want you to go."

"I no longer need an invitation," he said softly. "You are my wife."

"Once I was, a very long time ago. But no longer."

"You can't change the truth, Amiranth."

"You can't change my heart."

He picked up a lock of her hair, holding it, feeling the brilliance of it, faerie silk against his palm. She made no protest to his move, only kept her gaze steady upon him, as sober and wild as a forest creature come to the light. He broke away from that look, going back to the burnished gold entwined between his fingers.

"I've never seen such a color as this."

One shoulder lifted to a shrug, dismissive.

"It wasn't always this way," he said, remembering. "It was . . . lighter before." He looked up at her. "And—shorter?"

"No."

"More curl," he guessed, and then remembered. "Aye. It curled. All over." Tristan smiled, recalling that in his mind.

"It's only hair," she said, and with a small flick of her hand freed the lock he held, sweeping it over her shoulder to fall against the pillows again. Her look was sulky now; she avoided his gaze.

"Will you let me stay with you?" he asked.

"No."

"Would you deny me, Amiranth?"

Before she could reply he leaned over her, placing a hand against her cheek, feeling the burn there against him. Tristan captured her gaze, holding on to her unhappy look.

"Don't answer me yet. Think of this . . ." His hand slid down her cheek to her throat, the delicacy of her collarbone. With the center of his palm on her chest he could feel her heart beating, passionate, the opposite of what her face told him. "We have a desire between us, Amiranth. It's been this way since Safere, and you know it as well as I. Whatever else our past has been, we have this now. It's no sin. It's what we were meant to do."

"No."

"No? You don't like this?" His touch turned to a caress, skimming her skin and the softness of her gown, finding the weight of her breast, cupping it. Her nipple hardened against him.

"No," she said again, tighter.

He smiled down at her. "You're a bad liar, my love."

"You didn't think so before." She pushed away his hand.

Tristan sat back, taking a deep breath to regain his control, to fight the selfish thing in him that told him to take her now, to smother her protests because they were not real, to bring forth her passion the way they both wanted him to. . . .

The curtains drifted silently against him, cool floating.

"Another child," he said, concentrating on them. "Another baby. Wouldn't you like that?"

She did not reply. He waited, looking back at her

only when he heard a muffled sound, nearly impercep-
tible.

She had turned her face away, a hand over her
mouth, eyes squeezed shut.

"Amiranth," he said, dismayed. He went to her in the
shelter of the bed, touching her arm, her shoulder.
"No, love—I'm sorry. I thought—"

What the hell had he thought? That she would relent
to him for that? That she shared his hidden hope for a
family; that if nothing else mattered, it would be
enough to stay her? He had meant to say the right thing
and only said everything wrong. Tristan found her free
hand and brought it to his lips, and then his cheek,
holding it fast.

"Amiranth. I love you."

He knew instantly that he had made another mistake—
even before she took her hand from her mouth, blinking
back the wetness that had come to her eyes. She tugged at
the hand he held and he released it, watching as she sat up
amid her pillows, the sheath of her gown shadowed
against her.

"Love," she scoffed, her eyes bitter bright. "It's not
love you feel for me, Tristan Geraint."

He fumbled for the right reply, afraid of making
some new blunder.

"I do," he said anyway, because he had to. "I do love
you. You don't have to believe me. It is still true."

"Do you know what love means?" Her voice had a
tremble. "Do you know how it wounds? You don't!
You think only of yourself, and your title! You think you

need me, when all you really want from me is what you could buy at a common whorehouse."

He drew back, staring. She gave a brittle smile.

"Do you truly think I don't understand? From the moment I met Lily I wanted to be her. I could not even hate her for her beauty, because she was always so kind, and so good to me. I loved her. I admired her. I still do." She took a deep breath. "And so do you."

"You don't know what you're saying."

"You see before you the image of my cousin. It's God's jest, mayhap—you found her fair then, as you do now. But it's only me! It's still my own heart, my lord. I haven't changed from that plain little damsel you married. I am still her inside, with all her fears, and her lost dreams. In time you'll grow bored with me, no matter how I look now."

"Amiranth—it's not true."

"I don't trust you. I don't know if I ever could."

"I *love* you," he said fiercely. *"You."*

"You love the face of a ghost. Not me."

"You're wrong. Dammit, Amiranth—"

He found himself kissing her, holding her hard though she gave no resistance, his lips on hers, willful, as if he could prove himself through this. When he moved away it was only to catch his breath—to toss away the blankets over her, to cover her with himself, more kisses, a thousand, a million—however many it took to melt the ice that had come over her, and make her understand his heart.

She did not struggle, she did not kiss him back, she did not do anything. She only turned her face away, gazing out at the hazy dark room beyond the curtains. Tristan paused, fervent and ready, focused on her expression, the passive blankness to her eyes.

"Hurry," she said, listless. "Do it, if you must."

"What?"

"I won't stop you. But leave me after. At least give me that."

He stared down at her, the passion still singing through him, heightened by the sense of her body beneath his, soft and warm, scented of the night and of her. Slowly she drew her legs into an arch on either side of him, cradling him close.

"Hurry," she said again, distant.

Tristan pulled away from her, away from the bed. The curtains swirled at his touch, whispering in the night, tugging at the air behind him as he left her room, left his wife alone in her bed, with only her blankets to comfort her—and no comfort for him at all.

Chapter Thirteen

⟨∾⟩

THE WINDOW OF THE SITTING ROOM WAS NOT CLOSED
as securely as it should have been. It allowed Amiranth
to hear more than she wanted of the party gathered in
the bailey for the hunt about to take place. She kept her
back to it, resolute, and concentrated on her embroidery,
fashioning tiny, sparkling stars with thread of precious silver against a dark-stitched night.

The noises outside were rowdy and robust, men gathered with their horses, laughing, their voices coming to
the room as a low roar.

It was the fourth and final day of Tristan's celebration.
Tonight would be the last banquet, and then they would
depart, all those jocular knights and their sharp-witted
ladies. Amiranth would not be sorry to see them go.

The only people she might miss were her brother
and sister-in-law. Not because they had been overly

warm with her; more that they were vestiges of the familiar, a buffer she had set between Tristan and herself. She had spent more company with Constanz than perhaps either of them had liked, but the thought of being alone—vulnerable—in this enormous place was more than Amiranth could bear just now.

They sat together, she and Constanz and a few of the women of the castle, sewing quietly as the men outside mounted and the horns sounded. The barking of the dogs was especially loud, rising up the walls of the keep to fill the room.

She caught herself straining to hear Tristan among the chaos, and forced herself to stop, frowning at a corner of her embroidery.

"A merry hunt," commented one of the women timidly.

"Indeed," replied Constanz, after a moment.

Amiranth had invited herself into the circle of women in this room. She knew they met here daily, the minor ladies of the realm, young wives of knights sworn to the earldom—the earldom Liam had ruled, not his brother.

It bothered her, that she was so avoided by them. It annoyed her, rather. So she had taken her sewing and Constanz and dragged her to this door, then greeted their whispers and perfume and thread as if it were the veriest surprise to discover them here.

Constanz had mellowed with her years, apparently. She had said naught to any of them beyond the shortest of comments. Which was more than Amiranth herself felt like saying now.

A red-haired lady spoke. "Does my lord the earl enjoy the hunt?"

"I do not know," Amiranth replied, curt.

One hound began a particularly mournful bay, prompting an echo of others.

"Does my lady hunt?" asked the same woman.

"Nay."

A heavy pause; the women settled back into their sewing.

Tristan had not attempted to come to her bed again. She had considered dragging something heavy to block the door every night, and abandoned the idea as childish. If he wanted to, he would find a way in. She would not resist him in body—only in her soul, the place he would not think to find.

It made her breath short to consider it. It made her stomach ache, to remember that night, the look on his face when she had spurned him. And then, when she had retreated into herself, and left her body to him.

She would *not* be sorry for it, Amiranth thought. She would *not* feel this remorse now as she remembered him, dusky and enticing, his eyes of jet, the sensual curve of his lips right before he kissed her. . . .

Amiranth stabbed her needle into the cloth again, missing her mark. She set her jaw and slowly worked the needle back through the fabric to undo her mistake.

She was not sorry. She would not give in to him. She would not believe him.

He did not love her.

The needle stuck; she jabbed her finger against the tip of it, and jerked her hand away to suck at the blood.

Damn him anyway, even to say such a thing! Damn him for his looks and charm and soft, sly words! For making her think such impossible thoughts.

The hunters in the bailey began to ride out, the sound of hooves bringing thunder to the sitting room, the howling of the dogs fading in thin, baleful notes.

She pitied the creature they were to kill today. She pitied herself.

"A surfeit of blood sport is never good for a castle," commented one of the women, without glancing up from her work. She paused, then added lightly, "So I have heard."

Amiranth looked at her, guarded, uncertain of her meaning.

"Quite so," said a second lady, a woman with a head-dress wrapped in pink satin. "Men sport in blood, but too often the consequences turn tragic—do they not, my lady?"

Amiranth answered in the same nonchalant tone. "However do you mean?"

The woman's eyes widened, feigned innocence. "Why, only that life is full of danger; we all know of that. And when men thirst for the hunt, accidents may occur."

"Accidents?"

"Aye. Was not my lord's older brother killed in a hunt?" The woman turned to the others in the circle, as if to seek confirmation.

"Was he?" Amiranth bent her head over her cloth again, pretending to work with her needle. "I cannot recall."

"Aye," said a third woman, in a coy drawl. "It's true. I recall hearing of it. A tragic time indeed. The old earl had died with his countess, from a strange sickness none could explain. And then their eldest son, the new earl of the land, so hastily undone in a hunt. He had drawn away from the main party. He had gone off . . . alone?" Her voice rose slightly, doubtful, an invitation to contradiction.

Amiranth narrowed her eyes, the sliver of needle pressed hard against the pads of her fingers—her hands were too stiff to sew, but she could not seem to loosen them.

"Alone?" The pink satin woman shook her head. "I think not, Vanessa. I remember that *someone* was with him . . . only one other person, also from the hunt. Now, who could it have been?" Her voice turned cunning. "Ah! I have it now! It was our very lord, in fact! Aye, it was his brother *Tristan* with the earl when he died." She placed a hand over her chest, a frown puckering her forehead. "How dreadful!"

"Dreadful, indeed," said Constanz, dry. "More dreadful still that such a tale would be living yet in this castle."

"Why, it is no tale, my lady. It is fact!"

"Fact or no, it is certainly no fit subject for this room."

"My lady, I only—"

"Were you there?" Constanz demanded. "No, you were not. I wager you were still in the nursery at the time, clinging to your wet nurse. I suggest, madam, you let the past lie, as it should."

The women around them exchanged slanted looks, a few beginning to blush.

"I am done." Amiranth dropped her needle and cloth into the basket at her side and stood; all the ladies except Constanz stood as well, bobbing curtsies. Constanz merely nodded, her eyes going to the other faces in the chamber.

"I believe I'll stay. I find the light here very fine."

Amiranth nodded in return, sweeping from the room, trying very hard not to slam the door behind her.

SHE WALKED, AIMLESS AND RESTLESS, DOWN THE long hall before her, her sewing basket on her arm, her thoughts turned round and round.

Amiranth was not fooled by the light tones and arch words of the women she had just left. They did not like her, and she saw no reason to attempt to like them.

But she had not known that Tristan was the sole witness to his brother's death. She only barely recalled the rumors—back then she herself had been but a child. No one had openly discussed any of it with her.

Not that it mattered. A rumor was only that: hearsay. She was not fool enough to worry over it. Tristan had his secrets. She had known that about him from the moment she had first seen him in the king's hall, washed in sunlight, laughing and not laughing. His soul was deep and still; he was a mystery, yes, filled with both fury and gentle humor . . . he had led a life she was almost afraid to imagine—but that was no cause to brand him a murderer.

Yet here in the depths of the long hallway she had an image of him, defending her in the yard of the inn. His struggle with the innkeeper, his threat to the lanterned man. The savagery she had glimpsed behind his eyes. How she had so believed him, that he would do it, kill them all to keep her safe—

"My lady."

Amiranth let out a small cry, whirling to confront the voice behind her.

Lord Liam looked at her with consternation. "I beg your forgiveness."

She had wandered deeper into the keep than she had meant to. But for them, the hall was empty, only a series of torches giving off dull light for comfort. All the doors before her were closed.

"I fear I've made an ill habit of startling you," Liam continued, rueful.

"No. No . . . I was merely in heavy thought." She shifted the basket over her arm. "Did you require something, my lord?"

"Only a word, if it pleases my lady."

But he said nothing more, only gazed down at her. In the torchlight she saw it again, traces of his brother in him, but softer, younger, more like the boy Tristan had been once.

"Speak, then," she said.

"Not here. Mayhap we might . . ." He tested the handle of the door nearest them. It opened, silent as a crypt. Darkness waited beyond.

Amiranth looked down the hall. Still no one else came. The only sound to be heard was the faint sizzle of the torches.

"If this time does not suit you . . ." Liam said, hesitant.

"It does." She walked past him into the room, inky thick shadows and a chill that sent bumps across her skin. No one had been here for some time, she would guess. Dust lay heavy on the table she passed. There were no rushes on the floor. Two chairs faced each other beside a closed chest; Amiranth ignored them, turning back to Liam.

He was staring down at his hands, clasped loosely before him, saying nothing at all. The cold around her seemed to swell.

She asked, "Do you not hunt, my lord?"

"Not today."

"An unfavorable day?"

"A simple hunt." He shrugged. "Today it's merely deer. I prefer . . . a greater challenge."

She nodded, falling into silence herself, glancing uneasily behind him, to where the door let in the meager light.

"It is not my place," he finally began, and then stopped himself with a small laugh. "I hear myself saying that to you yet again. I am afraid you'll find me too bold in my speech, my lady."

"If your thoughts are not bold, neither will be your speech," she replied, keeping a careful distance between them.

"Aye." His eyes flashed up at her, brown and hazel, direct into hers. "But they are bold thoughts."

"Then perhaps you should not speak after all." She began to brush past him, out to the hallway again.

"No, wait." He caught her arm, halting her easily with a firm touch. Amiranth pulled away from him, back into the room, since he blocked the doorway. He must have noted the expression on her face; he spoke quickly now. "Please—I beg your pardon once more. But I must talk with you. It is about your husband."

She kept her basket clutched over her stomach, watching him closely. Liam sighed and ran both hands through his hair—another trait of his brother's, familiar, unaware.

"I need to ask you—do you truly know Tristan, my lady?"

"I am hardly likely to forget my own husband, sir," she said tartly.

"Of course. I meant, how well do you know him?"

"Well enough!"

"I have offended you. I apologize. Please believe that I speak only out of concern for you, countess."

She arched a brow at him, unable to move, trying to find her regal poise again, because it seemed the best defense against him and what he might say. Liam turned to the door, placing one hand upon the edge of it so that it crept nearly closed. His shadow grew vague across the floor. She watched that, rather than his face, the unsettled look there that sent a faint thrill of fear through her bones.

"I have very few memories of my childhood." He

spoke to the darkness around them, somber. "I left Glynwallen at an early age—only ten—and what I do recall of this place is limited. But there are some things I shall never forget. My father's voice. My mother's touch. And Tristan—his temper."

His hand released the door; it stayed open by a bare crease.

"Many times he seemed jolly to me. I remember he would laugh, and it made me laugh as well. But when he grew angry . . . my lady, it was a fearsome thing. He made the servants scatter, he would send my mother to tears. I would hear my father shouting at him, our eldest brother, and Tristan shouting in return."

"Every family has disagreements," Amiranth said steadily. "I fought with my own brother."

"Did you?" He looked at her, a hint of a smile. "I cannot imagine such a thing. You seem so kind."

"Then I suppose you cannot trust the first appearance of things."

His smile faded. "No. You cannot."

"My lord, what is it precisely that you mean to say to me?"

"Be careful." His voice dropped. "Be careful, my lady. Your life has been sheltered, properly so. You cannot realize—I know your husband has been gone many years, to France, he says. But how much can he have changed? I remember his fits and anger. I remember the weeping he caused. He was not . . . rational."

"With all respect, my lord, these are the memories of a child."

"But true memories, nonetheless."

"I thank you for your thoughts, Lord Liam. However, you must excuse me now. I am late for an appointment."

He did not move from the doorway, even when she walked up close to him and waited, striving to look calm, unruffled. A frown came to him, his eyes falling from hers, so that all she saw was the length of his lashes.

"You are so lovely," he said, almost under his breath. "I would not see my lady harmed."

"Harmed by whom?" Her voice turned sharp. "By my husband, do you mean? I assure you—"

"Where has he been all this while?" Liam looked up again, almost pleading. "He told us prison, but I swear to you there was no call for ransom for him!"

Amiranth took a step back and he found her arm once more, following. "Yet if it were true, if it *were* prison, surely they would have wanted his wealth. But we heard nothing!"

"Release me!"

"It was a lie, my lady! He stayed away, alone, for his own mad reasons. Or perhaps it *was* prison—he was jailed for crimes committed—"

She tore away from him; the contents of her basket scattered between them, gleaming pins tumbling with tiny *plinks*, drifting cloth, the thread of silver coming unspooled, floating in slow sparkles to the ground.

They watched it together, motionless, as Amiranth's embroidery settled in folds by her feet.

"I'm sorry," Liam said, strained. "I did not mean—I only wanted to warn you, Amiranth."

"First names," said a new voice, lazy and ominous. "I

did not realize you were on such intimate terms with my wife, brother."

The door slipped open. Tristan stood there leaning against the wood, arms crossed, a dangerous smile on his face. He did not look at Amiranth.

"A presumption on my part," Liam said, very calm. "She did not grant me that right. Forgive me, my lady."

She nodded, not trusting her tongue.

"Are you not needed elsewhere, Liam?" Tristan prompted softly.

Liam faced her again, a silent look of warning before he bowed to them both and left, his footsteps hollow down the hall.

Amiranth threw Tristan one furtive glance but could not make out his face, lost to shadows and the thin light behind him. She knelt, gathering up her belongings. The silver thread tangled, glittery, around her cold fingers.

Tristan knelt as well, picking up the long design of her embroidery, staring at it.

"I know this," he said, holding it to the light. "I have seen this before."

She snatched it from his hands, tucking it swiftly into the basket.

"At Safere," he continued, watching her. "I saw it there, abandoned, I thought."

Amiranth stood, brushing out her skirts, not replying.

"You brought it with you. It must be important."

"It isn't," she said, and finally managed to leave that dark room, hoping she was headed in the right direction down the hallway. Tristan fell into step beside her, graceful and fleet, the back of his hand skimming hers, then taking hold of it, pulling her to a halt. The glow of a torch just behind him spread lustrous gold across his hair.

"Did he distress you, my lady?"

The edge of danger to him had returned. Amiranth avoided his look. "No, not at all."

"A strange thing, to find my wife meeting alone—in the dark—with my brother."

"An accident. He came upon me by chance."

He waited, and so she went on, nervous, "He only wanted to—speak of his childhood."

"How very . . . unlikely."

Her fingers curled against his grip. "It is truth."

"Is that all?"

"He is just a boy, my lord."

"He is a man, my love. Don't mistake it." His fingers locked with hers, warm and strong, almost too tight. "You have a man already, Amiranth. I dislike competition."

"He's not . . ." She couldn't finish her sentence, the words choked in her throat.

"No," Tristan agreed, silky threat. "He's not."

THEY BADE THE GUESTS FAREWELL TOGETHER, AS GROUP by group they left Glynwallen, causing a great clamor in the bailey and confusion in the stables, high-stepping horses and the din of impatient lords.

Amiranth stood by her husband and wished them all

well in a slight voice, not bothering much to be heard. Tristan himself was much more hale; he grinned and waved and joked them gone, until at last there was only Augustin and his party left to depart.

And after they were gone, it would be only she and Tristan at the castle, surrounded by the crafty whispers of the people who dwelled here.

She embraced her brother and then Constanz, stepping back to let them mount amid their knights, the blue and white of their house flashing bright across them all, from the horses to the smallest pennon banners.

From atop her mare Constanz gestured to her. Amiranth approached, trying not to look as morose as she felt.

Constanz leaned down from her saddle, her voice pitched low. "Disperse those women, Amiranth. They will do you no good." She ran a gloved hand down the neck of her steed, her eyes serious. "Were I you I would send them away as soon as may be. They are shallow, biting creatures, unfit for you."

The response came easily, an old habit resumed: "Yes, Constanz."

And then Constanz smiled at her suddenly, open and friendly—the first time Amiranth had ever seen such a look for her on her sister-in-law's face. "I think you'll do well here, child. I'm pleased you've found your love again. Watch your back. God keep."

She pulled away. Amiranth, astonished, watched her turn her mount to Augustin's, all of them riding off to the accompaniment of great fanfare from the players on the wall-walk above.

———— ഗ്രാ ————

SHE STAYED AWAY FROM HER QUARTERS UNTIL SHE couldn't any longer, until it became ridiculous to avoid the night, and the sleep that had befallen the rest of the castle. Tristan's men lay sprawled across the great room, on benches and the rushes, close to the hearths. Pages and squires slept curled together in corners like litters of puppies. It seemed to Amiranth that the hounds of the keep had the better deal: they nestled among everyone, hording warmth, a few raising their heads to watch her as she passed by the doors.

Tristan would not be there, asleep with his men. He would make good use of the luxury of his rooms, she knew that, a soft bed, private comfort comparable only to her own quarters. . . .

And he had a key. As much as she hated to think it, she had no way to prevent him from using it. Again.

Without the disorder of the visitors the keep seemed much emptier than it had before. In such a large place it could not be surprising to feel a little small, even if she was supposed to be the mistress here. But it was not her smallness that Amiranth feared; it was that there were fewer people between her and Tristan now, less distraction, less protection.

She drifted into her chambers on silent feet, moving as softly as she could manage. The hearth had been lit for her, her bed turned down.

Tristan lounged in a chair by the fire, studying something he held in his hands. He did not look up at her arrival.

"My lady," he greeted her, quiet reserve.

He wore a robe again, this one a subtle wool of darkest green, a narrow design of gold and lapis blue traced along the edges of it. It lay open carelessly, showing her no tunic beneath, only the fine expanse of his chest, the muscles there warmly sculpted in firelight.

"Your work is excellent," he said to her, finally looking up. She did not need to move closer to him to see what he held: her swan embroidery, as old as their marriage itself—older, in fact—born from the mists of her infatuated girlhood.

"It is late," Amiranth said.

"Aye." But he did not rise from the chair. His gaze returned to the cloth, the curl to his lips so serious.

She walked toward him, holding out her hand for the material. He ignored her gesture.

"Why do I know this?" he asked, musing. "Why is it so familiar to me?"

Her hand remained out. "You said you saw it at Safere."

"Aye. But more than that. Could I have seen it before?"

"No."

He looked at her from beneath his lashes; the line to his mouth changed again, lightening, roguish once more. His fingers followed the edges of the cloth, pulling it taut, releasing it again, stroking the material in a rhythm she found disturbing for no reason. Amiranth drew close and grabbed it from him.

"I wish you to leave, my lord."

"I do not wish to leave," he replied, relaxing back into the chair. "I am most comfortable here."

"And will you spend the night there?" she asked, sarcastic.

"Oh no." His voice had a hidden laugh. "I'm not *that* comfortable. Not yet."

She let out her breath in frustration, snapping away from him, taking the embroidery to the basket she had left on a side table, rolling it up to put away.

Without warning he was behind her, his hand over hers, stopping her. The heat of him against her back felt like a welcome. She stared down at the basket, trying not to think, not to feel him so close to her, his arm following hers, the colors of his sleeve lapping over her forearm.

"You are most gifted," Tristan said, his hand still on hers, cupping it, turning it so that both their palms faced up. The embroidery slipped from her fingers and fell at an angle across the basket, unrolling to show the full scene. Amiranth frowned at it, trying to focus on that, the lake and the swan and the stars. She had used the silver thread unsparingly across it all, so that now the entire cloth seemed to glitter against the surrounding night.

She didn't know what it was going to be, this sparkling piece. It had started small, a little daydream she stitched together, over the years growing larger, more complex. It was almost as big as two pillows now, an altar cloth, perhaps—and still she had not finished it. She did not know when she would be able to stop.

Tristan had wrapped his fingers around her own, stepping closer, so that the presence of his body behind hers became intimate, and she could feel his breath against her temple. She did not dare move. She did not dare turn her head.

"I began it long ago," she said for a distraction, concentrating on the swan. "Years ago, actually. Before our marriage. Before the plague came, and everyone began to die."

His lips brushed where his breath had been, still light, fleeting. His other hand stole around her waist, holding her there.

"It's you," Amiranth said, fighting the urge to close her eyes, to lean back against him. She took her hand from his and placed it on the cloth, pointed to the elegant silver swan on its sapphire lake. "It was how I used to see you."

Tristan paused. His lips lifted from her temple, although he did not move away.

"This?" he asked, quiet puzzlement. "You saw me as this?"

Her voice grew slender. "I used to watch you from a distance at court. I used to admire you. You seemed so handsome to me. So alone. I pictured stars and night around you. You were . . . untouchable."

Another pause, longer; she felt him tilt his head, giving the cloth another look. Amiranth reached for it, pushing it back into the basket, embarrassed.

"It was just some girlish foolishness. Do not heed it, my lord."

"What if I wish to?" he asked, soft.

"Then you are a bigger fool than I was." She moved out of the circle of his arms. "I'm only finishing it now because it vexes me to have it remain undone."

"So . . . how do you see me now, Amiranth?"

She tried a cold smile. "Better not to ask."

He came to her, the light fully upon him now, revealing his face in orange and gold, growing bright in his eyes. She backed away until she caught herself doing it, then stopped, standing her ground. He smiled at her—a distant, distracted look—and took her by the shoulders, his fingers curving into her. His head lowered; he placed a kiss at the crest of her shoulder, at the edge of her gown. One hand slid down her back, forcing her to lean closer to him. He spoke against her skin.

"But I *am* asking."

She swallowed, keeping her hands clenched in her skirts. "Stop."

"How do you see me?" he asked, persistent, as he kissed her again, higher, a heated path up her neck.

"I—" She could not finish the thought. He had taken it from her, stolen her reason with his touch, the feel of his lips on her, the soft huff of his breath warming her.

"Let's make it fair. I will tell you first what I see," he said, all velvet and honey. "A woman beyond beauty, with a gentle heart and the quick mind of a strategist. A woman I never forgot, not even in death, Amiranth. The woman I love."

"Liar." She was dizzy with him, she was burning. "You don't love me."

"Come with me," Tristan whispered, drawing her to him, pulling her along so that she barely felt her feet moving—not to her bed but across the chamber, to the door that led to his. "I can prove it."

At the open archway they stopped. He brought his hands to her face and kissed her, not as soft as before, but with a hunger to it that awakened that part of her she did not want to consider. She grasped at her wits, trying not to succumb to the sweet humming call of him.

"Shallow man. You did not like me nearly so well when I was plain."

That hurt him, she could see that it did. But he hid it well, giving her no clue to his pain beyond the flash in his eyes. His forehead lowered to hers; his face blurred out of focus. "Amiranth." His voice was deep, almost grieving. "I did not like *myself*."

Before she could respond to that he was kissing her again, achingly tender. She felt restless, too hot in her skin, her gown too tight. She wanted to go forward with him and she did not. He took the choice from her by lifting her up suddenly, moving them both across the room to his bed.

It was massive, like his keep, fitting for the lord of this place. It was heavy and old, with thick, dark wood and curtains of its own—not sheer, but glimmering cloth-of-gold that fell all the way to the floor in weighted folds.

She felt the curtains slide against her as they passed,

and then she was in the bed itself, lost to the furs and rich blankets, fragrant, luscious. Her hand encountered something unfamiliar: rose petals, scattered across the sheets.

She frowned at them, watching them drift from her fingers in dabs of pink and cream and deep, deep red.

Tristan came down beside her, so close the folds of his robe settled over her, dusky green against her gown. He reached for the knots of her jeweled belt and she stopped him, their gazes locked, her hand tense around his.

"You said I could," he pointed out, reasonable.

She had. But she had not meant it like this—in his bed, with petals and softness and the teasing contact of his body against hers.

His hand moved anyway, not waiting for her response, sliding out of her grip to the belt again, simple knots, easy to unravel. The cloth-of-gold framed him, unreal, a shimmering crown to a pagan king.

The belt loosened; he pulled it free, pressing a kiss to her there, the curve of her waist, then took her hands and lifted her to sit, so that they faced each other in the pagan bed. Without a word he put his arms around her, no kisses now, his gaze holding hers, entrancing. She felt his fingers nimble against her back, finding the ties there, pulling them free. The tightness of her gown eased away, drawn over her head, fluttering to the floor. She wore only her undertunic now, a thin wool, fleecy white.

His hands grazed her, barely touching, her shoulders, her breasts. Her stomach, her thighs . . . back up again, drawing teasing circles against the shape of her. She was unable to look away from it, the tan of his skin against the white.

"How do you see me now, Amiranth?" His voice was husky, close to her ear. His lips touched her there, found her earlobe, withdrew. His hands were stroking, moving down her legs, his palms flat against her, drawing down, down . . . her calves, her ankles. With great care he lifted one slippered foot, and then the slipper was gone. The other foot. He traced her calves again, pushing up her tunic to reveal the stockings she wore, plain and warm. He scooped up a handful of rose petals and let them glide across her body, a contrast of colors.

"I see a dream," he murmured, watching his hands, the petals. "I see my dreams. How do you see me?"

She could not answer. There was a hardness in her throat; she could not speak at all. Tristan glanced up at her, dark and wild. She knew this look about him now. Aye, she did.

His robe had come open even more, held in place now by only the slash of his belt. The muscles of his stomach rippled as he moved; she had a glimpse of his shoulder, smooth skin, hard curves. With slow solemnity he ran one finger under the garter on her leg, testing the ties of it, then tugged it down and away, tossed to the shadowed room. The stocking unrolled against his palms, his fingers trailing along the tender flesh of her thighs, a caress disguised . . . down the length of her leg, exploring the shape of her beneath the plain fabric. She bit her lip as he did it all over again, her other leg now, and could not hide the shiver that took her.

With the stockings gone Tristan began to raise her tunic, until she had no choice but to lift her arms, helping him. Another shiver went through her as he finished. There was nothing about her now but the coverings of the bed, and him, his warmth faint against her. Amiranth clasped her arms over her chest and then released them, determined not to show her shyness, not to let him know the secret song that was awakening through her.

If he noticed her response he gave no hint of it. His hands and gaze had gone to her hair, pinned up in tight fashion since this morning. With great care he loosened the pins, pulling them from her one at a time until her hair fell free about her shoulders, down her arms, helping to hide her. The pins joined her slippers on the floor.

Now he paused to look at her openly, every bit of her, rose petals and unbound hair, a long, bold examination that sent an unwanted blush blossoming through her. Then he turned away, and all she had was his back, swathed in green, the black of his own hair falling against it. When he turned again he held something in his hands. A bowl, polished silver. His fingers dipped into it, and came out stained dark, wet. He held a gleaming blackberry between his fingertips.

He brought it to her, leaning over to place it against her lips. Amiranth felt the juice of it slipping into her mouth.

His gaze was almost slumberous, focused on the berry, her lips, that roguish look turned rapt across his face.

"I see my dreams," Tristan said again, slow and musing, as if he could not quite be sure.

She opened her mouth—she meant to protest, to say *something,* but instead she felt the blackberry, plump with juice, touching her tongue, his fingers against her lips. It was sweet and tangy, ripe with liquid. She had no choice but to accept it.

He brought her another, again placing it against her lips. Amiranth faltered, uncertain if she should continue, what it might mean, but even as she hesitated he met her eyes, intent and commanding.

She ate the berry, watching him, the way he smiled at that, completely sensual, knowing. When he leaned close she was perfectly still. Their lips met, slick with juice. She tasted the blackberry and him at once, and could not seem to breathe. Tristan pulled at her lower lip gently with his teeth, then kissed her deeply, finding her tongue, encouraging her to kiss him back.

He shifted. She felt his fingers against her, very cool, and when she looked down he had taken more berries, the dark liquid of them sliding down her body.

How do you see me?

He bent his head, following the juice, licking her skin, soft tongue, a heated sucking, to her breasts, her nipples. She watched as her hands came up to hold him there, her fingers lost in the waves of his hair. Swirls of deep purple decorated her skin, his mark upon her, his hands clutching at her, greedy, elegant fingers painting her stomach. Lower.

How did she see him?

Like fire darkly turned, a cool burning, painful and wanted.

She lay flat in the covers, tilting her head back, feeling him, his robe gone, his body lean, masculine, all that she did not know—that she wanted to learn. He moved on top of her and she felt the liquid run between them, crushed berries. He found her lips, and he tasted of untamed things, the wild forest, purple sugar.

Like the wind, a force she could not master, only feel.

Her body arched against his, eager for the weight of him, solid muscles and supple tension. The song of before—a deep thrumming, half forgotten—grew stronger in her, overwhelming. She pressed her lips to him, his shoulder, seeing her own hands adorned by blackberry juice, fluid sweetness that transferred to him, to her tongue, finding him, feeling the hard beating of his heart as she began her own exploration.

Like satin, like steel.

Rose petals clung to them both, their perfume heavy. She adored the tapered lines of her husband, how he moved, slow and sure, old memories coming back to her—but better, finer, her own secret dream returning, and no unhappy endings this time.

They were sitting up together. They were kissing as his hands skimmed her, urging her closer. She felt his legs come around her, her own around his waist, until their chests were crushed together, and the hard, urgent part of him stayed stiff against her belly.

Like sunlight over mist, too bright and beautiful to take in.

She watched his face, comely and fine, a devil's smile for her, black eyes that glittered. He grasped her buttocks and moved her against him, rubbing them together, and the song in her turned fell and potent. She held him fast. She threw her head back and closed her eyes, smiling her own fierce smile as Tristan bent his head and tasted her again.

Like the ocean, strong and sweet and salt, bitter and clean, she could not catch her breath from him.

They moved together easily, effortlessly, and she was down on her back amid the petals, and he was above her with her legs still wrapped around him, craving him. He entered her quickly, a delicious push, and it didn't hurt—not like before, no agony. She didn't even have time to flinch; there was only a strange stinging under the pleasure, and then not even that . . . just the feel of him inside her, building their rhythm, a long, slow sliding that began to quicken, sharpening the craving.

Like the sun itself, beyond her comprehension.

They were entangled. They were entwined, they were lost together. It was roses and sugar and a strong building ache, a thing she could not name. It was Tristan, wild and pagan, gold behind him, raven hair, eyes of jet. It was his body over hers. It was his teeth against her skin, his words, ragged murmurs she could not make out, breathless, her name—her true name—worshipful.

Like her soul.

She fell apart around him, with great tremors and bright joy. She felt him find his own release, holding her even closer than before, his body pumping against hers, a sound like anguish low in his throat. She took him in and kept him there as it happened, her arms clasped around his back, her face turned away where he could not see, and guess what lay behind her eyes.

Like love.

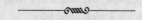

TRISTAN WATCHED HER AS SHE SLEPT, HIS ROSE-TUMBLED wife. She was painted in indigo by him; they were both bedecked with soft petals, artful patterns along their limbs. It was full dark at last, the heart of the night, and yet he could still see her. She was more radiant than the night, she glowed amber and ivory before him. He held her and cherished her warmth beneath the scented sheets.

His dreams had come true. By fate or good fortune, he didn't know, he didn't care. All that mattered was here with him now. The past eight years were naught but a distant nightmare.

She slept so peacefully as Tristan kept his quiet watch, admiring her, everything about her.

His wife. Amiranth.

The nightingale outside his window began a lilting song as he settled back in the bed, bringing her close.

Chapter Fourteen

TRISTAN WAS TEMPTED TO LET AMIRANTH AVOID him again the next morning. He had had to leave before she woke, and she seemed flustered at the breakfast, avoiding his eyes, her cheeks flagged with color.

By accident or design, strands of her hair had slipped free from their knots; they joined to become a curl down the side of her face, falling into a deep spiral, darkened gold against delicate pink.

Only hair, he thought abruptly, remembering her words. Yet he would never say such a thing about it—not the burnished, rich amber gracing her, the way it shone and sparkled. The way it had felt to him last night, both silky and fine, the way it slid through his fingers, fantasy turned true. How it had felt on his face, the scent of it, of her, amid the sweet layers of blonde, heavy and warm. *Only hair,* she had said. But to him it was a part of *her,* and so a part of something nearly in-comprehensible: lush womanhood, the promise of sanc-tuary in her arms. The rapture of last night, and all his unspoken dreams of her.

So Tristan smiled at her at the table and decided to overcome her morning shyness, making certain she kept close to him, that their fingers would touch, that he spoke to her in words he almost did not listen to, dis-tracted by the faded smudge of blue on her skin he could see just above the cut of her bodice—blackberry juice, scrubbed faint but not quite gone.

That made him smile again. She noticed. He watched her take a long breath, and found the new blush that washed over her completely captivating.

Tristan was not the only man at the table to take note of it. His casual glance found his brother staring at Amiranth, his brows drawn together. One of the hounds came up beside him, sniffing for food—Liam ran a hand over its head absently, then pushed it away, still fixed on Amiranth. Almost slowly he looked up and discovered Tristan's glare.

Liam looked quickly down at the table. When the dog came again, he cuffed it, keeping his face lowered.

Very deliberately Tristan drew Amiranth's hand from her lap, bringing it to his lips. When she turned to him he captured her face and kissed her lips—there, in the open, for all to see.

She pulled back; the pink of her cheeks deepened. He could not tell if it was passion or embarrassment. It did not matter. He would not suffer another man—*any* man—to think his wife open for claiming.

The meal progressed quietly, sleepy servants and yawning nobles, desultory conversation. Even the dogs seemed lethargic. Many people were still recovering from the festivities of the days before. It would be a while before the castle found its routine again, before the people settled back into their accustomed places. . . .

Or rather, not. With the help of Silas James, Tristan had been making quiet plans for those brash young knights who had served his brother. He knew they were restless, ill tempered with the shift in their lives. He was not blind to the sharp looks thrown to him, to the clusters of men and women who watched him with disgruntled faces. He almost could not blame them—they were young and impetuous, bolder than they thought the world to be. Sooner or later they might be foolish enough to start more than just the evil rumors he had been hearing.

He would not abide such surly thoughts, much less any action against him. Indeed, he did not have to.

He was going to send them all away—every one of them—with their wives and horses and belongings, whatever they had brought to his castle. He would deed one of his estates to Liam, on the condition that they all remain there, forever. Let them stew in their resentment far from Glynwallen.

Perhaps he would give them Safere. He felt a biting irony at that.

"My lord, I have a thought," said his brother, underneath the steady murmur of the meal.

Tristan came back to the moment, taking a sip of ale, inviting Liam to continue with a wave of his hand.

"I had thought perhaps that I might leave Glynwallen."

Tristan set down the ale. "Indeed?"

"Aye." Liam kept his gaze straight on Tristan, not glancing for even a moment at Amiranth, who had stilled with focused attention on him. "I have a yearning to travel—and you do not need me here, after all." He spoke carefully, as if considering his words. "A few of the knights would like the same—if it pleases my lord."

Tristan studied him, hiding his surprise. "I see no reason why not. It is a vast world, brother."

"It is," agreed Liam, more quickly now. "I thought we might tour the country, and stay awhile at one of the estates."

Tristan nodded. "Which one?"

"Whichever you decide. Merlyff, I thought."

Beside him Amiranth drew up straighter, her hands clenched against the edge of the table. Liam talked on, oblivious.

"It is a distance from here, and has not been attended to in some time, I fear."

"And so could use a guiding hand," Tristan finished for him, assessing.

"Aye. Or so I thought."

"I think it a most excellent idea." He spoke over Amiranth's gasp. "Perhaps you might need more than a few men, after all. Perhaps you might need . . . a good number of them. And their wives. To make the place habitable again."

Liam raised his brows. "Do you think so, my lord?"

"I do." Tristan gave him a measuring look. "I think your plan should be enacted with all haste, in fact. I dread the thought of any property of *mine* being misused. I am sure with you there, all will be set to right again."

Liam gazed back at him, not quite a challenge, breaking it off only when Amiranth spoke in an overbright voice.

"Merlyff. I have heard much of the promised beauty of this estate. Perhaps I might join you there, Lord Liam."

There was an awkward pause. Liam seemed startled, the other people around them uncertain. Tristan turned to her and she was staring back at him, haughty. The flush marking her now was clearly anger.

"You will always be most welcome, my lady," Liam finally said, gallant. "But it is indeed a long journey. I think it best if you wait to visit, until we may be certain the manor is fit for your grace."

"Yes," said Tristan flatly. "It will be some time before my lady will be able to see the place."

Amiranth clamped her lips closed, her eyes flashing as she took in his face. She rose stiffly, dipping a brief curtsy, leaving the table, and then the hall.

Tristan watched her go—they all did, staring. There could be no glib excuses for her withdrawal this time; he didn't even bother to try. Instead he fought the feeling that was flooding through him now: jealousy, caustic and undeniable.

She only wanted the manor, he told himself. It was not the man, merely the place. He had promised it to her once—or rather, promised it to her cousin—and now that she was thwarted again, she had struck back. She did not truly want to be with Liam over him.

But the jealousy stayed, black and bubbling. Tristan found it impossible to look at his brother again, and see the thoughtful expression on his handsome young face.

———— ◦〰◦ ————

AMIRANTH PACED AWAY AND FOUND HERSELF OUT-side the keep, into the clouds and thick fog of the early day, fuming.

How dare he! How dare he give away *her* estate—as if by last night all scores had settled between them. They were not! Last night had been only . . .

She did not know precisely what last night had been. She could not—would not—say. It had been inevitable, she knew that. It had been only what she had come to realize had to happen between them.

No, she thought, stopping outside the walls of the granary. She was lying to herself. Last night had been anything but expected.

She had known she had no real right to refuse him. He was her husband—she had declared it to all—and so had the law of both the church and the land behind him. Better to submit to that, and avoid the torment she kept feeling around him, the yearning, her self-disdain at reaching for him, again and again.

She had thought it would be as it had been the first time, pain and humiliation, a terrible hurt she would nurse to healing. She almost welcomed it, the rough ending to her soft reveries. Indeed, part of her had thought to use it as a weapon against him in her heart . . . to take the pain and turn it into hatred, if she could. Amiranth wanted to hate still. It would be an easier thing than how she truly felt.

All she had known of physical love had been her wedding night. How could she have anticipated how it had actually been between them? Rose petals and black-berries, firelight and furs. Cloth-of-gold all around them as Tristan came to her, and touched her, and made her feel such things . . . such vivid pleasure she might have screamed with it. . . .

Perhaps she had. It was a delicious haze to her in this cool misted morning, a memory both warmer and less tangible than the fog she walked through now.

And there might be a baby from it. Amiranth hugged her arms around herself, dreaming of that, of what might come.

She heard the call of a rider not too distant, the re-turning shout of the sentinel over the gate. Through the haze on the ground figures turned murky; the outline of a man on a horse seemed to materialize before her and then fade off again, so close she heard the particular sharp strike of metal horseshoes against the stones.

She was turning away when she heard the man's voice again, the words muffled by fog.

"Where is my lord?" he asked urgently.

A boy answered him—presumably from the stables, taking charge of the horse.

"In the great hall, sir, breaking his fast."

"And where is Tristan Geraint?"

Amiranth froze, recognizing who it was that spoke: Hugh Fletcher, the discontented castellan.

The stableboy seemed confused. "I have told you, sir. In the great hall."

"I meant Lord *Liam,* stupid child," growled the man.

"In the great hall as well, I suppose." The boy sounded indifferent to the insult; she heard the clipped steps of the steed following him as he walked away.

Silence. Either the castellan was gone too, shrouded with fog, or he stood as she did, listening hard to the distant sounds of the bailey. She waited, breathing through her mouth, searching, searching—seeing nothing of a man before her, only patches of buildings revealed and engulfed again in slow drifts.

She could not say why she felt the tingle of alarm running through her. She could not explain why Hugh Fletcher's voice gave her a chill, why she felt so compelled to rush back to the keep, to find Tristan and tell him what had happened. She knew only that there was something ugly afoot, and that he deserved to know of it. She had heard naught of the old castellan for days, not since well before the feast—God knew what knavery he had invented in such a while. She had not come this far with Tristan to see it all fall apart through the sly pickings of a deposed servant.

Amiranth made her way through the mists back to the keep.

———————— ⌒⌐⌐ ————————

LIAM GERAINT WAS ON HIS WAY TO MASS, WALKING slowly down the cold stone corridor that led to the chapel. The knights and ladies he himself had brought to prominence now passed by him, avoiding his gaze, speaking in animated whispers about what they had overheard at breakfast: that they would be leaving, that he had surrendered to his brother, and was abandoning the estate to the usurper and his plebeian guard.

Liam gritted his teeth and let them gossip. No man would risk disputing him, not if he wished to keep this idle life Liam supplied. They could leave with him or go to the devil, he didn't care which.

That he was giving up Glynwallen put him in a foul temper; forfeiting the title of earl was bad enough, but to leave the castle, this rich and fortified place that he had made his own. . . .

For all that Merlyff was a little jewel of a manor, it was meager consolation for what he had relinquished. But a consolation was better than nothing at all. He had no choice; too much of his life could return to haunt him beneath the steady scrutiny of others. No matter how it galled him, he knew he would do well to re-member that.

Rapid footsteps behind him, a hand on his arm. He turned to find his castellan before him, bowing, speaking under his breath.

"My lord! My liege lord—"

"Where the devil have you been?" Liam shook off the man's hand, irritated.

Hugh Fletcher came closer, beaded with moisture,

his eyes burning. "I have news of your brother and his wife, my lord. Such news—I have learned a thing that will surely undo them both. I have proof that the man who claims to be Tristan Geraint lives a lie, at the very least!"

Liam quickly scanned the passageway, then pulled Hugh back against the wall, letting the others walk by.

"Tell me all," he commanded, and the castellan began to speak.

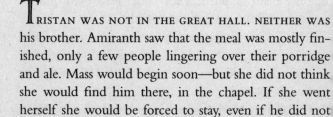

Tristan was not in the great hall. Neither was his brother. Amiranth saw that the meal was mostly finished, only a few people lingering over their porridge and ale. Mass would begin soon—but she did not think she would find him there, in the chapel. If she went herself she would be forced to stay, even if he did not attend. Better to check any other likely place first. If he was at Mass, they could not speak anyway.

Not in his rooms, or hers.

People stared at her as she passed by; she did not care for their veiled curiosity, she did not have time to worry about them. She could not even find Tristan's steward. It must be Mass after all, she decided, and turned back to find the chapel, keeping her eyes and ears sharp for any clue of Hugh Fletcher. He was as absent as the rest.

She checked the great hall one last time, and saw then what she had not before: a flash of color above her, movement in the depths of the solar, overlooking the chamber. She searched closer, seeking the betrayal of motion again, and was finally rewarded—darkened colors, a dark face. Her husband up there, taken by shadows, looking down at her. He made no sign that he saw her.

Amiranth had not been to the solar before. It was Tristan's domain, and she had not felt comfortable enough to go exploring there. But she found the stairs to it easily, narrow and twisting, ending in a landing with a solid wooden door before her, shut tight.

She opened the door.

A hushed place, unlit, not very unlike the solar at Iving. Long columns at the end of it, stately and cold. A single window at the other end, braced by chiseled pillars. Grand furnishings, tapestries and rushes and chairs strewn with cushions. There were elaborate iron braziers empty of coal. There were carved tables inlaid with pearl, and a board of chess set up with heavy marble pieces that turned ghostly before her.

"My lord?"

He appeared from behind one of the columns, quiet, part of the dimness. She faltered for a moment, seeing him so suddenly, and tried to capture what it was about him that had changed since she saw him last, not so very long ago.

Same tunic, midnight blue and black edging. Same hose, same boots. Same look upon his face, guarded, alert. His hair still fell unruly to his shoulders. His eyes were just as unreadable.

He wore a sword, she realized. Aye, a sword and scabbard, low on his hips, broad and thick with a plain silver handle. She had not seen him so armed since that day he rode out of Safere, off to vanish into France.

She wasn't certain what it meant, that sword. It did not match the elegance of the room, or his fine tunic. It was clearly a weapon made for war, for killing. When she paired it with the surly look on his face, the chill of before returned to her.

He brought up a hand and rubbed at his temple, still watching her.

"Are you well?" she asked, not at all what she had meant to say.

"Aye." His hand lowered, going to rest lightly on the hilt of the sword.

She gathered her senses. "We must talk."

A corner of his mouth lifted, sardonic, a subtle danger.

"You will not leave me, Amiranth."

"What?"

"You will not leave." He pushed off the pillar, moving toward her with that dark grace he had when he wished, a shadow come to life before her, looming tall, coming close. "Not to Merlyff, or anywhere else without me. You are mine now. You always were. Never think otherwise."

"I'll think what I please," she retorted, unnerved by the warning in his tone. She backed away a few steps, to keep space between them. "You do not control me."

"Mine," he repeated, and put more meaning into that single word than she had ever heard before: threat and hostility and possession, something black-edged and disturbed.

He was not rational. . . .

Liam's warning came back to her, and it seemed, in this instant, to be a very real thing, not mere idle words. Tristan was *not* rational. Not now—perhaps not truly ever. He was as inconstant as the shadows themselves, ever lapping and changing with the light.

He watched her with a smile turned mocking, almost not there, slight beneath the cold sparkle to his eyes. One hand reached out to her.

"Come here to me."

She felt her feet stay fixed to the floor, unable to run away, or go forward, to obey that hushed command.

"Amiranth," he said, shading her name with that darkness. "Come to me."

Her lips parted. She could find no words to express her dismay, her sudden loss of heart—the trickle of fear that sent her hands to fists, hidden in her skirts.

"Wife," he whispered, and took the first step himself, holding her easily with his gaze. "My lady wife. Do you think to escape me? Is that what you wish?"

"No," she breathed, and managed another step away.

"No," he echoed, still mocking, so quiet and deadly. "No, I think not. Come to me, Amiranth. Come now."

And she did, helpless, fearful that if she did not—if she turned and ran—he would only catch her, and unleash the black thing within him.

She stopped before him, staring not at his eyes, so strange and unfocused, but at the collar of his tunic, a logical thing: stitched seams and an intricate pattern, something she understood. Not his face, with that look of a lost soul upon it.

His hand came up, cupped her cheek, stroking downward to her breast, her waist, where he curved his fingers around her, forcing her to take the last halting step to him.

"There. Are you pleased?" she asked, in a voice that hardly trembled.

He did not reply; his other hand followed his first, enclosing the other half of her waist, so that his fingers nearly encircled her, an unsubtle measure of control. They remained like that, so close she could almost hear his heartbeat. Her own was the sound of a tempest in her head, to match the fear running through her.

"I killed a man once," Tristan said, a soft rush near her ear. "More than once, in fact. But this particular man was my friend. Did you know that?"

She shook her head.

"Of course you didn't. I've never told you. I've never told anyone. But it is true, Amiranth. I killed him because he betrayed me."

She found the nerve to meet his eyes. "Was it your brother?" she asked, and then could not believe she had said it.

His mocking smile returned, no comfort. "No."

"I—" She tried to pull away and he held her there, his grip no longer light against her, but firm, unyielding.

"He was my friend. You knew him once. Sir Gilbert, a vassal of mine. We went to France together."

A vision of a man's face came to her—a boy, almost, who had compared her to her cousin, and laughed at the thought of war.

"We were captured together," Tristan continued,

"and jailed together. We did it all together, my lady—squired, gamed, courted, sparred together. But what do you think happened in France, my wife? What do you think he did, when those damned French came to us, chained to our walls?"

Amiranth no longer moved, unable to resist the lure of his eyes, the cold blackness there, the winter look all about him. "I don't know," she whispered.

"Betrayal," he said down to her, cool as ice. "He let loose my name, and they snatched it from his lips, tore him up for it." His face turned harder, almost savage, a mask of a handsome man, feral in the darkness. "So I did it. As soon as they left—I found my way over to him, and did it. He was suffering, you see—the blood—so much damned *blood*—"

She braced her hands against his arms. "You're hurting me."

"They would have given him a slow death, so I gave him a quick one—I could not bear his moans—and he *thanked* me for it, as he died, he *thanked* me—"

"Stop!"

Her voice was broken, shrill with fear. It seemed to reach him at last; his hands loosened from her, then fell away. He blinked and stepped back, frowning down at her, rubbing his temple again. She took two rapid steps from him, not turning, staring at his face.

"I loved him," Tristan said to her, quiet. "I would have told them myself what they wanted, if he had not first."

She shivered, afraid but not, trying to forget the face

of the man named Gilbert, trying not to picture him in death, with Tristan beside him.

"I understand love, Amiranth. I understand it full well. Know that I love you. Know that you will not leave me. Not ever."

"I would not betray you," she said, trying to make it sound true.

"No," he agreed softly. "You would not."

"My lord?"

Neither of them turned at the new voice at the door. They stayed locked on each other, emotion spun taut between them.

"Forgive me, my lord." It was Liam.

Amiranth finally turned; Hugh Fletcher stood just behind Tristan's brother, his gaze direct to hers, the light to his eyes almost triumphant.

"I do not mean to interrupt," said Liam, very smooth. "Yet I fear I must discuss with you a matter of some urgency."

Amiranth glanced quickly back to Tristan, alarmed by both Liam's voice and that look of the castellan. She had not told him—he was not prepared, she had meant to warn him, and it had gotten swallowed in their moment, and now—

"My lady." Tristan nodded to her, a clear dismissal, ignoring her gaze.

"My lord," she responded, going to him. "I would stay."

His mouth tightened, forbidding. Amiranth maintained her stance, willing him to meet her eyes. At last he did; the emotions there made a connection she felt to her toes. Anger, confusion, turmoil—pain.

He gave her a short nod of his head. She half turned to the two other men, keeping her eyes lowered, so that they could not read her face.

Liam spoke, an embarrassed laugh. "Well. This is most awkward. But I've had news of your wife, my lord. Strange news."

Amiranth looked up fully. Tristan shifted behind her, placing a hand upon her shoulder, light now, no sign of the terrible strength he had held her with before.

"What news?" he asked, impassive.

"My man has traveled to Safere." Liam took in Amiranth, almost regretful. "What he found there was most puzzling."

"Allow me to guess," said Tristan. From his voice she could imagine the expression on his face—arrogant, bored. "A deserted estate, no people, no plants or live-stock. It fell to the plague months past. I was there, brother. This is not news to me."

"Aye. The plague touched us all, I fear. But perhaps you can explain to me, my lord, why my lady stands here before us, yet her grave is back there."

Tristan's only reaction was fleeting tension through his fingers, so fast she might have imagined it.

"A most peculiar thing," Liam went on, keen as a hawk, "that the lady yet lives . . . or so you have claimed."

Amiranth heard her own response, her voice far more assured than she felt. "A simple mistake. The woman in that grave is in fact my noble cousin. When the plague first struck Safere, many were afflicted. I had gone to beg a service of prayer for us at a nearby convent. She died while I was gone—the grave digger was confused."

"And the stone cutter as well?" Liam asked pleasantly.

"It was a confusing time for all of us, I would say." She threw him a chilly smile, a reflection of the cold fright in her.

"And so it was." Tristan slipped his hand down her arm, a caress the other two followed with their eyes, his fingers finding her waist again, still light, still relaxed. "I must remember to send someone to Safere to remedy this sad mistake. But do not trouble yourselves over the past of my wife, good sirs. She is safe now with me."

It was a challenge, cloaked in velvet but still quite apparent. Amiranth felt her smile frozen in place, praying they would bow to it, and not demand more proof.

"A most woeful tale," commented Lord Liam, still pleasant. "God grant your cousin peace, my lady. Perhaps you might know the answer to another riddle that pesters me."

She waited, careful of her breathing, that it would not expose the racing of her heart.

"My man heard strange stories on the road. Stories of a couple who traveled the countryside. Thieves, they were called. A man and a woman—a dark man, and a very fair woman—gone from town to town, stealing food, stealing horses. . . ."

"How distressing," Amiranth said, unemotional.

"Indeed. Even more distressing to consider that they

appeared to start from the general direction of Safere, and slowly make their way to this castle."

"What are you saying, my lord?"

"They were, by all accounts, dangerous thieves, my lady. Liars, outlaws, pretending to be what they were not. Did you perchance come across them in your travels?"

"Certainly not." Tristan's hand had gone tighter on her waist; she could not see his face, and tell if he was closer to rage, or just fear, as she was. From the corner of her eye she caught the gleam of his sword, long and heavy against his leg. "I do not consort with common thieves."

"A whore," growled Hugh Fletcher, breaking his silence. "She was a whore, they said. She stole money and a fine mare, marked just as the one you rode—"

She felt Tristan's hand leave her and turned to him, but she was too slow, and it was too late. He had his sword drawn, the slither of steel sharp against the scabbard. It flashed before her, a slash of silver death cutting through the air around her, aimed for the castellan.

Fletcher stumbled backward and Tristan followed him easily. The tip of the sword came to rest against the center of the man's chest.

"I don't believe I understand you, peasant. Do you dare insult my wife?" The sword remained steady; Amiranth swallowed her cry. Tristan was centered with full menace on the castellan. Liam had fallen back into the depths of the room, silent.

"I would not insult the Countess of Haverlocke,"

Hugh said, and the implication in his voice was clear: *This is not she.*

"My lord." Amiranth stepped close to her husband, watching the blade, the way the very end of it had become lost in the man's brown tunic. Tristan paid her no attention. All the danger of before had come back to him, manifested in the shine of his sword, the way his fingers flushed red and white around the hilt. Yet when he spoke, his words were perfectly civil.

"I know not what you heard on your travels. I care not. I want you gone from my demesne. Now. And never return, or I swear to you by my oath you will be sorry for it."

A pause, both men staring at each other.

Then Tristan pulled the sword away with a flourish, a skillful move that belied the stark threat of the moment, sheathing it again. He looked at Liam, pressed back against a table, and his words to him were no less cordial.

"Will you join your spy, brother? Or shall you keep your unseemly thoughts to yourself from this day on?"

Liam's eyes flew to Amiranth, then to the castellan, pallid beneath his beard. He straightened.

"A thousand apologies. I had a mystery, that was all. My lady has explained it well."

Tristan nodded. "What an excellent conclusion. Upon consideration, Liam, I have decided it would be best if you left for Merlyff immediately. Gather your men and leave soon—no later than this week." He glanced back to Hugh Fletcher. "And both of you know this: I will not tolerate any gossip regarding the countess. It appears I have an insufferable temper when it comes to my wife."

Without even a bow Fletcher left, and then Liam, until there was only Amiranth left to stare at her husband, wondering at the thin, savage smile on his face.

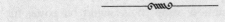

H E DID NOT COME TO HER THAT NIGHT.

She had dreaded his visit; she had coveted it. Amiranth hardly knew what she thought any longer. Tristan had turned her emotions inside out; she did not know him, or even herself.

He had said he loved her. In the depths of danger in his solar she believed him at last—how else to explain the look in his eyes, the awful grief there, the anger? How else to explain his conduct, the words and deeds of a man gone beyond reason?

He had confessed himself a killer. Yet she felt no fear of him—not like that. He had lived through a thing so wrenching she could not fathom it in her worst imaginings. His life had been stolen from him as surely as he had been stolen from her, by war or fate, it hardly mattered.

He threatened her and the people around him. He acted wildly, almost madly.

Yet she yearned for him. She waited in her bed for a husband who did not appear, and fell asleep only when she could no longer struggle against the night.

She did not dream. And in the morning, he was still gone.

Amiranth went to breakfast, missing him, but he was not there, either. Half the great hall remained empty; she had heard the grumblings of the young nobles as she walked the halls. She passed the ladies' quarters and noted the many harried maids within, the barbed voices of the noblewomen directing the packing. They complained loudly at how soon they would be gone, the undue haste of this move, the slowness of the maids, the unfairness of their lives. . . .

Good. Let them depart, and take their complaints with them.

But where was Tristan? Why did she feel so desolate without him?

Lord Liam was missing from breakfast as well, along with his treacherous castellan. Only one trusted face remained: Silas James stayed close to her. He had seated her at the table, sent quick orders for her food. She felt his steady watch behind her as she ate, and gathered a small comfort from it. A part of her wanted to ask him of Tristan, but pride kept her mute, and so she ate in silence.

Amiranth caught herself examining the solar balcony, but there was no shadow-man standing over her today. It was empty—she confirmed it after the meal, just to be certain. Perhaps he had returned to his room by now. . . .

Down the main hallway she heard a strange rise in noise, sharper than the usual murmur of gossip. She followed it to the source, her pace quickening, quickening, until she stood at the entrance to the keep garden, a place she had not visited since that afternoon days ago, when Tristan had discovered her true self, and made a vow to bind her to him forever.

The garden appeared little changed. The grass was just as green, the trees as tall and leafy. The flowers still gave off their summer fragrance beneath a clear blue sky.

But there was a crowd of people spilling over the path, trampling the elegant maze of plants and pebbles. Amiranth made her way though them, all the way up to the curtain of willow leaves waving with the breeze. She saw then what everyone else did.

A man lay curled beneath the strands of willow, his body limp, his face gone slack and ghastly. It was Hugh Fletcher, and a great pool of blood had spread black beneath him, staining the lush grass.

Chapter Fifteen

━━━━━━━━⟨ᴗᴜᴜᴗ⟩━━━━━━━━

AMIRANTH STARED AT THE BODY, FEELING ODDLY calm. She turned around, seeing no one she knew, and so addressed the man nearest her, a redheaded fellow gone almost as white as the dead man.

"Bring Silas James here. At once!" she added, when he did not move. The man started, bowing, then retreated through the people.

She glanced back at the perfect peace of the garden, green willow leaves rising to the sky, sunlight warm on her head, and almost could not bring herself to look down again. Hugh Fletcher still lay there—most clearly murdered.

"Step back," she ordered, facing the crowd. "Back, I say!"

She got them to shift as one, the mass of them moving reluctantly, not far, and not for long.

With her back to them she bent down to the body, her skirts clutched high in one hand, avoiding the blooded grass. She touched the brown tunic above the blood, lifting it to see the gash that had severed the cloth: a single cut, as if from the solitary thrust of a blade, entering his ribs. She knew enough of knives to realize that this was not the work of a dagger—only a sword could have done such a thing.

Amiranth dropped the tunic, standing, fighting the nausea that wanted to rise in her. She could not seem to take a deep enough breath.

"Sweet Mary, what has happened here?"

Liam at her side, his voice loud and stunned, his gaze to her horrified.

"He is dead," she said, witless, a conspicuous truth.

"My lady—do not look at such a thing! Come away!"

"No." She shook her head at him, pulling at the grip he had on her arm. "I'm waiting. The steward will soon come."

"My lady—Amiranth—please." Liam's voice lowered; the sunlight angled across him. In her jumbled state of mind she thought she saw Tristan for an instant, just as he had appeared that first time in the royal court. She raised a hand to her eyes, wavering, and when she looked up it was Liam again.

"I pray you, at least sit down," he said, and led her to a bench she had not even noticed nearby, a simple block of hewn granite, speckled with leafy shadow. She sat, ignoring Liam now, ignoring them all, her attention fixed on the terrible shape by the willow.

And Silas James did come. Liam left her to speak with him, and then the people crowded close again, and she could not see any of it. Her gaze fell to her lap, to her hands, clenched against her skirts. The colors of the grass at her feet seemed too bright at once, hurting her eyes. She closed them.

A new voice, prompting a hush in all the others. She knew who it would be. She knew his pitch, the inflection of his words, such easy command.

Her eyes opened. Tristan was by the body, nearly a head taller than everyone else. She saw him turn to see her, a cautious look, and then away again.

Amiranth stared at a rose bush to her left, marking the entrance back to the path. It had blooms the color of sea coral. The petals were small and delicate, the centers dabs of yellow. There was a bit of cloth caught against one of the thorns.

Not just any cloth. A beautiful velvet, in fact. Bicolored, indigo and dark crimson stitched together. The colors of two great houses, merged as one.

Everything else faded away. She saw only the velvet, a slender, tattered piece, obviously ripped from something much larger.

A mantle.

Almost listlessly she reached for it, plucking it from the thorn, pressing it into her palm, and then her palm into her skirts.

"What did you find, my lady?"

Liam stood before her, concerned, a throng of people behind him.

"Nothing. Only a leaf."

"And this!" cried Liam, triumphant. She watched, sickened, as he bent to the sea coral bush again, and from the thorns produced a second bit of velvet she had not seen, this one mostly indigo, the crimson a mere threading along one side.

"What is it?" asked someone.

Amiranth shrugged, her heart in her throat.

"Velvet," mused Liam. He held it up to Tristan, so that all could see. "What colors, my lord? They seem familiar to me."

Amiranth felt turned to stone, as mindless and cold as the granite bench. She saw Tristan walk close, examine the cloth. Their eyes met across the grass. His were blacker than night, inscrutable.

She rose, still keeping her own shred of velvet clutched tight in her fist, and pushed past the people, out of the garden, back into the dim corridors of the keep. She walked sedately, no hurry, aware of the looks she garnered, the speculation behind her.

After rounding two corners and finding herself at last alone, she broke into a run.

Her room was empty. She shut the door, pressing her back to it, then turned and locked it, her fingers trembling. Gulping air, she raced to the door that connected their quarters, swinging it wide—empty again.

The lock on his door was harder to turn, but she managed it, grimacing with the effort. When it was done she stared wildly around his chamber, her hands clenched up in her hair.

Where was it? Where would it be? Oh God, she had to find it.

His trunks were all together, and she found it in th
second one, right on top, tossed there carelessly, no
even folded. Amiranth lifted the heavy cloak and held i
up to the light of the window.

There were two tears along the bottom, very close t
each other. She did not even have to match her own bi
of velvet to the rents, although she did it anyway, spread
ing it out on the floor, going to her knees, aligning th
exact fit of her little piece to the longer tear.

Amiranth gathered it all up, went back into he
room—where the fire in the hearth was still blazing—
and tossed the mantle in.

For a moment she feared she had smothered the fire
but no, it came back, flames dancing up to lick aroun
the edges of cloth, kindling slow, then faster, the color
of it gradually blackening before her.

She watched it burn, her hands pressed over he
heart, the heat of the fire growing hot upon her face.

In time she remembered the torn piece in her hand
she threw that in, as well.

The door to her chamber opened. The fire grev
brighter with the draft, and settled back again as th
door closed.

Tristan stood alone at the entrance, the key to he
room still visible in his hand. He was not watching he
but the leaping flames, the charred velvet, thick blacl
smoke rising to vanish behind the hood of the fireplace

She could not find words for him. She could not fin
anything—not thought or sense at the sight of him, th
tense angles of his face, the lift of his lips, a wry ac
knowledgment as he took in the mantle.

He approached her, dropping the key on a table as he passed, and the only thought that came clear to her was: *I hope he locked the door again.*

Then he was there in front of her, his hands at her shoulders. He held her carefully, lightly, as she stared up into his face.

He seemed about to speak but didn't, instead lowering his head to hers, a kiss that nearly bruised her, the careful touch of before gone with just a single beat of her heart, their bodies brought together, their own heat rediscovered.

It was as if she had gone up in flames herself. Her fears of before—of discovery, of him—turned to smoke under his hands, his lips, her body arching into his as he caught her to him harder still and held her fast. He was ungentle, grasping, surrounding her, pushing at her until Amiranth felt the wall behind her back, a cold contrast to Tristan. It did not satisfy him; he pushed at her still, his hips against hers, kissing her lips, her face, his hands tangled in her hair. His knee pushed her legs apart, roughly, as if she resisted him.

Amiranth turned her head away, dragging in the cool air. He tugged at her bodice now, a loose thing, pulling it tight down her shoulders so that he could find her skin there with his mouth.

"Wife," he said, a low whisper against her, gliding over her throat, her shoulders. Down to her breasts. "Wife, wife, wife . . ."

She kept her hands against him for balance, kissing him eagerly when he came back to her, glossy black hair against her fingers. He did not kiss her as he began

to lift her skirts, only stared into her eyes, both of ther
panting, captivated. She felt his hands against her leg
her thighs, skimming her hose, her garters—above tha
to her bare skin. The touch of his palms against he
there went through her like a jolt, how he followed th
curves of her, reaching higher, rubbing the edge of h
hand against the most sensitive part of her.

He kissed her again, deep and long, all the whi
teasing her, keeping up the rhythm of his hand until h
was covered in her wetness, and she was rocking int
him, a whimper in her throat.

He knew her so well—he did, he knew exactly hov
to touch her, what it meant when she pressed herself i
to him, feeling his arousal. But he kept up his tormen
until she moved her hands and stroked his hardnes
finding his shaft even past his tunic, learning the shap
of him through the soft cloth.

Tristan stilled, his breathing uneven, his eyes fierce
jet black that glittered. He took her hands and togethe
they sank to the carpet, Amiranth on top of him, strad
dling him, and his hands were at her hips, pulling
pulling. She needed no encouragement to find hir
again, to free him from the ties of his hose.

She felt him against her, smooth heat, pushing at he
tormenting. She placed her hand on his shaft and guide
him to the place where it felt best, a teasing contact, s
that she closed her eyes and bit her lip with the pleasur
of it.

Tristan groaned. He shoved her skirts aside, and wit
a quick thrust he entered her, straining to go deepe

Amiranth eased lower, her knees far apart, marveling at this new position, the incredible feel of him inside her. She began to move, slowly, languorously, until his hands at her hips forced her faster, exciting another whimper from her.

He watched her as they rocked together, her handsome dark husband, with his hair falling free behind him, his lips turned sensual, a carnal look. Amiranth bent over him as her climax shimmered through her, gasping against his shoulder, hiding her face.

Tristan wrapped his arms around her; with a lithe roll he was on top, his lips to her cheek, finding his own release within seconds. She heard him whisper her name in a long, ragged note.

Her gown was twisted around them both, their bodies still wet and shamelessly joined. He lifted his head and gazed down at her, out of breath, the fire smoldering behind him.

"I love you," Tristan said, defiant, and didn't wait for her response, kissing her again, slow and heavy, erotic. She tasted him and felt her heart fill her chest, aching.

She believed him; from the depths of her soul she believed him, and now, after all these years of longing for him, she did not know what it meant. He loved her, yes. It might be the love of a madman, of a killer, but it *was* love, a total and absolute claiming of her.

Madman or not, she was bound to him, and had been for nearly as long as she had known herself. It was a spell of her own making, her comely knight with a sobering past, and a touch that could enthrall her.

Amiranth brushed her fingers across his lips, feeling the words as he said them again, his eyes steady upon her.

"I love you."

"I know," she replied, hopeless.

He pulled away from her, leaving her with a rush of cold air, standing, adjusting his clothes. She sat up with a hand to her hair, feeling the mess of it, then tugged at her skirts.

"Why did you burn the cloak, Amiranth?"

She had no answer for him, could only look down at her lap, the wrinkled folds of her bliaut. He gave her a sideways look; she glanced at him from beneath her lashes and saw the arrogance marking him once more, recognizing it for what it was: a need, a hunger for her reassurance. But when he spoke all she heard was cool composure.

"I didn't do it. You know that."

She stood as well, going to the fireplace, witnessing the last of the wedding cloak turn to ash. He shifted behind her, coming close. She caught the scent of their lovemaking, heated around them both.

"Believe in me, Amiranth." It was a demand, not a plea.

"I do," she said. She shook her head, exhausted now, leaning against the stone wall. "God help me, but I do."

He touched her then, turning her to him with just his palm against her cheek, and began another kiss, another promise. Her weary fears fell away as Tristan took her to the bed, enthralling her once more.

---❦---

TRISTAN STUDIED THE LINES OF HIS SWORD, HOLD-ing the blade aloft in the soft light of his solar. A long beam of sunlight from the pillared window behind him fell across just the tip of it, highlighting the darkened red of blood that had dried against the steel.

The body of his brother's castellan had been removed from beneath the willow. He had supervised that him-self, before chasing after Amiranth. He knew also that the blood had been washed clean from the grass with buckets of water, so that now the keep garden appeared to have regained its peace, no lingering sign of the death that had taken place there.

He had walked by it this afternoon, making certain. He had inspected the area once again, finding nothing unordinary to reveal the killer—nothing beyond the telltale scrap of cloth that Liam had found.

But Amiranth had taken care of that particular prob-lem for him. For a moment Tristan let himself become lost in the memory of it, how she had looked when he unlocked the door and entered her room. Her face as she turned to him from that blazing fire. The sight of the mantle—the sure source of that damning cloth from the garden—going up in flames behind her.

Her eyes had been glowing dark; her skin had that cast of alabaster he recognized came to her whenever her emotions were deeply turned. He had realized, in that one extraordinary moment, what she had done.

That she had also recognized the indigo velvet, and had moved to act before he had thought to—to destroy the mantle. To hide the evidence.

To protect him.

His love for her seemed brighter than the flames, brighter than truth or lies, or faith or deceit. He had taken her then because he could not stop himself, and she had met his embrace with kisses that were as ardent and desperate as his own.

Tristan had left her sleeping in her bed, as deep in her dreams as if it were midnight, and not midday.

A smile came to him, even as he examined his sullied sword. She was spent. He liked to think he had something to do with that.

The sunbeam faded to nothing; a cloud passed by the window, pristine white blocking out the blue sky. In the new shadows the blood could have been mere rust against the steel—but Tristan knew better than that.

It was Hugh Fletcher's blood. This was the weapon that had pierced his heart.

He had found it tucked slyly beneath the cushions of a corner chair in his solar, not at all where he had left it last night—yet still in this chamber, the one place in the castle that was unequivocally all his own.

How long had it been since he had truly wielded a sword? Tristan wondered. It was both foreign and familiar, a strange weight in his hand, yet his arm knew how to manage it without any guidance at all. It was only yesterday morning he had first discovered this fine length of steel in a battered chest that had been lost to the solar shadows—his father's goods, long forgotten. He had strapped it on because it felt right to do so. Because it reminded him of who he used to be, and how he used to live.

And now the sword had been put to use, fulfilling its deadly purpose. Only not by him.

So who would kill Hugh Fletcher? Tristan could think of only one answer.

He went now to the trunk that held his father's old things, found a worn tunic inside. With great care he set to rubbing away the dried blood, letting it flake off into the tunic, polishing, polishing, until the white of the cloth was stained red, and the steel shone clean again.

He had thought he had moved swiftly enough to deflect his brother's resentment. He had thought he had been clever enough to rout out the unrest of his castle by offering a brilliant distraction: Merlyff. With it would come the gift of a life of leisure, in a place so fair it was coveted by kings. It would have been an opportunity many men would die for.

A black humor came to him: Perhaps Hugh Fletcher had.

Someone knocked on the door. Tristan slid the blade back into its scabbard, placing it again beneath the chair cushions where he had found it. He tossed the stained tunic into the trunk, then buried it deep within the other clothing, shutting the lid. Abruptly he wished for something new with which to wash his hands, but settled instead for running them down the sides of his hose.

Silas James was at the door, his eyes cautious, his face lined with what might have been worry, or just fatigue.

"The body has been taken to the chapel, my lord, as you instructed."

Tristan stepped aside and the other man entered, crossing to the center of the solar. Silas turned to him; the worry on his face did not wane.

"I fear there will be an inquiry, my lord."

Tristan nodded, expecting as much. "There usually is."

"It is an unfortunate thing."

"More so for Fletcher, I would say."

"Aye."

He could see that his steward wanted to say more, was weighing his words, as if uncertain. Tristan sat, then waved a hand to Silas, inviting him to do the same. The older man eased down slowly, a frown between his brows.

"Will you send for the king's men?" he finally asked.

Tristan sighed. "I suppose I will."

"You could refuse," Silas offered reluctantly.

Tristan did not reply, only stared up at the ceiling, the fitted stone, the beams of wood braced above him. He appreciated his steward's reluctance; they both knew the state of Glynwallen was uneasy at best. Under ordinary circumstances an investigation would proceed without anyone beyond the demesne ever the wiser; the castellan had not been of noble blood, so there was no true need to involve the king. As earl, Tristan could handle the crime himself. He could keep it all within the walls of the castle.

But life here now was far from ordinary. If Liam pressed for an official inquiry from the royal court—Tristan knew he would—there would be no good reason to refuse, either. And if word of his refusal got back to London, matters could become very ugly, very swiftly.

The clues had been set against him most carefully. The tattered mantle, the bloody sword . . . both Amiranth and his brother witness to his threat against the dead castellan. It was almost too perfect.

He was damned fortunate to have found the sword today; a glancing light over the tip of the scabbard was all that had revealed it to him in the far chair. It had been a stroke of pure luck, but he could not rely on luck alone. Who knew what unpleasant surprises tomorrow might hold for him?

Most of the young knights in his castle would gladly turn against him, without question. There was anger here, resentment, and even the promise of a new land had not calmed them. They all seemed to look to his brother, hungry for a thing no one yet dared say aloud. Tristan could not guess what they found there in Liam; leadership, perhaps, or just the yearning for what had once been. What he did know was that all he ever saw in his brother's eyes was a sharp cunning, combined with deceptive acquiescence.

He knew now that Merlyff was not going to be enough.

"Lord Liam is already talking," Silas said, hushed.

"Indeed?" He sounded tired—he felt it suddenly, at

the thought of Liam, and the murder, and all the danger that surrounded him still.

"Aye, my lord."

Silas did not volunteer further information, but Tristan did not have to ask. He could envision it clearly, how it would it happen: subtle hints dropped in corners and near gatherings of people. The uncertain looks aimed at him, the speculation in people's eyes. Liam's knights taking up the gossip, spreading it thick, transforming it to a darker rumor than even the ones before.

History was repeating itself at Glynwallen. Once again the whispers encircled him, calling him murderer, calling him mad. He had braved them well as a young man—what a fool he had been then, completely unaware of the fragility of his life. Tristan today was all too well aware of how easily his world could be broken.

If—when—the king's men came, they would catch the swell of murmured accusation within hours. They might even hear of Amiranth's false grave at Safere, the thieving couple who stole a fine mare, more seeds of doubt to be scattered and believed. . . .

There were too many black marks against him. There were too many questions surrounding him now for certain safety, and he knew it.

Who could say the slander of the past would not add conviction to the present? Who could say what might become of an earl said to be crazed, a killer of men, who had vanished for so long and then returned carrying wild tales of ransoms never issued, no proof to his words at all, save perhaps back in some dismal French prison?

Tristan knew he had much in this life. And under the right circumstances, he could lose much—his title, his home. His wife.

Amiranth. What would become of her without him?

Why, whispered his mind, *she had a ready substitute, did she not? Liam would be more than willing to comfort her over the loss of her mad husband, torn away from her, from his castle, to spend the rest of his miserable life in a dark London cell. She would not even have to leave Glynwallen— Liam could stay, and she could stay, and in time she might forget her sorrow completely, lost in the embrace of a tender new lord. . . .*

Tristan clenched his fists against his eyes, leaning his head back into the chair. His headache was creeping over him again, that throbbing menace in his skull that always seemed to surface in dire times. He fought it, trying to stay focused on what would happen next, what he must still do.

He might have enough power to deflect it all. He did still have the recognition of his brother-in-law and all his cronies from his past. It would be a tricky thing at best, to handle Liam amid all this treachery, but by God, he had been in worse circumstances than this before.

Glynwallen was *his.* So was Merlyff, and Layton, Staffordshire, Safere—*all* of it, and he would leave this place a dead man himself before he let them steal any of it from him.

Most especially before he let anyone steal Amiranth.

"Lord Liam asks when the king's officers will come," Silas said now, into the heavy quiet.

Tristan opened his eyes, and the ache in his head became a stabbing pain. The light from the window nearly blinded him, even with the soft clouds overhead.

"Send for them," he said. "Let them come. We will finish this once and forever."

Chapter Sixteen

———⟨∙⟩———

THE CASTLE SEEMED SUBDUED TO AMIRANTH, THE people brimming with repressed emotions. The servants skittered nervously through the halls; the nobles drifted about in perfumed clouds, pale faces and round eyes, watching her, talking about her.

For the fourth time today she raised a hand to her hair, running her fingers over the gold netting that held it in place, finding it secure. It was not her looks that drew their stares. It was what had happened this morning, the murder—her husband.

But they did not know of the cloak. They could not know of that.

Just as they could not know of what had happened after she had burned it. Tristan coming to her. Their lovemaking. The wild feelings that had taken her, fear and hope and deep, deep determination.

Tristan had not killed Hugh Fletcher. She didn't know who had. The castellan had not been a pleasant man, she could say that much, small of heart and mind—yet surely not deserving of death. The murderer had been someone from Glynwallen, almost certainly, but the choices here were vast. Perhaps he had enemies, a serf he had abused, or a disgruntled soldier, one of Liam's knights . . . or even Liam himself, with his avid gaze and cool smiles.

Amiranth pressed a hand over her eyes for a moment, blocking the terrible thought. She felt half mad herself today, unnerved by all the ghastly happenings.

Whoever it was, he had taken the trouble to find Tristan's mantle, to wear it, or even just to carry it to the murder—it didn't matter. The result was the same. To anyone who might have found it, it would be clear who had slain the castellan.

She considered the situation with a sort of wary resignation. There was no proof to back her faith in Tristan beyond the brutal honesty she found in his eyes—hardly convincing for anyone else. From any other point of view, it seemed all but certain that Tristan Geraint was what he had always been rumored to be: a merciless killer. He had confessed to her that he had taken the life of a friend; she prayed no one else discovered *that* particular fact.

It seemed, even after all these years, that her truest heart had not changed. She still believed he could not murder in cold blood. Not her husband.

No one else thought the same. Amiranth saw it on their faces, the curiosity of these brash knights and their ladies. She saw the gleam of hope in them, that with this new upset a new ending might come for them: stay at Glynwallen. Preserve their indolent lives here. Even Tristan's guard seemed uncertain, although Silas James kept stubbornly close to his lord, vigilant. She was pleased about that.

If Liam and his knights stayed, she would go. If Tristan left—was taken—she would follow. Nothing here mattered to her as he did. But Glynwallen was his legacy, and she would not bow to these wicked schemes around them without a good battle.

Supper was excruciating. Tristan sat beside her, silent, brooding. She said nothing beyond the most obvious comments on the meal, which he either ignored or replied to in curt acknowledgment. He kept rubbing at his temple, as if to soothe a pain there that would not go away.

The great hall was hushed, only the occasional drone of whispered words reaching her—things she did not want to hear. Things she would not believe.

Liam was seated down the table from her. Every now and again she caught his stare, the way he was examining her, a faint frown on his face. He appeared melancholy, sullen. It filled her with impatience, until she realized he might miss his former castellan. She felt shame that she had not mourned the loss of a man, even if he had been her enemy.

Just before the supper Tristan had told her he had sent word to London of the murder. That Edward would most likely be sending men to Glynwallen soon, and to be prepared for it.

Prepared, indeed. The resignation of before began to

slide over her again. She had never felt so unready for anything in her life.

Amiranth returned her gaze to her food, leaving Liam still staring.

What a mire. What a terrible, tragic mire.

Tristan left the meal early, before even the final course was served. He had squeezed her hand beneath the table, then rose without a word, walking away.

Amiranth stayed in her seat, baffled. Every person in the great hall stared after him, the figure of him vanishing out the main doors, and then—with almost perfect accord—swung back around to stare at her.

She turned to the page nearest her, lifting her hand for more wine, acting as if nothing unusual had happened.

With a patience she had not known she possessed she managed to finish the supper, to eat and drink calmly, and pretend that the unnatural silence that had settled over the people did not affect her in the least.

The food was tasteless. The wine did not quench her thirst.

She took only a few bites of the sugared almonds offered to her on a silver platter to end the night. When she rose, so did everyone else, but all waited for her to pass before following her out of the chamber.

She walked without a sense of where to go, very aware of the commotion of people behind her. Tristan might be in his solar again, or his rooms. . . .

The solar was closer. She would try there first.

Since she had passed the entrance, she turned, starting back through the crowd, ignoring them, walking boldly down their middle. They fell away easily, avoiding her gown, her shoulders, the gradual swing of her hands. Good.

The climb to the solar was dangerously dim; no torch had been lit for the stairs. She felt her way up, brushing her fingers over the stone, careful with her skirts. The dull noises of the great hall were still audible below her, but ahead was only dark quiet.

The door was open. There was more darkness inside, the bare illumination from the hall beyond the balcony chasing out a distant purple dusk from the window.

He was not here. His room, then.

She turned and ran into something solid and warm. Amiranth gasped, alarmed, and stepped back too quickly, treading on her skirts.

Strong hands caught her, kept her from falling. Liam was holding her, his grip still firm on her arms, his body still close. He spoke her name softly.

"Amiranth."

She pulled away, letting out a shaky laugh in spite of herself, and he echoed it, smiling.

"Once again—"

"Your apologies. I know." She took a deep breath, hoping he could not perceive the agitated depths of her. "What are you doing, my lord?"

"Looking for you."

His tone remained soft, almost too intimate, especially in the emptiness around them. She moved away from him, toward the pale yellow light of the balcony, which felt like safety.

"I followed you—I confess it," Liam said, his face sobering. "I had to speak with you. It is most urgent."

One of the columns of the balcony was close enough to touch. She fought the urge to press against it, seeking something hard against her back. He moved closer to her, growing clearer with the light.

"What is the urgency, my lord?"

"Your safety—your very life."

She kept her voice impersonal. "Both are well guarded, Lord Liam."

"So I pray. But even a life well guarded can fall to harm." His eyes went behind her, to the open space above the great hall. "Hugh Fletcher was a good man. He did not deserve to die."

Amiranth bit her tongue to keep her silence, to resist the temptation to fall into this conversation. He looked back at her again, the reflected light from below all but erasing the lines on his face, so that he appeared even younger than he was, a boy before her—with the eyes of a man, warm and suggestive.

"I fear for you," he said now, and the timbre of his voice had turned deep, beguiling.

"Really?" She tried a careless smile. "Only yesterday you thought me a fraud, as I recall."

"No, Amiranth. Not you." He gave a small shrug, and the smile returned, lightening his features. "The stories Hugh told me—I could not reconcile them with the woman I know. It was too much a puzzle to me. That was all."

"I assure you, my lord, you do not know me."

He sobered. "I'd like to," he said, in a strange voice. "Very much so."

"Alas. You leave soon for Merlyff. I'm afraid your wish must remain unfulfilled."

"Ah, Merlyff." Liam tilted his head, once again looking behind her. "A beautiful place. But mayhap my wishes shall be fulfilled here, instead."

"I doubt that. Better to seek your fortune elsewhere."

He turned from her, moving across the chamber into the darkness. Amiranth followed his silhouette against the long window behind him, a shape of a man before a sky of bruised violet. Then he was past the window, bending down to the depths of the room. She saw him reach for one of the chairs that sat against the far wall, the cushions of its seat.

With his back to her she dared a quick glimpse to the great hall beyond the pillars—scarce people, all busy cleaning. None looked up at her.

"I have something to show you," Liam said, and she faced him again.

When he returned she saw he held Tristan's sword in his hands, the plain silver hilt, the weathered leather scabbard.

The air seemed to grow very cold around her, her thoughts slowed with it, her heart pained. She did not know how Liam had found the weapon, why it would be in such a strange place as a chair—all she knew was that she did not, did *not* want to see him unsheathe it. But he would, of course he would, and she would see what she could not bear to, the blood of a dead man on Tristan's blade—

With a dull gleam the sword came free of the scabbard, a metallic slither that sent shivers across her skin. Liam held up the blade; Amiranth averted her gaze, despair rising through her.

"I discovered this only this morning. See here, Amiranth, I—"

He stopped abruptly, fixed on the sword, and after a moment she found the courage to look at it as well.

It was long and deadly sharp, almost bright despite the night, clean all the way down to its honed tip.

Clean.

She swallowed, the despair turned instantly to sweet relief, flooding her, making her almost lightheaded.

"Yes?" she prompted. In the silence of the solar her voice sounded loud. "You were going to show me something, Lord Liam?"

Slowly, gently, he eased the sword back into its sheath, his mouth odd—almost smiling—his eyes lowered. He stood motionless for a long while. Amiranth moved forward, taking the sword from his hands. She leaned it carefully against one of the pillars behind her.

"You are in danger," Liam said, from where she had left him. "We both know it. He is my family and my lord—I love him. But he's lost control. We both heard what he said to Hugh."

"Why should *I* be in danger, my lord?" She straightened, facing him. "My husband would never harm me."

"Ordinarily, perhaps not." He lifted his hands before him, graceful, just like his brother. "But he is not an ordinary man."

"No," she agreed. "He is not."

"Jealousy is a powerful emotion, Amiranth. I wonder if you know how powerful."

There was a new shade to him, something that had her immediately alert. She glanced to the open doorway, the hollow landing beyond it, then back to Liam. Amiranth began to move toward the door.

"Tristan has no need to be jealous, my lord."

"No, he hasn't, has he?" Liam appeared to anticipate her thoughts; it seemed to her he moved leisurely, but he was to the door before she was, directly in her path. "Tristan has everything. A castle, a title—a lovely wife . . ." One hand reached out. Before she could retreat he sent his fingers down her cheek, a gliding stroke. Amiranth caught his wrist, pushing it from her, but he only twisted in her grip to take her hand now, holding her tightly when she tried to tug away. They stayed like that for a breathless instant, eyes locked, very close.

"All those years you spent alone at Safere," Liam murmured, so soft. "I wonder that I never visited."

"I'm certain you were busy," she said past her teeth, and with a jerk pulled free of him, circling to the door.

Now Liam only watched her go. "He needs to be locked away, Amiranth, for his own safety, if not yours. The king's men will come soon for the death of Hugh. I will follow honor and tell them the truth about Tristan, and what he said to my castellan. Will you?"

Amiranth did not answer, turning instead to see the growing light of a lamp flickering up the walls of the stairway. Footsteps sounded now, strong and steady, and she knew, with all of her heart, who approached the solar.

She had time only to look swiftly back at Liam; he had moved away from her, far away, back to the columns again. She lost his face to the gloom.

Tristan topped the stairs, the lamp casting him with wild, dancing shadows, revealing the dark glitter to his eyes. He had a smile that sent chills down her arms, but as he entered the room all he said was, "Here you are at last." His eyes flicked to take them both in. Amiranth pressed her hands together nervously, then deliberately stopped, smoothing them down her skirts.

Tristan walked easily into the chamber, greeting his brother in that bland, even voice that deepened her chill.

"And here you are as well, my brother. What luck."

"My lord." Liam bowed. Amiranth hoped Tristan had not noticed the short glance he threw to her at the end of it.

"Amiranth." She turned to see Tristan seated in a great chair—not the one that had held the sword—one with cushions of soft green and deep gold, wide, dark arms of mahogany. The lamp glowed fitfully on the table beside him. He lifted a hand to her, beckoning. She could not read his expression.

She crossed to him slowly, filled with unreasonable guilt—to be caught here, in this place, with his brother—even though she had done nothing wrong. Even though she had defended him, had come here searching for him—

His skin felt very warm against her fingers; his own closed over hers completely, drawing her firmly closer, downward, so that she had to sit immodestly on his lap or else pull away from him. He kept his gaze fixed on hers, cold and bright. She was too afraid to look away.

Only when she was seated—awkward across his legs, blushing—did he release her hand and her eyes, looking back to Liam, who had not moved.

"Well met, brother. I wished to speak with you."

"My lord." Liam gave another bow, shorter.

"I am curious. Why have your people ceased preparations to depart my castle?"

"Have they? Perhaps it was the murder, my lord. They are unsettled."

"I see."

Amiranth felt Tristan's touch on her shoulder, his hand sliding down to her forearm, following the back of her hand to her waist. The heat of his palm seemed to burn through her there; he spread his fingers across her, then began to rub her midriff in a slow, lazy circle.

"You'll want to speak with them, then. Assure them all is well. I doubt very much there is any jeopardy to them."

With Tristan behind her she could not see his face, but she saw Liam's. He was staring at the movement, Tristan's hand against her, the circles steady, rhythmic. Her blush heightened.

"Soon the danger will be gone," Tristan continued, affable. "Don't you think so, Liam?"

"Aye. I hope it."

"I know it."

Amiranth attempted to shift position. Tristan halted her easily, his hand stilling, pressing her back to him. His other hand came around her, up by her neck. She felt him tug at a curl that had loosened from the delicate netting. It fell free down her chest, cool against the warmth of her skin.

"There was a time," Tristan said, contemplative, "when the thought of death pained me greatly. I did not even enjoy the hunt. Do you remember that, Liam?"

"If you say, my lord."

"What—you don't recall? It was one of the few things we had in common, I believe. You could not bear the sight of blood. You were terrified of knives, of death . . . just the sight of a bloodied stag always sent you crying as a boy. You used to beg me not to hunt, hanging on to my legs." He paused for a moment as his fingers slid through the lock of her hair, wrapping around the gold of it. "I fear I did not need much persuasion. There was always too much death in this castle for my taste. Unlike some, I did not revel in it." His fingers stilled. "Today I find it—not as troubling as before."

Liam leaned back against the pillar, crossing his arms. "The consequence of war, no doubt. You are at ease with killing now, I suppose."

She felt a new tension tighten through Tristan, his absolute quiet. Then his hand moved again, stroking, rubbing his knuckles against the swell of flesh above her bodice.

"No doubt," he said slowly. "But you've changed as well, Liam. I confess I am surprised at the differences the passing of time may bring about in a man."

"Are you, my lord? Well, it's been a very long while, after all. The years bring many changes to us all."

Tristan laughed, though it did not sound mirthful to Amiranth, but more of something icy and deep. "Aye, I suppose you're right. Eight years may do anything to anyone, I think. Indeed, some men might grow to become quite . . . covetous over such a time."

There was an edge of menace to the air now; it was not her imagination, and not trifling. She was not fooled by Tristan's casual words, or by the shameless stroking he continued across her breast. Liam was staring behind her now, stiff and tall, deliberately ignoring Tristan's repeated massage over her skin.

Tristan spoke again. "So. You've outgrown your childish fears of blood. You must find that very helpful for who you are today."

"Who I am, my lord?"

"Aye," replied Tristan lazily. "A murderer. Killer of your own castellan."

No one moved, no one spoke. From the great hall below Amiranth heard the faint, echoing sounds of the serfs, and the hush of her own breath, suspended.

"I found the sword, you know," Tristan continued, almost conversational. "And my wife found the cloak. Did you truly think such simple tricks could harm me?"

Liam's arms slowly uncrossed. Amiranth saw the flash of emotion on his face—anger or fear, she didn't know—quickly veiled, a swift glance to her and then back to Tristan again.

"You speak of nonsense, brother."

"Oh? I think not, *brother*."

With Tristan's light urging at her waist she stood, moving aside as he rose after her, walking around the chamber, coming close to Liam. The flame of the lamp seemed to dim as he passed.

"I was not the one who threatened Hugh Fletcher," Liam said quickly. "I was not the one who held a sword to him!"

"No," Tristan agreed, with a faint, wintry smile. "That was I, most certainly."

"You admit it!" Liam looked to her, his voice not as sure as it could be. "You admit you killed him!"

"I admit that I *would* have, had he crossed me further." Tristan's eyes narrowed, a sharp, wicked look—a devil look—coming over him. "I admit that he was in grave, grave danger from me. Shall I tell you why?"

Amiranth took a step forward. "Tristan—"

He ignored her, focused on the other man, speaking with steely calm. "Because he threatened my wife. That was all. Yet that, I assure you, was everything, and the only thing I needed to draw blood. I will not tolerate any threat to what is mine."

Liam glanced to her again, and there could be no mistaking his countenance now: sly triumph.

"Tristan," Amiranth said again, coming closer. "Stop talking."

Liam began to inch away in small, sideways steps as he watched Tristan, who only stared back at him, unmoving.

"But I did not kill him," her husband said, a dark shadow edged in golden light. "I did not, because you did it for me. Didn't you?"

"Be calm," Liam urged, still moving. "Be calm,

brother. You are confused. You don't know what you say—"

"I know exactly what I say. I know a killer when I see one. I know your face—in the past eight years I've seen a wealth of it, that deadness in your eyes. That gap in your soul. I know you very well indeed, killer."

The devil's look about Tristan grew keener, tense muscles and the whisper of cold danger all around him, of something darkly fleet, barely contained. He was taller than his brother, broader of shoulder, a clear and looming peril.

With deliberate care he lifted his hand to the dagger at his waist. Liam watched him do it, smiling now as if in disbelief. His voice took on the coaxing note meant to soothe a savage temper.

"Think clearly, brother. Of course I did not kill my man. Your time in Mirgaux has baffled your mind, that's all."

"Has it?" The dagger came free. It gleamed silver and yellow, seemed a natural extension of Tristan's hand.

Liam had his own knife, the hilt of it very visible, tucked into his belt. He did not reach for it, but Amiranth could see that he wanted to. He finally looked alarmed, as if only now realizing what might happen. His steps became stilted, easing around a large column, his eyes on Tristan's blade.

"Come, my lord—you are distressing your wife. Put down the dagger."

"My wife?" Tristan seemed fully at ease, moving with the shadows, a slow, relentless pursuit. "Oh yes.

My wife." His voice raised slightly. "Amiranth. What was the name of my prison in France?"

"I— What?" She tore her gaze from the terrible sliding gleam of his blade, back to his face, the demonic smile.

"The prison, my love."

She stared at him, confounded. "I don't know. Tristan, please—"

"Did you hear that, Liam? She does not know. Can you guess why?"

Amiranth began to approach them both. She didn't know what she could do; Tristan's face terrified her, a mask of ice, no emotions at all beyond that frightening cold. She could not allow him to harm Liam. She could not allow him to risk himself, his life, for that.

He halted her with a simple look, freezing her in place, ferocity barely contained behind his eyes. She caught a glimpse of eternity in the black of his gaze— torture, imprisonment—and understood then that whatever compelled him now would not be easily stopped.

He turned that gaze back to Liam. "Because I never told her. I never told *anyone* the name of that place. Mirgaux. I believe that's the very first time I've ever even said it aloud. So how do *you* know of it? Unless . . ."

Liam drew his blade. "You are mad!"

"Unless there was a ransom, after all," Tristan finished.

Amiranth made a noise, a sound of breathless horror. Liam risked another look to her, his eyes wide. His voice rang off the stones.

"There was no ransom!"

"Really?" Tristan did a trick with the dagger, twirling it in his fingers, so that the metal became a blur. Before she could blink he held it ready again, close to Liam. "Then how did you know the name?"

"You mentioned it!"

"No." A single word, total conviction.

"Stay back!" Liam lunged at him. Amiranth cried out, darting forward, but Tristan had already knocked the dagger aside. The two men grappled for a moment, struggling, slamming into her with heavy force. She staggered sideways, falling against one of the columns and then to the floor, landing across something long and flat, pressed hard into her ribs. Tristan's sword. Amiranth grasped it in an instant, pulling it to her, finding her feet again. When she turned, Tristan held Liam by an arm around his throat, his teeth bared, his face taut with effort. Liam had both hands around Tristan's arm, pulling, gaining nothing by it. A dagger glinted on the floor across the room.

Voices came from behind the solar door, muffled, worried. Liam focused instantly on her, one hand now stretched out, appealing.

"Amiranth! He *is* mad!"

Still hugging the sword, she ran to the door, slid the bolt home.

"My lord? My lady?"

She didn't know who that was. Past the panicked rush of her heartbeat, it could have been anyone. "All is well here," she called past the wood. "Go away."

"Are you certain?" Perhaps Silas's voice—or one of Liam's men, spying, close. . . .

"Begone!" she said sharply. "We will summon you when you are needed!"

Tristan watched her, fiendish handsome and glittering eyes, savagery in every line of him. He bent his head to speak softly into the other man's ear.

"Outnumbered, I fear. Admit the truth, Liam, and mayhap I'll let you live."

"Amiranth!"

Slowly she shook her head at Liam, staying back against the door.

"I have a taste for blood, you know," Tristan whispered. "It's what you've been saying all along, isn't it? I changed in prison. I held the hand of death and welcomed it. Admit what you did to Fletcher, or I vow you will suffer what I've learned."

"Nothing! I did nothing to him!"

"You've hardly convinced me, boy." He tightened his grip, and Amiranth watched as the other man's face grew distorted.

"I'll tell you! I will!" Liam took a gasping breath of air, trying to jerk away, but Tristan held him fast. "Let me free!"

Without warning Tristan released him, spinning him around, the point of his dagger appearing from nowhere to rest at the side of the man's neck.

"So. Talk."

But Liam said nothing, panting, holding his throat. His eyes darted around the chamber, furtive. She saw it then, saw it full and clear: the cunning on him, the

cruel twist to his mouth, brutal wrath no longer disguised.

"You did it, didn't you?" Amiranth asked quietly,
standing by the door. "Sweet Mary. Did you even think
twice about it? Killing an innocent man—for what?"

"For Glynwallen," Tristan answered her. "And for
you, I think, my lady. Little Liam grew up to become
quite an opportunist, it seems. He wanted far more than
Merlyff. He thought to take the chance to turn you
against me, and seize it all. He did it for wealth, and title, and a demesne any would envy. I know that feeling
well." Tristan gave a short laugh, acrid. "But you've lost,
boy. And so you've lost everything."

Liam charged suddenly, striking at Tristan, the hand
with the blade, and then the two of them were battling
again, fists flying.

Amiranth moved forward almost tranquilly, freeing
the sword she held from the scabbard, walking to them.
Pressing it against Liam's neck, and then his chest.

It checked both men instantly, panting, staring at her.
The blade felt surprisingly light in her hands, easy to
yield. She used the pressure of it to force Liam to back
away from her husband.

All her panicked fears of before were gone. It was a
peculiar feeling, to be unafraid of this moment, with the
promise of death so close all about them. Yet Amiranth
felt strong, impassive. There was only a black, unholy
thing rising through her, like the moon passing over the
sun, blocking out all light; she did not recognize herself
amid it.

Just one thought seemed to matter to her now, and so

Amiranth asked the question that fronted the mass of that eclipse within her:

"I want to know. How many demands of ransom were there for him?"

Liam did not answer. A thin line of blood was seeping from his nose. He glared at her, setting his jaw.

"How many?" she asked again, still so mild, and pressed harder with the sword. Liam flinched. She watched it, detached.

"Amiranth," Tristan murmured, just behind her.

"I want to know," she repeated, very composed. "I spent years waiting for you. I spent years dying, because you were dead. And now I want to know."

Silence; neither man spoke.

"How many demands?" she hissed, and suddenly knew the eclipse for what it was: wrath and fury, something well beyond her, dark and deep and reckless. She took a step toward Liam, her hands firm on the sword, and pushed at him a little harder, searching for blood.

"Two," said Liam, backing away. Amiranth followed, sword up, until he was pressed against a wall, his hands flat behind him. She kept her eyes on the tip of the blade, the blossom of crimson she saw just beginning to stain his tunic there.

"Three," he gasped, when she pushed at him again, and his face was moist with sweat.

"By heavens," she said calmly, "I think I'll kill you myself for that."

A hand closed over her own, tanned fingers, warm. She realized that she was shaking now, a distant trembling that had taken over her entire body. Tristan moved beside her, urging her back, his fingers slipping over hers, grasping the sword.

She allowed it, releasing her grip. She could not feel her arms any longer; she could not feel anything.

Tristan stood beside her now, keeping the sword aimed at the other man. He threw her one quick, hidden look—and then a shadowed smile.

"It seems we have a problem, don't we?" he said to Liam, who had slumped against the wall, clutching at his chest. "A true criminal in our midst. A member of my own family, God forgive you, turned murderer and thief." His smile grew thinner, a ruthless curl to his lips. "And people call *me* mad."

Liam lifted his hand from his tunic, staring at the blood across his palm. Then he looked at them both, his face turned rash, careless. "What of it? What do you think to do about it, my *dread* lord? You have no proof of any of it. None but Fletcher and I knew of the ransom demands. And I can easily find a dozen men to vouch for me the night he died—twice as many to swear to your madness!"

"True," Tristan said, musing. The blade of the sword tilted in the light, an adept twist back and forth, shining steel and distant gold, a drop of bright red at the tip of it. "When the king's men come, it shall be your word against mine."

"And mine," vowed Amiranth, low and vehement. "And my brother's. You may be very certain the Earl of Iving will assure our king that my husband is right and sane."

Tristan lifted the sword slightly, turning it again, as if to examine the blade. Liam did not move.

"It appears your word won't suffice, brother. So I think we have a simple choice. Shall I kill you now? Or will you go? I offer you your life—which is more than you deserve, but I'm in a generous mood. Listen well. Take your knights—their wives, all of them—and leave my demesne tonight. In fact, you must leave England altogether. I suggest France." Tristan had a smile that was not a smile, gentle and cold, to match his voice. "You already have the name of a place there to live, don't you? Or stay, and take your chances now against me. I've already sent for the king's inquisitors. Another death will merely spare them a trip."

Liam seemed to falter, his eyes on the sword, a paleness coming over him, harsh against the red blood on his face.

"You don't dare harm me," he said, but Amiranth heard the doubt in his voice. "You don't dare kill me."

"I was alone in my husband's solar," she said evenly, "when Lord Liam came to me. He seemed crazed, frenzied. He spoke of nonsense—said he loved me beyond reason, though I tried to flee. He attacked me, tore at my gown, my hair. Praise God my husband came to defend me. Praise God my good lord was here to stop him. We wept for his death, but there was no choice."

Tristan nodded, thoughtful. Liam grew paler.

"It is time," Tristan said, matter-of-fact. "What say you? Life apart from these shores—or death now, and my own satisfaction?"

"If I go—they'll think I'm running, that I killed Hugh Fletcher!"

"So they will." Tristan smiled again. "But it is only the truth, is it not?"

"Damn you!"

Amiranth watched Liam struggle to accept it, the inevitable outcome. His eyes were glazed, his fingers curled to fists.

"I'll go," he spat finally.

"Now. With all your people," Tristan prompted.

"Aye."

"Excellent. Oh, and take this thought with you." Very smoothly Tristan aimed the blade to Liam's heart once again, his arm a straight line, clean and strong. "I know your face, boy. I know your name and those of all who travel with you, and I will have spies everywhere. Wherever you go, I will know it. Should you return to England, I will know it. I shall not be so merciful in the future. If the king's army does not catch you, I will."

He gave Liam a hard stare, adding softly, "And I vow there shall be no second or third chances for *you*."

He stepped back, sword still raised, then threw Amiranth another of his secret smiles.

"Let in my steward, love. He's waiting most anxiously behind that door, along with a good number of my men. They'll make a fine escort to the coast for my brother and his company."

FIVE DAYS HAD PASSED.

It was just after sunrise, and Amiranth had watched it come from atop the gatehouse, colored light spilling over the treetops, trimming the clouds with gold and pink and orange. There was no wind at all up here, not even the mildest of breezes, and so sounds carried well up the walls: the bustle of the workers in the bailey below, the soft whickering of the horses of Tristan's guard as they crossed the gate, the low voices of men, beginning only now to return from the shore.

Tristan was among them. He had left with sturdy Evan, the castellan, and a mighty contingent of his men, all of them armed and vigilant around the hostility of Liam and his group. They had departed in the deep of the night, just as Tristan said they would, the whole of them shuffled beyond the gates of the castle and into a future that none could predict.

She did not weep for them. Although she knew Tristan had taken from them all weapons, he had let them keep their goods and riches—they would not starve. It was a fairer fate than he himself had been condemned to, she thought.

They left in groups, both quiet and cursing, but Amiranth had no patience for their complaints. Such wily hearts would surely find their way in the world. As long as it was not here. As long as it spared her husband.

So the danger had fled the gates of Glynwallen, and Liam was truly gone, and now—at last—Amiranth caught sight of Tristan riding in, sitting splendid and tall on his destrier, a virtuous knight returning home from a journey that had seemed to Amiranth longer than time itself.

He lifted his face and found her amid the cream-colored stones. One arm raised, a greeting. She leaned out over the carved unicorn and waved back to him.

"My lord returns," said Silas James softly, at her side.

"Aye."

She waited for him up here alone, and it was not long before Tristan was striding to her along the wall-walk, handsome with the painted sky all around him. The lines on his face seemed deepened, his gait slower than usual beneath the glinting weight of his mail and plates. But the expression on his face was pure gladness—enough to catch her breath in her throat, an answering happiness coursing through her.

Amiranth took the final steps to him, pressing her face against his shoulder, metal and man, feeling his arms come around her and his head rest against hers. They did not speak for a long while. When she looked up again the sun had broken free of the clouds, and Tristan gazed down at her with eyes to match the fair morning, clear and warm.

"They're gone, out to sea, every one of them." He placed a kiss on her forehead, giving the smallest of sighs.

She said to his shoulder, "It does not seem fair, to let him go free. Not after what he did to you."

His reply was gentle. "Perhaps it isn't. But it is the wiser course. For all that he's done, he is yet my brother. And I don't believe I'm ready for another death . . . not even his."

"Unfair," she murmured anyway.

"Aye," he agreed, weary. "Life is full of such a fate. I have had my share of it, my lady."

"But no more." She raised her head and touched his face softly, carefully, tracing the lines around his mouth with the tips of her fingers.

His lashes lowered, comely features and golden sun, the aspect of a pagan king falling across him once again, a mythic grace that lingered as he lifted his eyes, a solemn look.

"Merlyff is free now." His hand came up, cupped her cheek. "If you want—if you wish it still, you may go."

He spoke carefully, dispassionately, but she could see what it cost him. She could see the suffering in his eyes.

"I won't keep you here, Amiranth. I don't want to hold you by force."

She started to speak and he stopped her, kissing her quick and hard before backing away. The first morning breeze came to them then, stirring his hair, lifting it to catch the sheen of the rising sun. With great care Tristan went to his knees before her—not pleading, but proud and slow, taking in her face. She stood silent as the breeze came again, pushing against her skirts.

"But if you stay," Tristan said, "I will make up for our past. I love you with all that I am. I love your heart, your spirit, and aye, your body. You make me feel such things I never knew. You make me realize I have good cause to live, and stay alive. You were with me all those years away, Amiranth, through all the pain and loneliness— you were there in my heart. You don't have to believe me, but I swear it's true." He shook his head, solemn, golden bright. "I know I don't deserve you, but I'll spend the rest of my life trying to be worthy of you."

When she did not move, he added simply, "I promise."

They stayed motionless for a moment. Her words were trapped in her throat; she could not speak, her hopes were so great.

"Please," he said, in a strained voice. "Please, Amiranth. Don't leave me alone. I don't want—I don't want to be without you again."

It was that which freed her, the anguish in him, lancing through her, deep and powerful. She went to him, taking up his hands, helping him to rise.

"I never stopped loving you," she said. "I tried, and could not." She shook her head, smiling up at him, sunlight in her eyes. "Since I was a girl, all I ever wanted was to spend my life with you, Tristan Geraint. I'm grown now, and not such a fool to let you go again."

He stared at her, and she followed the transformation in him as it happened: his stoic look turned to amazement, and then relief. His own smile came, glorious, and then Tristan gave a wondering laugh, bringing her to him, fast and certain.

"Oh, God." He rocked her close, his lips on her hair. "It seems I was fool enough for us both."

"Aye, my lord, you were. But fortune smiles on fools, I've heard."

He laughed again, a joyous sound that rumbled through her, and then pulled back to gaze into her eyes, so handsome and determined. "I'll take what fortune I can, if it means I get you."

"As will I, my brave knight."

Amiranth lifted her head for his kiss, delighting in it, the sweet sensation of her love, her husband—her hero—come home at last, cherishing her close.

Epilogue

———— ༺⚬꧂ ————

I N THE DEPTHS OF A DUSKY ROOM A COUPLE SLEPT
peacefully in a great bed, dark and fair intertwined, nestled together beneath sheets and furs. A gleaming canopy
of golden cloth swayed with the occasional draft, the
falling folds of it offering a soft rustling in the night.

The room was large and well furnished, filled with
elegant chairs and tables, large chests and gilded drawers. Roses and rushes turned the air fragrant, a gentle
reminder of the summer day that would come with the
dawn.

On the chair closest to the dwindling fire was a long,
embroidered cushion, tilted so that it caught the last of
the light. It glimmered even in the dimness, an intricate
scene of two swans side by side on a sapphire lake, their
heads curved together, sharing their secrets beneath the
sparkling stars.

About the Author

SHANA ABÉ is the award-winning author of eleven novels, including the bestselling Drákon series. She lives in Colorado with five rescued house rabbits and one big happy dog. Please support your local animal shelter and spay or neuter your pets.

Visit her website at www.shanaabe.com.